THOMAS HARDY

Selected Short Stories

D1459554

THOMAS HARDY

Selected Short Stories

SENATE

Thomas Hardy – Selected Short Stories

Complete edition first published in 1928 as
The Short Stories of Thomas Hardy by Macmillan &
Company, London

This edition published in 1995 by Senate,
an imprint of Tiger Books International PLC,
26A York Street, Twickenham,
Middlesex TW1 3LJ, United Kingdom

Copyright © 1928 Estate of Thomas Hardy

Cover design © Tiger Books International 1995

3 5 7 9 10 8 6 4 2

ISBN 1 85958 093 9

Printed and bound in the UK by
Cox & Wyman, Reading, England

CONTENTS

WESSEX TALES

LIFE'S LITTLE IRONIES

v

WESSEX TALES

PREFACE TO *WESSEX TALES*

AN apology is perhaps needed for the neglect of contrast
which is shown by presenting two stories of hangmen and
one of a military execution in such a small collection as
the following. But as to the former, in the neighbourhood
of county-towns hanging matters used to form a large
proportion of the local tradition; and though never
personally acquainted with any chief operator at such
scenes, the writer of these pages had as a boy the privilege
of being on speaking terms with a man who applied for
the office, and who sank into an incurable melancholy
because he failed to get it, some slight mitigation of his
grief being to dwell upon striking episodes in the lives of
those happier ones who had held it with success and renown.
His tale of disappointment used to cause his listener some
wonder why his ambition should have taken such an unfortunate form, by limiting itself to a profession of which
there could be only one practitioner in England at one
time, when it might have aimed at something more commonplace—that would have afforded him more chances—such
as the office of a judge, a bishop, or even a member of
Parliament—but its nobleness was never questioned. In
those days, too, there was still living an old woman who,
for the cure of some eating disease, had been taken in her
youth to have her 'blood turned' by a convict's corpse,
in the manner described in 'The Withered Arm.'

Since writing this story some years ago I have been
reminded by an aged friend who knew 'Rhoda Brook'
that, in relating her dream, my forgetfulness has weakened
the facts out of which the tale grew. In reality it was
while lying down on a hot afternoon that the incubus
oppressed her and she flung it off, with the results upon
the body of the original as described. To my mind the
occurrence of such a vision in the daytime is more impressive

than if it had happened in a midnight dream. Readers
are therefore asked to correct the misrelation, which affords
an instance of how our imperfect memories insensibly
formalize the fresh originality of living fact—from whose
shape they slowly depart, as machine-made castings depart
by degrees from the sharp hand-work of the mould.

Among the many devices for concealing smuggled goods
in caves and pits of the earth, that of planting an apple-tree
in a tray or box which was placed over the mouth of the
pit is, I believe, unique, and it is detailed in ' The Distracted
Preacher ' precisely as described by an old carrier of ' tubs '
—a man who was afterwards in my father's employ for
over thirty years. I never gathered from his reminiscences
what means were adopted for lifting the tree, which, with
its roots, earth, and receptacle, must have been of considerable weight. There is no doubt, however, that the thing
was done through many years. My informant often spoke,
too, of the horribly suffocating sensation produced by the
pair of spirit-tubs slung upon the chest and back, after
stumbling with the burden of them for several miles inland
over a rough country and in darkness. He said that
though years of his youth and young manhood were spent
in this irregular business, his profits from the same, taken
all together, did not average the wages he might have
earned in a steady employment, whilst the fatigues and
risks were excessive.

I may add that the action of this story is founded on
certain smuggling exploits that occurred between 1825 and
1830, and were brought to a close in the latter year by the
trial of the chief actors at the Assizes before Baron Bolland
for their desperate armed resistance to the Custom-house
officers during the landing of a cargo of spirits. This
happened only a little time after the doings recorded in
the narrative, in which some incidents that came out at
the trial are also embodied.

In the culminating affray the character called Owlett
was badly wounded, and several of the Preventive-men
would have lost their lives through being overpowered by
the far more numerous body of smugglers, but for the
forbearance and manly conduct of the latter. This served

them in good stead at their trial, in which the younger
Erskine prosecuted, their defence being entrusted to Erle.
Baron Bolland's summing up was strongly in their favour ;
they were merely ordered to enter into their own recog-
nizances for good behaviour and discharged. (See also as
to facts the note at the end of the tale.)

However, the stories are but dreams, and not records.
They were first collected and published under their present
title, in two volumes, in 1888.

April 1896—*May* 1912.

An experience of the writer in respect of the tale called
'A Tradition of Eighteen Hundred and Four' is curious
enough to be mentioned here. The incident of Napoleon's
visit to the English coast by night, with a view to discovering a convenient spot for landing his army of invasion, was
an invention of the author's on which he had some doubts
because of its improbability. This was in 1882, when it
was first published. Great was his surprise several years
later to be told that it was a real tradition. How far this
is true he is unaware.

T. H.

June 1919.

THE THREE STRANGERS

THE THREE STRANGERS

AMONG the few features of agricultural England which retain an appearance but little modified by the lapse of centuries, may be reckoned the long, grassy and furzy downs, coombs, or ewe-leases, as they are called according to their kind, that fill a large area of certain counties in the south and south-west. If any mark of human occupation is met with hereon, it usually takes the form of the solitary cottage of some shepherd.

Fifty years ago such a lonely cottage stood on such a down, and may possibly be standing there now. In spite of its loneliness, however, the spot, by actual measurement, was not three miles from a county-town. Yet that affected it little. Three miles of irregular upland, during the long inimical seasons, with their sleets, snows, rains, and mists, afford withdrawing space enough to isolate a Timon or a Nebuchadnezzar; much less, in fair weather, to please that less repellent tribe, the poets, philosophers, artists, and others who ' conceive and meditate of pleasant things.'

Some old earthen camp or barrow, some clump of trees, at least some starved fragment of ancient hedge is usually taken advantage of in the erection of these forlorn dwellings. But, in the present case, such a kind of shelter had been disregarded. Higher Crowstairs, as the house was called, stood quite detached and undefended. The only reason for its precise situation seemed to be the crossing of two footpaths at right angles hard by, which may have crossed there and thus for a good five hundred years. Hence the house was exposed to the elements on all sides. But, though the wind up here blew unmistakably when it did blow, and the rain hit hard whenever it fell, the various weathers of the winter season were not quite so formidable on the down as they were imagined to be by dwellers on low ground. The raw rimes were not so pernicious as in

9

the hollows, and the frosts were scarcely so severe. When the shepherd and his family who tenanted the house were pitied for their sufferings from the exposure, they said that upon the whole they were less inconvenienced by 'wuzzes and flames' (hoarses and phlegms) than when they had lived by the stream of a snug neighbouring valley.

The night of March 28, 182–, was precisely one of the nights that were wont to call forth these expressions of commiseration. The level rainstorm smote walls, slopes, and hedges like the clothyard shafts of Senlac and Crecy. Such sheep and outdoor animals as had no shelter stood with their buttocks to the winds; while the tails of little birds trying to roost on some scraggy thorn were blown inside-out like umbrellas. The gable-end of the cottage was stained with wet, and the eavesdroppings flapped against the wall. Yet never was commiseration for the shepherd more misplaced. For that cheerful rustic was entertaining a large party in glorification of the christening of his second girl.

The guests had arrived before the rain began to fall, and they were all now assembled in the chief or living-room of the dwelling. A glance into the apartment at eight o'clock on this eventful evening would have resulted in the opinion that it was as cosy and comfortable a nook as could be wished for in boisterous weather. The calling of its inhabitant was proclaimed by a number of highly-polished sheep-crooks without stems that were hung ornamentally over the fireplace, the curl of each shining crook varying from the antiquated type engraved in the patriarchal pictures of old family Bibles to the most approved fashion of the last local sheep-fair. The room was lighted by half-a-dozen candles, having wicks only a trifle smaller than the grease which enveloped them, in candlesticks that were never used but at high-days, holy-days, and family feasts. The lights were scattered about the room, two of them standing on the chimney-piece. This position of candles was in itself significant. Candles on the chimney-piece always meant a party.

On the hearth, in front of a back-brand to give substance,

blazed a fire of thorns, that crackled 'like the laughter of the fool.'

Nineteen persons were gathered here. Of these, five women, wearing gowns of various bright hues, sat in chairs along the wall; girls shy and not shy filled the window-bench; four men, including Charley Jake the hedge-carpenter, Elijah New the parish-clerk, and John Pitcher, a neighbouring dairyman, the shepherd's father-in-law, lolled in the settle; a young man and maid, who were blushing over tentative *pourparlers* on a life-companionship, sat beneath the corner-cupboard; and an elderly engaged man of fifty or upward moved restlessly about from spots where his betrothed was not to the spot where she was. Enjoyment was pretty general, and so much the more prevailed in being unhampered by conventional restrictions. Absolute confidence in each other's good opinion begat perfect ease, while the finishing stroke of manner, amounting to a truly princely serenity, was lent to the majority by the absence of any expression or trait denoting that they wished to get on in the world, enlarge their minds, or do any eclipsing thing whatever—which nowadays so generally nips the bloom and *bonhomie* of all except the two extremes of the social scale.

Shepherd Fennel had married well, his wife being a dairyman's daughter from a vale at a distance, who brought fifty guineas in her pocket—and kept them there, till they should be required for ministering to the needs of a coming family. This frugal woman had been somewhat exercised as to the character that should be given to the gathering. A sit-still party had its advantages; but an undisturbed position of ease in chairs and settles was apt to lead on the men to such an unconscionable deal of toping that they would sometimes fairly drink the house dry. A dancing-party was the alternative; but this, while avoiding the foregoing objection on the score of good drink, had a counterbalancing disadvantage in the matter of good victuals, the ravenous appetites engendered by the exercise causing immense havoc in the buttery. Shepherdess Fennel fell back upon the intermediate plan of mingling short dances with short periods of talk and

singing, so as to hinder any ungovernable rage in either.
But this scheme was entirely confined to her own gentle
mind : the shepherd himself was in the mood to exhibit
the most reckless phases of hospitality.

The fiddler was a boy of those parts, about twelve years
of age, who had a wonderful dexterity in jigs and reels,
though his fingers were so small and short as to necessitate
a constant shifting for the high notes, from which he
scrambled back to the first position with sounds not of
unmixed purity of tone. At seven the shrill tweedle-dee
of this youngster had begun, accompanied by a booming
ground-bass from Elijah New, the parish-clerk, who had
thoughtfully brought with him his favourite musical
instrument, the serpent. Dancing was instantaneous, Mrs.
Fennel privately enjoining the players on no account to
let the dance exceed the length of a quarter of an hour.

But Elijah and the boy in the excitement of their position
quite forgot the injunction. Moreover, Oliver Giles, a
man of seventeen, one of the dancers, who was enamoured
of his partner, a fair girl of thirty-three rolling years, had
recklessly handed a new crown-piece to the musicians, as
a bribe to keep going as long as they had muscle and wind.
Mrs. Fennel, seeing the steam begin to generate on the
countenances of her guests, crossed over and touched the
fiddler's elbow and put her hand on the serpent's mouth.
But they took no notice, and fearing she might lose her
character of genial hostess if she were to interfere too
markedly, she retired and sat down helpless. And so the
dance whizzed on with cumulative fury, the performers
moving in their planet-like courses, direct and retrograde,
from apogee to perigee, till the hand of the well-kicked
clock at the bottom of the room had travelled over the
circumference of an hour.

While these cheerful events were in course of enactment
within Fennel's pastoral dwelling an incident having
considerable bearing on the party had occurred in the
gloomy night without. Mrs. Fennel's concern about the
growing fierceness of the dance corresponded in point of
time with the ascent of a human figure to the solitary hill
of Higher Crowstairs from the direction of the distant town.

This personage strode on through the rain without a pause, following the little-worn path which, further on in its course, skirted the shepherd's cottage.

It was nearly the time of full moon, and on this account, though the sky was lined with a uniform sheet of dripping cloud, ordinary objects out of doors were readily visible. The sad wan light revealed the lonely pedestrian to be a man of supple frame; his gait suggested that he had somewhat passed the period of perfect and instinctive agility, though not so far as to be otherwise than rapid of motion when occasion required. At a rough guess, he might have been about forty years of age. He appeared tall, but a recruiting sergeant, or other person accustomed to the judging of men's heights by the eye, would have discerned that this was chiefly owing to his gauntness, and that he was not more than five-feet-eight or nine.

Notwithstanding the regularity of his tread there was caution in it, as in that of one who mentally feels his way; and despite the fact that it was not a black coat nor a dark garment of any sort that he wore, there was something about him which suggested that he naturally belonged to the black-coated tribes of men. His clothes were of fustian, and his boots hobnailed, yet in his progress he showed not the mud-accustomed bearing of hobnailed and fustianed peasantry.

By the time that he had arrived abreast of the shepherd's premises the rain came down, or rather came along, with yet more determined violence. The outskirts of the little settlement partially broke the force of wind and rain, and this induced him to stand still. The most salient of the shepherd's domestic erections was an empty sty at the forward corner of his hedgeless garden, for in these latitudes the principle of masking the homelier features of your establishment by a conventional frontage was unknown. The traveller's eye was attracted to this small building by the pallid shine of the wet slates that covered it. He turned aside, and, finding it empty, stood under the pent-roof for shelter.

While he stood the boom of the serpent within the adjacent house, and the lesser strains of the fiddler, reached

the spot as an accompaniment to the surging hiss of the
flying rain on the sod, its louder beating on the cabbage-
leaves of the garden, on the straw hackles of eight or ten
beehives just discernible by the path, and its dripping
from the eaves into a row of buckets and pans that had
been placed under the walls of the cottage. For at Higher
Crowstairs, as at all such elevated domiciles, the grand
difficulty of housekeeping was an insufficiency of water ;
and a casual rainfall was utilized by turning out, as catchers,
every utensil that the house contained. Some queer stories
might be told of the contrivances for economy in suds and
dish-waters that are absolutely necessitated in upland
habitations during the droughts of summer. But at this
season there were no such exigencies ; a mere acceptance
of what the skies bestowed was sufficient for an abundant
store.

At last the notes of the serpent ceased and the house was
silent. This cessation of activity aroused the solitary
pedestrian from the reverie into which he had lapsed, and,
emerging from the shed, with an apparently new intention,
he walked up the path to the house-door. Arrived here,
his first act was to kneel down on a large stone beside the
row of vessels, and to drink a copious draught from one
of them. Having quenched his thirst he rose and lifted
his hand to knock, but paused with his eye upon the panel.
Since the dark surface of the wood revealed absolutely.
nothing, it was evident that he must be mentally looking
through the door, as if he wished to measure thereby all
the possibilities that a house of this sort might include,
and how they might bear upon the question of his entry.

In his indecision he turned and surveyed the scene
around. Not a soul was anywhere visible. The garden-
path stretched downward from his feet, gleaming like the
track of a snail ; the roof of the little well (mostly dry),
the well-cover, the top rail of the garden-gate, were
varnished with the same dull liquid glaze ; while, far away
in the vale, a faint whiteness of more than usual extent
showed that the rivers were high in the meads. Beyond
all this winked a few bleared lamplights through the beating
drops—lights that denoted the situation of the county-

town from which he had appeared to come. The absence of all notes of life in that direction seemed to clinch his intentions, and he knocked at the door.

Within, a desultory chat had taken the place of movement and musical sound. The hedge-carpenter was suggesting a song to the company, which nobody just then was inclined to undertake, so that the knock afforded a not unwelcome diversion.

' Walk in ! ' said the shepherd promptly.

The latch clicked upward, and out of the night our pedestrian appeared upon the door-mat. The shepherd arose, snuffed two of the nearest candles, and turned to look at him.

Their light disclosed that the stranger was dark in complexion and not unprepossessing as to feature. His hat, which for a moment he did not remove, hung low over his eyes, without concealing that they were large, open, and determined, moving with a flash rather than a glance round the room. He seemed pleased with his survey, and, baring his shaggy head, said, in a rich deep voice, ' The rain is so heavy, friends, that I ask leave to come in and rest awhile.'

' To be sure, stranger,' said the shepherd. ' And faith, you've been lucky in choosing your time, foɪ we are having a bit of a fling for a glad cause—though, to be sure, a man could hardly wish that glad cause to happen more than once a year.'

' Nor less,' spoke up a woman. ' For 'tis best to get your family over and done with, as soon as you can, so as to be all the earlier out of the fag o't.'

' And what may be this glad cause ? ' asked the stranger.

' A birth and christening,' said the shepherd.

The stranger hoped his host might not be made unhappy either by too many or too few of such episodes, and being invited by a gesture to a pull at the mug, he readily acquiesced. His manner, which, before entering. had been so dubious, was now altogether that of a careless and candid man.

' Late to be traipsing athwart this coomb—hey ? ' said the engaged man of fifty.

'Late it is. master, as you say.—I'll take a seat in the
chimney-corner, if you have nothing to urge against it,
ma'am ; for I am a little moist on the side that was next
the rain.'

Mrs. Shepherd Fennel assented, and made room for the
self-invited comer, who, having got completely inside the
chimney-corner, stretched out his legs and his arms with
the expansiveness of a person quite at home.

'Yes, I am rather cracked in the vamp,' he said freely,
seeing that the eyes of the shepherd's wife fell upon his
boots, 'and I am not well fitted either. I have had some
rough times lately, and have been forced to pick up what
I can get in the way of wearing, but I must find a suit
better fit for working-days when I reach home.'

'One of hereabouts ? ' she inquired.

'Not quite that—further up the country.'

'I thought so. And so be I ; and by your tongue you
come from my neighbourhood.'

'But you would hardly have heard of me,' he said
quickly. 'My time would be long before yours, ma'am,
you see.'

This testimony to the youthfulness of his hostess had
the effect of stopping her cross-examination.

'There is only one thing more wanted to make me
happy,' continued the new-comer. 'And that is a little
baccy, which I am sorry to say I am out of.'

'I'll fill your pipe,' said the shepherd.

'I must ask you to lend me a pipe likewise.'

'A smoker, and no pipe about 'ee ? '

'I have dropped it somewhere on the road.'

The shepherd filled and handed him a new clay pipe,
saying, as he did so, 'Hand me your baccy-box— I'll fill
that too, now I am about it.'

The man went through the movement of searching his
pockets.

'Lost that too ? ' said his entertainer, with some surprise.

'I am afraid so,' said the man with some confusion.
'Give it to me in a screw of paper.' Lighting his pipe at
the candle with a suction that drew the whole flame into
the bowl, he resettled himself in the corner and bent his

looks upon the faint steam from his damp legs, as if he wished to say no more.

Meanwhile the general body of guests had been taking little notice of this visitor by reason of an absorbing discussion in which they were engaged with the band about a tune for the next dance. The matter being settled, they were about to stand up when an interruption came in the shape of another knock at the door.

At sound of the same the man in the chimney-corner took up the poker and began stirring the brands as if doing it thoroughly were the one aim of his existence; and a second time the shepherd said, 'Walk in!' In a moment another man stood upon the straw-woven door-mat. He too was a stranger.

This individual was one of a type radically different from the first. There was more of the commonplace in his manner, and a certain jovial cosmopolitanism sat upon his features. He was several years older than the first arrival, his hair being slightly frosted, his eyebrows bristly, and his whiskers cut back from his cheeks. His face was rather full and flabby, and yet it was not altogether a face without power. A few grog-blossoms marked the neigh-bourhood of his nose. He flung back his long drab great-coat, revealing that beneath it he wore a suit of cinder-gray shade throughout, large heavy seals, of some metal or other that would take a polish, dangling from his fob as his only personal ornament. Shaking the water-drops from his low-crowned glazed hat, he said, 'I must ask for a few minutes' shelter, comrades, or I shall be wetted to my skin before I get to Casterbridge.'

'Make yourself at home, master,' said the shepherd, perhaps a trifle less heartily than on the first occasion. Not that Fennel had the least tinge of niggardliness in his composition; but the room was far from large, spare chairs were not numerous, and damp companions were not altogether desirable at close quarters for the women and girls in their bright-coloured gowns.

However, the second comer, after taking off his great-coat, and hanging his hat on a nail in one of the ceiling-beams as if he had been specially invited to put it there,

advanced and sat down at the table. This had been
pushed so closely into the chimney-corner, to give all
available room to the dancers, that its inner edge grazed
the elbow of the man who had ensconced himself by the
fire ; and thus the two strangers were brought into close
companionship. They nodded to each other by way of
breaking the ice of unacquaintance, and the first stranger
handed his neighbour the family mug—a huge vessel of
brown ware, having its upper edge worn away like a
threshold by the rub of whole generations of thirsty lips
that had gone the way of all flesh, and bearing the following
inscription burnt upon its rotund side in yellow letters :—

THERE IS NO FUN
UNTILL i CUM

The other man, nothing loth, raised the mug to his lips,
and drank on, and on, and on—till a curious blueness
overspread the countenance of the shepherd's wife, who
had regarded with no little surprise the first stranger's
free offer to the second of what did not belong to him to
dispense.

'I knew it ! ' said the toper to the shepherd with much
satisfaction. ' When I walked up your garden before
coming in, and saw the hives all of a row, I said to myself,
" Where there's bees there's honey, and where there's honey
there's mead." But mead of such a truly comfortable
sort as this I really didn't expect to meet in my older days.'
He took yet another pull at the mug, till it assumed an
ominous elevation.

'Glad you enjoy it ! ' said the shepherd warmly.

'It is goodish mead,' assented Mrs. Fennel, with an
absence of enthusiasm which seemed to say that it was
possible to buy praise for one's cellar at too heavy a price.
'It is trouble enough to make—and really I hardly think
we shall make any more. For honey sells well, and we
ourselves can make shift with a drop o' small mead and
metheglin for common use from the comb-washings.'

'O, but you'll never have the heart ! ' reproachfully
cried the stranger in cinder-gray, after taking up the mug
a third time and setting it down empty. · 'I love mead,

when 'tis old like this, as I love to go to church o' Sundays
or to relieve the needy any day of the week.'

' Ha, ha, ha ! ' said the man in the chimney-corner, who,
in spite of the taciturnity induced by the pipe of tobacco,
could not or would not refrain from this slight testimony
to his comrade's humour.

Now the old mead of those days, brewed of the purest
first-year or maiden honey, four pounds to the gallon—
with its due complement of white of eggs, cinnamon, ginger,
cloves, mace, rosemary, yeast, and processes of working,
bottling, and cellaring—tasted remarkably strong ; but it
did not taste so strong as it actually was. Hence, presently,
the stranger in cinder-gray at the table, moved by its
creeping influence, unbuttoned his waistcoat, threw himself
back in his chair, spread his legs, and made his presence
felt in various ways.

' Well, well, as I say,' he resumed, ' I am going to Casterbridge, and to Casterbridge I must go. I should have been
almost there by this time ; but the rain drove me into
your dwelling, and I'm not sorry for it.'

' You don't live in Casterbridge ? ' said the shepherd.

' Not as yet ; though I shortly mean to move there.'

' Going to set up in trade, perhaps ? '

' No, no,' said the shepherd's wife. ' It is easy to see
that the gentleman is rich, and don't want to work at
anything.'

The cinder-gray stranger paused, as if to consider
whether he would accept that definition of himself. He
presently rejected it by answering, ' Rich is not quite the
word for me, dame. I do work, and I must work. And
even if I only get to Casterbridge by midnight I must begin
work there at eight to-morrow morning. Yes, het or wet,
blow or snow, famine or sword, my day's work to-morrow
must be done.'

' Poor man ! Then, in spite o' seeming, you be worse
off than we ? ' replied the shepherd's wife.

' 'Tis the nature of my trade, men and maidens. 'Tis
the nature of my trade more than my poverty. . . . But
really and truly I must up and off, or I shan't get a lodging
in the town.' However, the speaker did not move, and

directly added, 'There's time for one more draught of friendship before I go ; and I'd perform it at once if the mug were not dry.'

'Here's a mug o' small,' said Mrs. Fennel. 'Small, we call it, though to be sure 'tis only the first wash o' the combs.'

'No,' said the stranger disdainfully. 'I won't spoil your first kindness by partaking o' your second.'

'Certainly not,' broke in Fennel. 'We don't increase and multiply every day, and I'll fill the mug again.' He went away to the dark place under the stairs where the barrel stood. The shepherdess followed him.

'Why should you do this ? ' she said reproachfully, as soon as they were alone. 'He's emptied it once, though it held enough for ten people ; and now he's not contented wi' the small, but must needs call for more o' the strong ! And a stranger unbeknown to any of us. For my part, I don't like the look o' the man at all.'

'But he's in the house, my honey ; and 'tis a wet night, and a christening. Daze it, what's a cup of mead more or less ? There'll be plenty more next bee-burning.'

'Very well—this time, then,' she answered, looking wistfully at the barrel. 'But what is the man's calling, and where is he one of, that he should come in and join us like this ? '

'I don't know. I'll ask him again.'

The catastrophe of having the mug drained dry at one pull by the stranger in cinder-gray was effectually guarded against this time by Mrs. Fennel. She poured out his allowance in a small cup, keeping the large one at a discreet distance from him. When he had tossed off his portion the shepherd renewed his inquiry about the stranger's occupation.

The latter did not immediately reply, and the man in the chimney-corner, with sudden demonstrativeness, said, 'Anybody may know my trade—I'm a wheelwright.'

'A very good trade for these parts,' said the shepherd.

'And anybody may know mine—if they've the sense to find it out,' said the stranger in cinder-gray.

'You may generally tell what a man is by his claws,

observed the hedge-carpenter, looking at his own hands.
' My fingers be as full of thorns as an old pin-cushion is of
pins.'

The hands of the man in the chimney-corner instinctively
sought the shade, and he gazed into the fire as he resumed
his pipe. The man at the table took up the hedge-
carpenter's remark, and added smartly, ' True ; but the
oddity of my trade is that, instead of setting a mark upon
me, it sets a mark upon my customers.'

No observation being offered by anybody in elucidation
of this enigma the shepherd's wife once more called for a
song. The same obstacles presented themselves as at the
former time—one had no voice, another had forgotten the
first verse. The stranger at the table, whose soul had now
risen to a good working temperature, relieved the difficulty
by exclaiming that, to start the company, he. would sing
himself. Thrusting one thumb into the arm-hole of his
waistcoat, he waved the other hand in the air, and, with
an extemporizing gaze at the shining sheep-crooks above
the mantelpiece, began :—

> O my trade it is the rarest one,
>   Simple shepherds all—
>   My trade is a sight to see ;
> For my customers I tie, and take them up on high,
>   And waft 'em to a far countree ! '

The room was silent when he had finished the verse—
with one exception, that of the man in the chimney-
corner, who, at the singer's word, ' Chorus ! ' joined him
in a deep bass voice of musical relish—

> ' And waft 'em to a far countree ! '

Oliver Giles, John Pitcher the dairyman, the parish-
clerk, the engaged man of fifty, the row of young women
against the wall, seemed lost in thought not of the gayest
kind. The shepherd looked meditatively on the ground,
the shepherdess gazed keenly at the singer, and with.
some suspicion ; she was doubting whether this stranger
were merely singing an old song from recollection, or was
composing one there and then for the occasion. All were
as perplexed at the obscure revelation as the guests at

Belshazzar's Feast, except the man in the chimney-corner,
who quietly said, 'Second verse, stranger,' and smoked
on.

The singer thoroughly moistened himself from his lips
inwards, and went on with the next stanza as requested :—

> ' My tools are but common ones,
> Simple shepherds all—
> My tools are no sight to see :
> A little hempen string, and a post whereon to swing,
> Are implements enough for me ! '

Shepherd Fennel glanced round. There was no longer
any doubt that the stranger was answering his question
rhythmically. The guests one and all started back with
suppressed exclamations. The young woman engaged to
the man of fifty fainted half-way, and would have proceeded, but finding him wanting in alacrity for catching
her she sat down trembling.

' O, he's the——! ' whispered the people in the background, mentioning the name of an ominous public officer.
' He's come to do it ! 'Tis to be at Casterbridge jail
to-morrow—the man for sheep-stealing—the poor clock-
maker we heard of, who used to live away at Shottsford
and had no work to do—Timothy Summers, whose family
were a-starving, and so he went out of Shottsford by the
high-road, and took a sheep in open daylight, defying the
farmer and the farmer's wife and the farmer's lad, and
every man jack among 'em. He ' (and they nodded
towards the stranger of the deadly trade) ' is come from up
the country to do it because there's not enough to do
in his own county-town, and he's got the place here now
our own county man's dead ; he's going to live in the same
cottage under the prison wall.'

The stranger in cinder-gray took no notice of this whispered string of observations, but again wetted his lips.
Seeing that his friend in the chimney-corner was the only
one who reciprocated his joviality in any way, he held out
his cup towards that appreciative comrade, who also
held out his own. They clinked together, the eyes of the
rest of the room hanging upon the singer's actions. He
parted his lips for the third verse ; but at that moment

another knock was audible upon the door. This time the
knock was faint and hesitating.

The company seemed scared; the shepherd looked
with consternation towards the entrance, and it was with
some effort that he resisted his alarmed wife's deprecatory
glance, and uttered for the third time the welcoming words,
' Walk in ! '

The door was gently opened, and another man stood
upon the mat. He, like those who had preceded him, was
a stranger. This time it was a short, small personage, of
fair complexion, and dressed in a decent suit of dark clothes.

' Can you tell me the way to——? ' he began : when,
gazing round the room to observe the nature of the company amongst whom he had fallen, his eyes lighted on the
stranger in cinder-gray. It was just at the instant when
the latter, who had thrown his mind into his song with
such a will that he scarcely heeded the interruption,
silenced all whispers and inquiries by bursting into his
third verse :—

> ' To-morrow is my working day,
> Simple shepherds all—
> To-morrow is a working day for me :
> For the farmer's sheep is slain, and the lad who did it ta'en,
> And on his soul may God ha' merc-y ! '

The stranger in the chimney-corner, waving cups with
the singer so heartily that his mead splashed over on the
hearth, repeated in his bass voice as before :—

> ' And on his soul may God ha' merc-y ! '

All this time the third stranger had been standing
in the doorway. Finding now that he did not come
forward or go on speaking, the guests particularly regarded
him. They noticed to their surprise that he stood before
them the picture of abject terror—his knees trembling,
his hand shaking so violently that the door-latch by which
he supported himself rattled audibly : his white lips were
parted, and his eyes fixed on the merry officer of justice
in the middle of the room. A moment more and he had
turned, closed the door, and fled.

' What a man can it be ? ' said the shepherd.

The rest, between the awfulness of their late discovery and the odd conduct of this third visitor, looked as if they knew not what to think, and said nothing. Instinctively they withdrew further and further from the grim gentleman in their midst, whom some of them seemed to take for the Prince of Darkness himself, till they formed a remote circle, an empty space of floor being left between them and him—

> '. . . circulus, cujus centrum diabolus.'

The room was so silent—though there were more than twenty people in it—that nothing could be heard but the patter of the rain against the window-shutters, accompanied by the occasional hiss of a stray drop that fell down the chimney into the fire, and the steady puffing of the man in the corner, who had now resumed his pipe of long clay.

The stillness was unexpectedly broken. The distant sound of a gun reverberated through the air—apparently from the direction of the county-town.

'Be jiggered!' cried the stranger who had sung the song, jumping up.

'What does that mean?' asked several.

'A prisoner escaped from the jail—that's what it means.'

All listened. The sound was repeated, and none of them spoke but the man in the chimney-corner, who said quietly, 'I've often been told that in this county they fire a gun at such times; but I never heard it till now.'

'I wonder if it is *my* man?' murmured the personage in cinder-gray.

'Surely it is!' said the shepherd involuntarily. 'And surely we've zeed him! That little man who looked in at the door by now, and quivered like a leaf when he zeed ye and heard your song!'

'His teeth chattered, and the breath went out of his body,' said the dairyman.

'And his heart seemed to sink within him like a stone,' said Oliver Giles.

'And he bolted as if he'd been shot at,' said the hedge-carpenter.

'True—his teeth chattered, and his heart seemed to sink ; and he bolted as if he'd been shot at,' slowly summed up the man in the chimney-corner.

'I didn't notice it,' remarked the hangman.

'We were all a-wondering what made him run off in such a fright,' faltered one of the women against the wall, 'and now 'tis explained !'

The firing of the alarm-gun went on at intervals, low and sullenly, and their suspicions became a certainty. The sinister gentleman in cinder-gray roused himself. 'Is there a constable here ? ' he asked, in thick tones. 'If so, let him step forward.'

The engaged man of fifty stepped quavering out from the wall, his betrothed beginning to sob on the back of the chair.

'You are a sworn constable ? '

'I be, sir.'

'Then pursue the criminal at once, with assistance, and bring him back here. He can't have gone far.'

'I will, sir, I will—when I've got my staff. I'll go home and get it, and come sharp here, and start in a body.'

'Staff !—never mind your staff ; the man'll be gone ! '

'But I can't do nothing without my staff—can I, William, and John, and Charles Jake ? No ; for there's the king's royal crown a painted on en in yaller and gold, and the lion and the unicorn, so as when I raise en up and hit my prisoner, 'tis made a lawful blow thereby. I wouldn't 'tempt to take up a man without my staff—no, not I. If I hadn't the law to gie me courage, why, instead o' my taking up him he might take up me ! '

'Now, I'm a king's man myself, and can give you authority enough for this,' said the formidable officer in gray. 'Now then, all of ye, be ready. Have ye any lanterns ? '

'Yes—have ye any lanterns ?—I demand it ! ' said the constable.

'And the rest of you able-bodied——'

'Able-bodied men—yes—the rest of ye ! ' said the constable.

'Have you some good stout staves and pitchforks——'

' Staves and pitchforks—in the name o' the law ! And
take 'em in yer hands and go in quest, and do as we in
authority tell ye ! '

Thus aroused, the men prepared to give chase. The
evidence was, indeed, though circumstantial, so con-
vincing, that but little argument was needed to show the
shepherd's guests that after what they had seen it would
look very much like connivance if they did not instantly
pursue the unhappy third stranger, who could not as yet
have gone more than a few hundred yards over such un-
even country.

A shepherd is always well provided with lanterns ; and,
lighting these hastily, and with hurdle-staves in their
hands, they poured out of the door, taking a direction
along the crest of the hill, away from the town, the rain
having fortunately a little abated.

Disturbed by the noise, or possibly by unpleasant
dreams of her baptism, the child who had been christened
began to cry heart-brokenly in the room overhead. These
notes of grief came down through the chinks of the floor
to the ears of the women below, who jumped up one by one,
and seemed glad of the excuse to ascend and comfort the
baby, for the incidents of the last half-hour greatly oppressed them. Thus in the space of two or three minutes
the room on the ground-floor was deserted quite.

But it was not for long. Hardly had the sound of footsteps died away when a man returned round the corner of
the house from the direction the pursuers had taken.
Peeping in at the door, and seeing nobody there, he entered
leisurely. It was the stranger of the chimney-corner, who
had gone out with the rest. The motive of his return
was shown by his helping himself to a cut piece of skimmer-
cake that lay on a ledge beside where he had sat, and
which he had apparently forgotten to take with him.
He also poured out half a cup more mead from the quantity that remained, ravenously eating and drinking these
as he stood. He had not finished when another figure
came in just as quietly—his friend in cinder-gray.

' O—you here ? ' said the latter, smiling. ' I thought
you had gone to help in the capture.' And this speaker

also revealed the object of his return by looking soli-citously round for the fascinating mug of old mead.

'And I thought you had gone,' said the other, con-tinuing his skimmer-cake with some effort.

'Well, on second thoughts, I felt there were enough without me,' said the first confidentially, 'and such a night as it is, too. Besides, 'tis the business o' the Govern-ment to take care of its criminals—not mine.'

'True; so it is. And I felt as you did, that there were enough without me.'

'I don't want to break my limbs running over the humps and hollows of this wild country.'

'Nor I neither, between you and me.'

'These shepherd-people are used to it—simple-minded souls, you know, stirred up to anything in a moment. They'll have him ready for me before the morning, and no trouble to me at all.'

'They'll have him, and we shall have saved ourselves all labour in the matter.'

'True, true. Well, my way is to Casterbridge; and 'tis as much as my legs will do to take me that far. Going the same way?'

'No, I am sorry to say! I have to get home over there' (he nodded indefinitely to the right), 'and I feel as you do, that it is quite enough for my legs to do before bedtime.'

The other had by this time finished the mead in the mug, after which, shaking hands heartily at the door, and wishing each other well, they went their several ways.

In the meantime the company of pursuers had reached the end of the hog's-back elevation which dominated this part of the down. They had decided on no particular plan of action; and, finding that the man of the baleful trade was no longer in their company, they seemed quite unable to form any such plan now. They descended in all directions down the hill, and straightway several of the party fell into the snare set by Nature for all misguided midnight ramblers over this part of the cretaceous for-mation. The 'lanchets,' or flint slopes, which belted the escarpment at intervals of a dozen yards, took the less cautious ones unawares, and losing their footing on the rubbly steep they slid sharply downwards, the lanterns rolling from their hands to the bottom, and there lying on their sides till the horn was scorched through.

When they had again gathered themselves together the shepherd, as the man who knew the country best, took the lead, and guided them round these treacherous inclines. The lanterns, which seemed rather to dazzle their eyes and warn the fugitive than to assist them in the exploration, were extinguished, due silence was observed; and in this more rational order they plunged into the vale. It was a grassy, briery, moist defile, affording some shelter to any person who had sought it; but the party perambulated it in vain, and ascended on the other side. Here they wandered apart, and after an interval closed together again to report progress. At the second time of closing in they found themselves near a lonely ash, the single tree on this part of the coomb, probably sown there by a passing bird some fifty years before. And here, standing a little to one side of the trunk, as motionless as the trunk itself, appeared the man they were in quest of, his outline being well defined against the sky beyond. The band noiselessly drew up and faced him.

'Your money or your life!' said the constable sternly to the still figure.

'No, no,' whispered John Pitcher. ''Tisn't our side ought to say that. That's the doctrine of vagabonds like him, and we be on the side of the law.'

'Well, well,' replied the constable impatiently; 'I must say something, mustn't I? and if you had all the weight o' this undertaking upon your mind, perhaps you'd say the wrong thing too!—Prisoner at the bar, surrender, in the name of the Father—the Crown, I mane!'

The man under the tree seemed now to notice them for the first time, and, giving them no opportunity whatever for exhibiting their courage, he strolled slowly towards them. He was, indeed, the little man, the third stranger; but his trepidation had in a great measure gone.

'Well, travellers,' he said, 'did I hear ye speak to me?'

'You did: you've got to come and be our prisoner

at once ! ' said the constable. ' We arrest 'ee on the charge
of not biding in Casterbridge jail in a decent proper manner
to be hung to-morrow morning. Neighbours, do your duty,
and seize the culpet ! '

On hearing the charge the man seemed enlightened, and,
saying not another word, resigned himself with preter-
natural civility to the search-party, who, with their staves
in their hands, surrounded him on all sides, and marched
him back towards the shepherd's cottage.

It was eleven o'clock by the time they arrived. The
light shining from the open door, a sound of men's voices
within, proclaimed to them as they approached the house
that some new events had arisen in their absence. On
entering they discovered the shepherd's living-room to be
invaded by two officers from Casterbridge jail, and a well-
known magistrate who lived at the nearest country-seat,
intelligence of the escape having become generally circulated.

' Gentlemen,' said the constable, ' I have brought back
your man—not without risk and danger ; but every one
must do his duty ! He is inside this circle of able-bodied
persons, who have lent me useful aid, considering their
ignorance of Crown work. Men, bring forward your
prisoner ! ' And the third stranger was led to the light.

' Who is this ? ' said one of the officials.

' The man,' said the constable.

' Certainly not,' said the turnkey ; and the first corroborated his statement.

' But how can it be otherwise ? ' asked the constable.
' Or why was he so terrified at sight o' the singing instrument of the law who sat there ? ' Here he related the
strange behaviour of the third stranger on entering the
house during the hangman's song.

' Can't understand it,' said the officer coolly. ' All I
know is that it is not the condemned man. He's quite a
different character from this one ; a gauntish fellow, with
dark hair and eyes, rather good-looking, and with a musical
bass voice that if you heard it once you'd never mistake as
long as you lived.'

' Why, souls—'twas the man in the chimney-corner ! '

' Hey—what ? ' said the magistrate, coming forward

after inquiring particulars from the shepherd in the background. ' Haven't you got the man after all ? '

' Well, sir,' said the constable, ' he's the man we were in search of, that's true ; and yet he's not the man we were in search of. For the man we were in search of was not the man we wanted, sir, if you understand my every-day way ; for 'twas the man in the chimney-corner ! '

' A pretty kettle of fish altogether ! ' said the magistrate. ' You had better start for the other man at once.'

The prisoner now spoke for the first time. The mention of the man in the chimney-corner seemed to have moved him as nothing else could do. ' Sir,' he said, stepping forward to the magistrate, ' take no more trouble about me. The time is come when I may as well speak. I have done nothing ; my crime is that the condemned man is my brother. Early this afternoon I left home at Shottsford to tramp it all the way to Casterbridge jail to bid him farewell. I was benighted, and called here to rest and ask the way. When I opened the door I saw before me the very man, my brother, that I thought to see in the condemned cell at Casterbridge. He was in this chimney-corner ; and jammed close to him, so that he could not have got out if he had tried, was the executioner who'd come to take his life, singing a song about it and not knowing that it was his victim who was close by, joining in to save appearances. My brother threw a glance of agony at me, and I knew he meant, " Don't reveal what you see ; my life depends on it." I was so terror-struck that I could hardly stand, and, not knowing what I did, I turned and hurried away.'

The narrator's manner and tone had the stamp of truth, and his story made a great impression on all around.

' And do you know where your brother is at the present time ? ' asked the magistrate.

' I do not. I have never seen him since I closed this door.'

' I can testify to that, for we've been between ye ever since,' said the constable.

' Where does he think to fly to ?—what is his occupation ? '

' He's a watch-and-clock-maker, sir.'

' 'A said 'a was a wheelwright—a wicked rogue,' said the constable.

' The wheels of clocks and watches he meant, no doubt,' said Shepherd Fennel. ' I thought his hands were palish for's trade.'

' Well, it appears to me that nothing can be gained by retaining this poor man in custody,' said the magistrate ; ' your business lies with the other, unquestionably.'

And so the little man was released off-hand ; but he looked nothing the less sad on that account, it being beyond the power of magistrate or constable to raze out the written troubles in his brain, for they concerned another whom he regarded with more solicitude than himself. When this was done, and the man had gone his way, the night was found to be so far advanced that it was deemed useless to renew the search before the next morning.

Next day, accordingly, the quest for the clever sheep-stealer became general and keen, to all appearance at least. But the intended punishment was cruelly disproportioned to the transgression, and the sympathy of a great many country-folk in that district was strongly on the side of the fugitive. Moreover, his marvellous coolness and daring in hob-and-nobbing with the hangman, under the unprecedented circumstances of the shepherd's party, won their admiration. So that it may be questioned if all those who ostensibly made themselves so busy in exploring woods and fields and lanes were quite so thorough when it came to the private examination of their own lofts and out-houses. Stories were afloat of a mysterious figure being occasionally seen in some old overgrown trackway or other, remote from turnpike roads ; but when a search was instituted in any of these suspected quarters nobody was found. Thus the days and weeks passed without tidings.

In brief, the bass-voiced man of the chimney-corner was never recaptured. Some said that he went across the sea, others that he did not, but buried himself in the depths of a populous city. At any rate, the gentleman in cinder-gray never did his morning's work at Casterbridge, nor met anywhere at all, for business purposes, the genial comrade with whom he had passed an hour of relaxation in the lonely house on the slope of the coomb.

The grass has long been green on the graves of Shepherd Fennel and his frugal wife ; the guests who made up the christening party have mainly followed their entertainers to the tomb ; the baby in whose honour they all had met is a matron in the sere and yellow leaf. But the arrival of the three strangers at the shepherd's that night, and the details connected therewith, is a story as well known as ever in the country about Higher Crowstairs.

March 1883.

A TRADITION OF
EIGHTEEN HUNDRED AND FOUR

A TRADITION OF
EIGHTEEN HUNDRED AND FOUR

THE widely discussed possibility of an invasion of England through a Channel tunnel has more than once recalled old Solomon Selby's story to my mind.

The occasion on which I numbered myself among his audience was one evening when he was sitting in the yawning chimney-corner of the inn-kitchen, with some others who had gathered there, and I entered for shelter from the rain. Withdrawing the stem of his pipe from the dental notch in which it habitually rested, he leaned back in the recess behind him and smiled into the fire. The smile was neither mirthful nor sad, not precisely humorous nor altogether thoughtful. We who knew him recognized it in a moment : it was his narrative smile. Breaking off our few desultory remarks we drew up closer, and he thus began :—

' My father, as you mid know, was a shepherd all his life, and lived out by the Cove four miles yonder, where I was born and lived likewise, till I moved here shortly afore I was married. The cottage that first knew me stood on the top of the down, near the sea ; there was no house within a mile and a half of it ; it was built o' purpose for the farm-shepherd, and had no other use. They tell me that it is now pulled down, but that you can see where it stood by the mounds of earth and a few broken bricks that are still lying about. It was a bleak and dreary place in winter-time, but in summer it was well enough, though the garden never came to much, because we could not get up a good shelter for the vegetables and currant bushes ; and where there is much wind they don't thrive.

' Of all the years of my growing up the ones that bide clearest in my mind were eighteen hundred and three, four, and five. This was for two reasons : I had just then

35

grown to an age when a child's eyes and ears take in and
note down everything about him, and there was more at
that date to bear in mind than there ever has been since
with me.   It was, as I need hardly tell ye, the time after
the first peace, when Bonaparte was scheming his descent
upon England.   He had crossed the great Alp mountains,
fought in Egypt, drubbed the Turks, the Austrians, and
the Prooossians, and now thought he'd have a slap at us.
On the other side of the Channel, scarce out of sight and
hail of a man standing on our English shore, the French
army of a hundred and sixty thousand men and fifteen
thousand horses had been brought together from all parts,
and were drilling every day.   Bonaparte had been three
years a-making his preparations ; and to ferry these soldiers
and cannon and horses across he had contrived a couple
of thousand flat-bottomed boats.   These boats were small
things, but wonderfully built.   A good few of 'em were so
made as to have a little stable on board each for the two
horses that were to haul the cannon carried at the stern.
To get in order all these, and other things required, he had
assembled there five or six thousand fellows that worked
at trades—carpenters, blacksmiths, wheelwrights, saddlers,
and what not.   O 'twas a curious time !

' Every morning Neighbour Boney would muster his
multitude of soldiers on the beach, draw 'em up in line,
practise 'em in the manœuvre of embarking, horses and
all, till they could do it without a single hitch.   My father
drove a flock of ewes up into Sussex that year, and as he
went along the drover's track over the high downs thereabout he could see this drilling actually going on—the
accoutrements of the rank and file glittering in the sun
like silver.   It was thought and always said by my uncle
Job, sergeant of foot (who used to know all about these
matters), that Bonaparte meant to cross with oars on a
calm night.   The grand query with us, was, Where would
my gentleman land ?   Many of the common people thought
it would be at Dover ; others, who knew how unlikely it
was that any skilful general would make a business of
landing just where he was expected, said he'd go either
east into the River Thames, or west'ard to some convenient

place, most likely one of the little bays inside the Isle of
Portland, between the Beal and St. Alban's Head—and
for choice the three-quarter-round Cove, screened from
every mortal eye, that seemed made o' purpose, out by
where we lived, and which I've climmed up with two tubs
of brandy across my shoulders on scores o' dark nights in
my younger days. Some had heard that a part o' the
French fleet would sail right round Scotland, and come up
the Channel to a suitable haven. However, there was
much doubt upon the matter; and no wonder, for after-
years proved that Bonaparte himself could hardly make up
his mind upon that great and very particular point, where
to land. His uncertainty came about in this wise, that
he could get no news as to where and how our troops
lay in waiting, and that his knowledge of possible places
where flat-bottomed boats might be quietly run ashore,
and the men they brought marshalled in order, was dim
to the last degree. Being flat-bottomed, they didn't require a harbour for unshipping their cargo of men, but a
good shelving beach away from sight, and with a fair open
road toward London. How the question posed that great
Corsican tyrant (as we used to call him), what pains he
took to settle it, and, above all, what a risk he ran on one
particular night in trying to do so, were known only to
one man here and there; and certainly to no maker of
newspapers or printer of books, or my account o't would
not have had so many heads shaken over it as it has by
gentry who only believe what they see in printed lines.

' The flocks my father had charge of fed all about the
downs near our house, overlooking the sea and shore each
way for miles. In winter and early spring father was up
a deal at nights, watching and tending the lambing. Often
he'd go to bed early, and turn out at twelve or one; and
on the other hand, he'd sometimes stay up till twelve or
one, and then turn in to bed. As soon as I was old enough
I used to help him, mostly in the way of keeping an eye
upon the ewes while he was gone home to rest. This is
what I was doing in a particular month in either the year
four or five—I can't certainly fix which, but it was long
before I was took away from the sheepkeeping to be

bound prentice to a trade. Every night at that time I
was at the fold, about half a mile, or it may be a little more,
from our cottage, and no living thing at all with me but
the ewes and young lambs. Afeard? No; I was never
afeared of being alone at these times; for I had been
reared in such an out-step place that the lack o' human
beings at night made me less fearful than the sight of 'em.
Directly I saw a man's shape after dark in a lonely place
I was frightened out of my senses.

' One day in that month we were surprised by a visit
from my uncle Job, the sergeant in the Sixty-first foot,
then in camp on the downs above King George's watering-
place, several miles to the west yonder. Uncle Job dropped
in about dusk, and went up with my father to the fold
for an hour or two. Then he came home, had a drop to
drink from the tub of sperrits that the smugglers kept us
in for housing their liquor when they'd made a run, and for
burning 'em off when there was danger. After that he
stretched himself out on the settle to sleep. I went to
bed: at one o'clock father came home, and waking me
to go and take his place, according to custom, went to
bed himself. On my way out of the house I passed Uncle
Job on the settle. He opened his eyes, and upon my
telling him where I was going he said it was a shame
that such a youngster as I should go up there all alone;
and when he had fastened up his stock and waist-belt
he set off along with me, taking a drop from the
sperrit-tub in a little flat bottle that stood in the corner-
cupboard.

' By and by we drew up to the fold, saw that all was
right, and then, to keep ourselves warm, curled up in a
heap of straw that lay inside the thatched hurdles we had
set up to break the stroke of the wind when there was any.
To-night, however, there was none. It was one of those
very still nights when, if you stand on the high hills anywhere within two or three miles of the sea, you can hear
the rise and fall of the tide along the shore, coming and
going every few moments like a sort of great snore of the
sleeping world. Over the lower ground there was a bit of
a mist, but on the hill where we lay the air was clear, and

the moon, then in her last quarter, flung a fairly good light
on the grass and scattered straw.

'While we lay there Uncle Job amused me by telling
me strange stories of the wars he had served in and the
wownds he had got. He had already fought the French
in the Low Countries, and hoped to fight 'em again. His
stories lasted so long that at last I was hardly sure that I
was not a soldier myself, and had seen such service as he
told of. The wonders of his tales quite bewildered my
mind, till I fell asleep and dreamed of battle, smoke, and
flying soldiers, all of a kind with the doings he had been
bringing up to me.

'How long my nap lasted I am not prepared to say.
But some faint sounds over and above the rustle of the
ewes in the straw, the bleat of the lambs, and the tinkle
of the sheep-bell brought me to my waking senses. Uncle
Job was still beside me ; but he too had fallen asleep. I
looked out from the straw, and saw what it was that had
aroused me. Two men, in boat-cloaks, cocked hats, and
swords, stood by the hurdles about twenty yards off.

'I turned my ear thitherward to catch what they were
saying, but though I heard every word o't, not one did I
understand. They spoke in a tongue that was not ours
—in French, as I afterward found. But if I could not
gain the meaning of a word, I was shrewd boy enough to
find out a deal of the talkers' business. By the light o'
the moon I could see that one of 'em carried a roll of
paper in his hand, while every moment he spoke quick
to his comrade, and pointed right and left with the other
hand to spots along the shore. There was no doubt that
he was explaining to the second gentleman the shapes and
features of the coast. What happened soon after made
this still clearer to me.

'All this time I had not waked Uncle Job, but now I
began to be afeared that they might light upon us, because
uncle breathed so heavily through's nose. I put my mouth
to his ear and whispered, " Uncle Job."

' " What is it, my boy ? " he said, just as if he hadn't
been asleep at all.

' " Hush ! " says I. " Two French generals—"

' " French ? " says he.

' " Yes," says I. " Come to see where to land their army ! "

' I pointed 'em out ; but I could say no more, for the pair were coming at that moment much nearer to where we lay. As soon as they got as near as eight or ten yards, the officer with a roll in his hand stooped down to a slanting hurdle, unfastened his roll upon it, and spread it out. Then suddenly he sprung a dark lantern open on the paper, and showed it to be a map.

' " What be they looking at ? " I whispered to Uncle Job.

' " A chart of the Channel," says the sergeant (knowing about such things).

' The other French officer now stooped likewise, and over the map they had a long consultation, as they pointed here and there on the paper, and then hither and thither at places along the shore beneath us. I noticed that the manner of one officer was very respectful toward the other, who seemed much his superior, the second in rank calling him by a sort of title that I did not know the sense of. The head one, on the other hand, was quite familiar with his friend, and more than once clapped him on the shoulder.

' Uncle Job had watched as well as I, but though the map had been in the lantern-light, their faces had always been in shade. But when they rose from stooping over the chart the light flashed upward, and fell smart upon one of 'em's features. No sooner had this happened than Uncle Job gasped, and sank down as if he'd been in a fit.

' " What is it—what is it, Uncle Job ? " said I.

' " O good God ! " says he, under the straw.

' " What ? " says I.

' " Boney ! " he groaned out.

' " Who ? " says I.

' " Bonaparty," he said. " The Corsican ogre. O that I had got but my new-flinted firelock, that there man should die ! But I haven't got my new-flinted firelock, and that there man must live. So lie low, as you value your life ! "

' I did lie low, as you mid suppose. But I couldn't help

peeping. And then I too, lad as I was, knew that it was the face of Bonaparte. Not know Boney? I should think I did know Boney. I should have known him by half the light o' that lantern. If I had seen a picture of his features once, I had seen it a hundred times. There was his bullet head, his short neck, his round yaller cheeks and chin, his gloomy face, and his great glowing eyes. He took off his hat to blow himself a bit, and there was the forelock in the middle of his forehead, as in all the draughts of him. In moving, his cloak fell a little open, and I could see for a moment his white-fronted jacket and one of the epaulets.

' But none of this lasted long. In a minute he and his general had rolled up the map, shut the lantern, and turned to go down toward the shore.

' Then Uncle Job came to himself a bit. "Slipped across in the night-time to see how to put his men ashore," he said. " The like o' that man's coolness eyes will never again see ! Nephew, I must act in this, and immediate, or England's lost ! "

' When they were over the brow, we crope out, and went some little way to look after them. Half-way down they were joined by two others, and six or seven minutes brought them to the shore. Then, from behind a rock, a boat came out into the weak moonlight of the Cove, and they jumped in ; it put off instantly, and vanished in a few minutes between the two rocks that stand at the mouth of the Cove as we all know. We climmed back to where we had been before, and I could see, a short way out, a larger vessel, though still not very large. The little boat drew up alongside, was made fast at the stern as I suppose, for the largest sailed away, and we saw no more.

' My uncle Job told his officers as soon as he got back to camp ; but what they thought of it I never heard—neither did he. Boney's army never came, and a good job for me ; for the Cove below my father's house was where he meant to land, as this secret visit showed. We coast-folk should have been cut down one and all, and I should not have sat here to tell this tale.'

We who listened to old Selby that night have been

familiar with his simple grave-stone for these ten years past. Thanks to the incredulity of the age his tale has been seldom repeated. But if anything short of the direct testimony of his own eyes could persuade an auditor that Bonaparte had examined these shores for himself with a view to a practicable landing-place, it would have been Solomon Selby's manner of narrating the adventure which befell him on the down.

Christmas, 1882.

THE MELANCHOLY HUSSAR OF THE GERMAN
LEGION

THE MELANCHOLY HUSSAR OF THE GERMAN LEGION

I

HERE stretch the downs, high and breezy and green, absolutely unchanged since those eventful days. A plough has never disturbed the turf, and the sod that was uppermost then is uppermost now. Here stood the camp; here are distinct traces of the banks thrown up for the horses of the cavalry, and spots where the midden-heaps lay are still to be observed. At night, when I walk across the lonely place, it is impossible to avoid hearing, amid the scourings of the wind over the grass-bents and thistles, the old trumpet and bugle calls, the rattle of the halters; to help seeing rows of spectral tents and the *impedimenta* of the soldiery. From within the canvases come guttural syllables of foreign tongues, and broken songs of the fatherland; for they were mainly regiments of the King's German Legion that slept round the tent-poles hereabout at that time.

It was nearly ninety years ago. The British uniform of the period, with its immense epaulettes, queer cocked-hat, breeches, gaiters, ponderous cartridge-box, buckled shoes, and what not, would look strange and barbarous now. Ideas have changed; invention has followed invention. Soldiers were monumental objects then. A divinity still hedged kings here and there; and war was considered a glorious thing.

Secluded old manor-houses and hamlets lie in the ravines and hollows among these hills, where a stranger had hardly ever been seen till the King chose to take the baths yearly at the sea-side watering-place a few miles to the south; as a consequence of which battalions descended in a cloud upon the open country around. Is it necessary to add that the echoes of many characteristic tales, dating from

that picturesque time, still linger about here in more or
less fragmentary form, to be caught by the attentive ear ?
Some of them I have repeated ; most of them I have
forgotten ; one I have never repeated, and assuredly can
never forget.

Phyllis told me the story with her own lips. She was
then an old lady of seventy-five, and her auditor a lad of
fifteen. She enjoined silence as to her share in the incident,
till she should be ' dead, buried, and forgotten.' Her life
was prolonged twelve years after the day of her narration,
and she has now been dead nearly twenty. The oblivion
which in her modesty and humility she courted for herself
has only partially fallen on her, with the unfortunate
result of inflicting an injustice upon her memory ; since
such fragments of her story as got abroad at the time,
and have been kept alive ever since, are precisely those
which are most unfavourable to her character.

It all began with the arrival of the York Hussars, one
of the foreign regiments above alluded to. Before that
day scarcely a soul had been seen near her father's house
for weeks. When a noise like the brushing skirt of a
visitor was heard on the doorstep, it proved to be a scudding
leaf ; when a carriage seemed to be nearing the door, it
was her father grinding his sickle on the stone in the garden
for his favourite relaxation of trimming the box-tree borders
to the plots. A sound like luggage thrown down from the
coach was a gun far away at sea ; and what looked like a
tall man by the gate at dusk was a yew bush cut into a
quaint and attenuated shape. There is no such solitude
in country places now as there was in those old days.

Yet all the while King George and his Court were at his
favourite sea-side resort, not more than five miles off.

The daughter's seclusion was great, but beyond the
seclusion of the girl lay the seclusion of the father. If
her social condition was twilight, his was darkness. Yet
he enjoyed his darkness, while her twilight oppressed her.
Dr. Grove had been a professional man whose taste
for lonely meditation over metaphysical questions had
diminished his practice till it no longer paid him to keep
it going ; after which he had relinquished it and hired at

a nominal rent the small, dilapidated, half farm, half manor-house of this obscure inland nook, to make a sufficiency of an income which in a town would have been inadequate for their maintenance. He stayed in his garden the greater part of the day, growing more and more irritable with the lapse of time, and the increasing perception that he had wasted his life in the pursuit of illusions He saw his friends less and less frequently. Phyllis became so shy that if she met a stranger anywhere in her short rambles she felt ashamed at his gaze, walked awkwardly, and blushed to her shoulders.

Yet Phyllis was discovered even here by an admirer, and her hand most unexpectedly asked in marriage.

The King, as aforesaid, was at the neighbouring town, where he had taken up his abode at Gloucester Lodge ; and his presence in the town naturally brought many county people thither. Among these idlers—many of whom professed to have connections and interests with the Court—was one Humphrey Gould, a bachelor ; a personage neither young nor old ; neither good-looking nor positively plain. Too steady-going to be ' a buck ' (as fast and unmarried men were then called), he was an approximately fashionable man of a mild type. This bachelor of thirty found his way to the village on the down : beheld Phyllis ; made her father's acquaintance in order to make hers ; and by some means or other she sufficiently inflamed his heart to lead him in that direction almost daily ; till he became engaged to marry her.

As he was of an old local family, some of whose members were held in respect in the county, Phyllis, in bringing him to her feet, had accomplished what was considered a brilliant move for one in her constrained position. How she had done it was not quite known to Phyllis herself. In those days unequal marriages were regarded rather as a violation of the laws of nature than as a mere infringement of convention, the more modern view, and hence when Phyllis, of the watering-place *bourgeoisie*, was chosen by such a gentlemanly fellow, it was as if she were going to be taken to heaven, though perhaps the uninformed would have seen no great difference in the respective

positions of the pair, the said Gould being as poor as a
crow.

This pecuniary condition was his excuse—probably a
true one—for postponing their union, and as the winter
drew nearer, and the King departed for the season, Mr.
Humphrey Gould set out for Bath, promising to return
to Phyllis in a few weeks. The winter arrived, the date
of his promise passed, yet Gould postponed his coming,
on the ground that he could not very easily leave his father
in the city of their sojourn, the elder having no other
relative near him. Phyllis, though lonely in the extreme,
was content. The man who had asked her in marriage
was a desirable husband for her in many ways ; her father
highly approved of his suit ; but this neglect of her was
awkward, if not painful, for Phyllis. Love him in the
true sense of the word she assured me she never did, but
she had a genuine regard for him ; admired a certain
methodical and dogged way in which he sometimes took
his pleasure ; valued his knowledge of what the Court
was doing, had done, or was about to do ; and she was not
without a feeling of pride that he had chosen her when
he might have exercised a more ambitious choice.

But he did not come ; and the spring developed. His
letters were regular though formal ; and it is not to be
wondered that the uncertainty of her position, linked with
the fact that there was not much passion in her thoughts
of Humphrey, bred an indescribable dreariness in the heart
of Phyllis Grove. The spring was soon summer, and the
summer brought the King ; but still no Humphrey Gould.
All this while the engagement by letter was maintained
intact.

At this point of time a golden radiance flashed in upon
the lives of people here, and charged all youthful thought
with emotional interest. This radiance was the aforesaid
York Hussars.

II

The present generation has probably but a very dim
notion of the celebrated York Hussars of ninety years ago.
They were one of the regiments of the King's German

Legion, and (though they somewhat degenerated later on)
their brilliant uniform, their splendid horses, and above
all, their foreign air and mustachios (rare appendages then),
drew crowds of admirers of both sexes wherever they went.
These with other regiments had come to encamp on the
downs and pastures, because of the presence of the King
in the neighbouring town.

The spot was high and airy, and the view extensive,
commanding Portland—the Isle of Slingers—in front, and
reaching to St. Aldhelm's Head eastward, and almost to
the Start on the west.

Phyllis, though not precisely a girl of the village, was
as interested as any of them in this military investment.
Her father's home stood somewhat apart, and on the
highest point of ground to which the lane ascended, so
that it was almost level with the top of the church tower
in the lower part of the parish. Immediately from the
outside of the garden-wall the grass spread away to a
great distance, and it was crossed by a path which came
close to the wall. Ever since her childhood it had been
Phyllis's pleasure to clamber up this fence and sit on the
top—a feat not so difficult as it may seem, the walls in
this district being built of rubble, without mortar, so
that there were plenty of crevices for small toes.

She was sitting up here one day, listlessly surveying the
pasture without, when her attention was arrested by a
solitary figure walking along the path. It was one of the
renowned German Hussars, and he moved onward with
his eyes on the ground, and with the manner of one who
wished to escape company. His head would probably
have been bent like his eyes but for his stiff neck-gear.
On nearer view she perceived that his face was marked
with deep sadness. Without observing her, he advanced
by the footpath till it brought him almost immediately
under the wall.

Phyllis was much surprised to see a fine, tall soldier
in such a mood as this. Her theory of the military, and
of the York Hussars in particular (derived entirely from
hearsay, for she had never talked to a soldier in her life),
was that their hearts were as gay as their accoutrements.

At this moment the Hussar lifted his eyes and noticed her on her perch, the white muslin neckerchief which covered her shoulders and neck where left bare by her low gown, and her white raiment in general, showing conspicuously in the bright sunlight of this summer day. He blushed a little at the suddenness of the encounter, and without halting a moment from his pace passed on.

All that day the foreigner's face haunted Phyllis; its aspect was so striking, so handsome, and his eyes were so blue, and sad, and abstracted. It was perhaps only natural that on some following day at the same hour she should look over that wall again, and wait till he had passed a second time. On this occasion he was reading a letter, and at the sight of her his manner was that of one who had half expected or hoped to discover her. He almost stopped, smiled, and made a courteous salute. The end of the meeting was that they exchanged a few words. She asked him what he was reading, and he readily informed her that he was re-perusing letters from his mother in Germany; he did not get them often, he said, and was forced to read the old ones a great many times. This was all that passed at the present interview, but others of the same kind followed.

Phyllis used to say that his English, though not good, was quite intelligible to her, so that their acquaintance was never hindered by difficulties of speech. Whenever the subject became too delicate, subtle, or tender, for such words of English as were at his command, the eyes no doubt helped out the tongue, and—though this was later on—the lips helped out the eyes. In short, this acquaintance, unguardedly made, and rash enough on her part, developed and ripened. Like Desdemona, she pitied him, and learnt his history.

His name was Matthäus Tina, and Saarbrück his native town, where his mother was still living. His age was twenty-two, and he had already risen to the grade of corporal, though he had not long been in the army. Phyllis used to assert that no such refined or well-educated young man could have been found in the ranks of the purely English regiments, some of these foreign soldiers having rather the graceful manner and presence of our native officers than of our rank and file.

She by degrees learnt from her foreign friend a circumstance about himself and his comrades which Phyllis would least have expected of the York Hussars. So far from being as gay as its uniform, the regiment was pervaded by a dreadful melancholy, a chronic home-sickness, which depressed many of the men to such an extent that they could hardly attend to their drill. The worst sufferers were the younger soldiers who had not been over here long. They hated England and English life; they took no interest whatever in King George and his island kingdom, and they only wished to be out of it and never to see it any more. Their bodies were here, but their hearts and minds were always far away in their dear fatherland, of which—brave men and stoical as they were in many ways—they would speak with tears in their eyes. One of the worst of the sufferers from this home-woe, as he called it in his own tongue, was Matthäus Tina, whose dreamy musing nature felt the gloom of exile still more intensely from the fact that he had left a lonely mother at home with nobody to cheer her.

Though Phyllis, touched by all this, and interested in his history, did not disdain her soldier's acquaintance, she declined (according to her own account, at least) to permit the young man to overstep the line of mere friendship for a long while—as long, indeed, as she considered herself likely to become the possession of another; though it is probable that she had lost her heart to Matthäus before she was herself aware. The stone wall of necessity made anything like intimacy difficult; and he had never ventured to come, or to ask to come, inside the garden, so that all their conversation had been overtly conducted across this boundary.

III

But news reached the village from a friend of Phyllis's father concerning Mr. Humphrey Gould, her remarkably cool and patient betrothed. This gentleman had been heard to say in Bath that he considered his overtures to

Miss Phyllis Grove to have reached only the stage of a half-understanding ; and in view of his enforced absence on his father's account, who was too great an invalid now to attend to his affairs, he thought it best that there should be no definite promise as yet on either side. He was not sure, indeed, that he might not cast his eyes elsewhere.

This account—though only a piece of hearsay, and as such entitled to no absolute credit—tallied so well with the infrequency of his letters and their lack of warmth, that Phyllis did not doubt its truth for one moment ; and from that hour she felt herself free to bestow her heart as she should choose. Not so her father ; he declared the whole story to be a fabrication. He had known Mr. Gould's family from his boyhood ; and if there was one proverb which expressed the matrimonial aspect of that family well, it was ' Love me little, love me long.' Humphrey was an honourable man, who would not think of treating his engagement so lightly. ' Do you wait in patience,' he said ; ' all will be right enough in time.'

From these words Phyllis at first imagined that her father was in correspondence with Mr. Gould ; and her heart sank within her ; for in spite of her original intentions she had been relieved to hear that her engagement had come to nothing. But she presently learnt that her father had heard no more of Humphrey Gould than she herself had done ; while he would not write and address her affianced directly on the subject, lest it should be deemed an imputation on that bachelor's honour.

' You want an excuse for encouraging one or other of those foreign fellows to flatter you with his unmeaning attentions,' her father exclaimed, his mood having of late been a very unkind one towards her. ' I see more than I say. Don't you ever set foot outside that garden-fence without my permission. If you want to see the camp I'll take you myself some Sunday afternoon.'

Phyllis had not the smallest intention of disobeying him in her actions, but she assumed herself to be independent with respect to her feelings. She no longer checked her fancy for the Hussar, though she was far from regarding him as her lover in the serious sense in which an Englishman might have been regarded as such. The young foreign soldier was almost an ideal being to her, with none of the appurtenances of an ordinary house-dweller; one who had descended she knew not whence, and would disappear she knew not whither; the subject of a fascinating dream—no more.

They met continually now—mostly at dusk—during the brief interval between the going down of the sun and the minute at which the last trumpet-call summoned him to his tent. Perhaps her manner had become less restrained latterly; at any rate that of the Hussar was so; he had grown more tender every day, and at parting after these hurried interviews she reached down her hand from the top of the wall that he might press it. One evening he held it such a while that she exclaimed, ' The wall is white, and somebody in the field may see your shape against it ! '

He lingered so long that night that it was with the greatest difficulty that he could run across the intervening stretch of ground and enter the camp in time. On the next occasion of his awaiting her she did not appear in her usual place at the usual hour. His disappointment was unspeakably keen; he remained staring blankly at the spot, like a man in a trance. The trumpets and tattoo sounded, and still he did not go.

She had been delayed purely by an accident. When she arrived she was anxious because of the lateness of the hour, having heard as well as he the sounds denoting the closing of the camp. She implored him to leave immediately.

' No,' he said gloomily. ' I shall not go in yet—the moment you come—I have thought of your coming all day.'

' But you may be disgraced at being after time ? '

' I don't mind that. I should have disappeared from the world some time ago if it had not been for two persons —my beloved, here, and my mother in Saarbrück. I hate the army. I care more for a minute of your company than for all the promotion in the world.'

Thus he stayed and talked to her, and told her inter-

esting details of his native place, and incidents of his
childhood, till she was in a simmer of distress at his recklessness in remaining. It was only because she insisted
on bidding him good-night, and leaving the wall, that he
returned to his quarters.

The next time that she saw him he was without the
stripes that had adorned his sleeve. He had been broken
to the level of private for his lateness that night ; and as
Phyllis considered herself to be the cause of his disgrace
her sorrow was great. But the position was now reversed ;
it was his turn to cheer her.

' Don't grieve, meine Liebliche ! ' he said. ' I have got
a remedy for whatever comes. First, even supposing I
regain my stripes, would your father allow you to marry
a non-commissioned officer in the York Hussars ? '

She flushed. This practical step had not been in her
mind in relation to such an unrealistic person as he was ;
and a moment's reflection was enough for it. ' My father
would not—certainly would not,' she answered unflinchingly.
' It cannot be thought of ! My dear friend, please do forget me : I fear I am ruining you and your prospects ! '

' Not at all ! ' said he. ' You are giving this country
of yours just sufficient interest to me to make me care
to keep alive in it. If my dear land were here also, and
my old parent, with you, I could be happy as I am, and
would do my best as a soldier. But it is not so. And now
listen. This is my plan. That you go with me to my own
country, and be my wife there, and live there with my
mother and me. I am not a Hanoverian, as you know,
though I entered the army as such ; my country is by the
Saar, and is at peace with France, and if I were once in it
I should be free.'

' But how get there ? ' she asked. Phyllis had been
rather amazed than shocked at his proposition. Her
position in her father's house was growing irksome and
painful in the extreme ; his parental affection seemed to
be quite dried up. She was not a native of the village,
like all the joyous girls around her ; and in some way
Matthäus Tina had infected her with his own passionate
longing for his country, and mother, and home.

'But how?' she repeated, finding that he did not answer. 'Will you buy your discharge?'

'Ah, no,' he said. 'That's impossible in these times. No; I came here against my will; why should I not escape? Now is the time, as we shall soon be striking camp, and I might see you no more. This is my scheme. I will ask you to meet me on the highway two miles off, on some calm night next week that may be appointed. There will be nothing unbecoming in it, or to cause you shame; you will not fly alone with me, for I will bring with me my devoted young friend, Christoph, an Alsatian, who has lately joined the regiment, and who has agreed to assist in this enterprise. We shall have come from yonder harbour, where we shall have examined the boats, and found one suited to our purpose. Christoph has already a chart of the Channel, and we will then go to the harbour, and at midnight cut the boat from her moorings, and row away round the point out of sight; and by the next morning we are on the coast of France, near Cherbourg. The rest is easy, for I have saved money for the land journey, and can get a change of clothes. I will write to my mother, who will meet us on the way.'

He added details in reply to her inquiries, which left no doubt in Phyllis's mind of the feasibility of the undertaking. But its magnitude almost appalled her; and it is questionable if she would ever have gone further in the wild adventure if, on entering the house that night, her father had not accosted her in the most significant terms.

'How about the York Hussars?' he said.

'They are still at the camp; but they are soon going away, I believe.'

'It is useless for you to attempt to cloak your actions in that way. You have been meeting one of those fellows; you have been seen walking with him—foreign barbarians, not much better than the French themselves! I have made up my mind—don't speak a word till I have done, please!—I have made up my mind that you shall stay here no longer while they are on the spot. You shall go to your aunt's.'

It was useless for her to protest that she had never taken

a walk with any soldier or man under the sun except himself. Her protestations were feeble, too, for though he was not literally correct in his assertion, he was virtually only half in error.

The house of her father's sister was a prison to Phyllis. She had quite recently undergone experience of its gloom; and when her father went on to direct her to pack what would be necessary for her to take, her heart died within her. In after-years she never attempted to excuse her conduct during this week of agitation; but the result of her self-communing was that she decided to join in the scheme of her lover and his friend, and fly to the country which he had coloured with such lovely hues in her imagination. She always said that the one feature in his proposal which overcame her hesitation was the obvious purity and straightforwardness of his intentions. He showed himself to be so virtuous and kind; he treated her with a respect to which she had never before been accustomed; and she was braced to the obvious risks of the voyage by her confidence in him.

IV

It was on a soft, dark evening of the following week that they engaged in the adventure. Tina was to meet her at a point in the highway at which the lane to the village branched off. Christoph was to go ahead of them to the harbour where the boat lay, row it round the Nothe —or Look-out as it was called in those days—and pick them up on the other side of the promontory, which they were to reach by crossing the harbour-bridge on foot, and climbing over the Look-out hill.

As soon as her father had ascended to his room she left the house, and, bundle in hand, proceeded at a trot along the lane. At such an hour not a soul was afoot anywhere in the village, and she reached the junction of the lane with the highway unobserved. Here she took up her position in the obscurity formed by the angle of a fence, whence she could discern every one who approached along the turnpike-road, without being herself seen.

She had not remained thus waiting for her lover longer

than a minute—though from the tension of her nerves the lapse of even that short time was trying—when, instead of the expected footsteps, the stage-coach could be heard descending the hill. She knew that Tina would not show himself till the road was clear, and waited impatiently for the coach to pass. Nearing the corner where she was it slackened speed, and, instead of going by as usual, drew up within a few yards of her. A passenger alighted, and she heard his voice. It was Humphrey Gould's.

He had brought a friend with him, and luggage. The luggage was deposited on the grass, and the coach went on its route to the royal watering-place.

'I wonder where that young man is with the horse and trap?' said her former admirer to his companion. 'I hope we shan't have to wait here long. I told him half-past nine o'clock precisely.'

'Have you got her present safe?'

'Phyllis's? O, yes. It is in this trunk. I hope it will please her.'

'Of course it will. What woman would not be pleased with such a handsome peace-offering?'

'Well—she deserves it. I've treated her rather badly. But she has been in my mind these last two days much more than I should care to confess to everybody. Ah, well; I'll say no more about that. It cannot be that she is so bad as they make out. I am quite sure that a girl of her good wit would know better than to get entangled with any of those Hanoverian soldiers. I won't believe it of her, and there's an end on't.'

More words in the same strain were casually dropped as the two men waited; words which revealed to her, as by a sudden illumination, the enormity of her conduct. The conversation was at length cut off by the arrival of the man with the vehicle. The luggage was placed in it, and they mounted, and were driven on in the direction from which she had just come.

Phyllis was so conscience-stricken that she was at first inclined to follow them; but a moment's reflection led her to feel that it would only be bare justice to Matthäus to wait till he arrived, and explain candidly that she had changed her mind—difficult as the struggle would be when she stood face to face with him. She bitterly reproached herself for having believed reports which represented Humphrey Gould as false to his engagement, when, from what she now heard from his own lips, she gathered that he had been living full of trust in her. But she knew well enough who had won her love. Without him her life seemed a dreary prospect, yet the more she looked at his proposal the more she feared to accept it—so wild as it was, so vague, so venturesome. She had promised Humphrey Gould, and it was only his assumed faithlessness which had led her to treat that promise as nought. His solicitude in bringing her these gifts touched her ; her promise must be kept, and esteem must take the place of love. She would preserve her self-respect. She would stay at home, and marry him, and suffer.

Phyllis had thus braced herself to an exceptional fortitude when, a few minutes later, the outline of Matthäus Tina appeared behind a field-gate, over which he lightly leapt as she stepped forward. There was no evading it, he pressed her to his breast.

' It is the first and last time ! ' she wildly thought as she stood encircled by his arms.

How Phyllis got through the terrible ordeal of that night she could never clearly recollect. She always attributed her success in carrying out her resolve to her lover's honour, for as soon as she declared to him in feeble words that she had changed her mind, and felt that she could not, dared not, fly with him, he forbore to urge her, grieved as he was at her decision. Unscrupulous pressure on his part, seeing how romantically she had become attached to him, would no doubt have turned the balance in his favour. But he did nothing to tempt her unduly or unfairly.

On her side, fearing for his safety, she begged him to remain. This, he declared, could not be. ' I cannot break faith with my friend,' said he. Had he stood alone he would have abandoned his plan. But Christoph, with the boat and compass and chart, was waiting on the shore ;

the tide would soon turn ; his mother had been warned of his coming ; go he must.

Many precious minutes were lost while he tarried, unable to tear himself away. Phyllis held to her resolve, though it cost her many a bitter pang. At last they parted, and he went down the hill. Before his footsteps had quite died away she felt a desire to behold at least his outline once more, and running noiselessly after him regained view of his diminishing figure. For one moment she was sufficiently excited to be on the point of rushing forward and linking her fate with his. But she could not. The courage which at the critical instant failed Cleopatra of Egypt could scarcely be expected of Phyllis Grove.

A dark shape, similar to his own, joined him in the highway. It was Christoph, his friend. She could see no more ; they had hastened on in the direction of the town and harbour, four miles ahead. With a feeling akin to despair she turned and slowly pursued her way homeward.

Tattoo sounded in the camp ; but there was no camp for her now. It was as dead as the camp of the Assyrians after the passage of the Destroying Angel.

She noiselessly entered the house, seeing nobody, and went to bed. Grief, which kept her awake at first, ulti-mately wrapped her in a heavy sleep. The next morning her father met her at the foot of the stairs.

' Mr. Gould is come ! ' he said triumphantly.

Humphrey was staying at the inn, and had already called to inquire for her. He had brought her a present of a very handsome looking-glass in a frame of *repoussé* silverwork, which her father held in his hand. He had promised to call again in the course of an hour, to ask Phyllis to walk with him.

Pretty mirrors were rarer in country-houses at that day than they are now, and the one before her won Phyllis's admiration. She looked into it, saw how heavy her eyes were, and endeavoured to brighten them. She was in that wretched state of mind which leads a woman to move mechanically onward in what she conceives to be her allotted path. Mr. Humphrey had, in his undemonstrative way,

been adhering all along to the old understanding ; it was
for her to do the same, and to say not a word of her own
lapse. She put on her bonnet and tippet, and when he
arrived at the hour named she was at the door awaiting
him.

v

Phyllis thanked him for his beautiful gift ; but the talking was soon entirely on Humphrey's side as they walked
along. He told her of the latest movements of the world
of fashion—a subject which she willingly discussed to the
exclusion of anything more personal—and his measured
language helped to still her disquieted heart and brain.
Had not her own sadness been what it was she must have
observed his embarrassment. At last he abruptly changed
the subject.

' I am glad you are pleased with my little present,' he said.
' The truth is that I brought it to propitiate 'ee, and
to get you to help me out of a mighty difficulty.'

It was inconceivable to Phyllis that this independent
bachelor—whom she admired in some respects—could
have a difficulty.

' Phyllis—I'll tell you my secret at once ; for I have a
monstrous secret to confide before I can ask your counsel.
The case is, then, that I am married : yes, I have privately
married a dear young belle ; and if you knew her, and I
hope you will, you would say everything in her praise.
But she is not quite the one that my father would have
chose for me—you know the paternal idea as well as I
—and I have kept it secret. There will be a terrible noise,
no doubt ; but I think that with your help I may get over
it. If you would only do me this good turn—when I have
told my father, I mean—say that you never could have
married me, you know, or something of that sort—'pon
my life it will help to smooth the way vastly. I am so
anxious to win him round to my point of view, and not to
cause any estrangement.'

What Phyllis replied she scarcely knew, or how she
counselled him as to his unexpected situation. Yet the
relief that his announcement brought her was perceptible.

To have confided her trouble in return was what her aching
heart longed to do ; and had Humphrey been a woman
she would instantly have poured out her tale. But to him
she feared to confess ; and there was a real reason for
silence, till a sufficient time had elapsed to allow her
lover and his comrade to get out of harm's way.

As soon as she reached home again she sought a solitary
place, and spent the time in half regretting that she had
not gone away, and in dreaming over the meetings with
Matthäus Tina from their beginning to their end. In his
own country, amongst his own countrywomen, he would
possibly soon forget her, even to her very name.

Her listlessness was such that she did not go out of the
house for several days. There came a morning which broke
in fog and mist, behind which the dawn could be discerned
in greenish grey ; and the outlines of the tents, and the
rows of horses at the ropes. The smoke from the canteen
fires drooped heavily.

The spot at the bottom of the garden where she had
been accustomed to climb the wall to meet Matthäus
was the only inch of English ground in which she took any
interest ; and in spite of the disagreeable haze prevailing
she walked out there till she reached the well-known corner.
Every blade of grass was weighted with little liquid globes,
and slugs and snails had crept out upon the plots. She
could hear the usual faint noises from the camp, and in
the other direction the trot of farmers on the road to
the town, for it was market-day. She observed that her
frequent visits to this corner had quite trodden down the
grass in the angle of the wall, and left marks of garden
soil on the stepping-stones by which she had mounted to
look over the top. Seldom having gone there till dusk,
she had not considered that her traces might be visible by
day. Perhaps it was these which had revealed her trysts
to her father.

While she paused in melancholy regard, she fancied
that the customary sounds from the tents were changing
their character. Indifferent as Phyllis was to camp doings
now, she mounted by the steps to the old place. What
she beheld at first awed and perplexed her ; then she stood

rigid, her fingers hooked to the wall, her eyes staring out of her head, and her face as if hardened to stone.

On the open green stretching before her all the regiments in the camp were drawn up in line, in the mid-front of which two empty coffins lay on the ground. The unwonted sounds which she had noticed came from an advancing procession. It consisted of the band of the York Hussars playing a dead march ; next two soldiers of that regiment in a mourning coach, guarded on each side, and accompanied by two priests. Behind came a crowd of rustics who had been attracted by the event. The melancholy procession marched along the front of the line, returned to the centre, and halted beside the coffins, where the two condemned men were blindfolded, and each placed kneeling on his coffin ; a few minutes' pause was now given while they prayed.

A firing-party of twenty-four men stood ready with levelled carbines. The commanding officer, who had his sword drawn, waved it through some cuts of the sword-exercise till he reached the downward stroke, whereat the firing-party discharged their volley. The two victims fell, one upon his face across his coffin, the other backwards.

As the volley resounded there arose a shriek from the wall of Dr. Grove's garden, and some one fell down inside ; but nobody among the spectators without noticed it at the time. The two executed Hussars were Matthäus Tina and his friend Christoph. The soldiers on guard placed the bodies in the coffins almost instantly ; but the colonel of the regiment, an Englishman, rode up and exclaimed in a stern voice : ' Turn them out—as an example to the men ! '

The coffins were lifted endwise, and the dead Germans flung out upon their faces on the grass. Then all the regiments wheeled in sections, and marched past the spot in slow time. When the survey was over the corpses were again coffined, and borne away.

Meanwhile Dr. Grove, attracted by the noise of the volley, had rushed out into his garden, where he saw his wretched daughter lying motionless against the wall. She was taken indoors, but it was long before she recovered consciousness; and for weeks they despaired of her reason.

It transpired that the luckless deserters from the York Hussars had cut the boat from her moorings in the adjacent harbour, according to their plan, and, with two other comrades who were smarting under ill-treatment from their colonel, had sailed in safety across the Channel. But mistaking their bearings they steered into Jersey, thinking that island the French coast. Here they were perceived to be deserters, and delivered up to the authorities. Matthäus and Christoph interceded for the other two at the court-martial, saying that it was entirely by the former's representations that these were induced to go. Their sentence was accordingly commuted to flogging, the death punishment being reserved for their leaders.

The visitor to the well-known old Georgian watering-place, who may care to ramble to the neighbouring village under the hills, and examine the register of burials, will there find two entries in these words:—

' Matth : Tina (Corpl.) in His Majesty's Regmt. of York Hussars, and Shot for Desertion, was Buried June 30th, 1801, aged 22 years. Born in the town of Sarrbruk, Germany.
' Christoph Bless, belonging to His Majesty's Regmt. of York Hussars, who was Shot for Desertion, was Buried June 30th, 1801, aged 22 years. Born at Lothaargen, Alsatia.'

Their graves were dug at the back of the little church, near the wall. There is no memorial to mark the spot, but Phyllis pointed it out to me. While she lived she used to keep their mounds neat; but now they are overgrown with nettles, and sunk nearly flat. The older villagers, however, who know of the episode from their parents, still recollect the place where the soldiers lie. Phyllis lies near.

October 1889.

THE WITHERED ARM

THE WITHERED ARM

A LORN MILKMAID

I

IT was an eighty-cow dairy, and the troop of milkers, regular and supernumerary, were all at work; for, though the time of year was as yet but early April, the feed lay entirely in water-meadows, and the cows were ' in full pail.' The hour was about six in the evening, and three-fourths of the large, red, rectangular animals having been finished off, there was opportunity for a little conversation.

' He do bring home his bride to-morrow, I hear. They've come as far as Anglebury to-day.'

The voice seemed to proceed from the belly of the cow called Cherry, but the speaker was a milking-woman, whose face was buried in the flank of that motionless beast.

' Hav' anybody seen her ? ' said another.

There was a negative response from the first. ' Though they say she's a rosy-cheeked, tisty-tosty little body enough,' she added; and as the milkmaid spoke she turned her face so that she could glance past her cow's tail to the other side of the barton, where a thin, fading woman of thirty milked somewhat apart from the rest.

' Years younger than he, they say,' continued the second, with also a glance of reflectiveness in the same direction.

' How old do you call him, then ? '

' Thirty or so.'

' More like forty,' broke in an old milkman near, in a long white pinafore or ' wropper,' and with the brim of his hat tied down, so that he looked like a woman. ' 'A was born before our Great Weir was builded, and I hadn't man's wages when I laved water there.'

The discussion waxed so warm that the purr of the milk-streams became jerky, till a voice from another cow's belly

67

cried with authority, ' Now then, what the Turk do it matter to us about Farmer Lodge's age, or Farmer Lodge's new mis'ess ? I shall have to pay him nine pound a year for the rent of every one of these milchers, whatever his age or hers. Get on with your work, or 'twill be dark afore we have done. The evening is pinking in a'ready.' This speaker was the dairyman himself, by whom the milkmaids and men were employed.

Nothing more was said publicly about Farmer Lodge's wedding, but the first woman murmured under her cow to her next neighbour, ' 'Tis hard for *she*,' signifying the thin worn milkmaid aforesaid.

' O no,' said the second. ' He ha'n't spoke to Rhoda Brook for years.'

When the milking was done they washed their pails and hung them on a many-forked stand made as usual of the peeled limb of an oak-tree, set upright in the earth, and resembling a colossal antlered horn. The majority then dispersed in various directions homeward. The thin woman who had not spoken was joined by a boy of twelve or thereabout, and the twain went away up the field also.

Their course lay apart from that of the others, to a lonely spot high above the water-meads, and not far from the border of Egdon Heath, whose dark countenance was visible in the distance as they drew nigh to their home.

' They've just been saying down in barton that your father brings his young wife home from Anglebury to-morrow,' the woman observed. ' I shall want to send you for a few things to market, and you'll be pretty sure to meet 'em.'

' Yes, mother,' said the boy. ' Is father married then ? '

' Yes . . . You can give her a look, and tell me what she's like, if you do see her.'

' Yes, mother.'

' If she's dark or fair, and if she's tall—as tall as I. And if she seems like a woman who has ever worked for a living, or one that has been always well off, and has never done anything, and shows marks of the lady on her, as I expect she do.'

' Yes.'

They crept up the hill in the twilight and entered the cottage. It was built of mud-walls, the surface of which had been washed by many rains into channels and depressions that left none of the original flat face visible; while here and there in the thatch above a rafter showed like a bone protruding through the skin.

She was kneeling down in the chimney-corner, before two pieces of turf laid together with the heather inwards, blowing at the red-hot ashes with her breath till the turves flamed. The radiance lit her pale cheek, and made her dark eyes, that had once been handsome, seem handsome anew. 'Yes,' she resumed, 'see if she is dark or fair, and if you can, notice if her hands be white; if not, see if they look as though she had ever done housework, or are milker's hands like mine.'

The boy again promised, inattentively this time, his mother not observing that he was cutting a notch with his pocket-knife in the beech-backed chair.

THE YOUNG WIFE

II

THE road from Anglebury to Holmstoke is in general level; but there is one place where a sharp ascent breaks its monotony. Farmers homeward-bound from the former market-town, who trot all the rest of the way, walk their horses up this short incline.

The next evening while the sun was yet bright a handsome new gig, with a lemon-coloured body and red wheels, was spinning westward along the level highway at the heels of a powerful mare. The driver was a yeoman in the prime of life, cleanly shaven like an actor, his face being toned to that bluish-vermilion hue which so often graces a thriving farmer's features when returning home after successful dealings in the town. Beside him sat a woman, many years his junior—almost, indeed, a girl. Her face too was fresh in colour, but it was of a totally different quality—soft and evanescent, like the light under a heap of rose-petals.

Few people travelled this way, for it was not a main

road, and the long white riband of gravel that stretched before them was empty, save of one small scarce-moving speck, which presently resolved itself into the figure of a boy, who was creeping on at a snail's pace, and continually looking behind him—the heavy bundle he carried being some excuse for, if not the reason of, his dilatoriness. When the bouncing gig-party slowed at the bottom of the incline above mentioned, the pedestrian was only a few yards in front. Supporting the large bundle by putting one hand on his hip, he turned and looked straight at the farmer's wife as though he would read her through and through, pacing along abreast of the horse.

The low sun was full in her face, rendering every feature, shade, and contour distinct, from the curve of her little nostril to the colour of her eyes. The farmer, though he seemed annoyed at the boy's persistent presence, did not order him to get out of the way; and thus the lad preceded them, his hard gaze never leaving her, till they reached the top of the ascent, when the farmer trotted on with relief in his lineaments—having taken no outward notice of the boy whatever.

'How that poor lad stared at me!' said the young wife.

'Yes, dear; I saw that he did.'

'He is one of the village, I suppose?'

'One of the neighbourhood. I think he lives with his mother a mile or two off.'

'He knows who we are, no doubt?'

'O yes. You must expect to be stared at just at first, my pretty Gertrude.'

'I do,—though I think the poor boy may have looked at us in the hope we might relieve him of his heavy load, rather than from curiosity.'

'O no,' said her husband off-handedly. 'These country lads will carry a hundredweight once they get it on their backs; besides, his pack had more size than weight in it. Now, then, another mile and I shall be able to show you our house in the distance—if it is not too dark before we get there.' The wheels spun round, and particles flew from their periphery as before, till a white house of ample

dimensions revealed itself, with farm-buildings and ricks
at the back.

Meanwhile the boy had quickened his pace, and turning
up a by-lane some mile and half short of the white farm-
stead, ascended towards the leaner pastures, and so on to
the cottage of his mother.

She had reached home after her day's milking at the
outlying dairy, and was washing cabbage at the doorway
in the declining light. ' Hold up the net a moment,' she
said, without preface, as the boy came up.

He flung down his bundle, held the edge of the cabbage-
net, and as she filled its meshes with the dripping leaves
she went on, ' Well, did you see her ? '

' Yes ; quite plain.'

' Is she ladylike ? '

' Yes ; and more. A lady complete.'

' Is she young ? '

' Well, she's growed up, and her ways be quite a woman's.'

' Of course. What colour is her hair and face ? '

' Her hair is lightish, and her face as comely as a live
doll's.'

' Her eyes, then, are not dark like mine ? '

' No—of a bluish turn, and her mouth is very nice and
red ; and when she smiles, her teeth show white.'

' Is she tall ? ' said the woman sharply.

' I couldn't see. She was sitting down.'

' Then do you go to Holmstoke church to-morrow morning : she's sure to be there. Go early and notice her
walking in, and come home and tell me if she's taller
than I.'

' Very well, mother. But why don't you go and see for
yourself ? '

' *I* go to see her ! I wouldn't look up at her if she were
to pass my window this instant. She was with Mr. Lodge,
of course. What did he say or do ? '

' Just the same as usual.'

' Took no notice of you ? '

' None.'

Next day the mother put a clean shirt on the boy, and
started him off for Holmstoke church. He reached the

ancient little pile when the door was just being opened
and he was the first to enter. Taking his seat by the
font, he watched all the parishioners file in. The well-to-
do Farmer Lodge came nearly last, and his young wife,
who accompanied him, walked up the aisle with the shyness natural to a modest woman who had appeared thus
for the first time. As all other eyes were fixed upon her,
the youth's stare was not noticed now.

When he reached home his mother said, ' Well ? ' before
he had entered the room.

' She is not tall. She is rather short,' he replied.

' Ah ! ' said his mother, with satisfaction.

' But she's very pretty—very. In fact, she's lovely.'
The youthful freshness of the yeoman's wife had evidently
made an impression even on the somewhat hard nature of
the boy.

' That's all I want to hear,' said his mother quickly.
' Now, spread the tablecloth. The hare you wired is very
tender ; but mind that nobody catches you.—You've
never told me what sort of hands she had.'

' I have never seen 'em. She never took off her gloves.'

' What did she wear this morning ? '

' A white bonnet and a silver-coloured gownd. It
whewed and whistled so loud when it rubbed against the
pews that the lady coloured up more than ever for very
shame at the noise, and pulled it in to keep it from touching ; but when she pushed into her seat, it whewed more
than ever. Mr. Lodge, he seemed pleased, and his waistcoat stuck out, and his great golden seals hung like a lord's ;
but she seemed to wish her noisy gownd anywhere but on
her.'

' Not she ! However, that will do now.'

These descriptions of the newly-married couple were
continued from time to time by the boy at his mother's
request, after any chance encounter he had had with them.
But Rhoda Brook, though she might easily have seen
young Mrs. Lodge for herself by walking a couple of miles,
would never attempt an excursion towards the quarter
where the farmhouse lay. Neither did she, at the daily
milking in the dairyman's yard on Lodge's outlying second

farm, ever speak on the subject of the recent marriage.
The dairyman, who rented the cows of Lodge, and knew
perfectly the tall milkmaid's history, with manly kindliness
always kept the gossip in the cow-barton from annoying
Rhoda. But the atmosphere thereabout was full of the
subject during the first days of Mrs. Lodge's arrival, and
from her boy's description and the casual words of the
other milkers, Rhoda Brook could raise a mental image of
the unconscious Mrs. Lodge that was realistic as a photograph.

A VISION

III

ONE night, two or three weeks after the bridal return,
when the boy was gone to bed, Rhoda sat a long time
over the turf ashes that she had raked out in front of her
to extinguish them. She contemplated so intently the
new wife, as presented to her in her mind's eye over the
embers, that she forgot the lapse of time. At last, wearied
with her day's work, she too retired.

But the figure which had occupied her so much during
this and the previous days was not to be banished at night.
For the first time Gertrude Lodge visited the supplanted
woman in her dreams. Rhoda Brook dreamed—since her
assertion that she really saw, before falling asleep, was not
to be believed—that the young wife, in the pale silk dress
and white bonnet, but with features shockingly distorted,
and wrinkled as by age, was sitting upon her chest as she
lay. The pressure of Mrs. Lodge's person grew heavier ;
the blue eyes peered cruelly into her face, and then the
figure thrust forward its left hand mockingly, so as to
make the wedding-ring it wore glitter in Rhoda's eyes.
Maddened mentally, and nearly suffocated by pressure,
the sleeper struggled ; the incubus, still regarding her,
withdrew to the foot of the bed, only, however, to come
forward by degrees, resume her seat, and flash her left
hand as before.

Gasping for breath, Rhoda, in a last desperate effort,
swung out her right hand, seized the confronting spectre

by its obtrusive left arm, and whirled it backward to the
floor, starting up herself as she did so with a low cry.

' O, merciful heaven ! ' she cried, sitting on the edge of
the bed in a cold sweat ; ' that was not a dream—she was
here ! '

She could feel her antagonist's arm within her grasp even
now—the very flesh and bone of it, as it seemed. She
looked on the floor whither she had whirled the spectre,
but there was nothing to be seen.

Rhoda Brook slept no more that night, and when she
went milking at the next dawn they noticed how pale and
haggard she looked. The milk that she drew quivered
into the pail ; her hand had not calmed even yet, and still
retained the feel of the arm. She came home to breakfast
as wearily as if it had been supper-time.

' What was that noise in your chimmer, mother, last
night ? ' said her son. ' You fell off the bed, surely ? '

' Did you hear anything fall ? At what time ? '

' Just when the clock struck two.'

She could not explain, and when the meal was done
went silently about her household work, the boy assisting
her, for he hated going afield on the farms, and she indulged
his reluctance. Between eleven and twelve the garden-
gate clicked, and she lifted her eyes to the window. At the
bottom of the garden, within the gate, stood the woman
of her vision. Rhoda seemed transfixed.

' Ah, she said she would come ! ' exclaimed the boy, also
observing her.

' Said so—when ? How does she know us ? '

' I have seen and spoken to her. I talked to her yesterday.'

' I told you,' said the mother, flushing indignantly, ' never
to speak to anybody in that house, or go near the place.'

' I did not speak to her till she spoke to me. And I
did not go near the place. I met her in the road.'

' What did you tell her ? '

' Nothing. She said, " Are you the poor boy who had
to bring the heavy load from market ? " And she looked
at my boots, and said they would not keep my feet dry if
it came on wet, because they were so cracked. I told her

I lived with my mother, and we had enough to do to keep
ourselves, and that's how it was ; and she said then, " I'll
come and bring you some better boots, and see your mother."
She gives away things to other folks in the meads besides
us.'

Mrs. Lodge was by this time close to the door—not in
her silk, as Rhoda had dreamt of in the bed-chamber, but
in a morning hat, and gown of common light material,
which became her better than silk.   On her arm she carried
a basket.

The impression remaining from the night's experience
was still strong.   Brook had almost expected to see the
wrinkles, the scorn, and the cruelty on her visitor's face.
She would have escaped an interview had escape been
possible.   There was, however, no backdoor to the cottage,
and in an instant the boy had lifted the latch to Mrs.
Lodge's gentle knock.

' I see I have come to the right house,' said she, glancing
at the lad, and smiling.   ' But I was not sure till you opened
the door.'

The figure and action were those of the phantom ; but
her voice was so indescribably sweet, her glance so winning,
her smile so tender, so unlike that of Rhoda's midnight
visitant, that the latter could hardly believe the evidence
of her senses.   She was truly glad that she had not hidden
away in sheer aversion, as she had been inclined to do.
In her basket Mrs. Lodge brought the pair of boots that
she had promised to the boy, and other useful articles.

At these proofs of a kindly feeling towards her and hers
Rhoda's heart reproached her bitterly.   This innocent
young thing should have her blessing and not her curse.
When she left them a light seemed gone from the dwelling.
Two days later she came again to know if the boots fitted,
and less than a fortnight after that paid Rhoda another
call.   On this occasion the boy was absent.

' I walk a good deal,' said Mrs. Lodge, ' and your house
is the nearest outside our own parish.   I hope you are well.
You don't look quite well.'

Rhoda said she was well enough, and, indeed, though
the paler of the two, there was more of the strength that

endures in her well-defined features and large frame than
in the soft-cheeked young woman before her. The conversation became quite confidential as regarded their powers
and weaknesses ; and when Mrs. Lodge was leaving, Rhoda
said, ' I hope you will find this air agree with you, ma'am,
and not suffer from the damp of the water-meads.'

The younger one replied that there was not much doubt
of it, her general health being usually good. ' Though,
now you remind me,' she added, ' I have one little ailment
which puzzles me. It is nothing serious, but I cannot
make it out.'

She uncovered her left hand and arm, and their outline
confronted Rhoda's gaze as the exact original of the limb
she had beheld and seized in her dream. Upon the pink
round surface of the arm were faint marks of an unhealthy
colour, as if produced by a rough grasp. Rhoda's eyes
became riveted on the discolorations ; she fancied that
she discerned in them the shape of her own four fingers.

' How did it happen ? ' she said mechanically.

' I cannot tell,' replied Mrs. Lodge, shaking her head.
' One night when I was sound asleep, dreaming I was away
in some strange place, a pain suddenly shot into my arm
there, and was so keen as to awaken me. I must have
struck it in the daytime, I suppose, though I don't remember doing so.' She added, laughing, ' I tell my dear husband that it looks just as if he had flown into a rage and
struck me there. O, I daresay it will soon disappear.'

' Ha, ha ! Yes. . . . On what night did it come ? '

Mrs. Lodge considered, and said it would be a fortnight
ago on the morrow. ' When I awoke I could not remember
where I was,' she added, ' till the clock striking two reminded
me.'

She had named the night and the hour of Rhoda's spectral encounter, and Brook felt like a guilty thing. The
artless disclosure startled her ; she did not reason on the
freaks of coincidence, and all the scenery of that ghastly
night returned with double vividness to her mind.

' O, can it be,' she said to herself, when her visitor had
departed, ' that I exercise a malignant power over people
against my own will ? ' She knew that she had been slily

called a witch since her fall ; but never having understood
why that particular stigma had been attached to her, it
had passed disregarded. Could this be the explanation,
and had such things as this ever happened before ?

A SUGGESTION

IV

THE summer drew on, and Rhoda Brook almost dreaded
to meet Mrs. Lodge again, notwithstanding that her feeling
for the young wife amounted wellnigh to affection. Something in her own individuality seemed to convict Rhoda of
crime. Yet a fatality sometimes would direct the steps of
the latter to the outskirts of Holmstoke whenever she left
her house for any other purpose than her daily work, and
hence it happened that their next encounter was out of
doors. Rhoda could not avoid the subject which had so
mystified her, and after the first few words she stammered,
' I hope your—arm is well again, ma'am ? ' She had perceived with consternation that Gertrude Lodge carried her
left arm stiffly.

' No ; it is not quite well. Indeed, it is no better at
all ; it is rather worse. It pains me dreadfully sometimes.'

' Perhaps you had better go to a doctor, ma'am.'

She replied that she had already seen a doctor. Her
husband had insisted upon her going to one. But the
surgeon had not seemed to understand the afflicted limb
at all ; he had told her to bathe it in hot water, and she
had bathed it, but the treatment had done no good.

' Will you let me see it ? ' said the milkwoman.

Mrs. Lodge pushed up her sleeve and disclosed the place,
which was a few inches above the wrist. As soon as Rhoda
Brook saw it, she could hardly preserve her composure.
There was nothing of the nature of a wound, but the arm
at that point had a shrivelled look, and the outline of the
four fingers appeared more distinct than at the former
time. Moreover, she fancied that they were imprinted in
precisely the relative position of her clutch upon the arm
in the trance : the first finger towards Gertrude's wrist,
and the fourth towards her elbow.

What the impress resembled seemed to have struck Gertrude herself since their last meeting. ' It looks almost like finger-marks,' she said ; adding with a faint laugh, ' My husband says it is as if some witch, or the devil himself, had taken hold of me there, and blasted the flesh.'

Rhoda shivered. ' That's fancy,' she said hurriedly. ' I wouldn't mind it, if I were you.'

' I shouldn't so much mind it,' said the younger, with hesitation, ' if—if I hadn't a notion that it makes my husband—dislike me—no, love me less. Men think so much of personal appearance.'

' Some do—he for one.'

' Yes ; and he was very proud of mine, at first.'

' Keep your arm covered from his sight.'

' Ah—he knows the disfigurement is there ! ' She tried to hide the tears that filled her eyes.

' Well, ma'am, I earnestly hope it will go away soon.'

And so the milkwoman's mind was chained anew to the subject by a horrid sort of spell as she returned home. The sense of having been guilty of an act of malignity increased, affect as she might to ridicule her superstition. In her secret heart Rhoda did not altogether object to a slight diminution of her successor's beauty, by whatever means it had come about ; but she did not wish to inflict upon her physical pain. For though this pretty young woman had rendered impossible any reparation which Lodge might have made Rhoda for his past conduct, everything like resentment at the unconscious usurpation had quite passed away from the elder's mind.

If the sweet and kindly Gertrude Lodge only knew of the dream-scene in the bed-chamber, what would she think ? Not to inform her of it seemed treachery in the presence of her friendliness ; but tell she could not of her own accord—neither could she devise a remedy.

She mused upon the matter the greater part of the night, and the next day, after the morning milking, set out to obtain another glimpse of Gertrude Lodge if she could, being held to her by a gruesome fascination. By

watching the house from a distance the milkmaid was
presently able to discern the farmer's wife in a ride she was
taking alone—probably to join her husband in some distant field. Mrs. Lodge perceived her, and cantered in her
direction.

' Good morning, Rhoda ! ' Gertrude said, when she had
come up. ' I was going to call.'

Rhoda noticed that Mrs. Lodge held the reins with some
difficulty.

' I hope—the bad arm,' said Rhoda.

' They tell me there is possibly one way by which I
might be able to find out the cause, and so perhaps the
cure, of it,' replied the other anxiously. ' It is by going
to some clever man over in Egdon Heath. They did not
know if he was still alive—and I cannot remember his
name at this moment ; but they said that you knew more
of his movements than anybody else hereabout, and could
tell me if he were still to be consulted. Dear me—what
was his name ? But you know.'

' Not Conjuror Trendle ? ' said her thin companion, turning pale.

' Trendle—yes. Is he alive ? '

' I believe so,' said Rhoda, with reluctance.

' Why do you call him conjuror ? '

' Well—they say—they used to say he was a—he had
powers other folks have not.'

' O, how could my people be so superstitious as to recommend a man of that sort ! I thought they meant some
medical man. I shall think no more of him.'

Rhoda looked relieved, and Mrs. Lodge rode on. The
milkwoman had inwardly seen, from the moment she heard
of her having been mentioned as a reference for this man,
that there must exist a sarcastic feeling among the work-
folk that a sorceress would know the whereabouts of the
exorcist. They suspected her, then. A short time ago
this would have given no concern to a woman of her common sense. But she had a haunting reason to be superstitious now ; and she had been seized with sudden dread
that this Conjuror Trendle might name her as the malignant influence which was blasting the fair person of Ger-

trude and so lead her friend to hate her for ever, and to treat her as some fiend in human shape.

But all was not over. Two days after, a shadow intruded into the window-pattern thrown on Rhoda Brook's floor by the afternoon sun. The woman opened the door at once, almost breathlessly.

'Are you alone?' said Gertrude. She seemed to be no less harassed and anxious than Brook herself.

'Yes,' said Rhoda.

'The place on my arm seems worse, and troubles me!' the young farmer's wife went on. 'It is so mysterious! I do hope it will not be an incurable wound. I have again been thinking of what they said about Conjuror Trendle. I don't really believe in such men, but I should not mind just visiting him, from curiosity—though on no account must my husband know. Is it far to where he lives?'

'Yes—five miles,' said Rhoda backwardly. 'In the heart of Egdon.'

'Well, I should have to walk. Could not you go with me to show me the way—say to-morrow afternoon?'

'O, not I; that is——,' the milkwoman murmured, with a start of dismay. Again the dread seized her that something to do with her fierce act in the dream might be revealed, and her character in the eyes of the most useful friend she had ever had be ruined irretrievably.

Mrs. Lodge urged, and Rhoda finally assented, though with much misgiving. Sad as the journey would be to her, she could not conscientiously stand in the way of a possible remedy for her patron's strange affliction. It was agreed that, to escape suspicion of their mystic intent, they should meet at the edge of the heath at the corner of a plantation which was visible from the spot where they now stood.

CONJUROR TRENDLE

V

By the next afternoon Rhoda would have done anything to escape this inquiry. But she had promised to go. Moreover, there was a horrid fascination at times in becom-

ing instrumental in throwing such possible light on her
own character as would reveal her to be something greater
in the occult world than she had ever herself suspected.

She started just before the time of day mentioned between
them, and half-an-hour's brisk walking brought her to the
south-eastern extension of the Egdon tract of country,
where the fir plantation was. A slight figure, cloaked
and veiled, was already there. Rhoda recognized, almost
with a shudder, that Mrs. Lodge bore her left arm in a
sling.

They hardly spoke to each other, and immediately set
out on their climb into the interior of this solemn country,
which stood high above the rich alluvial soil they had left
half-an-hour before. It was a long walk; thick clouds
made the atmosphere dark, though it was as yet only
early afternoon; and the wind howled dismally over the
slopes of the heath—not improbably the same heath which
had witnessed the agony of the Wessex King Ina, presented
to after-ages as Lear. Gertrude Lodge talked most, Rhoda
replying with monosyllabic preoccupation. She had a
strange dislike to walking on the side of her companion
where hung the afflicted arm, moving round to the other
when inadvertently near it. Much heather had been
brushed by their feet when they descended upon a cart-
track, beside which stood the house of the man they sought.

He did not profess his remedial practices openly, or care
anything about their continuance, his direct interests being
those of a dealer in furze, turf, 'sharp sand,' and other
local products. Indeed, he affected not to believe largely
in his own powers, and when warts that had been shown
him for cure miraculously disappeared—which it must be
owned they infallibly did—he would say lightly, 'O, I
only drink a glass of grog upon 'em at your expense—
perhaps it's all chance,' and immediately turn the subject.

He was at home when they arrived, having in fact seen
them descending into his valley. He was a grey-bearded
man, with a reddish face, and he looked singularly at
Rhoda the first moment he beheld her. Mrs. Lodge told
him her errand; and then with words of self-disparagement
he examined her arm.

'Medicine can't cure it,' he said promptly. ' 'Tis the work of an enemy.'

Rhoda shrank into herself, and drew back.

'An enemy? What enemy?' asked Mrs. Lodge.

He shook his head. 'That's best known to yourself,' he said. 'If you like, I can show the person to you, though I shall not myself know who it is. I can do no more; and don't wish to do that.'

She pressed him; on which he told Rhoda to wait outside where she stood, and took Mrs. Lodge into the room. It opened immediately from the door; and, as the latter remained ajar, Rhoda Brook could see the proceedings without taking part in them. He brought a tumbler from the dresser, nearly filled it with water, and fetching an egg, prepared it in some private way; after which he broke it on the edge of the glass, so that the white went in and the yolk remained. As it was getting gloomy, he took the glass and its contents to the window, and told Gertrude to watch the mixture closely. They leant over the table together, and the milkwoman could see the opaline hue of the egg-fluid changing form as it sank in the water, but she was not near enough to define the shape that it assumed.

'Do you catch the likeness of any face or figure as you look?' demanded the conjuror of the young woman.

She murmured a reply, in tones so low as to be inaudible to Rhoda, and continued to gaze intently into the glass. Rhoda turned, and walked a few steps away.

When Mrs. Lodge came out, and her face was met by the light, it appeared exceedingly pale—as pale as Rhoda's —against the sad dun shades of the upland's garniture. Trendle shut the door behind her, and they at once started homeward together. But Rhoda perceived that her companion had quite changed.

'Did he charge much?' she asked tentatively.

'O no—nothing. He would not take a farthing,' said Gertrude.

'And what did you see?' inquired Rhoda.

'Nothing I—care to speak of.' The constraint in her manner was remarkable; her face was so rigid as to wear an oldened aspect, faintly suggestive of the face in Rhoda's bed-chamber.

' Was it you who first proposed coming here ? ' Mrs. Lodge suddenly inquired, after a long pause. ' How very odd, if you did ! '

' No. But I am not sorry we have come, all things considered,' she replied. For the first time a sense of triumph possessed her, and she did not altogether deplore that the young thing at her side should learn that their lives had been antagonized by other influences than their own.

The subject was no more alluded to during the long and dreary walk home. But in some way or other a story was whispered about the many-dairied lowland that winter that Mrs. Lodge's gradual loss of the use of her left arm was owing to her being ' overlooked ' by Rhoda Brook. The latter kept her own counsel about the incubus, but her face grew sadder and thinner ; and in the spring she and her boy disappeared from the neighbourhood of Holmstoke.

A SECOND ATTEMPT

VI

HALF a dozen years passed away, and Mr. and Mrs. Lodge's married experience sank into prosiness, and worse. The farmer was usually gloomy and silent ; the woman whom he had wooed for her grace and beauty was contorted and disfigured in the left limb ; moreover, she had brought him no child, which rendered it likely that he would be the last of a family who had occupied that valley for some two hundred years. He thought of Rhoda Brook and her son ; and feared this might be a judgment from heaven upon him.

The once blithe-hearted and enlightened Gertrude was changing into an irritable, superstitious woman, whose whole time was given to experimenting upon her ailment with every quack remedy she came across. She was honestly attached to her husband, and was ever secretly hoping against hope to win back his heart again by regaining some at least of her personal beauty. Hence it arose that her closet was lined with bottles, packets, and ointment-pots of every description—nay, bunches of mystic herbs, charms, and books of necromancy, which in her schoolgirl time she would have ridiculed as folly.

'Damned if you won't poison yourself with these apothecary messes and witch mixtures some time or other,' said her husband, when his eye chanced to fall upon the multitudinous array.

She did not reply, but turned her sad, soft glance upon him in such heart-swollen reproach that he looked sorry for his words, and added, 'I only meant it for your good, you know, Gertrude.'

'I'll clear out the whole lot, and destroy them,' said she huskily, 'and try such remedies no more!'

'You want somebody to cheer you,' he observed. 'I once thought of adopting a boy; but he is too old now. And he is gone away I don't know where.'

She guessed to whom he alluded; for Rhoda Brook's story had in the course of years become known to her; though not a word had ever passed between her husband and herself on the subject. Neither had she ever spoken to him of her visit to Conjuror Trendle, and of what was revealed to her, or she thought was revealed to her, by that solitary heathman.

She was now five-and-twenty; but she seemed older. 'Six years of marriage, and only a few months of love,' she sometimes whispered to herself. And then she thought of the apparent cause, and said, with a tragic glance at her withering limb, 'If I could only again be as I was when he first saw me!'

She obediently destroyed her nostrums and charms; but there remained a hankering wish to try something else—some other sort of cure altogether. She had never revisited Trendle since she had been conducted to the house of the solitary by Rhoda against her will; but it now suddenly occurred to Gertrude that she would, in a last desperate effort at deliverance from this seeming curse, again seek out the man, if he yet lived. He was entitled to a certain credence, for the indistinct form he had raised in the glass had undoubtedly resembled the only woman in the world who—as she now knew, though not then—

could have a reason for bearing her ill-will. The visit
should be paid.

This time she went alone, though she nearly got lost
on the heath, and roamed a considerable distance out of
her way. Trendle's house was reached at last, however ;
he was not indoors, and instead of waiting at the cottage,
she went to where his bent figure was pointed out to her
at work a long way off. Trendle remembered her, and
laying down the handful of furze-roots which he was gathering and throwing into a heap, he offered to accompany
her in her homeward direction, as the distance was considerable and the days were short. So they walked together, his head bowed nearly to the earth, and his form
of a colour with it.

'You can send away warts and other excrescences, I
know,' she said ; ' why can't you send away this ? ' And
the arm was uncovered.

'You think too much of my powers ! ' said Trendle ;
' and I am old and weak now, too. No, no ; it is too much
for me to attempt in my own person. What have ye
tried ? '

She named to him some of the hundred medicaments
and counterspells which she had adopted from time to
time. He shook his head.

'Some were good enough,' he said approvingly ; ' but
not many of them for such as this. This is of the nature
of a blight, not of the nature of a wound, and if you ever
do throw it off, it will be all at once.'

'If I only could ! '

'There is only one chance of doing it known to me. It
has never failed in kindred afflictions—that I can declare.
But it is hard to carry out, and especially for a woman.'

'Tell me ! ' said she.

'You must touch with the limb the neck of a man who's
been hanged.'

She started a little at the image he had raised.

'Before he's cold—just after he's cut down,' continued
the conjuror impassively.

'How can that do good ? '

'It will turn the blood and change the constitution.

But, as I say, to do it is hard. You must go to the jail
when there's a hanging, and wait for him when he's brought
off the gallows. Lots have done it, though perhaps not
such pretty women as you. I used to send dozens for
skin complaints. But that was in former times. The last
I sent was in '13—near twelve years ago.'

He had no more to tell her, and, when he had put
her into a straight track homeward, turned and left her,
refusing all money as at first.

A RIDE

VII

THE communication sank deep into Gertrude's mind. Her
nature was rather a timid one; and probably of all remedies
that the white wizard could have suggested there was not
one which would have filled her with so much aversion as
this, not to speak of the immense obstacles in the way of
its adoption.

Casterbridge, the county-town, was a dozen or fifteen
miles off; and though in those days, when men were executed
for horse-stealing, arson, and burglary, an assize seldom
passed without a hanging, it was not likely that she could
get access to the body of the criminal unaided. And the
fear of her husband's anger made her reluctant to breathe
a word of Trendle's suggestion to him or to anybody about
him.

She did nothing for months, and patiently bore her disfigurement as before. But her woman's nature, craving
for renewed love, through the medium of renewed beauty
(she was but twenty-five), was ever stimulating her to try
what, at any rate, could hardly do her any harm. 'What
came by a spell will go by a spell surely,' she would say.
Whenever her imagination pictured the act she shrank in
terror from the possibility of it; then the words of the
conjuror, ' It will turn your blood,' were seen to be capable
of a scientific no less than a ghastly interpretation; the
mastering desire returned, and urged her on again.

There was at this time but one county paper, and that
her husband only occasionally borrowed. But old-fash-

ioned days had old-fashioned means, and news was extensively conveyed by word of mouth from market to market,
or from fair to fair, so that, whenever such an event as an
execution was about to take place, few within a radius of
twenty miles were ignorant of the coming sight; and, so far
as Holmstoke was concerned, some enthusiasts had been
known to walk all the way to Casterbridge and back in
one day, solely to witness the spectacle. The next assizes
were in March; and when Gertrude Lodge heard that they
had been held, she inquired stealthily at the inn as to the
result, as soon as she could find opportunity.

She was, however, too late. The time at which the
sentences were to be carried out had arrived, and to make
the journey and obtain admission at such short notice
required at least her husband's assistance. She dared not
tell him, for she had found by delicate experiment that
these smouldering village beliefs made him furious if mentioned, partly because he half entertained them himself.
It was therefore necessary to wait for another opportunity.

Her determination received a fillip from learning that
two epileptic children had attended from this very village
of Holmstoke many years before with beneficial results,
though the experiment had been strongly condemned by
the neighbouring clergy. April, May, June passed; and
it is no overstatement to say that by the end of the last-
named month Gertrude wellnigh longed for the death of a
fellow-creature. Instead of her formal prayers each night,
her unconscious prayer was, ' O Lord, hang some guilty
or innocent person soon ! '

This time she made earlier inquiries, and was altogether
more systematic in her proceedings. Moreover, the season
was summer, between the haymaking and the harvest,
and in the leisure thus afforded him her husband had been
holiday-taking away from home.

The assizes were in July, and she went to the inn as
before. There was to be one execution—only one—for
arson.

Her greatest problem was not how to get to Casterbridge, but what means she should adopt for obtaining
admission to the jail. Though access for such purposes

had formerly never been denied, the custom had fallen
into desuetude ; and in contemplating her possible difficulties, she was again almost driven to fall back upon her
husband.   But, on sounding him about the assizes, he was
so uncommunicative, so more than usually cold, that she did
not proceed, and decided that whatever she did she would
do alone.

Fortune, obdurate hitherto, showed her unexpected
favour.   On the Thursday before the Saturday fixed for
the execution, Lodge remarked to her that he was going
away from home for another day or two on business at a
fair, and that he was sorry he could not take her with him.

She exhibited on this occasion so much readiness to
stay at home that he looked at her in surprise.   Time
had been when she would have shown deep disappointment at the loss of such a jaunt.   However, he lapsed
into his usual taciturnity, and on the day named left
Holmstoke.

It was now her turn.   She at first had thought of driving, but on reflection held that driving would not do, since
it would necessitate her keeping to the turnpike-road, and
so increase by tenfold the risk of her ghastly errand being
found out.   She decided to ride, and avoid the beaten
track, notwithstanding that in her husband's stables
there was no animal just at present which by any stretch
of imagination could be considered a lady's mount, in
spite of his promise before marriage to always keep a mare
for her.   He had, however, many cart-horses, fine ones of
their kind ; and among the rest was a serviceable creature,
an equine Amazon, with a back as broad as a sofa, on which
Gertrude had occasionally taken an airing when unwell.
This horse she chose.

On Friday afternoon one of the men brought it round.
She was dressed, and before going down looked at her
shrivelled arm.   ' Ah ! ' she said to it, ' if it had not been
for you this terrible ordeal would have been saved me ! '

When strapping up the bundle in which she carried a
few articles of clothing, she took occasion to say to the
servant, ' I take these in case I should not get back to-
night from the person I am going to visit.   Don't be alarmed

if I am not in by ten, and close up the house as usual.
I shall be at home to-morrow for certain.' She meant
then to tell her husband privately; the deed accomplished
was not like the deed projected.   He would almost certainly
forgive her.

And then the pretty palpitating Gertrude Lodge went
from her husband's homestead ; but though her goal was
Casterbridge she did not take the direct route thither
through Stickleford.   Her cunning course at first was in
precisely the opposite direction.   As soon as she was out
of sight, however, she turned to the left, by a road which
led into Egdon, and on entering the heath wheeled round,
and set out in the true course, due westerly.   A more
private way down the county could not be imagined ;
and as to direction, she had merely to keep her horse's head
to a point a little to the right of the sun.   She knew that she
would light upon a furze-cutter or cottager of some sort
from time to time, from whom she might correct her bearing.

Though the date was comparatively recent, Egdon
was much less fragmentary in 'character than now.   The
attempts—successful and otherwise—at cultivation on
the lower slopes, which intrude and break up the original
heath into small detached heaths, had not been carried
far ;   Enclosure Acts had not taken effect, and the banks
and fences which now exclude the cattle of those villagers
who formerly enjoyed rights of commonage thereon, and
the carts of those who had turbary privileges which kept
them in firing all the year round, were not erected.   Gertrude, therefore, rode along with no other obstacles than
the prickly furze-bushes, the mats of heather, the white
water-courses, and the natural steeps and declivities of the
ground.

Her horse was sure, if heavy-footed and slow, and though
a draught animal, was easy-paced ; had it been otherwise,
she was not a woman who could have ventured to ride over
such a bit of country with a half-dead arm.   It was therefore nearly eight o'clock when she drew rein to breathe
her bearer on the last outlying high point of heath-land
towards Casterbridge, previous to leaving Egdon for the
cultivated valleys.

She halted before a pool called Rushy-pond, flanked by the ends of two hedges; a railing ran through the centre of the pond, dividing it in half. Over the railing she saw the low green country; over the green trees the roofs of the town; over the roofs a white flat façade, denoting the entrance to the county jail. On the roof of this front specks were moving about; they seemed to be workmen erecting something. Her flesh crept. She descended slowly, and was soon amid corn-fields and pastures. In another half-hour, when it was almost dusk, Gertrude reached the White Hart, the first inn of the town on that side.

Little surprise was excited by her arrival; farmers' wives rode on horseback then more than they do now; though, for that matter, Mrs. Lodge was not imagined to be a wife at all; the innkeeper supposed her some harum-skarum young woman who had come to attend 'hang-fair' next day. Neither her husband nor herself ever dealt in Casterbridge market, so that she was unknown. While dismounting she beheld a crowd of boys standing at the door of a harness-maker's shop just above the inn, looking inside it with deep interest.

'What is going on there?' she asked of the ostler.

'Making the rope for to-morrow.'

She throbbed responsively, and contracted her arm.

''Tis sold by the inch afterwards,' the man continued. 'I could get you a bit, miss, for nothing, if you'd like?'

She hastily repudiated any such wish, all the more from a curious creeping feeling that the condemned wretch's destiny was becoming interwoven with her own; and having engaged a room for the night, sat down to think.

Up to this time she had formed but the vaguest notions about her means of obtaining access to the prison. The words of the cunning-man returned to her mind. He had implied that she should use her beauty, impaired though it was, as a pass-key. In her inexperience she knew little about jail functionaries; she had heard of a high-sheriff and an under-sheriff, but dimly only. She knew, however, that there must be a hangman, and to the hangman she determined to apply.

A WATER-SIDE HERMIT

VIII

AT this date, and for several years after, there was a hangman to almost every jail. Gertrude found, on inquiry, that the Casterbridge official dwelt in a lonely cottage by a deep slow river flowing under the cliff on which the prison buildings were situate—the stream being the self-same one, though she did not know it, which watered the Stickleford and Holmstoke meads lower down in its course.

Having changed her dress, and before she had eaten or drunk—for she could not take her ease till she had ascertained some particulars—Gertrude pursued her way by a path along the water-side to the cottage indicated. Passing thus the outskirts of the jail, she discerned on the level roof over the gateway three rectangular lines against the sky, where the specks had been moving in her distant view ; she recognized what the erection was, and passed quickly on. Another hundred yards brought her to the executioner's house, which a boy pointed out. It stood close to the same stream, and was hard by a weir, the waters of which emitted a steady roar.

While she stood hesitating the door opened, and an old man came forth, shading a candle with one hand. Locking the door on the outside, he turned to a flight of wooden steps fixed against the end of the cottage, and began to ascend them, this being evidently the staircase to his bedroom. Gertrude hastened forward, but by the time she reached the foot of the ladder he was at the top. She called to him loudly enough to be heard above the roar of the weir ; he looked down and said, ' What d'ye want here ? '

' To speak to you a minute.'

The candle-light, such as it was, fell upon her imploring, pale, upturned face, and Davies (as the hangman was called) backed down the ladder. ' I was just going to bed,' he said. ' " Early to bed and early to rise," but I don't mind stopping a minute for such a one as you. Come into house.' He reopened the door, and preceded her to the room within.

The implements of his daily work, which was that of a

jobbing gardener, stood in a corner, and seeing probably
that she looked rural, he said, ' If you want me to undertake country work I can't come, for I never leave Casterbridge for gentle nor simple—not I. My real calling is
officer of justice,' he added formally.

' Yes, yes ! That's it. To-morrow ! '

' Ah ! I thought so. Well, what's the matter about
that ? 'Tis no use to come here about the knot—folks
do come continually, but I tell 'em one knot is as merciful
as another if ye keep it under the ear. Is the unfortunate
man a relation ; or, I should say, perhaps ' (looking at
her dress) ' a person who's been in your employ ? '

' No. What time is the execution ? '

' The same as usual—twelve o'clock, or as soon after as
the London mail-coach gets in. We always wait for that,
in case of a reprieve.'

' O—a reprieve—I hope not ! ' she said involuntarily.

' Well,—hee, hee !—as a matter of business, so do
I ! But still, if ever a young fellow deserved to be let off,
this one does ; only just turned eighteen, and only present
by chance when the rick was fired. Howsomever, there's
not much risk of it, as they are obliged to make an example
of him, there having been so much destruction of property
that way lately.'

' I mean,' she explained, ' that I want to touch him
for a charm, a cure of an affliction, by the advice of a
man who has proved the virtue of the remedy.'

' O yes, miss ! Now I understand. I've had such
people come in past years. But it didn't strike me that
you looked of a sort to require blood-turning. What's
the complaint ? The wrong kind for this, I'll be bound.'

' My arm.' She reluctantly showed the withered skin.

' Ah !—'tis all a-scram ! ' said the hangman, examining it.

' Yes,' said she.

' Well,' he continued, with interest, ' that *is* the class
o' subject, I'm bound to admit ! I like the look of the
wownd ; it is truly as suitable for the cure as any I ever
saw. 'Twas a knowing-man that sent 'ee, whoever he was.'

' You can contrive for me all that's necessary ? ' she said
breathlessly.

'You should really have gone to the governor of the jail, and your doctor with 'ee, and given your name and address—that's how it used to be done, if I recollect. Still, perhaps, I can manage it for a trifling fee.'

'O, thank you! I would rather do it this way, as I should like it kept private.'

'Lover not to know, eh?'

'No—husband.'

'Aha! Very well. I'll get 'ee a touch of the corpse.'

'Where is it now?' she said, shuddering.

'It?—*he*, you mean; he's living yet. Just inside that little small winder up there in the glum.' He signified the jail on the cliff above.

She thought of her husband and her friends. 'Yes, of course,' she said; 'and how am I to proceed?'

He took her to the door. 'Now, do you be waiting at the little wicket in the wall, that you'll find up there in the lane, not later than one o'clock. I will open it from the inside, as I shan't come home to dinner till he's cut down. Good-night. Be punctual; and if you don't want anybody to know 'ee, wear a veil. Ah—once I had such a daughter as you!'

She went away, and climbed the path above, to assure herself that she would be able to find the wicket next day. Its outline was soon visible to her—a narrow opening in the outer wall of the prison precincts. The steep was so great that, having reached the wicket, she stopped a moment to breathe; and, looking back upon the water-side cot, saw the hangman again ascending his outdoor staircase. He entered the loft or chamber to which it led, and in a few minutes extinguished his light.

The town clock struck ten, and she returned to the White Hart as she had come.

A RENCOUNTER

IX

It was one o'clock on Saturday. Gertrude Lodge, having been admitted to the jail as above described, was sitting in a waiting-room within the second gate, which stood

under a classic archway of ashlar, then comparatively
modern, and bearing the inscription, ' COVNTY JAIL : 1793.'
This had been the façade she saw from the heath the day
before. Near at hand was a passage to the roof on which
the gallows stood.

The town was thronged, and the market suspended ;
but Gertrude had seen scarcely a soul. Having kept her
room till the hour of the appointment, she had proceeded
to the spot by a way which avoided the open space below
the cliff where the spectators had gathered ; but she
could, even now, hear the multitudinous babble of their
voices, out of which rose at intervals the hoarse croak of a
single voice uttering the words, ' Last dying speech and
confession ! ' There had been no reprieve, and the execution was over ; but the crowd still waited to see the body
taken down.

Soon the persistent woman heard a trampling overhead,
then a hand beckoned to her, and, following directions,
she went out and crossed the inner paved court beyond
the gatehouse, her knees trembling so that she could
scarcely walk. One of her arms was out of its sleeve, and
only covered by her shawl.

On the spot at which she had now arrived were two
trestles, and before she could think of their purpose she
heard heavy feet descending stairs somewhere at her back.
Turn her head she would not, or could not, and, rigid
in this position, she was conscious of a rough coffin passing
her shoulder, borne by four men. It was open, and in it
lay the body of a young man, wearing the smockfrock of a
rustic, and fustian breeches. The corpse had been thrown
into the coffin so hastily that the skirt of the smockfrock
was hanging over. The burden was temporarily deposited
on the trestles.

By this time the young woman's state was such that a
gray mist seemed to float before her eyes, on account of
which, and the veil she wore, she could scarcely discern
anything : it was as though she had nearly died, but was
held up by a sort of galvanism.

' Now ! ' said a voice close at hand, and she was just
conscious that the word had been addressed to her.

By a last strenuous effort she advanced, at the same time hearing persons approaching behind her. She bared her poor curst arm; and Davies, uncovering the face of the corpse, took Gertrude's hand, and held it so that her arm lay across the dead man's neck, upon a line the colour of an unripe blackberry, which surrounded it.

Gertrude shrieked: 'the turn o' the blood,' predicted by the conjuror, had taken place. But at that moment a second shriek rent the air of the enclosure: it was not Gertrude's, and its effect upon her was to make her start round.

Immediately behind her stood Rhoda Brook, her face drawn, and her eyes red with weeping. Behind Rhoda stood Gertrude's own husband; his countenance lined, his eyes dim, but without a tear.

'D——n you! what are you doing here?' he said hoarsely.

'Hussy—to come between us and our child now!' cried Rhoda. 'This is the meaning of what Satan showed me in the vision! You are like her at last!' And clutching the bare arm of the younger woman, she pulled her unresistingly back against the wall. Immediately Brook had loosened her hold the fragile young Gertrude slid down against the feet of her husband. When he lifted her up she was unconscious.

The mere sight of the twain had been enough to suggest to her that the dead young man was Rhoda's son. At that time the relatives of an executed convict had the privilege of claiming the body for burial, if they chose to do so; and it was for this purpose that Lodge was awaiting the inquest with Rhoda. He had been summoned by her as soon as the young man was taken in the crime, and at different times since; and he had attended in court during the trial. This was the 'holiday' he had been indulging in of late. The two wretched parents had wished to avoid exposure; and hence had come themselves for the body, a waggon and sheet for its conveyance and covering being in waiting outside.

Gertrude's case was so serious that it was deemed advisable to call to her the surgeon who was at hand. She was taken out of the jail into the town ; but she never reached home alive. Her delicate vitality, sapped perhaps by the paralyzed arm, collapsed under the double shock that followed the severe strain, physical and mental, to which she had subjected herself during the previous twenty-four hours. Her blood had been ' turned ' indeed—too far. Her death took place in the town three days after.

Her husband was never seen in Casterbridge again ; once only in the old market-place at Anglebury, which he had so much frequented, and very seldom in public anywhere. Burdened at first with moodiness and remorse, he eventually changed for the better, and appeared as a chastened and thoughtful man. Soon after attending the funeral of his poor young wife he took steps towards giving up the farms in Holmstoke and the adjoining parish, and, having sold every head of his stock, he went away to Port-Bredy, at the other end of the county, living there in solitary lodgings till his death two years later of a painless decline. It was then found that he had bequeathed the whole of his not inconsiderable property to a reformatory for boys, subject to the payment of a small annuity to Rhoda Brook, if she could be found to claim it.

For some time she could not be found ; but eventually she reappeared in her old parish,—absolutely refusing, however, to have anything to do with the provision made for her. Her monotonous milking at the dairy was resumed, and followed for many long years, till her form became bent, and her once abundant dark hair white and worn away at the forehead—perhaps by long pressure against the cows. Here, sometimes, those who knew her experiences would stand and observe her, and wonder what sombre thoughts were beating inside that impassive, wrinkled brow, to the rhythm of the alternating milk-streams.

' *Blackwood's Magazine*,'
January 1888.

FELLOW-TOWNSMEN

FELLOW-TOWNSMEN

I

THE shepherd on the east hill could shout out lambing intelligence to the shepherd on the west hill, over the intervening town chimneys, without great inconvenience to his voice, so nearly did the steep pastures encroach upon the burghers' backyards. And at night it was possible to stand in the very midst of the town and hear from their native paddocks on the lower levels of greensward the mild lowing of the farmer's heifers, and the profound, warm blowings of breath in which those creatures indulge. But the community which had jammed itself in the valley thus flanked formed a veritable town, with a real mayor and corporation, and a staple manufacture.

During a certain damp evening five-and-thirty years ago, before the twilight was far advanced, a pedestrian of professional appearance, carrying a small bag in his hand and an elevated umbrella, was descending one of these hills by the turnpike road when he was overtaken by a phaeton.

'Hullo, Downe—is that you?' said the driver of the vehicle, a young man of pale and refined appearance. 'Jump up here with me, and ride down to your door.'

The other turned a plump, cheery, rather self-indulgent face over his shoulder towards the hailer.

'O, good evening, Mr. Barnet—thanks,' he said, and mounted beside his acquaintance.

They were fellow-burgesses of the town which lay beneath them, but though old and very good friends they were differently circumstanced. Barnet was a richer man than the struggling young lawyer Downe, a fact which was to some extent perceptible in Downe's manner towards his companion, though nothing of it ever showed in Barnet's manner towards the solicitor. Barnet's position

in the town was none of his own making; his father had
been a very successful flax-merchant in the same place,
where the trade was still carried on as briskly as the small
capacities of its quarters would allow. Having acquired
a fair fortune, old Mr. Barnet had retired from business,
bringing up his son as a gentleman-burgher, and, it must
be added, as a well-educated, liberal-minded young man.

'How is Mrs. Barnet?' asked Downe.

'Mrs. Barnet was very well when I left home,' the other
answered constrainedly, exchanging his meditative regard
of the horse for one of self-consciousness.

Mr. Downe seemed to regret his inquiry, and immediately took up another thread of conversation. He con-
gratulated his friend on his election as a councilman;
he thought he had not seen him since that event took
place; Mrs. Downe had meant to call and congratulate Mrs.
Barnet, but he feared that she had failed to do so as yet.

Barnet seemed hampered in his replies. 'We should
have been glad to see you. I—my wife would welcome
Mrs. Downe at any time, as you know. . . . Yes, I am a
member of the corporation—rather an inexperienced
member, some of them say. It is quite true; and I should
have declined the honour as premature—having other
things on my hands just now, too—if it had not been
pressed upon me so very heartily.'

'There is one thing you have on your hands which
I can never quite see the necessity for,' said Downe, with
good-humoured freedom. 'What the deuce do you want
to build that new mansion for, when you have already got
such an excellent house as the one you live in?'

Barnet's face acquired a warmer shade of colour; but
as the question had been idly asked by the solicitor while
regarding the surrounding flocks and fields, he answered
after a moment with no apparent embarrassment—

'Well, we wanted to get out of the town, you know;
the house I am living in is rather old and inconvenient.'

Mr. Downe declared that he had chosen a pretty site for
the new building. They would be able to see for miles
and miles from the windows. Was he going to give it a
name? He supposed so.

Barnet thought not. There was no other house near that was likely to be mistaken for it. And he did not care for a name.

' But I think it has a name ! ' Downe observed : ' I went past—when was it ?—this morning ; and I saw something, —" Château Ringdale," I think it was, stuck up on a board ! '

' It was an idea she—we had for a short time,' said Barnet hastily. ' But we have decided finally to do without a name—at any rate such a name as that. It must have been a week ago that you saw it. It was taken down last Saturday. . . . Upon that matter I am firm ! ' he added grimly.

Downe murmured in an unconvinced tone that he thought he had seen it yesterday.

Talking thus they drove into the town. The street was unusually still for the hour of seven in the evening ; an increasing drizzle from the sea had prevailed since the afternoon, and now formed a gauze across the yellow lamps, and trickled with a gentle rattle down the heavy roofs of stone tile, that bent the house-ridges hollow-backed with its weight, and in some instances caused the walls to bulge outwards in the upper story. Their route took them past the little town-hall, the Black-Bull Hotel, and onward to the junction of a small street on the right, consisting of a row of those two-and-two windowed brick residences of no particular age, which are exactly alike wherever found, except in the people they contain.

' Wait—I'll drive you up to your door,' said Barnet, when Downe prepared to alight at the corner. He thereupon turned into the narrow street, when the faces of three little girls could be discerned close to the panes of a lighted window a few yards ahead, surmounted by that of a young matron, the gaze of all four being directed eagerly up the empty street. ' You are a fortunate fellow, Downe,' Barnet continued, as mother and children disappeared from the window to run to the door. ' You must be happy if any man is. I would give a hundred such houses as my new one to have a home like yours.'

' Well—yes, we get along pretty comfortably,' replied Downe complacently.

'That house, Downe, is none of my ordering,' Barnet broke out, revealing a bitterness hitherto suppressed, and checking the horse a moment to finish his speech before delivering up his passenger. 'The house I have already is good enough for me, as you supposed. It is my own freehold; it was built by my grandfather, and is stout enough for a castle. My father was born there, lived there, and died there. I was born there, and have always lived there; yet I must needs build a new one.'

'Why do you?' said Downe.

'Why do I? To preserve peace in the household. I do anything for that; but I don't succeed. I was firm in resisting "Château Ringdale," however; not that I would not have put up with the absurdity of the name, but it was too much to have your house christened after Lord Ringdale, because your wife once had a fancy for him. If you only knew everything, you would think all attempt at reconciliation hopeless. In your happy home you have had no such experiences; and God forbid that you ever should. See, here they are all ready to receive you!'

'Of course! And so will your wife be waiting to receive you,' said Downe. 'Take my word for it she will! And with a dinner prepared for you far better than mine.'

'I hope so,' Barnet replied dubiously.

He moved on to Downe's door, which the solicitor's family had already opened. Downe descended, but being encumbered with his bag and umbrella, his foot slipped, and he fell upon his knees in the gutter.

'O, my dear Charles!' said his wife, running down the steps; and, quite ignoring the presence of Barnet, she seized hold of her husband, pulled him to his feet, and kissed him, exclaiming, 'I hope you are not hurt, darling!' The children crowded round, chiming in piteously, 'Poor papa!'

'He's all right,' said Barnet, perceiving that Downe was only a little muddy, and looking more at the wife than at the husband. Almost at any other time—certainly during his fastidious bachelor years—he would have thought her a too demonstrative woman; but those recent circumstances of his own life to which he had just

alluded made Mrs. Downe's solicitude so affecting that his
eye grew damp as he witnessed it. Bidding the lawyer and
his family good-night he left them, and drove slowly into
the main street towards his own house.

The heart of Barnet was sufficiently impressionable
to be influenced by Downe's parting prophecy that he
might not be so unwelcome home as he imagined : the
dreary night might, at least on this one occasion, make
Downe's forecast true. Hence it was in a suspense that
he could hardly have believed possible that he halted at
his door. On entering his wife was nowhere to be seen,
and he inquired for her. The servant informed him that
her mistress had the dressmaker with her, and would be
engaged for some time.

' Dressmaker at this time of day ! '

' She dined early, sir, and hopes you will excuse her
joining you this evening.'

' But she knew I was coming to-night ? '

' O yes, sir.'

' Go up and tell her I am come.'

The servant did so ; but the mistress of the house
merely transmitted her former words.

Barnet said nothing more, and presently sat down to his
lonely meal, which was eaten abstractedly, the domestic
scene he had lately witnessed still impressing him by its
contrast with the situation here. His mind fell back into
past years upon a certain pleasing and gentle being whose
face would loom out of their shades at such times as these.
Barnet turned in his chair, and looked with unfocused
eyes in a direction southward from where he sat, as if he
saw not the room but a long way beyond. ' I wonder if she
lives there still ! ' he said.

II

He rose with a sudden rebelliousness, put on his hat
and coat, and went out of the house, pursuing his way
along the glistening pavement while eight o'clock was
striking from St. Mary's tower, and the apprentices and
shopmen were slamming up the shutters from end to end
of the town. In two minutes only those shops which

could boast of no attendant save the master or the mistress remained with open eyes. These were ever somewhat less prompt to exclude customers than the others : for their owners' ears the closing hour had scarcely the cheerfulness that it possessed for the hired servants of the rest. Yet the night being dreary the delay was not for long, and their windows, too, blinked together one by one.

During this time Barnet had proceeded with decided step in a direction at right angles to the broad main thoroughfare of the town, by a long street leading due southward. Here, though his family had no more to do with the flax manufacture, his own name occasionally greeted him on gates and warehouses, being used allusively by small rising tradesmen as a recommendation, in such words as ' Smith, from Barnet & Co.'—' Robinson, late manager at Barnet's.' The sight led him to reflect upon his father's busy life, and he questioned if it had not been far happier than his own.

The houses along the road became fewer, and presently open ground appeared between them on either side, the track on the right hand rising to a higher level till it merged in a knoll. On the summit a row of builders' scaffold-poles probed the indistinct sky like spears, and at their bases could be discerned the lower courses of a building lately begun. Barnet slackened his pace and stood for a few moments without leaving the centre of the road, apparently not much interested in the sight, till suddenly his eye was caught by a post in the fore part of the ground bearing a white board at the top. He went to the rails, vaulted over, and walked in far enough to discern painted upon the board ' Château Ringdale.'

A dismal irony seemed to lie in the words, and its effect was to irritate him. Downe, then, had spoken truly. He stuck his umbrella into the sod, and seized the post with both hands, as if intending to loosen and throw it down. Then, like one bewildered by an opposition which would exist none the less though its manifestations were removed, he allowed his arms to sink to his side.

' Let it be,' he said to himself. ' I have declared there shall be peace—if possible.'

Taking up his umbrella, he quietly left the enclosure, and went on his way, still keeping his back to the town. He had advanced with more decision since passing the new building, and soon a hoarse murmur rose upon the gloom ; it was the sound of the sea. The road led to the harbour, at a distance of a mile from the town, from which the trade of the district was fed. After seeing the obnoxious name-board Barnet had forgotten to open his umbrella, and the rain tapped smartly on his hat, and occasionally stroked his face as he went on.

Though the lamps were still continued at the roadside they stood at wider intervals than before, and the pavement had given place to rough gravel. Every time he came to a lamp an increasing shine made itself visible upon his shoulders, till at last they quite glistened with wet. The murmur from the shore grew stronger, but it was still some distance off when he paused before one of the smallest of the detached houses by the wayside, standing in its own garden, the latter being divided from the road by a row of wooden palings. Scrutinizing the spot to ensure that he was not mistaken, he opened the gate and gently knocked at the cottage door.

When he had patiently waited minutes enough to lead any man in ordinary cases to knock again, the door was heard to open, though it was impossible to see by whose hand, there being no light in the passage. Barnet said at random, ' Does Miss Savile live here ? '

A youthful voice assured him that she did live there, and by a sudden afterthought asked him to come in. It would soon get a light, it said : but the night being wet, mother had not thought it worth while to trim the passage lamp.

' Don't trouble yourself to get a light for me,' said Barnet hastily ; ' it is not necessary at all. Which is Miss Savile's sitting-room ? '

The young person, whose white pinafore could just be discerned, signified a door in the side of the passage, and Barnet went forward at the same moment, so that no light should fall upon his face. On entering the room he closed the door behind him, pausing till he heard the retreating footsteps of the child.

He found himself in an apartment which was simply and neatly, though not poorly furnished ; everything, from the miniature chiffonnier to the shining little daguerreotype which formed the central ornament of the mantelpiece, being in scrupulous order. The picture was enclosed by a frame of embroidered card-board—evidently the work of feminine hands—and it was the portrait of a thin-faced, elderly lieutenant in the navy. From behind the lamp on the table a female form now rose into view, that of a young girl, and a resemblance between her and the portrait was early discoverable. She had been so absorbed in some occupation on the other side of the lamp as to have barely found time to realize her visitor's presence.

They both remained standing for a few seconds without speaking. The face that confronted Barnet had a beautiful outline ; the Raffaelesque oval of its contour was remarkable for an English countenance, and that countenance housed in a remote country-road to an unheard-of harbour. But her features did not do justice to this splendid beginning : Nature had recollected that she was not in Italy ; and the young lady's lineaments, though not so inconsistent as to make her plain, would have been accepted rather as pleasing than as correct. The preoccupied expression which, like images on the retina, remained with her for a moment after the state that caused it had ceased, now changed into a reserved, half-proud, and slightly indignant look, in which the blood diffused itself quickly across her cheek, and additional brightness broke the shade of her rather heavy eyes.

' I know I have no business here,' he said, answering the look. ' But I had a great wish to see you, and inquire how you were. You can give your hand to me, seeing how often I have held it in past days ? '

' I would rather forget than remember all that, Mr. Barnet,' she answered, as she coldly complied with the request. ' When I think of the circumstances of our last meeting, I can hardly consider it kind of you to allude to such a thing as our past—or, indeed, to come here at all.'

' There was no harm in it surely ? I don't trouble you often, Lucy.'

'I have not had the honour of a visit from you for a very long time, certainly, and I did not expect it now,' she said, with the same stiffness in her air. 'I hope Mrs. Barnet is very well?'

'Yes, yes!' he impatiently returned. 'At least, I suppose so—though I only speak from inference!'

'But she is your wife, sir,' said the young girl tremulously.

The unwonted tones of a man's voice in that feminine chamber had startled a canary that was roosting in its cage by the window; the bird awoke hastily, and fluttered against the bars. She went and stilled it by laying her face against the cage and murmuring a coaxing sound. It might partly have been done to still herself.

'I didn't come to talk of Mrs. Barnet,' he pursued; 'I came to talk of you, of yourself alone; to inquire how you are getting on since your great loss.' And he turned towards the portrait of her father.

'I am getting on fairly well, thank you.'

The force of her utterance was scarcely borne out by her look; but Barnet courteously reproached himself for not having guessed a thing so natural; and to dissipate all embarrassment added, as he bent over the table, 'What were you doing when I came?—painting flowers, and by candlelight?'

'O no,' she said, 'not painting them—only sketching the outlines. I do that at night to save time—I have to get three dozen done by the end of the month.'

Barnet looked as if he regretted it deeply. 'You will wear your poor eyes out,' he said, with more sentiment than he had hitherto shown. . 'You ought not to do it. There was a time when I should have said you must not. Well —I almost wish I had never seen light with my own eyes when I think of that!'

'Is this a time or place for recalling such matters?' she asked, with dignity. 'You used to have a gentlemanly respect for me, and for yourself. Don't speak any more as you have spoken, and don't come again. I cannot think that this visit is serious, or was closely considered by you.'

'Considered: well, I came to see you as an old and

good friend—not to mince matters, to visit a woman I
loved. Don't be angry! I could not help doing it, so
many things brought you into my mind. . . . This evening
I fell in with an acquaintance, and when I saw how happy
he was with his wife and family welcoming him home,
though with only one-tenth of my income and chances, and
thought what might have been in my case, it fairly broke
down my discretion, and off I came here. Now I am here
I feel that I am wrong to some extent. But the feeling
that I should like to see you, and talk of those we used
to know in common, was very strong.'

'Before that can be the case a little more time must
pass,' said Miss Savile quietly; 'a time long enough for
me to regard with some calmness what at present I remember far too impatiently—though it may be you almost
forget it. Indeed you must have forgotten it long before
you acted as you did.' Her voice grew stronger and more
vivacious as she added: 'But I am doing my best to forget
it too, and I know I shall succeed from the progress I have
made already!'

She had remained standing till now, when she turned
and sat down, facing half away from him.

Barnet watched her moodily. 'Yes, it is only what I
deserve,' he said. 'Ambition pricked me on—no, it was
not ambition, it was wrongheadedness! Had I but
reflected. . . .' He broke out vehemently: 'But always
remember this, Lucy: if you had written to me only one
little line after that misunderstanding, I declare I should
have come back to you. That ruined me!' He slowly
walked as far as the little room would allow him to go,
and remained with his eyes on the skirting.

'But, Mr. Barnet, how could I write to you? There
was no opening for my doing so.'

'Then there ought to have been,' said Barnet, turning.
'That was my fault!'

'Well, I don't know anything about that; but as there
had been nothing said by me which required any explanation by letter, I did not send one. Everything was so
indefinite, and feeling your position to be so much wealthier
than mine, I fancied I might have mistaken your meaning.

And when I heard of the other lady—a woman of whose family even you might be proud—I thought how foolish I had been, and said nothing.'

'Then I suppose it was destiny—accident—I don't know what, that separated us, dear Lucy. Anyhow, you were the woman I ought to have made my wife—and I let you slip, like the foolish man that I was!'

'O, Mr. Barnet,' she said, almost in tears, 'don't revive the subject to me; I am the wrong one to console you —think, sir,—you should not be here—it would be so bad for me if it were known!'

'It would—it would, indeed,' he said hastily. 'I am not right in doing this, and I won't do it again.'

'It is a very common folly of human nature, you know, to think the course you did *not* adopt must have been the best,' she continued, with gentle solicitude, as she followed him to the door of the room. 'And you don't know that I should have accepted you, even if you had asked me to be your wife.' At this his eye met hers, and she dropped her gaze. She knew that her voice belied her. There was a silence till she looked up to add, in a voice of soothing playfulness, 'My family was so much poorer than yours, even before I lost my dear father, that—perhaps your companions would have made it unpleasant for us on account of my deficiencies.'

'Your disposition would soon have won them round,' said Barnet.

She archly expostulated: 'Now, never mind my disposition; try to make it up with your wife! Those are my commands to you. And now you are to leave me at once.'

'I will. I must make the best of it all, I suppose,' he replied, more cheerfully than he had as yet spoken. 'But I shall never again meet with such a dear girl as you!' And he suddenly opened the door and left her alone. When his glance again fell on the lamps that were sparsely ranged along the dreary level road, his eyes were in a state which showed straw-like motes of light radiating from each flame into the surrounding air.

On the other side of the way Barnet observed a man

under an umbrella, walking parallel with himself. Presently this man left the footway, and gradually converged on Barnet's course. The latter then saw that it was Charlson, a surgeon of the town, who owed him money. Charlson was a man not without ability; yet he did not prosper. Sundry circumstances stood in his way as a medical practitioner: he was needy; he was not a coddle; he gossiped with men instead of with women; he had married a stranger instead of one of the town young ladies; and he was given to conversational buffoonery. Moreover, his look was quite erroneous. Those only proper features in the family doctor, the quiet eye, and the thin straight passionless lips which never curl in public either for laughter or for scorn, were not his; he had a full-curved mouth, and a bold black eye that made timid people nervous. His companions were what in old times would have been called boon companions—an expression which, though of irreproachable root, suggests fraternization carried to the point of unscrupulousness. All this was against him in the little town of his adoption.

Charlson had been in difficulties, and to oblige him Barnet had put his name to a bill; and, as he had expected, was called upon to meet it when it fell due. It had been only a matter of fifty pounds, which Barnet could well afford to lose, and he bore no ill-will to the thriftless surgeon on account of it. But Charlson had a little too much brazen indifferentism in his composition to be altogether a desirable acquaintance.

'I hope to be able to make that little bill-business right with you in the course of three weeks, Mr. Barnet,' said Charlson with hail-fellow friendliness.

Barnet replied good-naturedly that there was no hurry.

This particular three weeks had moved on in advance of Charlson's present with the precision of a shadow for some considerable time.

'I've had a dream,' Charlson continued. Barnet knew from his tone that the surgeon was going to begin his characteristic nonsense, and did not encourage him. 'I've had a dream,' repeated Charlson, who required no encouragement. 'I dreamed that a gentleman, who has been very kind to me, married a haughty lady in haste, before he had quite forgotten a nice little girl he knew before, and that one wet evening, like the present, as I was walking up the harbour-road, I saw him come out of that dear little girl's present abode.'

Barnet glanced towards the speaker. The rays from a neighbouring lamp struck through the drizzle under Charlson's umbrella, so as just to illumine his face against the shade behind, and show that his eye was turned up under the outer corner of its lid, whence it leered with impish jocoseness as he thrust his tongue into his cheek.

'Come,' said Barnet gravely, 'we'll have no more of that.'

'No, no—of course not,' Charlson hastily answered, seeing that his humour had carried him too far, as it had done many times before. He was profuse in his apologies, but Barnet did not reply. Of one thing he was certain —that scandal was a plant of quick root, and that he was bound to obey Lucy's injunction for Lucy's own sake.

III

He did so, to the letter ; and though, as the crocus followed the snowdrop and the daffodil the crocus in Lucy's garden, the harbour-road was a not unpleasant place to walk in, Barnet's feet never trod its stones, much less approached her door. He avoided a saunter that way as he would have avoided a dangerous dram, and took his airings a long distance northward, among severely square and brown ploughed fields, where no other townsman came. Sometimes he went round by the lower lanes of the borough, where the rope-walks stretched in which his family formerly had share, and looked at the rope-makers walking backwards, overhung by apple-trees and bushes, and intruded on by cows and calves, as if trade had established itself there at considerable inconvenience to Nature.

One morning, when the sun was so warm as to raise a steam from the south-eastern slopes of those flanking hills that looked so lovely above the old roofs, but made every low-chimneyed house in the town as smoky as Tophet, Barnet glanced from the windows of the town-council

room for lack of interest in what was proceeding within
Several members of the corporation were present, but
there was not much business doing, and in a few minutes
Downe came leisurely across to him, saying that he seldom
saw Barnet now.

Barnet owned that he was not often present.

Downe looked at the crimson curtain which hung down
beside the panes, reflecting its hot hues into their faces,
and then out of the window. At that moment there
passed along the street a tall commanding lady, in whom
the solicitor recognized Barnet's wife. Barnet had done
the same thing, and turned away.

'It will be all right some day,' said Downe, with cheering
sympathy.

'You have heard, then, of her last outbreak?'

Downe depressed his cheerfulness to its very reverse
in a moment. 'No, I have not heard of anything serious,'
he said, with as long a face as one naturally round could
be turned into at short notice. 'I only hear vague reports
of such things.'

'You may think it will be all right,' said Barnet drily.
'But I have a different opinion. . . . No, Downe, we must
look the thing in the face. Not poppy nor mandragora
—however, how are your wife and children?'

Downe said that they were all well, thanks; they were
out that morning somewhere; he was just looking to see
if they were walking that way. Ah, there they were,
just coming down the street; and Downe pointed to the
figures of two children with a nursemaid, and a lady
walking behind them.

'You will come out and speak to her?' he asked.

'Not this morning. The fact is I don't care to speak to
anybody just now.'

'You are too sensitive, Mr. Barnet. At school I remember you used to get as red as a rose if anybody uttered a
word that hurt your feelings.'

Barnet mused. 'Yes,' he admitted, 'there is a grain of
truth in that. It is because of that I often try to make
peace at home. Life would be tolerable then at any rate,
even if not particularly bright.'

'I have thought more than once of proposing a little plan to you,' said Downe with some hesitation. 'I don't know whether it will meet your views, but take it or leave it, as you choose. In fact, it was my wife who suggested it : that she would be very glad to call on Mrs. Barnet and get into her confidence. She seems to think that Mrs. Barnet is rather alone in the town, and without advisers. Her impression is that your wife will listen to reason. Emily has a wonderful way of winning the hearts of people of her own sex.'

'And of the other sex too, I think. She is a charming woman, and you were a lucky fellow to find her.'

'Well, perhaps I was,' simpered Downe, trying to wear an aspect of being the last man in the world to feel pride. 'However, she will be likely to find out what ruffles Mrs. Barnet. Perhaps it is some misunderstanding, you know —something that she is too proud to ask you to explain, or some little thing in your conduct that irritates her because she does not fully comprehend you. The truth is, Emily would have been more ready to make advances if she had been quite sure of her fitness for Mrs. Barnet's society, who has of course been accustomed to London people of good position, which made Emily fearful of intruding.'

Barnet expressed his warmest thanks for the well-intentioned proposition. There was reason in Mrs. Downe's fear—that he owned. 'But do let her call,' he said. 'There is no woman in England I would so soon trust on such an errand. I am afraid there will not be any brilliant result ; still, I shall take it as the kindest and nicest thing if she will try it, and not be frightened at a repulse.'

When Barnet and Downe had parted, the former went to the Town Savings-Bank, of which he was a trustee, and endeavoured to forget his troubles in the contemplation of low sums of money, and figures in a network of red and blue lines. He sat and watched the working-people making their deposits, to which at intervals he signed his name. Before he left in the afternoon Downe put his head inside the door.

'Emily has seen Mrs. Barnet,' he said in a low voice.

' She has got Mrs. Barnet's promise to take her for a drive down to the shore to-morrow, if it is fine. Good afternoon ! '

Barnet shook Downe by the hand without speaking, and Downe went away.

IV

The next day was as fine as the arrangement could possibly require. As the sun passed the meridian and declined westward, the tall shadows from the scaffold-poles of Barnet's rising residence streaked the ground as far as to the middle of the highway. Barnet himself was there inspecting the progress of the works for the first time during several weeks. A building in an old-fashioned town five-and-thirty years ago did not, as in the modern fashion, rise from the sod like a booth at a fair. The foundations and lower courses were put in and allowed to settle for many weeks before the superstructure was built up, and a whole summer of drying was hardly sufficient to do justice to the important issues involved. Barnet stood within a window-niche which had as yet received no frame, and thence looked down a slope into the road. The wheels of a chaise were heard, and then his handsome Xantippe, in the company of Mrs. Downe, drove past on their way to the shore. They were driving slowly ; there was a pleasing light in Mrs. Downe's face, which seemed faintly to reflect itself upon the countenance of her companion— that *politesse du cœur* which was so natural to her having possibly begun already to work results. But whatever the situation, Barnet resolved not to interfere, or do anything to hazard the promise of the day. He might well afford to trust the issue to another when he could never direct it but to ill himself. His wife's clenched rein-hand in its lemon-coloured glove, her stiff erect figure, clad in velvet and lace, and her boldly-outlined face, passed on, exhibiting their owner as one fixed for ever above the level of her companion—socially by her early breeding, and materially by her higher cushion.

Barnet decided to allow them a proper time to themselves, and then stroll down to the shore and drive them home. After lingering on at the house for another hour he started with this intention. A few hundred yards below 'Château Ringdale' stood the cottage in which the late lieutenant's daughter had her lodging. Barnet had not been so far that way for a long time, and as he approached the forbidden ground a curious warmth passed into him, which led him to perceive that, unless he were careful, he might have to fight the battle with himself about Lucy over again. A tenth of his present excuse would, how-ever, have justified him in travelling by that road to-day.

He came opposite the dwelling, and turned his eyes for a momentary glance into the little garden that stretched from the palings to the door. Lucy was in the enclosure ; she was walking and stooping to gather some flowers, pos-sibly for the purpose of painting them, for she moved about quickly, as if anxious to save time. She did not see him ; he might have passed unnoticed ; but a sensa-tion which was not in strict unison with his previous senti-ments that day led him to pause in his walk and watch her. She went nimbly round and round the beds of anemones, tulips, jonquils, polyanthuses, and other old-fashioned flowers, looking a very charming figure in her half-mourning bonnet, and with an incomplete nosegay in her left hand. Raising herself to pull down a lilac blossom she observed him.

'Mr. Barnet ! ' she said, innocently smiling. 'Why, I have been thinking of you many times since Mrs. Barnet went by in the pony-carriage, and now here you are ! '

'Yes, Lucy,' he said.

Then she seemed to recall particulars of their last meet-ing, and he believed that she flushed, though it might have been only the fancy of his own supersensitiveness.

'I am going to the harbour,' he added.

'Are you ? ' Lucy remarked simply. 'A great many people begin to go there now the summer is drawing on.'

Her face had come more into his view as she spoke, and he noticed how much thinner and paler it was than when he had seen it last. 'Lucy, how weary you look ! tell me, can I help you ? ' he was going to cry out.—' If I do,' he thought, ' it will be the ruin of us both ! ' He merely said that the afternoon was fine, and went on his way.

As he went a sudden blast of air came over the hill as if in contradiction to his words, and spoilt the previous quiet of the scene. The wind had already shifted violently, and now smelt of the sea.

The harbour-road soon began to justify its name. A gap appeared in the rampart of hills which shut out the sea, and on the left of the opening rose a vertical cliff, coloured a burning orange by the sunlight, the companion cliff on the right being livid in shade. Between these cliffs, like the Libyan bay which sheltered the shipwrecked Trojans, was a little haven, seemingly a beginning made by Nature herself of a perfect harbour, which appealed to the passer-by as only requiring a little human industry to finish it and make it famous, the ground on each side as far back as the daisied slopes that bounded the interior valley being a mere layer of blown sand. But the Port-Bredy burgesses a mile inland had, in the course of ten centuries, responded many times to that mute appeal, with the result that the tides had invariably choked up their works with sand and shingle as soon as completed. There were but few houses here : a rough pier, a few boats, some stores, an inn, a residence or two, a ketch unloading in the harbour, were the chief features of the settlement. On the open ground by the shore stood his wife's pony-carriage, empty, the boy in attendance holding the horse.

When Barnet drew nearer, he saw an indigo-coloured spot moving swiftly along beneath the radiant base of the eastern cliff, which proved to be a man in a jersey, running with all his might. He held up his hand to Barnet, as it seemed, and they approached each other. The man was local, but a stranger to him.

'What is it, my man ? ' said Barnet.

'A terrible calamity ! ' the boatman hastily explained. Two ladies had been capsized in a boat—they were Mrs. Downe and Mrs. Barnet of the old town ; they had driven down there that afternoon—they had alighted, and it was so fine, that, after walking about a little while, they had been tempted to go out for a short sail round the cliff.

Just as they were putting in to the shore, the wind shifted with a sudden gust, the boat listed over, and it was thought they were both drowned. How it could have happened was beyond his mind to fathom, for John Green knew how to sail a boat as well as any man there.

' Which is the way to the place ? ' said Barnet.

It was just round the cliff.

' Run to the carriage and tell the boy to bring it to the place as soon as you can. Then go to the Harbour Inn and tell them to ride to town for a doctor. Have they been got out of the water ? '

' One lady has.'

' Which ? '

' Mrs. Barnet. Mrs. Downe, it is feared, has fleeted out to sea.'

Barnet ran on to that part of the shore which the cliff had hitherto obscured from his view, and there discerned, a long way ahead, a group of fishermen standing. As soon as he came up one or two recognized him, and, not liking to meet his eye, turned aside with misgiving. He went amidst them and saw a small sailing-boat lying draggled at the water's edge; and, on the sloping shingle beside it, a soaked and sandy woman's form in the velvet dress and yellow gloves of his wife.

V

All had been done that could be done. Mrs. Barnet was in her own house under medical hands, but the result was still uncertain. Barnet had acted as if devotion to his wife were the dominant passion of his existence. There had been much to decide—whether to attempt restoration of the apparently lifeless body as it lay on the shore—whether to carry her to the Harbour Inn—whether to drive with her at once to his own house. The first course, with no skilled help or appliances near at hand, had seemed hopeless. The second course would have occupied nearly as much time as a drive to the town, owing to the intervening ridges of shingle, and the necessity of crossing the harbour by boat to get to the house, added to which much time must have elapsed before a doctor could have arrived

down there. By bringing her home in the carriage some
precious moments had slipped by ; but she had been laid
in her own bed in seven minutes, a doctor called to her
side, and every possible restorative brought to bear upon
her.

At what a tearing pace he had driven up that road,
through the yellow evening sunlight, the shadows flapping
irksomely into his eyes as each wayside object rushed past
between him and the west ! Tired workmen with their
baskets at their backs had turned on their homeward journey to wonder at his speed. Half-way between the shore
and Port-Bredy town he had met Charlson, who had been
the first surgeon to hear of the accident. He was accompanied by his assistant in a gig. Barnet had sent on the
latter to the coast in case that Downe's poor wife should
by that time have been reclaimed from the waves, and had
brought Charlson back with him to the house.

Barnet's presence was not needed here, and he felt it to
be his next duty to set off at once and find Downe, that
no other than himself might break the news to him.

He was quite sure that no chance had been lost for Mrs.
Downe by his leaving the shore. By the time that Mrs.
Barnet had been laid in the carriage a much larger group
had assembled to lend assistance in finding her friend,
rendering his own help superfluous. But the duty of
breaking the news was made doubly painful by the circumstance that the catastrophe which had befallen Mrs. Downe
was solely the result of her own and her husband's loving-
kindness towards himself.

He found Downe in his office. When the solicitor comprehended the intelligence he turned pale, stood up, and
remained for a moment perfectly still, as if bereft of his
faculties ; then his shoulders heaved, he pulled out his
handkerchief and began to cry like a child. His sobs
might have been heard in the next room. He seemed to
have no idea of going to the shore, or of doing anything ;
but when Barnet took him gently by the hand and proposed
to start at once, he quietly acquiesced, neither uttering
any further word nor making any effort to repress his
tears.

Barnet accompanied him to the shore, where, finding that no trace had as yet been seen of Mrs. Downe, and that his stay would be of no avail, he left Downe with his friends and the young doctor, and once more hastened back to his own house.

At the door he met Charlson. 'Well!' Barnet said.

'I have just come down,' said the doctor; 'we have done everything, but without result. I sympathize with you in your bereavement.'

Barnet did not much appreciate Charlson's sympathy, which sounded to his ears as something of a mockery from the lips of a man who knew what Charlson knew about his domestic relations. Indeed, there seemed an odd spark in Charlson's full black eye as he said the words; but that might have been imaginary.

'And, Mr. Barnet,' Charlson resumed, 'that little matter between us—I hope to settle it finally in three weeks at least.'

'Never mind that now,' said Barnet abruptly. He directed the surgeon to go to the harbour in case his services might even now be necessary there: and himself entered the house.

The servants were coming from his wife's chamber, looking helplessly at each other and at him. He passed them by and entered the room, where he stood regarding the shape on the bed for a few minutes, after which he walked into his own dressing-room adjoining, and there paced up and down. In a minute or two he noticed what a strange and total silence had come over the upper part of the house; his own movements, muffled as they were by the carpet, seemed noisy, and his thoughts to disturb the air like articulate utterances. His eye glanced through the window. Far down the road to the harbour a roof detained his gaze: out of it rose a red chimney, and out of the red chimney a curl of smoke, as from a fire newly kindled. He had often seen such a sight before. In that house lived Lucy Savile; and the smoke was from the fire which was regularly lighted at this time to make her tea.

After that he went back to the bedroom, and stood there some time regarding his wife's silent form. She was a woman some years older than himself, but had not by any means overpassed the maturity of good looks and vigour. Her passionate features, well-defined, firm, and statuesque in life, were doubly so now : her mouth and brow, beneath her purplish-black hair, showed only too clearly that the turbulency of character which had made a bear-garden of his house had been no temporary phase of her existence. While he reflected, he suddenly said to himself, I wonder if all has been done ?

The thought was led up to by his having fancied that his wife's features lacked in its completeness the expression which he had been accustomed to associate with the faces of those whose spirits have fled for ever. The effacement of life was not so marked but that, entering uninformed, he might have supposed her sleeping. Her complexion was that seen in the numerous faded portraits by Sir Joshua Reynolds ; it was pallid in comparison with life, but there was visible on a close inspection the remnant of what had once been a flush ; the keeping between the cheeks and the hollows of the face being thus preserved, although positive colour was gone. Long orange rays of evening sun stole in through chinks in the blind, striking on the large mirror, and being thence reflected upon the crimson hangings and woodwork of the heavy bedstead, so that the general tone of light was remarkably warm ; and it was probable that something might be due to this circumstance. Still the fact impressed him as strange. Charlson had been gone more than a quarter of an hour : could it be possible that he had left too soon, and that his attempts to restore her had operated so sluggishly as only now to have made themselves felt ? Barnet laid his hand upon her chest, and fancied that ever and anon a faint flutter of palpitation, gentle as that of a butterfly's wing, disturbed the stillness there—ceasing for a time, then struggling to go on, then breaking down in weakness and ceasing again.

Barnet's mother had been an active practitioner of the healing art among her poorer neighbours, and her inspirations had all been derived from an octavo volume of Domestic Medicine, which at this moment was lying, as it had lain for many years, on a shelf in Barnet's dressing-room.

He hastily fetched it, and there read under the head
' Drowning ' :—

' Exertions for the recovery of any person who has not been
immersed for a longer period than half-an-hour should be continued
for at least four hours, as there have been many cases in which
returning life has made itself visible even after a longer interval.
' Should, however, a weak action of any of the organs show itself
when the case seems almost hopeless, our efforts must be redoubled ;
the feeble spark in this case requires to be solicited ; it will certainly
disappear under a relaxation of labour.'

Barnet looked at his watch ; it was now barely two
hours and a half from the time when he had first heard
of the accident. He threw aside the book and turned
quickly to reach a stimulant which had previously been
used. Pulling up the blind for more light, his eye glanced
out of the window. There he saw that red chimney still
smoking cheerily, and that roof, and through the roof that
somebody. His mechanical movements stopped, his hand
remained on the blind-cord, and he seemed to become
breathless, as if he had suddenly found himself treading
a high rope.

While he stood a sparrow lighted on the window-sill,
saw him, and flew away. Next a man and a dog walked
over one of the green hills which bulged above the roofs
of the town. But Barnet took no notice.

We may wonder what were the exact images that passed
through his mind during those minutes of gazing upon
Lucy Savile's house, the sparrow, the man and the dog,
and Lucy Savile's house again. There are honest men
who will not admit to their thoughts, even as idle hypo-
theses, views of the future that assume as done a deed
which they would recoil from doing ; and there are other
honest men for whom morality ends at the surface of their
own heads, who will deliberate what the first will not so
much as suppose. Barnet had a wife whose presence distracted his home ; she now lay as in death ; by merely
doing nothing—by letting the intelligence which had gone
forth to the world lie undisturbed—he would effect such a
deliverance for himself as he had never hoped for, and open
up an opportunity of which till now he had never dreamed.

Whether the conjuncture had arisen through any unscrupulous, ill-considered impulse of Charlson to help out of a
strait the friend who was so kind as never to press him
for what was due could not be told ; there was nothing
to prove it ; and it was a question which could never be
asked. The triangular situation—himself—his wife—Lucy
Savile—was the one clear thing.

From Barnet's actions we may infer that he *supposed*
such and such a result, for a moment, but did not deliberate. He withdrew his hazel eyes from the scene without,
calmly turned, rang the bell for assistance, and vigorously
exerted himself to learn if life still lingered in that motionless frame. In a short time another surgeon was in attendance ; and then Barnet's surmise proved to be true. The
slow life timidly heaved again ; but much care and patience
were needed to catch and retain it, and a considerable
period elapsed before it could be said with certainty that
Mrs. Barnet lived. When this was the case, and there
was no further room for doubt, Barnet left the chamber.
The blue evening smoke from Lucy's chimney had died
down to an imperceptible stream, and as he walked about
downstairs he murmured to himself, ' My wife was dead,
and she is alive again.'

It was not so with Downe. After three hours' immer-
sion his wife's body had been recovered, life, of course,
being quite extinct. Barnet, on descending, went straight
to his friend's house, and there learned the result. Downe
was helpless in his wild grief, occasionally even hysterical.
Barnet said little, but finding that some guiding hand was
necessary in the sorrow-stricken household, took upon him
to supervise and manage till Downe should be in a state
of mind to do so for himself.

VI

One September evening, four months later, when Mrs.
Barnet was in perfect health, and Mrs. Downe but a weak-
ening memory, an errand-boy paused to rest himself in
front of Mr. Barnet's old house, depositing his basket on
one of the window-sills. The street was not yet lighted,
but there were lights in the house, and at intervals a flit-

ting shadow fell upon the blind at his elbow. Words also were audible from the same apartment, and they seemed to be those of persons in violent altercation. But the boy could not gather their purport, and he went on his way.

Ten minutes afterwards the door of Barnet's house opened, and a tall closely-veiled lady in a travelling-dress came out and descended the freestone steps. The servant stood in the doorway watching her as she went with a measured tread down the street. When she had been out of sight for some minutes Barnet appeared at the door from within.

'Did your mistress leave word where she was going?' he asked.

'No, sir.'

'Is the carriage ordered to meet her anywhere?'

'No, sir.'

'Did she take a latch-key?'

'No, sir.'

Barnet went in again, sat down in his chair, and leaned back. Then in solitude and silence he brooded over the bitter emotions that filled his heart. It was for this that he had gratuitously restored her to life, and made his union with another impossible! The evening drew on, and nobody came to disturb him. At bedtime he told the servants to retire, that he would sit up for Mrs. Barnet himself; and when they were gone he leaned his head upon his hand and mused for hours.

The clock struck one, two; still his wife came not, and, with impatience added to depression, he went from room to room till another weary hour had passed. This was not altogether a new experience for Barnet; but she had never before so prolonged her absence. At last he sat down again and fell asleep.

He awoke at six o'clock to find that she had not returned. In searching about the rooms he discovered that she had taken a case of jewels which had been hers before her marriage. At eight a note was brought him; it was from his wife, in which she stated that she had gone by the coach to the house of a distant relative near London, and expressed a wish that certain boxes, articles of clothing, and so on, might be sent to her forthwith. The note was brought to him by a waiter at the Black-Bull Hotel, and had been written by Mrs. Barnet immediately before she took her place in the stage.

By the evening this order was carried out, and Barnet, with a sense of relief, walked out into the town. A fair had been held during the day, and the large clear moon which rose over the most prominent hill flung its light upon the booths and standings that still remained in the street, mixing its rays curiously with those from the flaring naphtha lamps. The town was full of country-people who had come in to enjoy themselves, and on this account Barnet strolled through the streets unobserved. With a certain recklessness he made for the harbour-road, and presently found himself by the shore, where he walked on till he came to the spot near which his friend the kindly Mrs. Downe had lost her life, and his own wife's life had been preserved. A tremulous pathway of bright moonshine now stretched over the water which had engulfed them, and not a living soul was near.

Here he ruminated on their characters, and next on the young girl in whom he now took a more sensitive interest than at the time when he had been free to marry her. Nothing, so far as he was aware, had ever appeared in his own conduct to show that such an interest existed. He had made it a point of the utmost strictness to hinder that feeling from influencing in the faintest degree his attitude towards his wife ; and this was made all the more easy for him by the small demand Mrs. Barnet made upon his attentions, for which she ever evinced the greatest contempt ; thus unwittingly giving him the satisfaction of knowing that their severance owed nothing to jealousy, or, indeed, to any personal behaviour of his at all. Her concern was not with him or his feelings, as she frequently told him ; but that she had, in a moment of weakness, thrown herself away upon a common burgher when she might have aimed at, and possibly brought down, a peer of the realm. Her frequent depreciation of Barnet in these terms had at times been so intense that he was sorely tempted to retaliate on her egotism by owning that

he loved at the same low level on which he lived; but
prudence had prevailed, for which he was now thankful.

Something seemed to sound upon the shingle behind
him over and above the raking of the wave. He looked
round, and a slight girlish shape appeared quite close to
him. He could not see her face because it was in the direction of the moon.

'Mr. Barnet?' the rambler said, in timid surprise. The
voice was the voice of Lucy Savile.

'Yes,' said Barnet. 'How can I repay you for this
pleasure?'

'I only came because the night was so clear. I am now
on my way home.'

'I am glad we have met. I want to know if you will
let me do something for you, to give me an occupation, as
an idle man? I am sure I ought to help you, for I know
you are almost without friends.'

She hesitated. 'Why should you tell me that?' she
said.

'In the hope that you will be frank with me.'

'I am not altogether without friends here. But I am
going to make a little change in my life—to go out as a
teacher of freehand drawing and practical perspective, of
course I mean on a comparatively humble scale, because I
have not been specially educated for that profession. But
I am sure I shall like it much.'

'You have an opening?'

'I have not exactly got it, but I have advertised for
one.'

'Lucy, you must let me help you!'

'Not at all.'

'You need not think it would compromise you, or that
I am indifferent to delicacy. I bear in mind how we stand.
It is very unlikely that you will succeed as teacher of the
class you mention, so let me do something of a different
kind for you. Say what you would like, and it shall be
done.'

'No; if I can't be a drawing-mistress or governess, or
something of that sort, I shall go to India and join my
brother.'

'I wish I could go abroad, anywhere, everywhere with you, Lucy, and leave this place and its associations for ever!'

She played with the end of her bonnet-string, and hastily turned aside. 'Don't ever touch upon that kind of topic again,' she said, with a quick severity not free from anger. 'It simply makes it impossible for me to see you, much less receive any guidance from you. No, thank you, Mr. Barnet; you can do nothing for me at present; and as I suppose my uncertainty will end in my leaving for India, I fear you never will. If ever I think you *can* do anything, I will take the trouble to ask you. Till then, good-bye.'

The tone of her latter words was equivocal, and while he remained in doubt whether a gentle irony was or was not inwrought with their sound, she swept lightly round and left him alone. He saw her form get smaller and smaller along the damp belt of sea-sand between ebb and flood, and when she had vanished round the cliff into the harbour-road he himself followed in the same direction.

That her hopes from an advertisement should be the single thread which held Lucy Savile in England was too much for Barnet. On reaching the town he went straight to the residence of Downe, now a widower with four children. The young motherless brood had been sent to bed about a quarter of an hour earlier, and when Barnet entered he found Downe sitting alone. It was the same room as that from which the family had been looking out for Downe at the beginning of the year, when Downe had slipped into the gutter and his wife had been so enviably tender towards him. The old neatness had gone from the house; articles lay in places which could show no reason for their presence, as if momentarily deposited there some months ago, and forgotten ever since; there were no flowers; things were jumbled together on the furniture which should have been in cupboards; and the place in general had that stagnant, unrenovated air which usually pervades the maimed home of the widower.

Downe soon renewed his customary full-worded lament over his wife, and even when he had worked himself up

to tears, went on volubly, as if a listener were a luxury to
be enjoyed whenever he could be caught.

'She was a treasure beyond compare, Mr. Barnet! I
shall never see such another. Nobody now to nurse me—
nobody to console me in those daily troubles, you know,
Barnet, which make consolation so necessary to a nature
like mine. It would be unbecoming to repine, for her
spirit's home was elsewhere—the tender light in her eyes
always showed it ; but it is a long dreary time that I have
before me, and nobody else can ever fill the void left in
my heart by her loss—nobody—nobody ! ' And Downe
wiped his eyes again.

'She was a good woman in the highest sense,' gravely
answered Barnet, who, though Downe's words drew genuine
compassion from his heart, could not help feeling that a
tender reticence would have been a finer tribute to Mrs.
Downe's really sterling virtues than such a second-class
lament as this.

'I have something to show you,' Downe resumed, producing from a drawer a sheet of paper on which was an
elaborate design for a canopied tomb. 'This has been
sent me by the architect, but it is not exactly what I
want.'

'You have got Jones to do it, I see, the man who is
carrying out my house,' said Barnet, as he glanced at the
signature to the drawing.

'Yes, but it is not quite what I want. I want something more striking—more like a tomb I have seen in
St. Paul's Cathedral. Nothing less will do justice to my
feelings, and how far short of them that will fall ! '

Barnet privately thought the design a sufficiently impos-
ing one as it stood, even extravagantly ornate ; but, feeling that he had no right to criticize, he said gently, ' Downe,
should you not live more in your children's lives at the
present time, and soften the sharpness of regret for your
own past by thinking of their future ? '

'Yes, yes ; but what can I do more ? ' asked Downe,
wrinkling his forehead hopelessly.

It was with anxious slowness that Barnet produced his
reply—the secret object of his visit to-night. 'Did you

not say one day that you ought by right to get a governess
for the children ? '

Downe admitted that he had said so, but that he could
not see his way to it.   ' The kind of woman I should like
to have,' he said, ' would be rather beyond my means.
No ; I think I shall send them to school in the town when
they are old enough to go out alone.'

' Now, I know of something better than that.   The late
Lieutenant Savile's daughter, Lucy, wants to do something for herself in the way of teaching.   She would be
inexpensive, and would answer your purpose as well as
anybody for six or twelve months.   She would probably
come daily if you were to ask her, and so your housekeeping arrangements would not be much affected.'

' I thought she had gone away,' said the solicitor, musing.
' Where does she live ? '

Barnet told him, and added that, if Downe should think
of her as suitable, he would do well to call as soon as possible, or she might be on the wing.   ' If you do see her,'
he said, ' it would be advisable not to mention my name.
She is rather stiff in her ideas of me, and it might prejudice
her against a course if she knew that I recommended it.'

Downe promised to give the subject his consideration,
and nothing more was said about it just then.   But when
Barnet rose to go, which was not till nearly bedtime, he
reminded Downe of the suggestion and went up the street
to his own solitary home with a sense of satisfaction at
his promising diplomacy in a charitable cause.

VII

The walls of his new house were carried up nearly to their
full height.   By a curious though not infrequent reaction,
Barnet's feelings about that unnecessary structure had
undergone a change ; he took considerable interest in its
progress as a long-neglected thing, his wife before her
departure having grown quite weary of it as a hobby.
Moreover, it was an excellent distraction for a man in the
unhappy position of having to live in a provincial town
with nothing to do.   He was probably the first of his line
who had ever passed a day without toil, and perhaps some-

thing like an inherited instinct disqualifies such men for a
life of pleasant inaction, such as lies in the power of those
whose leisure is not a personal accident, but a vast his-
torical accretion which has become part of their natures.

Thus Barnet got into a way of spending many of his
leisure hours on the site of the new building, and he might
have been seen on most days at this time trying the temper
of the mortar by punching the joints with his stick, looking at the grain of a floor-board, and meditating where it
grew, or picturing under what circumstances the last fire
would be kindled in the at present sootless chimneys.
One day when thus occupied he saw three children pass by
in the company of a fair young woman, whose sudden
appearance caused him to flush perceptibly.

' Ah, she is there,' he thought.   ' That's a blessed thing.'

Casting an interested glance over the rising building
and the busy workmen, Lucy Savile and the little Downes
passed by; and after that time it became a regular though
almost unconscious custom of Barnet to stand in the half-
completed house and look from the ungarnished windows
at the governess as she tripped towards the sea-shore with
her young charges, which she was in the habit of doing
on most fine afternoons.   It was on one of these occasions,
when he had been loitering on the first-floor landing, near
the hole left for the staircase, not yet erected, that there
appeared above the edge of the floor a little hat, followed
by a little head.

Barnet withdrew through a doorway, and the child came
to the top of the ladder, stepping on to the floor and crying to her sisters and Miss Savile to follow.   Another head
rose above the floor, and another, and then Lucy herself
came into view.   The troop ran hither and thither through
the empty, shaving-strewn rooms, and Barnet came forward.

Lucy uttered a small exclamation : she was very sorry
that she had intruded ; she had not the least idea that Mr.
Barnet was there : the children had come up, and she had
followed.

Barnet replied that he was only too glad to see them
there.   ' And now, let me show you the rooms,' he said.

She passively assented, and he took her round. There
was not much to show in such a bare skeleton of a house,
but he made the most of it, and explained the different
ornamental fittings that were soon to be fixed here and
there. Lucy made but few remarks in reply, though she
seemed pleased with her visit, and stole away down the
ladder, followed by her companions.

After this the new residence became yet more of a hobby
for Barnet. Downe's children did not forget their first
visit, and when the windows were glazed, and the handsome staircase spread its broad low steps into the hall,
they came again, prancing in unwearied succession through
every room from ground-floor to attics, while Lucy stood
waiting for them at the door. Barnet, who rarely missed
a day in coming to inspect progress, stepped out from the
drawing-room.

' I could not keep them out,' she said, with an apologetic
blush. ' I tried to do so very much ; but they are rather
wilful, and we are directed to walk this way for the sea
air.'

' Do let them make the house their regular playground,
and you yours,' said Barnet. ' There is no better place
for children to romp and take their exercise in than an
empty house, particularly in muddy or damp weather such
as we shall get a good deal of now ; and this place will not
be furnished for a long long time—perhaps never. I am
not at all decided about it.'

' O, but it must ! ' replied Lucy, looking round at the
hall. ' The rooms are excellent, twice as high as ours, and
the views from the windows are so lovely.'

' I daresay, I daresay,' he said absently.

' Will all the furniture be new ? ' she asked.

' All the furniture be new—that's a thing I have not
thought of. In fact, I only come here and look on. My
father's house would have been large enough for me, but
another person had a voice in the matter, and it was settled
that we should build. However, the place grows upon
me ; its recent associations are cheerful, and I am getting
to like it fast.'

A certain uneasiness in Lucy's manner showed that the

conversation was taking too personal a turn for her. ' Still, as modern tastes develop, people require more room to gratify them in,' she said, withdrawing to call the children ; and serenely bidding him good-afternoon she went on her way.

Barnet's life at this period was singularly lonely, and yet he was happier than he could have expected. His wife's estrangement and absence, which promised to be permanent, left him free as a boy in his movements, and the solitary walks that he took gave him ample opportunity for chastened reflection on what might have been his lot if he had only shown wisdom enough to claim Lucy Savile when there was no bar between their lives, and she was to be had for the asking. He would occasionally call at the house of his friend Downe ; but there was scarcely enough in common between their two natures to make them more than friends of that excellent sort whose personal knowledge of each other's history and character is always in excess of intimacy, whereby they are not so likely to be severed by a clash of sentiment as in cases where intimacy springs up in excess of knowledge. Lucy was never visible at these times, being either engaged in the school-room, or in taking an airing out of doors ; but, knowing that she was now comfortable, and had given up the, to him, depressing idea of going off to the other side of the globe, he was quite content.

The new house had so far progressed that the gardeners were beginning to grass down the front. During an afternoon which he was passing in marking the curve for the carriage-drive, he beheld her coming in boldly towards him from the road. Hitherto Barnet had only caught her on the premises by stealth; and this advance seemed to show that at last her reserve had broken down.

A smile gained strength upon her face as she approached, and it was quite radiant when she came up, and said, without a trace of embarrassment, ' I find I owe you a hundred thanks—and it comes to me quite as a surprise ! It was through your kindness that I was engaged by Mr. Downe. Believe me, Mr. Barnet, I did not know it until yesterday, or I should have thanked you long and long ago ! '

' I had offended you—just a trifle—at the time, I think ? '
said Barnet, smiling, ' and it was best that you should not
know.'

' Yes, yes,' she returned hastily.   ' Don't allude to that ;
it is past and over, and we will let it be.   The house is
finished almost, is it not ?   How beautiful it will look
when the evergreens are grown !   Do you call the style
Palladian, Mr. Barnet ? '

' I—really don't quite know what it is.   Yes, it must be
Palladian, certainly.   But I'll ask Jones, the architect ;
for, to tell the truth, I had not thought much about the
style : I had nothing to do with choosing it, I am sorry
to say.'

She would not let him harp on this gloomy refrain, and
talked on bright matters till she said, producing a small
roll of paper which he had noticed in her hand all the while,
' Mr. Downe wished me to bring you this revised drawing
of the late Mrs. Downe's tomb, which the architect has
just sent him.   He would like you to look it over.'

The children came up with their hoops, and she went
off with them down the harbour-road as usual.   Barnet
had been glad to get those words of thanks ; he had been
thinking for many months that he would like her to know
of his share in finding her a home such as it was ; and what
he could not do for himself, Downe had now kindly done
for him.   He returned to his desolate house with a lighter
tread ; though in reason he hardly knew why his tread
should be light.

On examining the drawing, Barnet found that, instead
of the vast altar-tomb and canopy Downe had determined
on at their last meeting, it was to be a more modest
memorial even than had been suggested by the architect ;
a coped tomb of good solid construction, with no useless
elaboration at all.   Barnet was truly glad to see that Downe
had come to reason of his own accord ; and he returned
the drawing with a note of approval.

He followed up the house-work as before, and as he
walked up and down the rooms, occasionally gazing from
the windows over the bulging green hills and the quiet
harbour that lay between them, he murmured words and

fragments of words which, if listened to, would have revealed
all the secrets of his existence. Whatever his reason in
going there, Lucy did not call again : the walk to the shore
seemed to be abandoned : he must have thought it as
well for both that it should be so, for he did not go anywhere out of his accustomed ways to endeavour to discover
her.

VIII

The winter and the spring had passed, and the house was
complete. It was a fine morning in the early part of
June, and Barnet, though not in the habit of rising early,
had taken a long walk before breakfast; returning by way
of the new building. A sufficiently exciting cause of his
restlessness to-day might have been the intelligence which
had reached him the night before, that Lucy Savile was
going to India after all, and notwithstanding the representations of her friends that such a journey was unadvisable
in many ways for an unpractised girl, unless some more
definite advantage lay at the end of it than she could show
to be the case. Barnet's walk up the slope to the building
betrayed that he was in a dissatisfied mood. He hardly
saw that the dewy time of day lent an unusual freshness
to the bushes and trees which had so recently put on their
summer habit of heavy leafage, and made his newly-laid
lawn look as well established as an old manorial meadow.
The house had been so adroitly placed between six tall
elms which were growing on the site beforehand, that they
seemed like real ancestral trees ; and the rooks, young and
old, cawed melodiously to their visitor.

The door was not locked, and he entered. No workmen
appeared to be present, and he walked from sunny window
to sunny window of the empty rooms, with a sense of seclusion which might have been very pleasant but for the antecedent knowledge that his almost paternal care of Lucy
Savile was to be thrown away by her wilfulness. Footsteps echoed through an adjoining room ; and bending his
eyes in that direction, he perceived Mr. Jones, the architect.
He had come to look over the building before giving the
contractor his final certificate. They walked over the

house together. Everything was finished except the paper-
ing : there were the latest improvements of the period
in bell-hanging, ventilating, smoke-jacks, fire-grates, and
French windows. The business was soon ended, and Jones,
having directed Barnet's attention to a book of wall-paper
patterns which lay on a bench for his choice, was leaving
to keep another engagement, when Barnet said, ' Is the
tomb finished yet for Mrs. Downe ? '

' Well—yes : it is at last,' said the architect, coming
back and speaking as if he were in a mood to make a confidence. ' I have had no end of trouble in the matter,
and, to tell the truth, I am heartily glad it is over.'

Barnet expressed his surprise. ' I thought poor Downe
had given up those extravagant notions of his ? Then he
has gone back to the altar and canopy after all ? Well, he
is to be excused, poor fellow ! '

' O no—he has not at all gone back to them—quite the
reverse,' Jones hastened to say. ' He has so reduced design
after design that the whole thing has been nothing but
waste labour for me ; till in the end it has become a
common headstone, which a mason put up in half a day.'

' A common headstone ? ' said Barnet.

' Yes. I held out for some time for the addition of a
footstone at least. But he said, " O no—he couldn't afford
it." '

' Ah, well—his family is growing up, poor fellow, and
his expenses are getting serious.'

' Yes, exactly,' said Jones, as if the subject were none
of his. And again directing Barnet's attention to the wall-
papers, the bustling architect left him to keep some other
engagement.

' A common headstone,' murmured Barnet, left again to
himself. He mused a minute or two, and next began
looking over and selecting from the patterns ; but had not
long been engaged in the work when he heard another
footstep on the gravel without, and somebody enter the
open porch.

Barnet went to the door—it was his manservant in
search of him.

' I have been trying for some time to find you, sir,' he

said. 'This letter has come by the post, and it is marked immediate. And there's this one from Mr. Downe, who called just now wanting to see you.' He searched his pocket for the second.

Barnet took the first letter—it had a black border, and bore the London postmark. It was not in his wife's hand-writing, or in that of any person he knew; but conjecture soon ceased as he read the page, wherein he was briefly informed that Mrs. Barnet had died suddenly on the pre-vious day, at the furnished villa she had occupied near London.

Barnet looked vaguely round the empty hall, at the blank walls, out of the doorway. Drawing a long palpitat-ing breath, and with eyes downcast, he turned and climbed the stairs slowly, like a man who doubted their stability. The fact of his wife having, as it were, died once already, and lived on again, had entirely dislodged the possibility of her actual death from his conjecture. He went to the landing, leant over the balusters, and after a reverie, of whose duration he had but the faintest notion, turned to the window and stretched his gaze to the cottage further down the road, which was visible from his landing, and from which Lucy still walked to the solicitor's house by a cross path. The faint words that came from his moving lips were simply, 'At last!'

Then, almost involuntarily, Barnet fell down on his knees and murmured some incoherent words of thanks-giving. Surely his virtue in restoring his wife to life had been rewarded! But, as if the impulse struck uneasily on his conscience, he quickly rose, brushed the dust from his trousers, and set himself to think of his next move-ments. He could not start for London for some hours; and as he had no preparations to make that could not be made in half-an-hour, he mechanically descended and resumed his occupation of turning over the wall-papers. They had all got brighter for him, those papers. It was all changed—who would sit in the rooms that they were to line? He went on to muse upon Lucy's conduct in so frequently coming to the house with the children; her occasional blush in speaking to him; her evident interest

in him. What woman can in the long run avoid being
interested in a man whom she knows to be devoted to
her ? If human solicitation could ever effect anything,
there should be no going to India for Lucy now. All the
papers previously chosen seemed wrong in their shades,
and he began from the beginning to choose again.

While entering on the task he heard a forced ' Ahem ! '
from without the porch, evidently uttered to attract his
attention, and footsteps again advancing to the door. His
man, whom he had quite forgotten in his mental turmoil,
was still waiting there.

' I beg your pardon, sir,' the man said from round the
doorway ; ' but here's the note from Mr. Downe that you
didn't take. He called just after you went out, and as he
couldn't wait, he wrote this on your study-table.'

He handed in the letter—no black-bordered one now,
but a practical-looking note in the well-known writing of
the solicitor.

' DEAR BARNET '—it ran—' Perhaps you will be prepared for the
information I am about to give—that Lucy Savile and myself are
going to be married this morning. I have hitherto said nothing as
to my intention to any of my friends, for reasons which I am sure
you will fully appreciate. The crisis has been brought about by her
expressing her intention to join her brother in India. I then discovered that I could not do without her.

' It is to be quite a private wedding ; but it is my particular wish
that you come down here quietly at ten, and go to church with us ;
it will add greatly to the pleasure I shall experience in the ceremony,
and, I believe, to Lucy's also. I have called on you very early to
make the request, in the belief that I should find you at home ; but
you are beforehand with me in your early rising.—Yours sincerely,
                                                    ' C. DOWNE.'

' Need I wait, sir ? ' said the servant after a dead silence.
' That will do, William. No answer,' said Barnet calmly.
When the man had gone Barnet re-read the letter. Turning eventually to the wall-papers, which he had been at
such pains to select, he deliberately tore them into halves
and quarters, and threw them into the empty fireplace.
Then he went out of the house, locked the door, and stood
in the front awhile. Instead of returning into the town,
he went down the harbour-road and thoughtfully lingered

about by the sea, near the spot where the body of Downe's late wife had been found and brought ashore.

Barnet was a man with a rich capacity for misery, and there is no doubt that he exercised it to its fullest extent now. The events that had, as it were, dashed themselves together into one half-hour of this day showed that curious refinement of cruelty in their arrangement which often proceeds from the bosom of the whimsical god at other times known as blind Circumstance. That his few minutes of hope, between the reading of the first and second letters, had carried him to extraordinary heights of rapture was proved by the immensity of his suffering now. The sun blazing into his face would have shown a close watcher that a horizontal line, which had never been seen before, but which was never to be gone thereafter, was somehow gradually forming itself in the smooth of his forehead. His eyes, of a light hazel, had a curious look which can only be described by the word bruised; the sorrow that looked from them being largely mixed with the surprise of a man taken unawares.

The secondary particulars of his present position, too, were odd enough, though for some time they appeared to engage little of his attention. Not a soul in the town knew, as yet, of his wife's death; and he almost owed Downe the kindness of not publishing it till the day was over: the conjuncture, taken with that which had accompanied the death of Mrs. Downe, being so singular as to be quite sufficient to darken the pleasure of the impressionable solicitor to a cruel extent, if made known to him. But as Barnet could not set out on his journey to London, where his wife lay, for some hours (there being at this date no railway within a distance of many miles), no great reason existed why he should leave the town.

Impulse in all its forms characterized Barnet, and when he heard the distant clock strike the hour of ten his feet began to carry him up the harbour-road with the manner of a man who must do something to bring himself to life. He passed Lucy Savile's old house, his own new one, and came in view of the church. Now he gave a perceptible start, and his mechanical condition went away. Before

the church-gate were a couple of carriages, and Barnet
then could perceive that the marriage between Downe and
Lucy was at that moment being solemnized within. A
feeling of sudden, proud self-confidence, an indocile wish
to walk unmoved in spite of grim environments, plainly
possessed him, and when he reached the wicket-gate he
turned in without apparent effort. Pacing up the paved
footway he entered the church and stood for awhile in
the nave passage. A group of people was standing round
the vestry door; Barnet advanced through these and
stepped into the vestry.

There they were, busily signing their names. Seeing
Downe about to look round Barnet averted his somewhat
disturbed face for a second or two; when he turned again
front to front he was calm and quite smiling; it was a
creditable triumph over himself, and deserved to be remembered in his native town. He greeted Downe heartily,
offering his congratulations.

It seemed as if Barnet expected a half-guilty look upon
Lucy's face; but no · save the natural flush and flurry
engendered by the service just performed, there was nothing whatever in her bearing which showed a disturbed
mind: her gray-brown eyes carried in them now as at
other times the well-known expression of common-sensed
rectitude which never went so far as to touch on hardness.
She shook hands with him, and Downe said warmly, ' I
wish you could have come sooner : I called on purpose to
ask you. You'll drive back with us now? '

' No, no,' said Barnet; ' I am not at all prepared; but
I thought I would look in upon you for a moment, even
though I had not time to go home and dress. I'll stand
back and see you pass out, and observe the effect of the
spectacle upon myself as one of the public.'

Then Lucy and her husband laughed, and Barnet laughed
and retired; and the quiet little party went gliding down
the nave and towards the porch, Lucy's new silk dress
sweeping with a smart rustle round the base-mouldings of
the ancient font, and Downe's little daughters following
in a state of round-eyed interest in their position, and that
of Lucy, their teacher and friend.

So Downe was comforted after his Emily's death, which had taken place twelve months, two weeks, and three days before that time.

When the two flys had driven off and the spectators had vanished, Barnet followed to the door, and went out into the sun. He took no more trouble to preserve a spruce exterior; his step was unequal, hesitating, almost convulsive; and the slight changes of colour which went on in his face seemed refracted from some inward flame. In the churchyard he became pale as a summer cloud, and finding it not easy to proceed he sat down on one of the tombstones and supported his head with his hand.

Hard by was a sexton filling up a grave which he had not found time to finish on the previous evening. Observing Barnet, he went up to him, and recognizing him, said, ' Shall I help you home, sir ? '

' O no, thank you,' said Barnet, rousing himself and standing up. The sexton returned to his grave, followed by Barnet, who, after watching him awhile, stepped into the grave, now nearly filled, and helped to tread in the earth.

The sexton apparently thought his conduct a little singular, but he made no observation, and when the grave was full, Barnet suddenly stopped, looked far away, and with a decided step proceeded to the gate and vanished. The sexton rested on his shovel and looked after him for a few moments, and then began banking up the mound.

In those short minutes of treading in the dead man Barnet had formed a design, but what it was the inhabitants of that town did not for some long time imagine. He went home, wrote several letters of business, called on his lawyer, an old man of the same place who had been the legal adviser of Barnet's father before him, and during the evening overhauled a large quantity of letters and other documents in his possession. By eleven o'clock the heap of papers in and before Barnet's grate had reached formidable dimensions, and he began to burn them. This, owing to their quantity, it was not so easy to do as he had expected, and he sat long into the night to complete the task.

The next morning Barnet departed for London, leaving a

note for Downe to inform him of Mrs. Barnet's sudden
death, and that he was gone to bury her ; but when a
thrice-sufficient time for that purpose had elapsed, he was
not seen again in his accustomed walks, or in his new
house, or in his old one. He was gone for good, nobody
knew whither. It was soon discovered that he had em-
powered his lawyer to dispose of all his property, real and
personal, in the borough, and pay in the proceeds to the
account of an unknown person at one of the large London
banks. The person was by some supposed to be himself
under an assumed name ; but few, if any, had certain
knowledge of that fact.

The elegant new residence was sold with the rest of his
possessions ; and its purchaser was no other than Downe,
now a thriving man in the borough, and one whose growing family and new wife required more roomy accommodation than was afforded by the little house up the narrow
side street. Barnet's old habitation was bought by the
trustees of the Congregational Baptist body in that town,
who pulled down the time-honoured dwelling and built a
new chapel on its site. By the time the last hour of that,
to Barnet, eventful year had chimed, every vestige of him
had disappeared from the precincts of his native place,
and the name became extinct in the borough of Port-
Bredy, after having been a living force therein for more
than two hundred years.

IX

Twenty-one years and six months do not pass without
setting a mark even upon durable stone and triple brass ;
upon humanity such a period works nothing less than
transformation. In Barnet's old birthplace vivacious
young children with bones like india-rubber had grown up
to be stable men and women, men and women had dried
in the skin, stiffened, withered, and sunk into decrepitude ;
while selections from every class had been consigned to the
outlying cemetery. Of inorganic differences the greatest
was that a railway had invaded the town, tying it on to a
main line at a junction a dozen miles off. Barnet's house
on the harbour-road, once so insistently new, had acquired

a respectable mellowness, with ivy, Virginia creepers,
lichens, damp patches, and even constitutional infirmities
of its own like its elder fellows. Its architecture, once so
very improved and modern, had already become stale in
style, without having reached the dignity of being old-
fashioned. Trees about the harbour-road had increased
in circumference or disappeared under the saw ; while the
church had had such a tremendous practical joke played
upon it by some facetious restorer or other as to be scarce
recognizable by its dearest old friends.

During this long interval George Barnet had never
once been seen or heard of in the town of his fathers.

It was the evening of a market-day, and some half-
dozen middle-aged farmers and dairymen were lounging
round the bar of the Black-Bull Hotel, occasionally dropping a remark to each other, and less frequently to the
two barmaids who stood within the pewter-topped counter
in a perfunctory attitude of attention, these latter sighing
and making a private observation to one another at odd
intervals, on more interesting experiences than the present.

' Days get shorter,' said one of the dairymen, as he
looked towards the street, and noticed that the lamplighter
was passing by.

The farmers merely acknowledged by their countenances
the propriety of this remark, and finding that nobody else
spoke, one of the barmaids said ' yes,' in a tone of painful
duty.

' Come fair-day we shall have to light up before we start
for home-along.'

' That's true,' his neighbour conceded, with a gaze of
blankness.

' And after that we shan't see much further difference
all's winter.'

The rest were not unwilling to go even so far as this.

The barmaid sighed again, and raised one of her hands
from the counter on which they rested to scratch the smallest surface of her face with the smallest of her fingers.
She looked towards the door, and presently remarked,
' I think I hear the 'bus coming in from station.'

The eyes of the dairymen and farmers turned to the

glass door dividing the hall from the porch, and in a minute or two the omnibus drew up outside. Then there was a lumbering down of luggage, and then a man came into the hall, followed by a porter with a portmanteau on his poll, which he deposited on a bench.

The stranger was an elderly person, with curly ashen-white hair, a deeply-creviced outer corner to each eyelid, and a countenance baked by innumerable suns to the colour of terra-cotta, its hue and that of his hair contrast-ing like heat and cold respectively. He walked medita-tively and gently, like one who was fearful of disturbing his own mental equilibrium. But whatever lay at the bottom of his breast had evidently made him so accustomed to its situation there that it caused him little practical inconvenience.

He paused in silence while, with his dubious eyes fixed on the barmaids, he seemed to consider himself. In a moment or two he addressed them, and asked to be accom-modated for the night. As he waited he looked curiously round the hall, but said nothing. As soon as invited he disappeared up the staircase, preceded by a chambermaid and candle, and followed by a lad with his trunk. Not a soul had recognized him.

A quarter of an hour later, when the farmers and dairy-men had driven off to their homesteads in the country, he came downstairs, took a biscuit and one glass of wine, and walked out into the town, where the radiance from the shop-windows had grown so in volume of late years as to flood with cheerfulness every standing cart, barrow, stall, and idler that occupied the wayside, whether shabby or genteel. His chief interest at present seemed to lie in the names painted over the shop-fronts and on doorways, as far as they were visible ; these now differed to an ominous extent from what they had been one-and-twenty years before.

The traveller passed on till he came to the bookseller's, where he looked in through the glass door. A fresh-faced young man was standing behind the counter, otherwise the shop was empty. The gray-haired observer entered, asked for some periodical by way of paying for admission, and with his elbow on the counter began to turn over the pages he had bought, though that he read nothing was obvious.

At length he said, ' Is old Mr. Watkins still alive ? ' in a voice which had a curious youthful cadence in it even now.

' My father is dead, sir,' said the young man.

' Ah, I am sorry to hear it,' said the stranger. ' But it is so many years since I last visited this town that I could hardly expect it should be otherwise.' After a short silence he continued—' And is the firm of Barnet, Browse and Company still in existence ?—they used to be large flax-merchants and twine-spinners here ? '

' The firm is still going on, sir, but they have dropped the name of Barnet. I believe that was a sort of fancy name—at least, I never knew of any living Barnet. 'Tis now Browse and Co.'

' And does Andrew Jones still keep on as architect ? '

' He's dead, sir.'

' And the vicar of St. Mary's—Mr. Melrose ? '

' He's been dead a great many years.'

' Dear me ! ' He paused yet longer, and cleared his voice. ' Is Mr. Downe, the solicitor, still in practice ? '

' No, sir, he's dead. He died about seven years ago.'

Here it was a longer silence still ; and an attentive observer would have noticed that the paper in the stranger's hand increased its imperceptible tremor to a visible shake. That gray-haired gentleman noticed it himself, and rested the paper on the counter. ' Is *Mrs.* Downe still alive ? ' he asked, closing his lips firmly as soon as the words were out of his mouth, and dropping his eyes.

' Yes, sir, she's alive and well. She's living at the old place.'

' In East Street ? '

' O no ; at Château Ringdale. I believe it has been in the family for some generations.'

' She lives with her children, perhaps ? '

' No ; she has no children of her own. There were some Miss Downes ; I think they were Mr. Downe's daugh-

ters by a former wife; but they are married and living
in other parts of the town. Mrs. Downe lives alone.'

'Quite alone?'

'Yes, sir; quite alone.'

The newly-arrived gentleman went back to the hotel
and dined; after which he made some change in his dress,
shaved back his beard to the fashion that had prevailed
twenty years earlier, when he was young and interesting,
and once more emerging, bent his steps in the direction of
the harbour-road. Just before getting to the point where
the pavement ceased and the houses isolated themselves,
he overtook a shambling, stooping, unshaven man, who
at first sight appeared like a professional tramp, his shoulders
having a perceptible greasiness as they passed under the
gaslight. Each pedestrian momentarily turned and regarded the other, and the tramp-like gentleman started
back.

'Good—why—is that Mr. Barnet? 'Tis Mr. Barnet,
surely!'

'Yes; and you are Charlson?'

'Yes—ah—you notice my appearance. The Fates
have rather ill-used me. By-the-bye, that fifty pounds.
I never paid it, did I? . . . But I was not ungrateful!'
Here the stooping man laid one hand emphatically on the
palm of the other. 'I gave you a chance, Mr. George
Barnet, which many men would have thought full value
received—the chance to marry your Lucy. As far as the
world was concerned, your wife was a *drowned woman*,
hey?'

'Heaven forbid all that, Charlson!'

'Well, well, 'twas a wrong way of showing gratitude, I
suppose. And now a drop of something to drink for old
acquaintance' sake! And, Mr. Barnet, she's again free
—there's a chance now if you care for it—ha, ha!' And
the speaker pushed his tongue into his hollow cheek and
slanted his eye in the old fashion.

'I know all,' said Barnet quickly; and slipping a
small present into the hands of the needy, saddening man,
he stepped ahead and was soon in the outskirts of the
town.

He reached the harbour-road, and paused before the entrance to a well-known house. It was so highly bosomed in trees and shrubs planted since the erection of the building that one would scarcely have recognized the spot as that which had been a mere neglected slope till chosen as a site for a dwelling. He opened the swing-gate, closed it noiselessly, and gently moved into the semicircular drive, which remained exactly as it had been marked out by Barnet on the morning when Lucy Savile ran in to thank him for procuring her the post of governess to Downe's children. But the growth of trees and bushes which revealed itself at every step was beyond all expectation ; sun-proof and moon-proof bowers vaulted the walks, and the walls of the house were uniformly bearded with creeping plants as high as the first-floor windows.

After lingering for a few minutes in the dusk of the bending boughs, the visitor rang the door-bell, and on the servant appearing, he announced himself as ' an old friend of Mrs. Downe's.'

The hall was lighted, but not brightly, the gas being turned low, as if visitors were rare. There was a stagnation in the dwelling ; it seemed to be waiting. Could it really be waiting for him ? The partitions which had been probed by Barnet's walking-stick when the mortar was green, were now quite brown with the antiquity of their varnish, and the ornamental woodwork of the staircase, which had glistened with a pale yellow newness when first erected, was now of a rich wine-colour. During the servant's absence the following colloquy could be dimly heard through the nearly-closed door of the drawing-room.

' He didn't give his name ? '

' He only said " an old friend," ma'am.'

' What kind of gentleman is he ? '

' A staidish gentleman, with gray hair.'

The voice of the second speaker seemed to affect the listener greatly. After a pause, the lady said, ' Very well, I will see him.'

And the stranger was shown in face to face with the Lucy who had once been Lucy Savile. The round cheek

of that formerly young lady had, of course, alarmingly
flattened its curve in her modern representative; a pervasive
grayness overspread her once dark brown hair, like morning rime on heather. The parting down the middle was
wide and jagged; once it had been a thin white line, a
narrow crevice between two high banks of shade. But
there was still enough left to form a handsome knob behind, and some curls beneath inwrought with a few hairs
like silver wires were very becoming. In her eyes the
only modification was that their originally mild rectitude
of expression had become a little more stringent than heretofore. Yet she was still girlish—a girl who had been
gratuitously weighted by destiny with a burden of five-
and-forty years instead of her proper twenty.

'Lucy, don't you know me?' he said, when the servant
had closed the door.

'I knew you the instant I saw you!' she returned
cheerfully. 'I don't know why, but I always thought
you would come back to your old town again.'

She gave him her hand, and then they sat down. 'They
said you were dead,' continued Lucy, 'but I never thought
so. We should have heard of it for certain if you had
been.'

'It is a very long time since we met.'

'Yes; what you must have seen, Mr. Barnet, in all
these roving years, in comparison with what I have seen
in this quiet place!' Her face grew more serious. 'You
know my husband has been dead a long time? I am a
lonely old woman now, considering what I have been;
though Mr. Downe's daughters—all married—manage to
keep me pretty cheerful.'

'And I am a lonely old man, and have been any time
these twenty years.'

'But where have you kept yourself? And why did
you go off so mysteriously?'

'Well, Lucy, I have kept myself a little in America,
and a little in Australia, a little in India, a little at the
Cape, and so on; I have not stayed in any place for a
long time, as it seems to me, and yet more than twenty
years have flown. But when people get to my age two

years go like one !—Your second question, why did I go
away so mysteriously, is surely not necessary. You
guessed why, didn't you ? '

' No, I never once guessed,' she said simply ; ' nor
did Charles, nor did anybody as far as I know.'

' Well, indeed ! Now think it over again, and then look
at me, and say if you can't guess ? '

She looked him in the face with an inquiring smile.
' Surely not because of me ? ' she said, pausing at the
commencement of surprise.

Barnet nodded, and smiled again ; but his smile was
sadder than hers.

' Because I married Charles ? ' she asked.

' Yes ; solely because you married him on the day I
was free to ask you to marry me. My wife died four-and-
twenty hours before you went to church with Downe. The
fixing of my journey at that particular moment was because
of her funeral; but once away I knew I should have no
inducement to come back, and took my steps accordingly.'

Her face assumed an aspect of gentle reflection, and
she looked up and down his form with great interest in
her eyes. ' I never thought of it ! ' she said. ' I knew, of
course, that you had once implied some warmth of feeling
towards me, but I concluded that it passed off. And I
have always been under the impression that your wife was
alive at the time of my marriage. Was it not stupid of me !
—But you will have some tea or something ? I have never
dined late, you know, since my husband's death. I have
got into the way of making a regular meal of tea. You
will have some tea with me, will you not ? '

The travelled man assented quite readily, and tea was
brought in. They sat and chatted over the tray, regardless
of the flying hour. ' Well, well ! ' said Barnet presently,
as for the first time he leisurely surveyed the room ; ' how
like it all is, and yet how different ! Just where your
piano stands was a board on a couple of trestles, bearing
the patterns of wall-papers, when I was last here. I
was choosing them—standing in this way, as it might be.
Then my servant came in at the door, and handed me a
note, so. It was from Downe, and announced that you

were just going to be married to him. I chose no more
wall-papers—tore up all those I had selected, and left the
house. I never entered it again till now.'

' Ah, at last I understand it all,' she murmured.

They had both risen and gone to the fireplace. The
mantel came almost on a level with her shoulder, which
gently rested against it, and Barnet laid his hand upon the
shelf close beside her shoulder. ' Lucy,' he said, ' better
late than never. Will you marry me now ? '

She started back, and the surprise which was so obvious
in her wrought even greater surprise in him that it should
be so. It was difficult to believe that she had been quite
blind to the situation, and yet all reason and common
sense went to prove that she was not acting.

' You take me quite unawares by such a question ! '
she said, with a forced laugh of uneasiness. It was the first
time she had shown any embarrassment at all. ' Why,'
she added, ' I couldn't marry you for the world.'

' Not after all this ! Why not ? '

' It is—I would—I really think I may say it—I would
upon the whole rather marry you, Mr. Barnet, than any
other man I have ever met, if I ever dreamed of marriage
again. But I don't dream of it—it is quite out of my
thoughts ; I have not the least intention of marrying
again.'

' But—on my account—couldn't you alter your plans a
little ? Come ! '

' Dear Mr. Barnet,' she said with a little flutter, ' I
would on your account if on anybody's in existence. But
you don't know in the least what it is you are asking
—such an impracticable thing—I won't say ridiculous,
of course, because I see that you are really in earnest, and
earnestness is never ridiculous to my mind.'

' Well, yes,' said Barnet more slowly, dropping her hand,
which he had taken at the moment of pleading, ' I am in
earnest. The resolve, two months ago, at the Cape, to
come back once more was, it is true, rather sudden, and
as I see now, not well considered. But I am in earnest in
asking.'

' And I in declining. With all good feeling and all

kindness, let me say that I am quite opposed to the idea of marrying a second time.'

'Well, no harm has been done,' he answered, with the same subdued and tender humorousness that he had shown on such occasions in early life. 'If you really won't accept me, I must put up with it, I suppose.' His eye fell on the clock as he spoke. 'Had you any notion that it was so late ? ' he asked. 'How absorbed I have been ! '

She accompanied him to the hall, helped him to put on his overcoat, and let him out of the house herself.

'Good-night,' said Barnet, on the doorstep, as the lamp shone in his face. 'You are not offended with me ? '

'Certainly not. Nor you with me ? '

' I'll consider whether I am or not,' he pleasantly replied. ' Good-night.'

She watched him safely through the gate ; and when his footsteps had died away upon the road, closed the door softly and returned to the room. Here the modest widow long pondered his speeches, with eyes dropped to an unusually low level. Barnet's urbanity under the blow of her refusal greatly impressed her. After having his long period of probation rendered useless by her decision, he had shown no anger, and had philosophically taken her words as if he deserved no better ones. It was very gentlemanly of him, certainly ; it was more than gentlemanly : it was heroic and grand. The more she meditated, the more she questioned the virtue of her conduct in checking him so peremptorily ; and went to her bedroom in a mood of dissatisfaction. On looking in the glass she was reminded that there was not so much remaining of her former beauty as to make his frank declaration an impulsive natural homage to her cheeks and eyes ; it must undoubtedly have arisen from an old staunch feeling of his, deserving tenderest consideration. She recalled to her mind with much pleasure that he had told her he was staying at the Black-Bull Hotel ; so that if, after waiting a day or two, he should not, in his modesty, call again, she might then send him a nice little note. To alter her views for the present was far from her intention ; but she would allow herself to be induced to reconsider the case, as any generous woman ought to do.

The morrow came and passed, and Mr. Barnet did not drop in. At every knock, light youthful hues flew across her cheek ; and she was abstracted in the presence of her other visitors. In the evening she walked about the house, not knowing what to do with herself ; the conditions of existence seemed totally different from those which ruled only four-and-twenty short hours ago. What had been at first a tantalizing, elusive sentiment was getting acclimatized within her as a definite hope, and her person was so informed by that emotion that she might almost have stood as its emblematical representative by the time the clock struck ten. In short, an interest in Barnet precisely resembling that of her early youth led her present heart to belie her yesterday's words to him, and she longed to see him again.

The next day she walked out early, thinking she might meet him in the street. The growing beauty of her romance absorbed her, and she went from the street to the fields, and from the fields to the shore, without any consciousness of distance, till reminded by her weariness that she could go no further. He had nowhere appeared. In the evening she took a step which under the circumstances seemed justifiable ; she wrote a note to him at the hotel, inviting him to tea with her at six precisely, and signing her note ' Lucy.'

In a quarter of an hour the messenger came back. Mr. Barnet had left the hotel early in the morning of the day before, but he had stated that he would probably return in the course of the week.

The note was sent back, to be given to him immediately on his arrival.

There was no sign from the inn that this desired event hâd occurred, either on the next day or the day following. On both nights she had been restless, and had scarcely slept half-an-hour.

On the Saturday, putting off all diffidence, Lucy went herself to the Black-Bull, and questioned the staff closely.

Mr. Barnet had cursorily remarked when leaving that

he might return on the Thursday or Friday, but they were directed not to reserve a room for him unless he should write.

He had left no address.

Lucy sorrowfully took back her note, went home, and resolved to wait.

She did wait—years and years—but Barnet never reappeared.

April 1880.

INTERLOPERS AT THE KNAP

INTERLOPERS AT THE KNAP

I

THE north road from Casterbridge is tedious and lonely, especially in winter-time. Along a part of its course it connects with Long-Ash Lane, a monotonous track without a village or hamlet for many miles, and with very seldom a turning. Unapprized wayfarers who are too old, or too young, or in other respects too weak for the distance to be traversed, but who, nevertheless, have to walk it, say, as they look wistfully ahead, ' Once at the top of that hill, and I must surely see the end of Long-Ash Lane ! ' But they reach the hilltop, and Long-Ash Lane stretches in front as mercilessly as before.

Some few years ago a certain farmer was riding through this lane in the gloom of a winter evening. The farmer's friend, a dairyman, was riding beside him. A few paces in the rear rode the farmer's man. All three were well horsed on strong, round-barrelled cobs ; and to be well horsed was to be in better spirits about Long-Ash Lane than poor pedestrians could attain to during its passage.

But the farmer did not talk much to his friend as he rode along. The enterprise which had brought him there filled his mind ; for in truth it was important. Not altogether so important was it, perhaps, when estimated by its value to society at large ; but if the true measure of a deed be proportionate to the space it occupies in the heart of him who undertakes it, Farmer Charles Darton's business to-night could hold its own with the business of kings.

He was a large farmer. His turnover, as it is called, was probably thirty thousand pounds a year. He had a great many draught horses, a great many milch cows, and of sheep a multitude. This comfortable position was, however, none of his own making. It had been created by his father, a man of a very different stamp from the present representative of the line.

Darton, the father, had been a one-idea'd character, with a buttoned-up pocket and a chink-like eye brimming with commercial subtlety. In Darton the son, this trade subtlety had become transmuted into emotional, and the harshness had disappeared; he would have been called a sad man but for his constant care not to divide himself from lively friends by piping notes out of harmony with theirs. Contemplative, he allowed his mind to be a quiet meeting-place for memories and hopes. So that, naturally enough, since succeeding to the agricultural calling, and up to his present age of thirty-two, he had neither advanced nor receded as a capitalist—a stationary result which did not agitate one of his unambitious, unstrategic nature, since he had all that he desired. The motive of his expedition to-night showed the same absence of anxious regard for Number One.

The party rode on in the slow, safe trot proper to night-time and bad roads, Farmer Darton's head jigging rather unromantically up and down against the sky, and his motions being repeated with bolder emphasis by his friend Japheth Johns; while those of the latter were travestied in jerks still less softened by art in the person of the lad who attended them. A pair of whitish objects hung one on each side of the latter, bumping against him at each step, and still further spoiling the grace of his seat. On close inspection they might have been perceived to be open rush baskets—one containing a turkey, and the other some bottles of wine.

'D'ye feel ye can meet your fate like a man, neighbour Darton?' asked Johns, breaking a silence which had lasted while five-and-twenty hedgerow trees had glided by.

Mr. Darton with a half-laugh murmured, 'Ay—call it my fate! Hanging and wiving go by destiny.' And then they were silent again.

The darkness thickened rapidly, at intervals shutting down on the land in a perceptible flap, like the wave of a wing. The customary close of day was accelerated by a

simultaneous blurring of the air. With the fall of night
had come a mist just damp enough to incommode, but not
sufficient to saturate them. Countrymen as they were
—born, as may be said, with only an open door between
them and the four seasons—they regarded the mist but
as an added obscuration, and ignored its humid quality.

They were travelling in a direction that was enlivened
by no modern current of traffic, the place of Darton's
pilgrimage being an old-fashioned village—one of the
Hintocks (several villages of that name, with a distinctive
prefix or affix, lying thereabout)—where the people make
the best cider and cider-wine in all Wessex, and where the
dunghills smell of pomace instead of stable refuse as elsewhere. The lane was sometimes so narrow that the
brambles of the hedge, which hung forward like anglers'
rods over a stream, scratched their hats and hooked their
whiskers as they passed. Yet this neglected lane had been
a highway to Queen Elizabeth's subjects and the cavalcades
of the past. Its day was over now, and its history as a
national artery done for ever.

'Why I have decided to marry her,' resumed Darton
(in a measured musical voice of confidence which revealed
a good deal of his composition), as he glanced round to
see that the lad was not too near, 'is not only that I like
her, but that I can do no better, even from a fairly practical
point of view. That I might ha' looked higher is possibly
true, though it is really all nonsense. I have had experience enough in looking above me. "No more superior
women for me," said I—you know when. Sally is a
comely, independent, simple character, with no make-up
about her, who'll think me as much a superior to her as
I used to think—you know who I mean—was to me.'

'Ay,' said Johns. 'However, I shouldn't call Sally
Hall simple. Primary, because no Sally is ; secondary,
because if some could be, this one wouldn't. 'Tis a wrong
denomination to apply to a woman, Charles, and affects
me, as your best man, like cold water. 'Tis like recommending a stage play by saying there's neither murder,
villainy, nor harm of any sort in it, when that's what you've
paid your half-crown to see.'

' Well; may your opinion do you good. Mine's a
different one.' And turning the conversation from the
philosophical to the practical, Darton expressed a hope
that the said Sally had received what he'd sent on by the
carrier that day.

Johns wanted to know what that was.

' It is a dress,' said Darton. ' Not exactly a wedding-
dress; though she may use it as one if she likes. It is
rather serviceable than showy—suitable for the winter
weather.'

' Good,' said Johns. ' Serviceable is a wise word in a
bridegroom. I commend 'ee, Charles.'

' For,' said Darton, ' why should a woman dress up
like a rope-dancer because she's going to do the most
solemn deed of her life except dying? '

' Faith, why? But she will, because she will, I suppose,'
said Dairyman Johns.

' H'm,' said Darton.

The lane they followed had been nearly straight for
several miles, but they now left it for a smaller one which
after winding uncertainly for some distance forked into
two. By night country roads are apt to reveal ungainly
qualities which pass without observation during day;
and though Darton had travelled this way before, he had
not done so frequently, Sally having been wooed at the
house of a relative near his own. He never remembered
seeing at this spot a pair of alternative ways looking so
equally probable as these two did now. Johns rode on a
few steps.

' Don't be out of heart, sonny,' he cried. ' Here's a
handpost. Ezra—come and climm this post, and tell us the
way.'

The lad dismounted, and jumped into the hedge where the
post stood under a tree.

' Unstrap the baskets, or you'll smash up that wine! '
cried Darton, as the young man began spasmodically to
climb the post, baskets and all.

' Was there ever less head in a brainless world? ' said
Johns. ' Here, simple Ezzy, I'll do it.' He leapt off, and
with much puffing climbed the post, striking a match when

he reached the top, and moving the light along the arm, the lad standing and gazing at the spectacle.

' I have faced tantalization these twenty years with a temper as mild as milk ! ' said Japheth ; ' but such things as this don't come short of devilry ! ' And flinging the match away, he slipped down to the ground.

' What's the matter ? ' asked Darton.

' Not a letter, sacred or heathen—not so much as would tell us the way to the town of Smokeyhole—ever I should sin to say it ! Either the moss and mildew have eat away the words, or we have arrived in a land where the natyves have lost the art o' writing, and should ha' brought our compass like Christopher Columbus.'

' Let us take the straightest road,' said Darton placidly ; ' I shan't be sorry to get there—'tis a tiresome ride. I would have driven if I had known.'

' Nor I neither, sir,' said Ezra. ' These straps plough my shoulder like a zull. If 'tis much further to your lady's home, Maister Darton, I shall ask to be let carry half of these good things in my innerds—hee, hee ! '

' Don't you be such a reforming radical, Ezra,' said Johns sternly. ' Here, I'll take the turkey.'

This being done, they went forward by the right-hand lane, which ascended a hill, the left winding away under a plantation. The pit-a-pit of their horses' hoofs lessened up the slope ; and the ironical directing-post stood in solitude as before, holding out its blank arms to the raw breeze, which brought a snore from the wood as if Skrymir the Giant were sleeping there.

II

Three miles to the left of the travellers, along the road they had not followed, rose an old house with mullioned windows of Ham-hill stone, and chimneys of lavish solidity. It stood at the top of a slope beside King's-Hintock village-street, only a mile or two from King's-Hintock Court, yet quite shut away from that mansion and its precincts. Immediately in front of it grew a large sycamore tree, whose bared roots formed a convenient staircase from the road below to the front door of the dwelling. Its situation gave

the house what little distinctive name it possessed, namely,
'The Knap.' Some forty yards off a brook dribbled past,
which, for its size, made a great deal of noise. At the back
was a dairy barton, accessible for vehicles and live-stock
by a side 'drong.' Thus much only of the character of the
homestead could be divined out of doors at this shady
evening-time.

But within there was plenty of light to see by, as plenty
was construed at Hintock. Beside a Tudor fireplace,
whose moulded four-centred arch was nearly hidden by a
figured blue-cloth blower, were seated two women—mother
and daughter—Mrs. Hall, and Sarah, or Sally; for this
was a part of the world where the latter modification had
not as yet been effaced as a vulgarity by the march of
intellect. The owner of the name was the young woman
by whose means Mr. Darton proposed to put an end to his
bachelor condition on the approaching day.

The mother's bereavement had been so long ago as
not to leave much mark of its occurrence upon her now,
either in face or clothes. She had resumed the mob-cap
of her early married life, enlivening its whiteness by a few
rose-du-Barry ribbons. Sally required no such aids to
pinkness. Roseate good-nature lit up her gaze; her
features showed curves of decision and judgment; and
she might have been regarded without much mistake
as a warm-hearted, quick-spirited, handsome girl.

She did most of the talking, her mother listening with a
half-absent air, as she picked up fragments of red-hot wood
ember with the tongs, and piled them upon the brands.
But the number of speeches that passed was very small in
proportion to the meanings exchanged. Long experience
together often enabled them to see the course of thought
in each other's minds without a word being spoken. Behind them, in the centre of the room, the table was spread
for supper, certain whiffs of air laden with fat vapours,
which ever and anon entered from the kitchen, denoting
its preparation there.

'The new gown he was going to send you stays about
on the way like himself,' Sally's mother was saying.

'Yes, not finished, I daresay,' cried Sally independently.

'Lord, I shouldn't be amazed if it didn't come at all!
Young men make such kind promises when they are near
you, and forget 'em when they go away. But he doesn't
intend it as a wedding-gown—he gives it to me merely
as a gown to wear when I like—a travelling-dress is what it
would be called by some. Come rathe or come late it
don't much matter, as I have a dress of my own to fall
back upon. But what time is it?'

She went to the family clock and opened the glass,
for the hour was not otherwise discernible by night, and
indeed at all times was rather a thing to be investigated
than beheld, so much more wall than window was there
in the apartment. 'It is nearly eight,' said she.

'Eight o'clock, and neither dress nor man,' said Mrs.
Hall.

'Mother, if you think to tantalize me by talking like
that, you are much mistaken! Let him be as late as he
will—or stay away altogether—I don't care,' said Sally.
But a tender, minute quaver in the negation showed
that there was something forced in that statement.

Mrs. Hall perceived it, and drily observed that she was
not so sure about Sally not caring. 'But perhaps you
don't care so much as I do, after all,' she said. 'For I
see what you don't, that it is a good and flourishing match
for you; a very honourable offer in Mr. Darton. And I
think I see a kind husband in him. So pray God 'twill go
smooth, and wind up well.'

Sally would not listen to misgivings. Of course it would
go smoothly, she asserted. 'How you are up and down,
mother!' she went on. 'At this moment, whatever hin-
ders him, we are not so anxious to see him as he is to be
here, and his thought runs on before him, and settles down
upon us like the star in the east. Hark!' she exclaimed,
with a breath of relief, her eyes sparkling. 'I heard something. Yes—here they are!'

The next moment her mother's slower ear also distinguished the familiar reverberation occasioned by footsteps clambering up the roots of the sycamore.

'Yes, it sounds like them at last,' she said. 'Well,
it is not so very late after all, considering the distance.'

The footfall ceased, and they arose, expecting a knock. They began to think it might have been, after all, some neighbouring villager under Bacchic influence, giving the centre of the road a wide berth, when their doubts were dispelled by the new-comer's entry into the passage. The door of the room was gently opened, and there appeared, not the pair of travellers with whom we have already made acquaintance, but a pale-faced man in the garb of extreme poverty—almost in rags.

'O, it's a tramp—gracious me!' said Sally, starting back.

His cheeks and eye-orbits were deep concaves—rather, it might be, from natural weakness of constitution than irregular living, though there were indications that he had led no careful life. He gazed at the two women fixedly for a moment : then with an abashed, humiliated demeanour, dropped his glance to the floor, and sank into a chair without uttering a word.

Sally was in advance of her mother, who had remained standing by the fire. She now tried to discern the visitor across the candles.

'Why—mother,' said Sally faintly, turning back to Mrs. Hall. 'It is Phil, from Australia!'

Mrs. Hall started, and grew pale, and a fit of coughing seized the man with the ragged clothes. 'To come home like this!' she said. 'O, Philip—are you ill?'

'No, no, mother,' replied he impatiently, as soon as he could speak.

'But for God's sake how do you come here—and just now, too?'

'Well, I am here,' said the man. 'How it is I hardly know. I've come home, mother, because I was driven to it. Things were against me out there, and went from bad to worse.'

'Then why didn't you let us know?—you've not writ a line for the last two or three years.'

The son admitted sadly that he had not. He said that he had hoped and thought he might fetch up again, and be able to send good news. Then he had been obliged to abandon that hope, and had finally come home from sheer necessity—previously to making a new start. 'Yes, things are very bad with me,' he repeated, perceiving their commiserating glances at his clothes.

They brought him nearer the fire, took his hat from his thin hand, which was so small and smooth as to show that his attempts to fetch up again had not been in a manual direction. His mother resumed her inquiries, and dubiously asked if he had chosen to come that particular night for any special reason.

For no reason, he told her. His arrival had been quite at random. Then Philip Hall looked round the room, and saw for the first time that the table was laid somewhat luxuriously, and for a larger number than themselves; and that an air of festivity pervaded their dress. He asked quickly what was going on.

'Sally is going to be married in a day or two,' replied the mother; and she explained how Mr. Darton, Sally's intended husband, was coming there that night with the groomsman, Mr. Johns, and other details. 'We thought it must be their step when we heard you,' said Mrs. Hall.

The needy wanderer looked again on the floor. 'I see —I see,' he murmured. 'Why, indeed, should I have come to-night? Such folk as I are not wanted here at these times, naturally. And I have no business here— spoiling other people's happiness.'

'Phil,' said his mother, with a tear in her eye, but with a thinness of lip and severity of manner which were presumably not more than past events justified; 'since you speak like that to me, I'll speak honestly to you. For these three years you have taken no thought for us. You left home with a good supply of money, and strength and education, and you ought to have made good use of it all. But you come back like a beggar; and that you come in a very awkward time for us cannot be denied. Your return to-night may do us much harm. But mind—you are welcome to this home as long as it is mine. I don't wish to turn you adrift. We will make the best of a bad job; and I hope you are not seriously ill?'

'O no. I have only this infernal cough.'

She looked at him anxiously. 'I think you had better go to bed at once,' she said.

'Well—I shall be out of the way there,' said the son wearily. 'Having ruined myself, don't let me ruin you by being seen in these togs, for Heaven's sake. Who do you say Sally is going to be married to—a Farmer Darton?'

'Yes—a gentleman-farmer—quite a wealthy man. Far better in station than she could have expected. It is a good thing, altogether.'

'Well done, little Sal!' said her brother, brightening and looking up at her with a smile. 'I ought to have written; but perhaps I have thought of you all the more. But let me get out of sight. I would rather go and jump into the river than be seen here. But have you anything I can drink? I am confoundedly thirsty with my long tramp.'

'Yes, yes, we will bring something upstairs to you,' said Sally, with grief in her face.

'Ay, that will do nicely. But, Sally and mother——' He stopped, and they waited. 'Mother, I have not told you all,' he resumed slowly, still looking on the floor between his knees. 'Sad as what you see of me is, there's worse behind.'

His mother gazed upon him in grieved suspense, and Sally went and leant upon the bureau, listening for every sound, and sighing. Suddenly she turned round, saying, 'Let them come, I don't care! Philip, tell the worst, and take your time.'

'Well, then,' said the unhappy Phil, 'I am not the only one in this mess. Would to Heaven I were! But——'

'O, Phil!'

'I have a wife as destitute as I.'

'A wife?' said his mother.

'Unhappily!'

'A wife! Yes, that is the way with sons!'

'And besides——' said he.

'Besides! O, Philip, surely——'

'I have two little children.'

'Wife and children!' whispered Mrs. Hall, sinking down confounded.

'Poor little things!' said Sally involuntarily.

His mother turned again to him. 'I suppose these helpless beings are left in Australia ? '

' No. They are in England.'

' Well, I can only hope you've left them in a respectable place.'

' I have not left them at all. They are here—within a few yards of us. In short, they are in the stable.'

' Where ? '

' In the stable. I did not like to bring them indoors till I had seen you, mother, and broken the bad news a bit to you. They were very tired, and are resting out there on some straw.'

Mrs. Hall's fortitude visibly broke down. She had been brought up not without refinement, and was even more moved by such a collapse of genteel aims as this than a substantial dairyman's widow would in ordinary have been moved. ' Well, it must be borne,' she said, in a low voice, with her hands tightly joined.   ' A starving son, a starving wife, starving children ! Let it be. But why is this come to us now, to-day, to-night ? Could no other misfortune happen to helpless women than this, which will quite upset my poor girl's chance of a happy life ? Why have you done us this wrong, Philip ? What respectable man will come here, and marry open-eyed into a family of vagabonds ? '

' Nonsense, mother ! ' said Sally vehemently, while her face flushed. ' Charley isn't the man to desert me. But if he should be, and won't marry me because Phil's come, let him go and marry elsewhere. I won't be ashamed of my own flesh and blood for any man in England —not I ! ' And then Sally turned away and burst into tears.

' Wait till you are twenty years older and you will tell a different tale,' replied her mother.

The son stood up. ' Mother,' he said bitterly, ' as I have come, so I will go. All I ask of you is that you will allow me and mine to lie in your stable to-night. I give you my word that we'll be gone by break of day, and trouble you no further ! '

Mrs. Hall, the mother, changed at that. ' O no,' she

answered hastily; 'never shall it be said that I sent any
of my own family from my door. Bring 'em in, Philip, or
take me out to them.'

'We will put 'em all into the large bedroom,' said Sally,
brightening, 'and make up a large fire. Let's go and help
them in, and call Rebekah.' (Rebekah was the woman
who assisted at the dairy and housework; she lived in
a cottage hard by with her husband, who attended to the
cows.)

Sally went to fetch a lantern from the back-kitchen,
but her brother said, 'You won't want a light. I lit the
lantern that was hanging there.'

'What must we call your wife?' asked Mrs. Hall.

'Helena,' said Philip.

With shawls over their heads they proceeded towards
the back door.

'One minute before you go,' interrupted Philip. 'I—I
haven't confessed all.'

'Then Heaven help us!' said Mrs. Hall, pushing to
the door and clasping her hands in calm despair.

'We passed through Evershead as we came,' he continued, 'and I just looked in at the " Sow-and-Acorn "
to see if old Mike still kept on there as usual. The carrier
had come in from Sherton Abbas at that moment, and
guessing that I was bound for this place—for I think he
knew me—he asked me to bring on a dressmaker's parcel
for Sally that was marked " immediate." My wife had
walked on with the children. 'Twas a flimsy parcel, and
the paper was torn, and I found on looking at it that it was
a thick warm gown. I didn't wish you to see poor Helena
in a shabby state. I was ashamed that you should—'twas
not what she was born to. I untied the parcel in the road,
took it on to her where she was waiting in the Lower Barn,
and told her I had managed to get it for her, and that
she was to ask no question. She, poor thing, must have
supposed I obtained it on trust, through having reached a
place where I was known, for she put it on gladly enough.
She has it on now. Sally has other gowns, I daresay.'

Sally looked at her mother, speechless.

'You have others, I daresay!' repeated Phil, with a

sick man's impatience. ' I thought to myself, "Better Sally cry than Helena freeze." Well, is the dress of great consequence ? 'Twas nothing very ornamental, as far as I could see.'

' No—no ; not of consequence,' returned Sally sadly, adding in a gentle voice, ' You will not mind if I lend her another instead of that one, will you ? '

Philip's agitation at the confession had brought on another attack of the cough, which seemed to shake him to pieces. He was so obviously unfit to sit in a chair that they helped him upstairs at once ; and having hastily given him a cordial and kindled the bedroom fire, they descended to fetch their unhappy new relations.

III

It was with strange feelings that the girl and her mother lately so cheerful, passed out of the back door into the open air of the barton, laden with hay scents and the herby breath of cows. A fine sleet had begun to fall, and they trotted across the yard quickly. The stable-door was open ; a light shone from it—from the lantern which always hung there, and which Philip had lighted, as he said. Softly nearing the door, Mrs. Hall pronounced the name ' Helena ! '

There was no answer for the moment. Looking in she was taken by surprise. Two people appeared before her. For one, instead of the drabbish woman she had expected, Mrs. Hall saw a pale, dark-eyed, ladylike creature, whose personality ruled her attire rather than was ruled by it. She was in a new and handsome gown, Sally's own, and an old bonnet. She was standing up, agitated ; her hand was held by her companion—none else than Sally's affianced, Farmer Charles Darton, upon whose fine figure the pale stranger's eyes were fixed, as his were fixed upon her. His other hand held the rein of his horse, which was standing saddled as if just led in.

At sight of Mrs. Hall they both turned, looking at her in a way neither quite conscious nor unconscious, and without seeming to recollect that words were necessary as a solution to the scene. In another moment Sally entered also, when Mr. Darton dropped his companion's hand, led the horse aside, and came to greet his betrothed and Mrs. Hall.

'Ah!' he said, smiling—with something like forced composure—'this is a roundabout way of arriving, you will say, my dear Mrs. Hall. But we lost our way, which made us late. I saw a light here, and led in my horse at once—my friend Johns and my man have gone onward to the little inn with theirs, not to crowd you too much. No sooner had I entered than I saw that this lady had taken temporary shelter here—and found I was intruding.'

'She is my daughter-in-law,' said Mrs. Hall calmly. 'My son, too, is in the house, but he has gone to bed unwell.'

Sally had stood staring wonderingly at the scene until this moment, hardly recognizing Darton's shake of the hand. The spell that bound her was broken by her perceiving the two little children seated on a heap of hay. She suddenly went forward, spoke to them, and took one on her arm and the other in her hand.

'And two children?' said Mr. Darton, showing thus that he had not been there long enough as yet to understand the situation.

'My grandchildren,' said Mrs. Hall, with as much affected ease as before.

Philip Hall's wife, in spite of this interruption to her first rencounter, seemed scarcely so much affected by it as to feel anyone's presence in addition to Mr. Darton's. However, arousing herself by a quick reflection, she threw a sudden critical glance of her sad eyes upon Mrs. Hall, and, apparently finding her satisfactory, advanced to her in a meek initiative. Then Sally and the stranger spoke some friendly words to each other, and Sally went on with the children into the house. Mrs. Hall and Helena followed, and Mr. Darton followed these, looking at Helena's dress and outline, and listening to her voice like a man in a dream.

By the time the others reached the house Sally had already gone upstairs with the tired children. She rapped against the wall for Rebekah to come in and help to attend to them, Rebekah's house being a little 'spit-and-daub' cabin

leaning against the substantial stonework of Mrs. Hall's taller
erection.   When she came a bed was made up for the little
ones, and some supper given to them.   On descending
the stairs after seeing this done Sally went to the sitting-
room.   Young Mrs. Hall entered it just in advance of her,
having in the interim retired with her mother-in-law to
take off her bonnet, and otherwise make herself present-
able.   Hence it was evident that no further communication could have passed between her and Mr. Darton since
their brief interview in the stable.

Mr. Japheth Johns now opportunely arrived, and broke
up the restraint of the company, after a few orthodox
meteorological commentaries had passed between him and
Mrs. Hall by way of introduction.   They at once sat down
to supper, the present of wine and turkey not being produced for consumption to-night, lest the premature display
of those gifts should seem to throw doubt on Mrs. Hall's
capacities as a provider.

'Drink hearty, Mr. Johns—drink hearty,' said that
matron magnanimously.   'Such as it is there's plenty of.
But perhaps cider-wine is not to your taste?—though
there's body in it.'

'Quite the contrairy, ma'am—quite the contrairy,' said
the dairyman.   'For though I inherit the malt-liquor
principle from my father, I am a cider-drinker on my
mother's side.   She came from these parts, you know.
And there's this to be said for't—'tis a more peaceful
liquor, and don't lie about a man like your hotter drinks.
With care, one may live on it a twelve-month without
knocking down a neighbour, or getting a black eye from
an old acquaintance.'

The general conversation thus begun was continued
briskly, though it was in the main restricted to Mrs. Hall
and Japheth, who in truth required but little help from
anybody.   There being slight call upon Sally's tongue,
she had ample leisure to do what her heart most desired,
namely, watch her intended husband and her sister-in-law
with a view of elucidating the strange momentary scene
in which her mother and herself had surprised them in the
stable.   If that scene meant anything, it meant, at least,

that they had met before. That there had been no time
for explanations Sally could see, for their manner was still
one of suppressed amazement at each other's presence
there. Darton's eyes, too, fell continually on the gown
worn by Helena as if this were an added riddle to his perplexity; though to Sally it was the one feature in the
case which was no mystery. He seemed to feel that fate
had impishly changed his *vis-à-vis* in the lover's jig he
was about to foot; that while the gown had been expected
to enclose a Sally, a Helena's face looked out from the
bodice; that some long-lost hand met his own from the
sleeves.

Sally could see that whatever Helena might know of
Darton, she knew nothing of how the dress entered into
his embarrassment. And at moments the young girl would
have persuaded herself that Darton's looks at her sister-
in-law were entirely the fruit of the clothes query. But
surely at other times a more extensive range of speculation
and sentiment was expressed by her lover's eye than that
which the changed dress would account for.

Sally's independence made her one of the least jealous
of women. But there was something in the relations of
these two visitors which ought to be explained.

Japheth Johns continued to converse in his well-known
style, interspersing his talk with some private reflections
on the position of Darton and Sally, which, though the
sparkle in his eye showed them to be highly entertaining
to himself, were apparently not quite communicable to
the company. At last he withdrew for the night, going
off to the roadside inn half-a-mile ahead, whither Darton
promised to follow him in a few minutes.

Half-an-hour passed, and then Mr. Darton also rose to
leave, Sally and her sister-in-law simultaneously wishing
him good-night as they retired upstairs to their rooms.
But on his arriving at the front door with Mrs. Hall a
sharp shower of rain began to come down, when the widow
suggested that he should return to the fireside till the
storm ceased.

Darton accepted her proposal, but insisted that, as it
was getting late, and she was obviously tired, she should

not sit up on his account, since he could let himself out of
the house, and would quite enjoy smoking a pipe by the
hearth alone.   Mrs. Hall assented; and Darton was left
by himself.   He spread his knees to the brands, lit up his
tobacco as he had said, and sat gazing into the fire, and
at the notches of the chimney-crook which hung above.

An occasional drop of rain rolled down the chimney
with a hiss, and still he smoked on; but not like a man
whose mind was at rest.   In the long run, however, despite
his meditations, early hours afield and a long ride in the
open air produced their natural result.   He began to doze.

How long he remained in this half-unconscious state he
did not know.   He suddenly opened his eyes.   The back-
brand had burnt itself in two, and ceased to flame; the
light which he had placed on the mantelpiece had nearly
gone out.   But in spite of these deficiencies there was a
light in the apartment, and it came from elsewhere.   Turning his head he saw Philip Hall's wife standing at the
entrance of the room with a bed-candle in one hand, a
small brass tea-kettle in the other, and *his* gown, as it
certainly seemed, still upon her.

'Helena!' said Darton, starting up.

Her countenance expressed dismay, and her first words
were an apology.   'I—did not know you were here, Mr.
Darton,' she said, while a blush flashed to her cheek.   'I
thought every one had retired—I was coming to make a
little water boil; my husband seems to be worse.   But
perhaps the kitchen fire can be lighted up again.'

'Don't go on my account.   By all means put it on here
as you intended,' said Darton.   'Allow me to help you.'
He went forward to take the kettle from her hand, but she
did not allow him, and placed it on the fire herself.

They stood some way apart, one on each side of the
fireplace, waiting till the water should boil, the candle on
the mantel between them, and Helena with her eyes on
the kettle.   Darton was the first to break the silence.
'Shall I call Sally?' he said.

'O no,' she quickly returned.   'We have given trouble
enough already.   We have no right here.   But we are
the sport of fate, and were obliged to come.'

'No right here!' said he in surprise.

'None. I can't explain it now,' answered Helena.
'This kettle is very slow.'

There was another pause; the proverbial dilatoriness
of watched pots was never more clearly exemplified.

Helena's face was of that sort which seems to ask for
assistance without the owner's knowledge—the very anti-
podes of Sally's, which was self-reliance expressed. Darton's eyes travelled from the kettle to Helena's face, then
back to the kettle, then to the face for rather a longer
time. 'So I am not to know anything of the mystery
that has distracted me all the evening?' he said. 'How
is it that a woman, who refused me because (as I supposed)
my position was not good enough for her taste, is found
to be the wife of a man who certainly seems to be worse
off than I?'

'He had the prior claim,' said she.

'What! you knew him at that time?'

'Yes, yes! And he went to Australia, and sent for me,
and I joined him out there!'

'Ah—that was the mystery!'

'Please say no more,' she implored. 'Whatever my
errors, I have paid for them during the last five years!'

The heart of Darton was subject to sudden overflowings.
He was kind to a fault. 'I am sorry from my soul,' he
said, involuntarily approaching her. Helena withdrew a
step or two, at which he became conscious of his movement, and quickly took his former place. Here he stood
without speaking, and the little kettle began to sing.

'Well, you might have been my wife if you had chosen,'
he said at last. 'But that's all past and gone. However,
if you are in any trouble or poverty I shall be glad to be
of service, and as your relation by marriage I shall have a
right to be. Does your uncle know of your distress?'

'My uncle is dead. He left me without a farthing.
And now we have two children to maintain.'

'What, left you nothing? How could he be so cruel as
that?'

'I disgraced myself in his eyes.'

'Now,' said Darton earnestly, 'let me take care of the

children, at least while you are so unsettled. *You* belong
to another, so I cannot take care of you.'

'Yes, you can,' said a voice; and suddenly a third figure
stood beside them. It was Sally. 'You can, since you
seem to wish to,' she repeated. 'She no longer belongs
to another. . . . My poor brother is dead!'

Her face was red, her eyes sparkled, and all the woman
came to the front. 'I have heard it!' she went on to
him passionately. 'You can protect her now as well as
the children!' She turned then to her agitated sister-in-
law. 'I heard something,' said Sally (in a gentle murmur,
differing much from her previous passionate words), 'and
I went into his room. It must have been the moment
you left. He went off so quickly, and weakly, and it was
so unexpected, that I couldn't leave even to call you.'

Darton was just able to gather from the confused discourse which followed that, during his sleep by the fire,
Sally's brother whom he had never seen had become worse;
and that during Helena's absence for water the end had
unexpectedly come. The two young women hastened
upstairs, and he was again left alone.

After standing there a short time he went to the front
door and looked out; till, softly closing it behind him, he
advanced and stood under the large sycamore-tree. The
stars were flickering coldly, and the dampness which had
just descended upon the earth in rain now sent up a chill
from it. Darton was in a strange position, and he felt it.
The unexpected appearance, in deep poverty, of Helena—
a young lady, daughter of a deceased naval officer, who
had been brought up by her uncle, a solicitor, and had
refused Darton in marriage years ago—the passionate,
almost angry demeanour of Sally at discovering them, the
abrupt announcement that Helena was a widow; all this
coming together was a conjuncture difficult to cope with
in a moment, and made him question whether he ought to
leave the house or offer assistance. But for Sally's manner
he would unhesitatingly have done the latter.

He was still standing under the tree when the door in
front of him opened, and Mrs. Hall came out. She went

round to the garden-gate at the side without seeing him. Darton followed her, intending to speak. Pausing outside, as if in thought, she proceeded to a spot where the sun came earliest in spring-time, and where the north wind never blew ; it was where the row of beehives stood under the wall. Discerning her object, he waited till she had accomplished it.

It was the universal custom thereabout to wake the bees by tapping at their hives whenever a death occurred in the household, under the belief that if this were not done the bees themselves would pine away and perish during the ensuing year. As soon as an interior buzzing responded to her tap at the first hive Mrs. Hall went on to the second, and thus passed down the row. As soon as she came back he met her.

' What can I do in this trouble, Mrs. Hall ? ' he said.

' O—nothing, thank you, nothing,' she said in a tearful voice, now just perceiving him. ' We have called Rebekah and her husband, and they will do everything necessary.' She told him in a few words the particulars of her son's arrival, broken in health—indeed, at death's very door, though they did not suspect it—and suggested, as the result of a conversation between her and her daughter, that the wedding should be postponed.

' Yes, of course,' said Darton. ' I think now to go straight to the inn and tell Johns what has happened.' It was not till after he had shaken hands with her that he turned hesitatingly and added, ' Will you tell the mother of his children that, as they are now left fatherless, I shall be glad to take the eldest of them, if it would be any convenience to her and to you ? '

Mrs. Hall promised that her son's widow should be told of the offer, and they parted. He retired down the rooty slope and disappeared in the direction of the inn, where he informed Johns of the circumstances. Meanwhile Mrs. Hall had entered the house. Sally was downstairs in the sitting-room alone, and her mother explained to her that Darton had readily assented to the postponement.

' No doubt he has,' said Sally, with sad emphasis. ' It is not put off for a week, or a month, or a year. I shall never marry him, and she will ! '

IV

Time passed, and the household on the Knap became again serene under the composing influences of daily routine. A desultory, very desultory, correspondence dragged on between Sally Hall and Darton, who, not quite knowing how to take her petulant words on the night of her brother's death, had continued passive thus long. Helena and her children remained at the dairy-house, almost of necessity, and Darton therefore deemed it advisable to stay away.

One day, seven months later on, when Mr. Darton was as usual at his farm, twenty miles from King's-Hintock, a note reached him from Helena. She thanked him for his kind offer about her children, which her mother-in-law had duly communicated, and stated that she would be glad to accept it as regarded the eldest, the boy. Helena had, in truth, good need to do so, for her uncle had left her penniless, and all application to some relatives in the north had failed. There was, besides, as she said, no good school near Hintock to which she could send the child.

On a fine summer day the boy came. He was accompanied half-way by Sally and his mother—to the 'White Horse,' the fine old Elizabethan inn at Chalk Newton,[1] where he was handed over to Darton's bailiff in a shining spring-cart, who met them there.

He was entered as a day-scholar at a popular school at Casterbridge, three or four miles from Darton's, having first been taught by Darton to ride a forest-pony, on which he cantered to and from the aforesaid fount of knowledge, and (as Darton hoped) brought away a promising headful of the same at each diurnal expedition. The thoughtful taciturnity into which Darton had latterly fallen was quite dissipated by the presence of this boy.

When the Christmas holidays came it was arranged that he should spend them with his mother. The journey was, for some reason or other, performed in two stages, as at his coming, except that Darton in person took the place of the bailiff, and that the boy and himself rode on horseback.

[1] It is now pulled down, and its site occupied by a modern one in red brick (1912).

Reaching the renowned ' White Horse,' Darton inquired
if Miss and young Mrs. Hall were there to meet little Philip
(as they had agreed to be). He was answered by the
appearance of Helena alone at the door.

' At the last moment Sally would not come,' she faltered.

That meeting practically settled the point towards which
these long-severed persons were converging. But nothing
was broached about it for some time yet. Sally Hall had,
in fact, imparted the first decisive motion to events by
refusing to accompany Helena. She soon gave them a
second move by writing the following note :—

' [*Private.*]

' DEAR CHARLES,—Living here so long and intimately with
Helena, I have naturally learnt her history, especially that of it
which refers to you. I am sure she would accept you as a husband
at the proper time, and I think you ought to give her the opportunity. You inquire in an old note if I am sorry that I showed
temper (which it *wasn't*) that night when I heard you talking to her.
No, Charles, I am not sorry at all for what I said then.—Yours
sincerely,

' SALLY HALL.'

Thus set in train, the transfer of Darton's heart back
to its original quarters proceeded by mere lapse of time.
In the following July, Darton went to his friend Japheth
to ask him at last to fulfil the bridal office which had been
in abeyance since the previous January twelvemonths.

' With all my heart, man o' constancy ! ' said Dairy-
man Johns warmly. ' I've lost most of my genteel fair
complexion haymaking this hot weather, 'tis true, but
I'll do your business as well as them that look better.
There be scents and good hair-oil in the world yet, thank
God, and they'll take off the roughest o' my edge. I'll
compliment her. " Better late than never, Sally Hall,"
I'll say.'

' It is not Sally,' said Darton hurriedly. ' It is young
Mrs. Hall.'

Japheth's face, as soon as he really comprehended,
became a picture of reproachful dismay. ' Not Sally ? ' he
said. ' Why not Sally ? I can't believe it ! Young Mrs.
Hall ! Well, well—where's your wisdom ? '

Darton shortly explained particulars ; but Johns would not be reconciled. 'She was a woman worth having if ever woman was,' he cried. 'And now to let her go !'

'But I suppose I can marry where I like,' said Darton.

'H'm,' replied the dairyman, lifting his eyebrows expressively. 'This don't become you, Charles—it really do not. If I had done such a thing you would have sworn I was a curst no'thern fool to be drawn off the scent by such a red-herring doll-oll-oll.'

Farmer Darton responded in such sharp terms to this laconic opinion that the two friends finally parted in a way they had never parted before. Johns was to be no grooms- man to Darton after all. He had flatly declined. Darton went off sorry, and even unhappy, particularly as Japheth was about to leave that side of the county, so that the words which had divided them were not likely to be ex- plained away or softened down.

A short time after the interview Darton was united to Helena at a simple matter-of-fact wedding, and she and her little girl joined the boy who had already grown to look on Darton's house as home.

For some months the farmer experienced an unprece- dented happiness and satisfaction. There had been a flaw in his life, and it was as neatly mended as was humanly possible. But after a season the stream of events followed less clearly, and there were shades in his reveries. Helena was a fragile woman, of little staying-power, physically or morally, and since the time that he had originally known her—eight or ten years before—she had been severely tried. She had loved herself out, in short, and was now occasion- ally given to moping. Sometimes she spoke regretfully of the gentilities of her early life, and instead of comparing her present state with her condition as the wife of the unlucky Hall, she mused rather on what it had been before she took the first fatal step of clandestinely marrying him. She did not care to please such people as those with whom she was thrown as a thriving farmer's wife. She allowed the pretty trifles of agricultural domesticity to glide by her as sorry details, and had it not been for the children

Darton's house would have seemed but little brighter than
it had been before.

This led to occasional unpleasantness, until Darton sometimes declared to himself that such endeavours as his to
rectify early deviations of the heart by harking back to the
old point mostly failed of success. 'Perhaps Johns was
right,' he would say. 'I should have gone on with Sally.
Better go with the tide and make the best of its course
than stem it at the risk of a capsize.' But he kept these
unmelodious thoughts to himself, and was outwardly con-
siderate and kind.

This somewhat barren tract of his life had extended to
less than a year and a half when his ponderings were cut
short by the loss of the woman they concerned. When
she was in her grave he thought better of her than when
she had been alive; the farm was a worse place without
her than with her, after all. No woman short of divine
could have gone through such an experience as hers with
her first husband without becoming a little soured. Her
stagnant sympathies, her sometimes unreasonable manner,
had covered a heart frank and well-meaning, and originally
hopeful and warm. She left him a tiny red infant in white
wrappings. To make life as easy as possible to this touching object became at once his care.

As this child learnt to walk and talk Darton learnt to
see feasibility in a scheme which pleased him. Revolving
the experiment which he had hitherto made upon life, he
fancied he had gained wisdom from his mistakes and caution from his miscarriages.

What the scheme was needs no penetration to discover.
Once more he had opportunity to recast and rectify his
ill-wrought situations by returning to Sally Hall, who still
lived quietly on under her mother's roof at Hintock.
Helena had been a woman to lend pathos and refinement
to a home; Sally was the woman to brighten it. She
would not, as Helena did, despise the rural simplicities of a
farmer's fireside. Moreover, she had a pre-eminent quali-
fication for Darton's household; no other woman could
make so desirable a mother to her brother's two children
and Darton's one as Sally—while Darton, now that Helena

had gone, was a more promising husband for Sally than he had ever been when liable to reminders from an uncured sentimental wound.

Darton was not a man to act rapidly, and the working out of his reparative designs might have been delayed for some time. But there came a winter evening precisely like the one which had darkened over that former ride to Hintock, and he asked himself why he should postpone longer, when the very landscape called for a repetition of that attempt.

He told his man to saddle the mare, booted and spurred himself with a younger horseman's nicety, kissed the two youngest children, and rode off. To make the journey a complete parallel to the first, he would fain have had his old acquaintance Japheth Johns with him. But Johns, alas! was missing. His removal to the other side of the county had left unrepaired the breach which had arisen between him and Darton; and though Darton had forgiven him a hundred times, as Johns had probably forgiven Darton, the effort of reunion in present circumstances was one not likely to be made.

He screwed himself up to as cheerful a pitch as he could without his former crony, and became content with his own thoughts as he rode, instead of the words of a companion. The sun went down; the boughs appeared scratched in like an etching against the sky; old crooked men with faggots at their backs said ' Good-night, sir,' and Darton replied ' Good-night' right heartily.

By the time he reached the forking roads it was getting as dark as it had been on the occasion when Johns climbed the directing-post. Darton; made no mistake this time. ' Nor shall I be able to mistake, thank Heaven, when I arrive,' he murmured. It gave him peculiar satisfaction to think that the proposed marriage, like his first, was of the nature of setting in order things long awry, and not a momentary freak of fancy.

Nothing hindered the smoothness of his journey, which seemed not half its former length. Though dark, it was only between five and six o'clock when the bulky chimneys of Mrs. Hall's residence appeared in view behind the syca-

more tree. On second thoughts he retreated and put up
at the ale-house as in former time ; and when he had plumed
himself before the inn mirror, called for something to drink,
and smoothed out the incipient wrinkles of care, he walked
on to the Knap with a quick step.

V

That evening Sally was making ' pinners ' for the milkers,
who were now increased by two, for her mother and herself
no longer joined in milking the cows themselves. But
upon the whole there was little change in the household
economy, and not much in its appearance, beyond such
minor particulars as that the crack over the window, which
had been a hundred years coming, was a trifle wider ; that
the beams were a shade blacker ; that the influence of
modernism had supplanted the open chimney-corner by a
grate ; that Rebekah, who had worn a cap when she had
plenty of hair, had left it off now she had scarce any,
because it was reported that caps were not fashionable ;
and that Sally's face had naturally assumed a more womanly
and experienced cast.

Mrs. Hall was actually lifting coals with the tongs, as
she had used to do.

' Five years ago this very night, if I am not mistaken——'
she said, laying on an ember.

' Not this very night—though 'twas one night this week,'
said the correct Sally.

' Well, 'tis near enough. Five years ago Mr. Darton
came to marry you, and my poor boy Phil came home to
die.' She sighed. ' Ah, Sally,' she presently said, ' if you
had managed well Mr. Darton would have had you, Helena
or none.'

' Don't be sentimental about that, mother,' begged Sally.
' I didn't care to manage well in such a case. Though I
liked him, I wasn't so anxious. I would never have married the man in the midst of such a hitch as that was,' she
added with decision ; ' and I don't think I would if he
were to ask me now.'

' I am not sure about that, unless you have another in
your eye.'

'I wouldn't; and I'll tell you why. I could hardly marry him for love at this time o' day. And as we've quite enough to live on if we give up the dairy to-morrow, I should have no need to marry for any meaner reason. . . . I am quite happy enough as I am, and there's an end of it.'

Now it was not long after this dialogue that there came a mild rap at the door, and in a moment there entered Rebekah, looking as though a ghost had arrived. The fact was that that accomplished skimmer and churner (now a resident in the house) had overheard the desultory observations between mother and daughter, and on opening the door to Mr. Darton thought the coincidence must have a grisly meaning in it. Mrs. Hall welcomed the farmer with warm surprise, as did Sally, and for a moment they rather wanted words.

'Can you push up the chimney-crook for me, Mr. Darton?—the notches hitch,' said the matron. He did it, and the homely little act bridged over the awkward consciousness that he had been a stranger for four years.

Mrs. Hall soon saw what he had come for, and left the principals together while she went to prepare him a late tea, smiling at Sally's recent hasty assertions of indifference, when she saw how civil Sally was. When tea was ready she joined them. She fancied that Darton did not look so confident as when he had arrived; but Sally was quite light-hearted, and the meal passed pleasantly.

About seven he took his leave of them. Mrs. Hall went as far as the door to light him down the slope. On the doorstep he said frankly—

'I came to ask your daughter to marry me; chose the night and everything, with an eye to a favourable answer. But she won't.'

'Then she's a very ungrateful girl!' emphatically said Mrs. Hall.

Darton paused to shape his sentence, and asked, 'I—I suppose there's nobody else more favoured?'

'I can't say that there is, or that there isn't,' answered Mrs. Hall. 'She's private in some things. I'm on your side, however, Mr. Darton, and I'll talk to her.'

'Thank 'ee, thank 'ee!' said the farmer in a gayer accent; and with this assurance the not very satisfactory visit came to an end. Darton descended the roots of the sycamore, the light was withdrawn, and the door closed. At the bottom of the slope he nearly ran against a man about to ascend.

'Can a jack-o'-lent believe his few senses on such a dark night, or can't he?' exclaimed one whose utterance Darton recognized in a moment, despite its unexpectedness. 'I dare not swear he can, though I fain would!' The speaker was Johns.

Darton said he was glad of this opportunity, bad as it was, of putting an end to the silence of years, and asked the dairyman what he was travelling that way for.

Japheth showed the old jovial confidence in a moment. 'I'm going to see your—relations—as they always seem to me,' he said—'Mrs. Hall and Sally. Well, Charles, the fact is I find the natural barbarousness of man is much increased by a bachelor life, and, as your leavings were always good enough for me, I'm trying civilization here.' He nodded towards the house.

'Not with Sally—to marry her?' said Darton, feeling something like a rill of ice water between his shoulders.

'Yes, by the help of Providence and my personal charms. And I think I shall get her. I am this road every week— my present dairy is only four miles off, you know, and I see her through the window. 'Tis rather odd that I was going to speak practical to-night to her for the first time. You've just called?'

'Yes, for a short while. But she didn't say a word about you.'

'A good sign, a good sign. Now that decides me. I'll swing the mallet and get her answer this very night as I planned.'

A few more remarks, and Darton, wishing his friend joy of Sally in a slightly hollow tone of jocularity, bade him good-bye. Johns promised to write particulars, and ascended, and was lost in the shade of the house and tree. A rectangle of light appeared when Johns was admitted, and all was dark again.

'Happy Japheth!' said Darton. 'This then is the explanation!'

He determined to return home that night. In a quarter of an hour he passed out of the village, and the next day went about his swede-lifting and storing as if nothing had occurred.

He waited and waited to hear from Johns whether the wedding-day was fixed : but no letter came. He learnt not a single particular till, meeting Johns one day at a horse-auction, Darton exclaimed genially—rather more genially than he felt—' When is the joyful day to be ? '

To his great surprise a reciprocity of gladness was not conspicuous in Johns. 'Not at all,' he said, in a very subdued tone. ' 'Tis a bad job ; she won't have me.'

Darton held his breath till he said with treacherous solicitude, ' Try again—'tis coyness.'

' O no,' said Johns decisively. 'There's been none of that. We talked it over dozens of times in the most fair and square way. She tells me plainly, I don't suit her. 'Twould be simply annoying her to ask her again. Ah, Charles, you threw a prize away when you let her slip five years ago.'

' I did—I did,' said Darton.

He returned from that auction with a new set of feelings in play. He had certainly made a surprising mistake in thinking Johns his successful rival. It really seemed as if he might hope for Sally after all.

This time, being rather pressed by business, Darton had recourse to pen-and-ink, and wrote her as manly and straightforward a proposal as any woman could wish to receive. The reply came promptly :—

' DEAR MR. DARTON,—I am as sensible as any woman can be of the goodness that leads you to make me this offer a second time. Better women than I would be proud of the honour, for when I read your nice long speeches on mangold-wurzel, and such-like topics, at the Casterbridge Farmers' Club, I do feel it an honour, I assure you. But my answer is just the same as before. I will not try to explain what, in truth, I cannot explain—my reasons ; I will simply say that I must decline to be married to you. With good wishes as in former times, I am, your faithful friend,

' SALLY HALL.'

Darton dropped the letter hopelessly. Beyond the negative, there was just a possibility of sarcasm in it— 'nice long speeches on mangold-wurzel' had a suspicious sound. However, sarcasm or none, there was the answer, and he had to be content.

He proceeded to seek relief in a business which at this time engrossed much of his attention—that of clearing up a curious mistake just current in the county, that he had been nearly ruined by the recent failure of a local bank. A farmer named Darton had lost heavily, and the similarity of name had probably led to the error. Belief in it was so persistent that it demanded several days of letter-writing to set matters straight, and persuade the world that he was as solvent as ever he had been in his life. He had hardly concluded this worrying task when, to his delight, another letter arrived in the handwriting of Sally. Darton tore it open; it was very short.

'DEAR MR. DARTON,—We have been so alarmed these last few days by the report that you were ruined by the stoppage of ——'s Bank, that, now it is contradicted, I hasten, by my mother's wish, to say how truly glad we are to find there is no foundation for the report. After your kindness to my poor brother's children, I can do no less than write at such a moment. We had a letter from each of them a few days ago.—Your faithful friend,

'SALLY HALL.'

'Mercenary little woman!' said Darton to himself with a smile. 'Then that was the secret of her refusal this time—she thought I was ruined.'

Now, such was Darton, that as hours went on he could not help feeling too generously towards Sally to condemn her in this. What did he want in a wife? he asked himself. Love and integrity. What next? Worldly wisdom. And was there really more than worldly wisdom in her refusal to go aboard a sinking ship? She now knew it was otherwise. 'Begad,' he said, 'I'll try her again.'

The fact was he had so set his heart upon Sally, and Sally alone, that nothing was to be allowed to baulk him, and his reasoning was purely formal.

Anniversaries having been unpropitious, he waited on till a bright day late in May—a day when all animate

nature was fancying, in its trusting, foolish way, that it
was going to bask under blue sky for evermore. As he
rode through Long-Ash Lane it was scarce recognizable as
the track of his two winter journeys. No mistake could
be made now, even with his eyes shut. The cuckoo's note
was at its best, between April tentativeness and midsummer
decrepitude, and the reptiles in the sun behaved as win-
ningly as kittens on a hearth. Though afternoon, and
about the same time as on the last occasion, it was broad
day and sunshine when he entered Hintock, and the details
of the Knap dairy-house were visible far up the road. He
saw Sally in the garden, and was set vibrating. He had
first intended to go on to the inn; but ' No,' he said; ' I'll
tie my horse to the garden-gate. If all goes well it can
soon be taken round; if not, I mount and ride away.'

The tall shade of the horseman darkened the room in
which Mrs. Hall sat, and made her start, for he had ridden
by a side path to the top of the slope, where riders seldom
came. In a few seconds he was in the garden with Sally.

Five—ay, three minutes—did the business at the back
of that row of bees. Though spring had come, and heavenly
blue consecrated the scene, Darton succeeded not. ' No,'
said Sally firmly. ' I will never, never marry you, Mr.
Darton. I would have done it once; but now I never
can.'

' But——!' implored Mr. Darton. And with a burst of
real eloquence he went on to declare all sorts of things
that he would do for her. He would drive her to see her
mother every week—take her to London—settle so much
money upon her—Heaven knows what he did not promise,
suggest, and tempt her with. But it availed nothing.
She interposed with a stout negative which closed the course
of his argument like an iron gate across a highway. Darton
paused.

' Then,' said he simply, ' you hadn't heard of my supposed failure when you declined last time? '

' I had not,' she said. ' That you believed me capable
of refusing you for such a reason does not help your cause.'

' And 'tis not because of any soreness from my slighting
you years ago? '

'No.   That soreness is long past.'

'Ah—then you despise me, Sally!'

'No,' she slowly answered.   'I don't altogether despise you.   I don't think you quite such a hero as I once did —that's all.   The truth is, I am happy enough as I am, and I don't mean to marry at all.   Now, may *I* ask a favour, sir?'   She spoke with an ineffable charm, which, whenever he thought of it, made him curse his loss of her as long as he lived.

'To any extent.'

'Please do not put this question to me any more.   Friends as long as you like, but lovers and married never.'

'I never will,' said Darton.   'Not if I live a hundred years.'

And he never did.   That he had worn out his welcome in her heart was only too plain.

When his step-children had grown up and were placed out in life all communication between Darton and the Hall family ceased.   It was only by chance that, years after, he learnt that Sally, notwithstanding the solicitations her attractions drew down upon her, had refused several offers of marriage, and steadily adhered to her purpose of leading a single life.

May 1884.

THE DISTRACTED PREACHER

THE DISTRACTED PREACHER

HOW HIS COLD WAS CURED

I

SOMETHING delayed the arrival of the Wesleyan minister, and a young man came temporarily in his stead. It was on the thirteenth of January 183– that Mr. Stockdale, the young man in question, made his humble entry into the village, unknown, and almost unseen. But when those of the inhabitants who styled themselves of his connection became acquainted with him, they were rather pleased with the substitute than otherwise, though he had scarcely as yet acquired ballast of character sufficient to steady the consciences of the hundred-and-forty Methodists of pure blood who, at this time, lived in Nether-Moynton, and to give in addition supplementary support to the mixed race which went to church in the morning and chapel in the evening, or when there was a tea—as many as a hundred-and-ten people more, all told, and including the parish-clerk in the winter-time, when it was too dark for the vicar to observe who passed up the street at seven o'clock—which, to be just to him, he was never anxious to do.

It was owing to this overlapping of creeds that the cele-brated population-puzzle arose among the denser gentry of the district around Nether-Moynton : how could it be that a parish containing fifteen score of strong full-grown Episcopalians, and nearly thirteen score of well-matured Dissenters, numbered barely two-and-twenty score adults in all ?

The young man being personally interesting, those with whom he came in contact were content to waive for a while the graver question of his sufficiency. It is said that at this time of his life his eyes were affectionate, though without a ray of levity ; that his hair was curly, and his

189

figure tall; that he was, in short, a very lovable youth, who won upon his female hearers as soon as they saw and heard him, and caused them to say, ' Why didn't we know of this before he came, that we might have gi'ed him a warmer welcome ! '

The fact was that, knowing him to be only provisionally selected, and expecting nothing remarkable in his person or doctrine, they and the rest of his flock in Nether-Moynton had felt almost as indifferent about his advent as if they had been the soundest church-going parishioners in the country, and he their true and appointed parson.　Thus when Stockdale set foot in the place nobody had secured a lodging for him, and though his journey had given him a bad cold in the head he was forced to attend to that business himself.　On inquiry he learnt that the only possible accommodation in the village would be found at the house of one Mrs. Lizzy Newberry, at the upper end of the street.

It was a youth who gave this information, and Stockdale asked him who Mrs. Newberry might be.

The boy said that she was a widow-woman, who had got no husband, because he was dead.　Mr. Newberry, he added, had been a well-to-do man enough, as the saying was, and a farmer ; but he had gone off in a decline.　As regarded Mrs. Newberry's serious side, Stockdale gathered that she was one of the trimmers who went to church and chapel both.

' I'll go there,' said Stockdale, feeling that, in the absence of purely sectarian lodgings, he could do no better.

' She's a little particular, and won't hae gover'ment folks, or curates, or the pa'son's friends, or such like,' said the lad dubiously.

' Ah, that may be a promising sign : I'll call. Or no ; just you go up and ask first if she can find room for me. I have to see one or two persons on another matter.　You will find me down at the carrier's.'

In a quarter of an hour the lad came back, and said that Mrs. Newberry would have no objection to accommodate him, whereupon Stockdale called at the house.　It stood within a garden-hedge, and seemed to be roomy and comfortable.　He saw an elderly woman, with whom he

made arrangements to come the same night, since there
was no inn in the place, and he wished to house himself
as soon as possible ; the village being a local centre from
which he was to radiate at once to the different small
chapels in the neighbourhood. He forthwith sent his luggage to Mrs. Newberry's from the carrier's, where he had
taken shelter, and in the evening walked up to his temporary home.

As he now lived there, Stockdale felt it unnecessary to
knock at the door, and entering quietly he had the pleasure of hearing footsteps scudding away like mice into the
back quarters. He advanced to the parlour, as the front
room was called, though its stone floor was scarcely disguised by the carpet, which only overlaid the trodden
areas, leaving sandy deserts under the furniture. But the
room looked snug and cheerful. The firelight shone out
brightly, trembling on the bulging mouldings of the table-
legs. playing with brass knobs and handles, and lurking in
great strength on the under surface of the chimney-piece.
A deep arm-chair, covered with horsehair, and studded
with a countless throng of brass nails, was pulled up on
one side of the fireplace. The tea-things were on the table,
the teapot cover was open, and a little handbell had been
laid at that precise point towards which a person seated
in the great chair might be expected instinctively to stretch
his hand.

Stockdale sat down, not objecting to his experience of
the room thus far, and began his residence by tinkling the
bell. A little girl crept in at the summons, and made tea
for him. Her name, she said, was Marther Sarer, and she
lived out there, nodding towards the road and village
generally. Before Stockdale had got far with his meal a
tap sounded on the door behind him, and on his telling
the inquirer to come in, a rustle of garments caused him
to turn his head. He saw before him a fine and extremely
well-made young woman, with dark hair, a wide, sensible,
beautiful forehead, eyes that warmed him before he knew
it, and a mouth that was in itself a picture to all appreciative souls.

' Can I get you anything else for tea ? ' she said, coming

forward a step or two, an expression of liveliness on her
features, and her hand waving the door by its edge.

'Nothing, thank you,' said Stockdale, thinking less of
what he replied than of what might be her relation to the
household.

'You are quite sure?' said the young woman, apparently
aware that he had not considered his answer.

He conscientiously examined the tea-things, and found
them all there. 'Quite sure, Miss Newberry,' he said.

'It is Mrs. Newberry,' she said. 'Lizzy Newberry. I
used to be Lizzy Simpkins.'

'O, I beg your pardon, Mrs. Newberry.' And before he
had occasion to say more she left the room.

Stockdale remained in some doubt till Martha Sarah
came to clear the table. 'Whose house is this, my little
woman?' said he.

'Mrs. Lizzy Newberry's, sir.'

'Then Mrs. Newberry is not the old lady I saw this
afternoon?'

'No. That's Mrs. Newberry's mother. It was Mrs.
Newberry who comed in to you just by now, because she
wanted to see if you was good-looking.'

Later in the evening, when Stockdale was about to begin
supper, she came again. 'I have come myself, Mr. Stockdale,' she said. The minister stood up in acknowledgment
of the honour. 'I am afraid little Marther might not
make you understand. What will you have for supper?
—there's cold rabbit, and there's a ham uncut.'

Stockdale said he could get on nicely with those viands,
and supper was laid. He had no more than cut a slice
when tap-tap came to the door again. The minister had
already learnt that this particular rhythm in taps denoted
the fingers of his enkindling landlady, and the doomed
young fellow buried his first mouthful under a look of
receptive blandness.

'We have a chicken in the house, Mr. Stockdale—I
quite forgot to mention it just now. Perhaps you would
like Marther Sarer to bring it up?'

Stockdale had advanced far enough in the art of being a
young man to say that he did not want the chicken, unless

she brought it up herself; but when it was uttered he blushed at the daring gallantry of the speech, perhaps a shade too strong for a serious man and a minister. In three minutes the chicken appeared, but, to his great surprise, only in the hands of Martha Sarah. Stockdale was disappointed, which perhaps it was intended that he should be.

He had finished supper, and was not in the least anticipating Mrs. Newberry again that night, when she tapped and entered as before. Stockdale's gratified look told that she had lost nothing by not appearing when expected. It happened that the cold in the head from which the young man suffered had increased with the approach of night, and before she had spoken he was seized with a violent fit of sneezing which he could not anyhow repress.

Mrs. Newberry looked full of pity. ' Your cold is very bad to-night, Mr. Stockdale.'

Stockdale replied that it was rather troublesome.

' And I've a good mind——' she added archly, looking at the cheerless glass of water on the table, which the abstemious minister was going to drink.

' Yes, Mrs. Newberry ? '

' I've a good mind that you should have something more likely to cure it than that cold stuff.'

' Well,' said Stockdale, looking down at the glass, ' as there is no inn here, and nothing better to be got in the village, of course it will do.'

To this she replied, ' There is something better, not far off, though not in the house. I really think you must try it, or you may be ill. Yes, Mr. Stockdale, you shall.' She held up her finger, seeing that he was about to speak. ' Don't ask what it is ; wait, and you shall see.'

Lizzy went away, and Stockdale waited in a pleasant mood. Presently she returned with her bonnet and cloak on, saying, ' I am so sorry, but you must help me to get it. Mother has gone to bed. Will you wrap yourself up, and come this way, and please bring that cup with you ? '

Stockdale, a lonely young fellow, who had for weeks felt a great craving for somebody on whom to throw away superfluous interest, and even tenderness, was not sorry to join her, and followed his guide through the back door across the garden, to the bottom, where the boundary was a wall. This wall was low, and beyond it Stockdale discerned in the night shades several grey headstones, and the outlines of the church roof and tower.

' It is easy to get up this way,' she said, stepping upon a bank which abutted on the wall; then putting her foot on the top of the stonework, and descending by a spring inside, where the ground was much higher, as is the manner of graveyards to be. Stockdale did the same, and followed her in the dusk across the irregular ground till they came to the tower door, which, when they had entered, she softly closed behind them.

' You can keep a secret ? ' she said, in a musical voice.

' Like an iron chest ! ' said he fervently.

Then from under her cloak she produced a small lighted lantern, which the minister had not noticed that she carried at all. The light showed them to be close to the singing-gallery stairs, under which lay a heap of lumber of all sorts, but consisting mostly of decayed framework, pews, panels, and pieces of flooring, that from time to time had been removed from their original fixings in the body of the edifice and replaced by new.

' Perhaps you will drag some of those boards aside ? ' she said, holding the lantern over her head to light him better. ' Or will you take the lantern while I move them ? '

' I can manage it,' said the young man, and acting as she ordered, he uncovered, to his surprise, a row of little barrels bound with wood hoops, each barrel being about as large as the nave of a heavy waggon-wheel. When they were laid open Lizzy fixed her eyes on him, as if she wondered what he would say.

' You know what they are ? ' she asked, finding that he did not speak.

' Yes, barrels,' said Stockdale simply. He was an inland man, the son of highly respectable parents, and brought up with a single eye to the ministry, and the sight suggested nothing beyond the fact that such articles were there.

' You are quite right, they are barrels,' she said, in an

emphatic tone of candour that was not without a touch of
irony.

Stockdale looked at her with an eye of sudden misgiving.
'Not smugglers' liquor?' he said.

'Yes,' said she. 'They are tubs of spirit that have
accidentally floated over in the dark from France.'

In Nether-Moynton and its vicinity at this date people
always smiled at the sort of sin called in the outside world
illicit trading; and these little kegs of gin and brandy were
as well known to the inhabitants as turnips. So that
Stockdale's innocent ignorance, and his look of alarm when
he guessed the sinister mystery, seemed to strike Lizzy
first as ludicrous, and then as very awkward for the good
impression that she wished to produce upon him.

'Smuggling is carried on here by some of the people,'
she said in a gentle, apologetic voice. 'It has been their
practice for generations, and they think it no harm. Now,
will you roll out one of the tubs?'

'What to do with it?' said the minister.

'To draw a little from it to cure your cold,' she answered.
'It is so 'nation strong that it drives away that sort of
thing in a jiffy. O, it is all right about our taking it. I
may have what I like; the owner of the tubs says so. I
ought to have had some in the house, and then I shouldn't
ha' been put to this trouble; but I drink none myself, and
so I often forget to keep it indoors.'

'You are allowed to help yourself, I suppose, that you
may not inform where their hiding-place is?'

'Well, no; not that particularly; but I may take any
if I want it. So help yourself.'

'I will, to oblige you, since you have a right to it,' murmured the minister; and though he was not quite satisfied
with his part in the performance, he rolled one of the
'tubs' out from the corner into the middle of the tower
floor. 'How do you wish me to get it out—with a gimlet,
I suppose?'

'No, I'll show you,' said his interesting companion; and
she held up with her other hand a shoemaker's awl and a
hammer. 'You must never do these things with a gimlet,
because the wood-dust gets in; and when the buyers pour

out the brandy that would tell them that the tub had been broached. An awl makes no dust, and the hole nearly closes up again. Now tap one of the hoops forward.'

Stockdale took the hammer and did so.

' Now make the hole in the part that was covered by the hoop.'

He made the hole as directed. ' It won't run out,' he said.

' O yes it will,' said she. ' Take the tub between your knees, and squeeze the heads ; and I'll hold the cup.'

Stockdale obeyed ; and the pressure taking effect upon the tub, which seemed to be thin, the spirit spirted out in a stream. When the cup was full he ceased pressing, and the flow immediately stopped. ' Now we must fill up the keg with water,' said Lizzy, ' or it will cluck like forty hens when it is handled, and show that 'tis not full.'

' But they tell you you may take it ? '

' Yes, the *smugglers* ; but the *buyers* must not know that the smugglers have been kind to me at their expense.'

' I see,' said Stockdale doubtfully. ' I much question the honesty of this proceeding.'

By her direction he held the tub with the hole upwards, and while he went through the process of alternately pressing and ceasing to press, she produced a bottle of water, from which she took mouthfuls, conveying each to the keg by putting her pretty lips to the hole, where it was sucked in at each recovery of the cask from pressure. When it was again full he plugged the hole, knocked the hoop down to its place, and buried the tub in the lumber as before.

' Aren't the smugglers afraid that you will tell ? ' he asked, as they recrossed the churchyard.

' O no ; they are not afraid of that. I couldn't do such a thing.'

' They have put you into a very awkward corner,' said Stockdale emphatically. ' You must, of course, as an honest person, sometimes feel that it is your duty to inform —really you must.'

' Well, I have never particularly felt it as a duty ; and,

besides, my first husband——' She stopped, and there was some confusion in her voice. Stockdale was so honest and unsophisticated that he did not at once discern why she paused : but at last he did perceive that the words were a slip, and that no woman would have uttered ' first husband ' by accident unless she had thought pretty frequently of a second. He felt for her confusion, and allowed her time to recover and proceed. ' My husband,' she said, in a self-corrected tone, ' used to know of their doings, and so did my father, and kept the secret. I cannot inform, in fact, against anybody.'

' I see the hardness of it,' he continued, like a man who looked far into the moral of things. ' And it is very cruel that you should be tossed and tantalized between your memories and your conscience. I do hope, Mrs. Newberry, that you will soon see your way out of this unpleasant position.'

' Well, I don't just now,' she murmured.

By this time they had passed over the wall and entered the house, where she brought him a glass and hot water, and left him to his own reflections. He looked after her vanishing form, asking himself whether he, as a respectable man, and a minister, and a shining light, even though as yet only of the halfpenny-candle sort, were quite justified in doing this thing. A sneeze settled the question ; and he found that when the fiery liquid was lowered by the addition of twice or thrice the quantity of water, it was one of the prettiest cures for a cold in the head that he had ever known, particularly at this chilly time of the year.

Stockdale sat in the deep chair about twenty minutes sipping and meditating, till he at length took warmer views of things, and longed for the morrow, when he would see Mrs. Newberry again. He then felt that, though chronologically at a short distance, it would in an emotional sense be very long before to-morrow came, and walked restlessly round the room. His eye was attracted by a framed and glazed sampler in which a running ornament of fir-trees and peacocks surrounded the following pretty bit of sentiment :—

> 'Rose-leaves smell when roses thrive,
> Here's my work while I'm alive ;
> Rose-leaves smell when shrunk and shed,
> Here's my work when I am dead.

> 'Lizzy Simpkins. Fear God. Honour the King.
> 'Aged 11 years.'

' 'Tis hers,' he said to himself. 'Heavens, how I like that name !'

Before he had done thinking that no other name from Abigail to Zenobia would have suited his young landlady so well, tap-tap came again upon the door ; and the minister started as her face appeared yet another time, looking so disinterested that the most ingenious would have refrained from asserting that she had come to affect his feelings by her seductive eyes.

'Would you like a fire in your room, Mr. Stockdale, on account of your cold ? '

The minister, being still a little pricked in the conscience for countenancing her in watering the spirits, saw here a way to self-chastisement. 'No, I thank you,' he said firmly ; 'it is not necessary. I have never been used to one in my life, and it would be giving way to luxury too far.'

'Then I won't insist,' she said, and disconcerted him by vanishing instantly.

Wondering if she was vexed by his refusal, he wished that he had chosen to have a fire, even though it should have scorched him out of bed and endangered his self-discipline for a dozen days. However, he consoled himself with what was in truth a rare consolation for a budding lover, that he was under the same roof with Lizzy ; her guest, in fact, to take a poetical view of the term lodger ; and that he would certainly see her on the morrow.

The morrow came, and Stockdale rose early, his cold quite gone. He had never in his life so longed for the breakfast-hour as he did that day, and punctually at eight o'clock, after a short walk to reconnoitre the premises, he re-entered the door of his dwelling. Breakfast passed, and Martha Sarah attended, but nobody came voluntarily as on the night before to inquire if there were other wants which he had not mentioned, and which she would attempt to gratify. He was disappointed, and went out, hoping to see her at dinner. Dinner-time came ; he sat down to the meal, finished it, lingered on for a whole hour, although two new teachers were at that moment waiting at the chapel-door to speak to him by appointment. It was useless to wait longer, and he slowly went his way down the lane, cheered by the thought that, after all, he would see her in the evening, and perhaps engage again in the delightful tub-broaching in the neighbouring church tower, which proceeding he resolved to render more moral by steadfastly insisting that no water should be introduced to fill up, though the tub should cluck like all the hens in Christendom. But nothing could disguise the fact that it was a queer business ; and his countenance fell when he thought how much more his mind was interested in that matter than in his serious duties.

However, compunction vanished with the decline of day. Night came, and his tea and supper ; but no Lizzy Newberry, and no sweet temptations. At last the minister could bear it no longer, and said to his quaint little attendant, 'Where is Mrs. Newberry to-day ? ' judiciously handing a penny as he spoke.

' She's busy,' said Martha.

' Anything serious happened ? ' he asked, handing another penny, and revealing yet additional pennies in the background.

' O no—nothing at all ! ' said she, with breathless confidence. ' Nothing ever happens to her. She's only biding upstairs in bed because 'tis her way sometimes.'

Being a young man of some honour he would not question further, and assuming that Lizzy must have a bad headache, or other slight ailment, in spite of what the girl had said, he went to bed dissatisfied, not even setting eyes on old Mrs. Simpkins. ' I said last night that I should see her to-morrow,' he reflected ; ' but that was not to be ! '

Next day he had better fortune, or worse, meeting her at the foot of the stairs in the morning, and being favoured by a visit or two from her during the day—

once for the purpose of making kindly inquiries about his comfort, as on the first evening, and at another time to place a bunch of winter-violets on his table, with a promise to renew them when they drooped. On these occasions there was something in her smile which showed how conscious she was of the effect she produced, though it must be said that it was rather a humorous than a designing consciousness, and savoured more of pride than of vanity.

As for Stockdale, he clearly perceived that he possessed unlimited capacity for backsliding, and wished that tutelary saints were not denied to Dissenters. He set a watch upon his tongue and eyes for the space of one hour and a half, after which he found it was useless to struggle further, and gave himself up to the situation. ' The other minister will be here in a month,' he said to himself when sitting over the fire. ' Then I shall be off, and she will distract my mind no more ! . . . And then, shall I go on living by myself for ever ? No ; when my two years of probation are finished, I shall have a furnished house to live in, with a varnished door and a brass knocker ; and I'll march straight back to her, and ask her flat, as soon as the last plate is on the dresser ! '

Thus a titillating fortnight was passed by young Stockdale, during which time things proceeded much as such matters have done ever since the beginning of history. He saw the object of attachment several times one day, did not see her at all the next, met her when he least expected to do so, missed her when hints and signs as to where she should be at a given hour almost amounted to an appointment. This mild coquetry was perhaps fair enough under the circumstances of their being so closely lodged, and Stockdale put up with it as philosophically as he was able. Being in her own house she could, after vexing him or disappointing him of her presence, easily win him back by suddenly surrounding him with those little attentions which her position as his landlady put it in her power to bestow. When he had waited indoors half the day to see her, and on finding that she would not be seen, had gone off in a huff to the dreariest and dampest walk he could discover, she would restore equilibrium in the evening with ' Mr. Stockdale, I have fancied you must feel draught o' nights from your bedroom window, and so I have been putting up thicker curtains this afternoon while you were out ' ; or, ' I noticed that you sneezed twice again this morning, Mr. Stockdale. Depend upon it that cold is hanging about you yet ; I am sure it is—I have thought of it continually ; and you must let me make a posset for you.'

Sometimes in coming home he found his sitting-room rearranged, chairs placed where the table had stood, and the table ornamented with the few fresh flowers and leaves that could be obtained at this season, so as to add a novelty to the room. At times she would be standing on a chair outside the house, trying to nail up a branch of the monthly rose which the winter wind had blown down ; and of course he stepped forward to assist her, when their hands got mixed in passing the shreds and nails. Thus they became friends again after a disagreement. She would utter on these occasions some pretty and deprecatory remark on the necessity of her troubling him anew ; and he would straightway say that he would do a hundred times as much for her if she should so require.

HOW HE SAW TWO OTHER MEN

II

MATTERS being in this advancing state, Stockdale was rather surprised one cloudy evening, while sitting in his room, at hearing her speak in low tones of expostulation to some one at the door. It was nearly dark, but the shutters were not yet closed, nor the candles lighted ; and Stockdale was tempted to stretch his head towards the window. He saw outside the door a young man in clothes of a whitish colour, and upon reflection judged their wearer to be the well-built and rather handsome miller who lived below. The miller's voice was alternately low and firm, and sometimes it reached the level of positive entreaty ; but what the words were Stockdale could in no way hear.

Before the colloquy had ended, the minister's attention was attracted by a second incident. Opposite Lizzy's home grew a clump of laurels, forming a thick and permanent shade. One of the laurel boughs now quivered against the light background of sky, and in a moment the head of a man peered out, and remained still. He seemed to be also much interested in the conversation at the door, and was plainly lingering there to watch and listen. Had Stockdale stood in any other relation to Lizzy than that of a lover, he might have gone out and investigated the meaning of this : but being as yet but an unprivileged ally, he did nothing more than stand up and show himself against the firelight, whereupon the listener disappeared, and Lizzy and the miller spoke in lower tones.

Stockdale was made so uneasy by the circumstance, that as soon as the miller was gone, he said, ' Mrs. Newberry, are you aware that you were watched just now, and your conversation heard ? '

' When ? ' she said.

' When you were talking to that miller. A man was looking from the laurel-tree as jealously as if he could have eaten you.'

She showed more concern than the trifling event seemed to demand, and he added, ' Perhaps you were talking of things you did not wish to be overheard ? '

' I was talking only on business,' she said.

' Lizzy, be frank ! ' said the young man. ' If it was only on business, why should anybody wish to listen to you ? '

She looked curiously at him. ' What else do you think it could be, then ? '

' Well—the only talk between a young woman and man that is likely to amuse an eavesdropper.'

' Ah yes,' she said, smiling in spite of her preoccupation. ' Well, my cousin Owlett has spoken to me about matrimony, every now and then, that's true ; but he was not speaking of it then. I wish he had been speaking of it, with all my heart. It would have been much less serious for me.'

' O Mrs. Newberry ! '

' It would. Not that I should ha' chimed in with him, of course. I wish it for other reasons. I am glad, Mr.

Stockdale, that you have told me of that listener. It is a timely warning, and I must see my cousin again.'

'But don't go away till I have spoken,' said the minister. 'I'll out with it at once, and make no more ado. Let it be Yes or No between us, Lizzy; please do!' And he held out his hand, in which she freely allowed her own to rest, but without speaking.

'You mean Yes by that?' he asked, after waiting a while.

'You may be my sweetheart, if you will.'

'Why not say at once you will wait for me until I have a house and can come back to marry you.'

'Because I am thinking—thinking of something else,' she said with embarrassment. 'It all comes upon me at once, and I must settle one thing at a time.'

'At any rate, dear Lizzy, you can assure me that the miller shall not be allowed to speak to you except on business? You have never directly encouraged him?'

She parried the question by saying, 'You see, he and his party have been in the habit of leaving things on my premises sometimes, and as I have not denied him, it makes him rather forward.'

'Things—what things?'

'Tubs—they are called Things here.'

'But why don't you deny him, my dear Lizzy?'

'I cannot well.'

'You are too timid. It is unfair of him to impose so upon you, and get your good name into danger by his smuggling tricks. Promise me that the next time he wants to leave his tubs here you will let me roll them into the street?'

She shook her head. 'I would not venture to offend the neighbours so much as that,' said she, 'or do anything that would be so likely to put poor Owlett into the hands of the Customs-men.'

Stockdale sighed, and said that he thought hers a mistaken generosity when it extended to assisting those who cheated the king of his dues. 'At any rate, you will let me make him keep his distance as your lover, and tell him flatly that you are not for him?'

'Please not, at present,' she said. 'I don't wish to

offend my old neighbours. It is not only Mr. Owlett who is concerned.'

'This is too bad,' said Stockdale impatiently.

'On my honour, I won't encourage him as my lover,' Lizzy answered earnestly. 'A reasonable man will be satisfied with that.'

'Well, so I am,' said Stockdale, his countenance clearing.

THE MYSTERIOUS GREATCOAT

III

STOCKDALE now began to notice more particularly a feature in the life of his fair landlady, which he had casually observed but scarcely ever thought of before. It was that she was markedly irregular in her hours of rising. For a week or two she would be tolerably punctual, reaching the ground-floor within a few minutes of half-past seven. Then suddenly she would not be visible till twelve at noon, perhaps for three or four days in succession; and twice he had certain proof that she did not leave her room till half-past three in the afternoon. The second time that this extreme lateness came under his notice was on a day when he had particularly wished to consult with her about his future movements; and he concluded, as he always had done, that she had a cold, headache, or other ailment, unless she had kept herself invisible to avoid meeting and talking to him, which he could hardly believe. The former supposition was disproved, however, by her innocently saying, some days later, when they were speaking on a question of health, that she had never had a moment's heaviness, headache, or illness of any kind since the previous January twelvemonth.

'I am glad to hear it,' said he. 'I thought quite otherwise.'

'What, do I look sickly?' she asked, turning up her face to show the impossibility of his gazing on it and holding such a belief for a moment.

'Not at all; I merely thought so from your being sometimes obliged to keep your room through the best part of the day.'

'O, as for that—it means nothing,' she murmured, with a look which some might have called cold, and which was the worst look that he liked to see upon her. 'It is pure sleepiness, Mr. Stockdale.'

'Never!'

'It is, I tell you. When I stay in my room till half-past three in the afternoon, you may always be sure that I slept soundly till three, or I shouldn't have stayed there.'

'It is dreadful,' said Stockdale, thinking of the disastrous effects of such indulgence upon the household of a minister, should it become a habit of everyday occurrence.

'But then,' she said, divining his good and prescient thoughts, 'it only happens when I stay awake all night. I don't go to sleep till five or six in the morning sometimes.'

'Ah, that's another matter,' said Stockdale. 'Sleeplessness to such an alarming extent is real illness. Have you spoken to a doctor?'

'O no—there is no need for doing that—it is all natural to me.' And she went away without further remark.

Stockdale might have waited a long time to know the real cause of her sleeplessness, had it not happened that one dark night he was sitting in his bedroom jotting down notes for a sermon, which occupied him perfunctorily for a considerable time after the other members of the household had retired. He did not get to bed till one o'clock. Before he had fallen asleep he heard a knocking at the front door, first rather timidly performed, and then louder. Nobody answered it, and the person knocked again. As the house still remained undisturbed, Stockdale got out of bed, went to his window, which overlooked the door, and opening it, asked who was there.

A young woman's voice replied that Susan Wallis was there, and that she had come to ask if Mrs. Newberry could give her some mustard to make a plaster with, as her father was taken very ill on the chest.

The minister, having neither bell nor servant, was compelled to act in person. 'I will call Mrs. Newberry,' he said. Partly dressing himself, he went along the passage and tapped at Lizzy's door. She did not answer, and, thinking of her erratic habits in the matter of sleep, he

thumped the door persistently, when he discovered, by its
moving ajar under his knocking, that it had only been
gently pushed to. As there was now a sufficient entry
for the voice, he knocked no longer, but said in firm tones,
' Mrs. Newberry, you are wanted.'

The room was quite silent ; not a breathing, not a rustle,
came from any part of it. Stockdale now sent a positive
shout through the open space of the door : ' Mrs. Newberry ! '—still no answer, or movement of any kind within.
Then he heard sounds from the opposite room, that of
Lizzy's mother, as if she had been aroused by his uproar
though Lizzy had not, and was dressing herself hastily.
Stockdale softly closed the younger woman's door and
went on to the other, which was opened by Mrs. Simpkins
before he could reach it. She was in her ordinary clothes,
and had a light in her hand.

' What's the person calling about ? ' she said in alarm.
Stockdale told the girl's errand, adding seriously, ' I
cannot wake Mrs. Newberry.'

' It is no matter,' said her mother. ' I can let the girl
have what she wants as well as my daughter.' And she
came out of the room and went downstairs.

Stockdale retired towards his own apartment, saying,
however, to Mrs. Simpkins from the landing, as if on second
thoughts, ' I suppose there is nothing the matter with
Mrs. Newberry, that I could not wake her ? '

' O no,' said the old lady hastily. ' Nothing at all.'

Still the minister was not satisfied. ' Will you go
in and see ? ' he said. ' I should be much more at ease.'

Mrs. Simpkins returned up the staircase, went to her
daughter's room, and came out again almost instantly.
' There is nothing at all the matter with Lizzy,' she said ;
and descended again to attend to the applicant, who,
having seen the light, had remained quiet during this
interval.

Stockdale went into his room and lay down as before.
He heard Lizzy's mother open the front door, admit the
girl, and then the murmured discourse of both as they
went to the store-cupboard for the medicament required.
The girl departed, the door was fastened, Mrs. Simpkins

came upstairs, and the house was again in silence. Still the minister did not fall asleep. He could not get rid of a singular suspicion, which was all the more harassing in being, if true, the most unaccountable thing within his experience. That Lizzy Newberry was in her bedroom when he made such a clamour at the door he could not possibly convince himself, notwithstanding that he had heard her come upstairs at the usual time, go into her chamber, and shut herself up in the usual way. Yet all reason was so much against her being elsewhere, that he was constrained to go back again to the unlikely theory of a heavy sleep, though he had heard neither breath nor movement during a shouting and knocking loud enough to rouse the Seven Sleepers.

Before coming to any positive conclusion he fell asleep himself, and did not awake till day. He saw nothing of Mrs. Newberry in the morning, before he went out to meet the rising sun, as he liked to do when the weather was fine ; but as this was by no means unusual, he took no notice of it. At breakfast-time he knew that she was not far off by hearing her in the kitchen, and though he saw nothing of her person, that back apartment being rigorously closed against his eyes, she seemed to be talking, ordering, and bustling about among the pots and skimmers in so ordinary a manner, that there was no reason for his wasting more time in fruitless surmise.

The minister suffered from these distractions, and his extemporized sermons were not improved thereby. Already he often said Romans for Corinthians in the pulpit, and gave out hymns in strange cramped metres, that hitherto had always been skipped, because the congregation could not raise a tune to fit them. He fully resolved that as soon as his few weeks of stay approached their end he would cut the matter short, and commit himself by proposing a definite engagement, repenting at leisure if necessary.

With this end in view, he suggested to her on the evening after her mysterious sleep that they should take a walk together just before dark, the latter part of the proposition being introduced that they might return home unseen.

She consented to go ; and away they went over a stile, to
a shrouded footpath suited for the occasion. But, in spite
of attempts on both sides, they were unable to infuse much
spirit into the ramble. She looked rather paler than
usual, and sometimes turned her head away.

'Lizzy,' said Stockdale reproachfully, when they had
walked in silence a long distance.

'Yes,' said she.

'You yawned—much my company is to you!' He
put it in that way, but he was really wondering whether
her yawn could possibly have more to do with physical
weariness from the night before than mental weariness of
that present moment. Lizzy apologized, and owned that
she was rather tired, which gave him an opening for a
direct question on the point ; but his modesty would not
allow him to put it to her ; and he uncomfortably resolved
to wait.

The month of February passed with alternations of
mud and frost, rain and sleet, east winds and north-westerly
gales. The hollow places in the ploughed fields showed
themselves as pools of water, which had settled there from
the higher levels, and had not yet found time to soak
away. The birds began to get lively, and a single thrush
came just before sunset each evening, and sang hopefully
on the large elm-tree which stood nearest to Mrs. Newberry's house. Cold blasts and brittle earth had given
place to an oozing dampness more unpleasant in itself than
frost ; but it suggested coming spring, and its unpleasantness was of a bearable kind.

Stockdale had been going to bring about a practical
understanding with Lizzy at least half a dozen times ;
but, what with the mystery of her apparent absence
on the night of the neighbour's call, and her curious way
of lying in bed at unaccountable times, he felt a check
within him whenever he wanted to speak out. Thus they
still lived on as indefinitely affianced lovers, each of whom
hardly acknowledged the other's claim to the name of
chosen one. Stockdale persuaded himself that his hesitation was owing to the postponement of the ordained
minister's arrival, and the consequent delay in his own

departure, which did away with all necessity for haste in his courtship ; but perhaps it was only that his discretion was reasserting itself, and telling him that he had better get clearer ideas of Lizzy before arranging for the grand contract of his life with her. She, on her part, always seemed ready to be urged further on that question than he had hitherto attempted to go ; but she was none the less independent, and to a degree which would have kept from flagging the passion of a far more mutable man.

On the evening of the first of March he went casually into his bedroom about dusk, and noticed lying on a chair a greatcoat, hat, and breeches. Having no recollection of leaving any clothes of his own in that spot, he went and examined them as well as he could in the twilight, and found that they did not belong to him. He paused for a moment to consider how they might have got there. He was the only man living in the house ; and yet these were not his garments, unless he had made a mistake. No, they were not his. He called up Martha Sarah.

'How did these things come in my room ? ' he said, flinging the objectionable articles to the floor.

Martha said that Mrs. Newberry had given them to her to brush, and that she had brought them up there thinking they must be Mr. Stockdale's, as there was no other gentleman a-lodging there.

'Of course you did,' said Stockdale. 'Now take them down to your mis'ess, and say they are some clothes I have found here and know nothing about.'

As the door was left open he heard the conversation downstairs. 'How stupid ! ' said Mrs. Newberry, in a tone of confusion. 'Why, Marther Sarer, I did not tell you to take 'em to Mr. Stockdale's room ! '

'I thought they must be his as they was so muddy,' said Martha humbly.

'You should have left 'em on the clothes-horse,' said the young mistress severely ; and she came upstairs with the garments on her arm, quickly passed Stockdale's room, and threw them forcibly into a closet at the end of a passage. With this the incident ended, and the house was silent again.

There would have been nothing remarkable in finding such clothes in a widow's house had they been clean; or moth-eaten, or creased, or mouldy from long lying by; but that they should be splashed with recent mud bothered Stockdale a good deal. When a young pastor is in the aspen stage of attachment, and open to agitation at the merest trifles, a really substantial incongruity of this complexion is a disturbing thing. However, nothing further occurred at that time; but he became watchful, and given to conjecture, and was unable to forget the circumstance.

One morning, on looking from his window, he saw Mrs. Newberry herself brushing the tails of a long drab greatcoat, which, if he mistook not, was the very same garment as the one that had adorned the chair of his room. It was densely splashed up to the hollow of the back with neighbouring Nether-Moynton mud, to judge by its colour, the spots being distinctly visible to him in the sunlight. The previous day or two having been wet, the inference was irresistible that the wearer had quite recently been walking some considerable distance about the lanes and fields. Stockdale opened the window and looked out, and Mrs. Newberry turned her head. Her face became slowly red; she never had looked prettier, or more incomprehensible. He waved his hand affectionately, and said good-morning; she answered with embarrassment, having ceased her occupation on the instant that she saw him, and rolled up the coat half-cleaned.

Stockdale shut the window. Some simple explanation of her proceeding was doubtless within the bounds of possibility; but he himself could not think of one; and he wished that she had placed the matter beyond conjecture by voluntarily saying something about it there and then.

But, though Lizzy had not offered an explanation at the moment, the subject was brought forward by her at the next time of their meeting. She was chatting to him concerning some other event, and remarked that it happened about the time when she was dusting some old clothes that had belonged to her poor husband.

'You keep them clean out of respect to his memory ? ' said Stockdale tentatively.

'I air and dust them sometimes,' she said, with the most charming innocence in the world.

'Do dead men come out of their graves and walk in mud ? ' murmured the minister, in a cold sweat at the deception that she was practising.

'What did you say ? ' asked Lizzy.

'Nothing, nothing,' said he mournfully. 'Mere words —a phrase that will do for my sermon next Sunday.' It was too plain that Lizzy was unaware that he had seen fresh pedestrian splashes upon the skirts of the tell-tale overcoat, and that she imagined him to believe it had come direct from some chest or drawer.

The aspect of the case was now considerably darker. Stockdale was so much depressed by it that he did not challenge her explanation, or threaten to go off as a missionary to benighted islanders, or reproach her in any way whatever. He simply parted from her when she had done talking, and lived on in perplexity, till by degrees his natural manner became sad and constrained.

AT THE TIME OF THE NEW MOON

IV

THE following Thursday was changeable, damp, and gloomy ; and the night threatened to be windy and unpleasant. Stockdale had gone away to Knollsea in the morning, to be present at some commemoration service there, and on his return he was met by the attractive Lizzy in the passage. Whether influenced by the tide of cheerfulness which had attended him that day, or by the drive through the open air, or whether from a natural disposition to let bygones alone, he allowed himself to be fascinated into forgetfulness of the greatcoat incident, and upon the whole passed a pleasant evening ; not so much in her society as within sound of her voice, as she sat talking in the back parlour to her mother, till the latter went to bed. Shortly after this Mrs. Newberry retired, and then Stockdale prepared to go upstairs himself. But

before he left the room he remained standing by the dying
embers a while, thinking long of one thing and another ;
and was only aroused by the flickering of his candle in the
socket as it suddenly declined and went out. Knowing
that there were a tinder-box, matches, and another candle
in his bedroom, he felt his way upstairs without a light.
On reaching his chamber he laid his hand on every possible
ledge and corner for the tinder-box, but for a long time in
vain. Discovering it at length, Stockdale produced a
spark, and was kindling the brimstone, when he fancied that
he heard a movement in the passage. He blew harder
at the lint, the match flared up, and looking by aid of the
blue light through the door, which had been standing
open all this time, he was surprised to see a male figure
vanishing round the top of the staircase with the evident
intention of escaping unobserved. The personage wore
the clothes which Lizzy had been brushing, and something
in the outline and gait suggested to the minister that the
wearer was Lizzy herself.

But he was not sure of this ; and, greatly excited,
Stockdale determined to investigate the mystery, and to
adopt his own way for doing it. He blew out the match
without lighting the candle, went into the passage, and
proceeded on tiptoe towards Lizzy's room. A faint gray
square of light in the direction of the chamber-window as
he approached told him that the door was open, and at
once suggested that the occupant was gone. He turned
and brought down his fist upon the handrail of the staircase : ' It was she ; in her late husband's coat and hat ! '

Somewhat relieved to find that there was no intruder
in the case, yet none the less surprised, the minister crept
down the stairs, softly put on his boots, overcoat, and hat,
and tried the front door. It was fastened as usual ; he
went to the back door, found this unlocked, and emerged
into the garden. The night was mild and moonless, and
rain had lately been falling, though for the present it
had ceased. There was a sudden dropping from the
trees and bushes every now and then, as each passing wind
shook their boughs. Among these sounds Stockdale heard
the faint fall of feet upon the road outside, and he guessed

from the step that it was Lizzy's.   He followed the sound,
and, helped by the circumstance of the wind blowing from
the direction in which the pedestrian moved, he got nearly
close to her, and kept there, without risk of being overheard.
While he thus followed her up the street or lane, as it might
indifferently be called, there being more hedge than houses
on either side, a figure came forward to her from one of the
cottage doors.   Lizzy stopped ; the minister stepped upon
the grass and stopped also.

'Is that Mrs. Newberry ?' said the man who had come
out, whose voice Stockdale recognized as that of one of
the most devout members of his congregation.

'It is,' said Lizzy.

'I be quite ready—I've been here this quarter-hour.'

'Ah, John,' said she, 'I have bad news ; there is danger
to-night for our venture.'

'And d'ye tell o't !   I dreamed there might be.'

'Yes,' she said hurriedly ; 'and you must go at once
round to where the chaps are waiting, and tell them they
will not be wanted till to-morrow night at the same time.
I go to burn the lugger off.'

'I will,' he said ; and instantly went off through a
gate, Lizzy continuing her way.

On she tripped at a quickening pace till the lane turned
into the turnpike-road, which she crossed, and got into the
track for Ringsworth.   Here she ascended the hill without
the least hesitation, passed the lonely hamlet of Holworth,
and went down the vale on the other side.   Stockdale had
never taken any extensive walks in this direction, but he
was aware that if she persisted in her course much longer
she would draw near to the coast, which was here between
two and three miles distant from Nether-Moynton ; and
as it had been about a quarter-past eleven o'clock when
they set out, her intention seemed to be to reach the shore
about midnight.

Lizzy soon ascended a small mound, which Stockdale
at the same time adroitly skirted on the left ; and a dull
monotonous roar burst upon his ear.   The hillock was about
fifty yards from the top of the cliffs, and by day it apparently commanded a full view of the bay.   There was light

enough in the sky to show her disguised figure against it when she reached the top, where she paused, and afterwards sat down. Stockdale, not wishing on any account to alarm her at this moment, yet desirous of being near her, sank upon his hands and knees, crept a little higher up, and there stayed still.

The wind was chilly, the ground damp, and his position one in which he did not care to remain long. However, before he had decided to leave it, the young man heard voices behind him. What they signified he did not know ; but, fearing that Lizzy was in danger, he was about to run forward and warn her that she might be seen, when she crept to the shelter of a little bush which maintained a precarious existence in that exposed spot ; and her form was absorbed in its dark and stunted outline as if she had become part of it. She had evidently heard the men as well as he. They passed near him, talking in loud and careless tones, which could be heard above the uninterrupted washings of the sea, and which suggested that they were not engaged in any business at their own risk. This proved to be the fact ; some of their words floated across to him, and caused him to forget at once the coldness of his situation.

'What's the vessel ? '

'A lugger, about fifty tons.'

'From Cherbourg, I suppose ? '

'Yes, 'a b'lieve.'

'But it don't all belong to Owlett ? '

'O no. He's only got a share. There's another or two in it—a farmer and such like, but the names I don't know.'

The voices died away, and the heads and shoulders of the men diminished towards the cliff, and dropped out of sight.

'My darling has been tempted to buy a share by that unbeliever Owlett,' groaned the minister, his honest affection for Lizzy having quickened to its intensest point during these moments of risk to her person and name. 'That's why she's here,' he said to himself. 'O, it will be the ruin of her ! '

His perturbation was interrupted by the sudden bursting out of a bright and increasing light from the spot where

Lizzy was in hiding. A few seconds later, and before it had reached the height of a blaze, he heard her rush past him down the hollow like a stone from a sling, in the direction of home. The light now flared high and wide, and showed its position clearly. She had kindled a bough of furze and stuck it into the bush under which she had been crouching ; the wind fanned the flame, which crackled fiercely, and threatened to consume the bush as well as the bough. Stockdale paused just long enough to notice thus much, and then followed rapidly the route taken by the young woman. His intention was to overtake her, and reveal himself as a friend ; but run as he would he could see nothing of her. Thus he flew across the open country about Holworth, twisting his legs and ankles in unexpected fissures and descents, till, on coming to the gate between the downs and the road, he was forced to pause to get breath. There was no audible movement either in front or behind him, and he now concluded that she had not outrun him, but that, hearing him at her heels, and believing him one of the excise party, she had hidden herself somewhere on the way, and let him pass by.

He went on at a more leisurely pace towards the village. On reaching the house he found his surmise to be correct, for the gate was on the latch, and the door unfastened, just as he had left them. Stockdale closed the door behind him, and waited silently in the passage. In about ten minutes he heard the same light footstep that he had heard in going out ; it paused at the gate, which opened and shut softly, and then the door-latch was lifted, and Lizzy came in.

Stockdale went forward and said at once, ' Lizzy, don't be frightened. I have been waiting up for you.'

She started, though she had recognized the voice. ' It is Mr. Stockdale, isn't it ? ' she said.

' Yes,' he answered, becoming angry now that she was safe indoors, and not alarmed. ' And a nice game I've found you out in to-night. You are in man's clothes, and I am ashamed of you ! '

Lizzy could hardly find a voice to answer this unexpected reproach.

' I am only partly in man's clothes,' she faltered, shrinking back to the wall. ' It is only his greatcoat and hat
and breeches that I've got on, which is no harm, as he was
my own husband ; and I do it only because a cloak blows
about so, and you can't use your arms. I have got my own
dress under just the same—it is only tucked in ! Will you
go away upstairs and let me pass ? I didn't want you to
see me at such a time as this ! '

' But I have a right to see you ! How do you think
there can be anything between us now ? ' Lizzy was silent.
' You are a smuggler,' he continued sadly.

' I have only a share in the run,' she said.

' That makes no difference. Whatever did you engage
in such a trade as that for, and keep it such a secret from
me all this time ? '

' I don't do it always. I only do it in winter-time when
'tis new moon.'

' Well, I suppose that's because it can't be done any-
when else. . . . You have regularly upset me, Lizzy.'

' I am sorry for that,' Lizzy meekly replied.

' Well now,' said he more tenderly, ' no harm is done as
yet. Won't you for the sake of me give up this blameable
and dangerous practice altogether ? '

' I must do my best to save this run,' said she, getting
rather husky in the throat. ' I don't want to give you
up—you know that ; but I don't want to lose my venture.
I don't know what to do now ! Why I have kept it so
secret from you is that I was afraid you would be angry if
you knew.'

' I should think so ! I suppose if I had married you
without finding this out you'd have gone on with it just the
same ? '

' I don't know. I did not think so far ahead. I only
went to-night to burn the folks off, because we found that
the Preventive-men knew where the tubs were to be
landed.'

' It is a pretty mess to be in altogether, is this,' said
the distracted young minister. ' Well, what will you do
now ? '

Lizzy slowly murmured the particulars of their plan, the

chief of which were that they meant to try their luck at some other point of the shore the next night ; that three landing-places were always agreed upon before the run was attempted, with the understanding that, if the vessel was 'burnt off' from the first point, which was Ringsworth, as it had been by her to-night, the crew should attempt to make the second, which was Lulwind Cove, on the second night ; and if there, too, danger threatened, they should on the third night try the third place, which was behind a headland further west.

'Suppose the officers hinder them landing there, too ? ' he said, his attention to this interesting programme displacing for a moment his concern at her share in it.

'Then we shan't try anywhere else all this dark—that's what we call the time between moon and moon—and perhaps they'll string the tubs to a stray-line, and sink 'em a little-ways from shore, and take the bearings ; and then when they have a chance they'll go to creep for 'em.'

'What's that ? '

'O, they'll go out in a boat and drag a creeper—that's a grapnel—along the bottom till it catch hold of the stray-line.'

The minister stood thinking ; and there was no sound within doors but the tick of the clock on the stairs, and the quick breathing of Lizzy, partly from her walk and partly from agitation, as she stood close to the wall, not in such complete darkness but that he could discern against its whitewashed surface the greatcoat, breeches, and broad hat which covered her.

'Lizzy, all this is very wrong,' he said. 'Don't you remember the lesson of the tribute-money ? " Render unto Cæsar the things that are Cæsar's." Surely you have heard that read times enough in your growing up ? '

'He's dead,' she pouted.

'But the spirit of the text is in force just the same.'

'My father did it, and so did my grandfather, and almost everybody in Nether-Moynton lives by it, and life would be so dull if it wasn't for that, that I should not care to live at all.'

' I am nothing to live for, of course,' he replied bitterly.
' You would not think it worth while to give up this wild
business and live for me alone ? '

' I have never looked at it like that.'

' And you won't promise and wait till I am ready ? '

' I cannot give you my word to-night.'   And, looking
thoughtfully down, she gradually moved and moved away,
going into the adjoining room, and closing the door between them.   She remained there in the dark till he was
tired of waiting, and had gone up to his own chamber.

Poor Stockdale was dreadfully depressed all the next
day by the discoveries of the night before.   Lizzy was
unmistakably a fascinating young woman, but as a minister's wife she was hardly to be contemplated.   ' If I
had only stuck to father's little grocery business, instead
of going in for the ministry, she would have suited me
beautifully ! ' he said sadly, until he remembered that
in that case he would never have come from his distant
home to Nether-Moynton, and never have known her.

The estrangement between them was not complete, but
it was sufficient to keep them out of each other's company.
Once during the day he met her in the garden-path, and
said, turning a reproachful eye upon her, ' Do you promise,
Lizzy ? '   But she did not reply.   The evening drew on,
and he knew well enough that Lizzy would repeat her
excursion at night—her half-offended manner had shown
that she had not the slightest intention of altering her plans
at present.   He did not wish to repeat his own share of the
adventure ; but, act as he would, his uneasiness on her
account increased with the decline of day.   Supposing
that an accident should befall her, he would never forgive
himself for not being there to help, much as he disliked
the idea of seeming to countenance such unlawful escapades.

HOW THEY WENT TO LULWIND COVE

V

As he had expected, she left the house at the same hour
at night, this time passing his door without stealth, as if
she knew very well that he would be watching, and were

resolved to brave his displeasure. He was quite ready,
opened the door quickly, and reached the back door almost
as soon as she.

'Then you will go, Lizzy?' he said as he stood on the
step beside her, who now again appeared as a little man
with a face altogether unsuited to his clothes.

'I must,' she said, repressed by his stern manner.

'Then I shall go, too,' said he.

'And I am sure you will enjoy it!' she exclaimed
in more buoyant tones. 'Everybody does who tries it.'

'God forbid that I should! he said. 'But I must look
after you.'

They opened the wicket and went up the road abreast
of each other, but at some distance apart, scarcely a word
passing between them. The evening was rather less
favourable to smuggling enterprise than the last had been,
the wind being lower, and the sky somewhat clear towards
the north.

'It is rather lighter,' said Stockdale.

''Tis, unfortunately,' said she. 'But it is only from
those few stars over there. The moon was new to-day at
four o'clock, and I expected clouds. I hope we shall be
able to do it this dark, for when we have to sink 'em for
long it makes the stuff taste bleachy, and folks don't like
it so well.'

Her course was different from that of the preceding
night, branching off to the left over Lord's Barrow as soon
as they had got out of the lane and crossed the highway.
By the time they reached Shaldon Down, Stockdale,
who had been in perplexed thought as to what he should
say to her, decided that he would not attempt expostulation
now, while she was excited by the adventure, but wait
till it was over, and endeavour to keep her from such
practices in future. It occurred to him once or twice, as
they rambled on, that should they be surprised by the
Preventive-guard, his situation would be more awkward
than hers, for it would be difficult to prove his true motive
in coming to the spot; but the risk was a slight consideration beside his wish to be with her.

They now arrived at a ravine which lay on the outskirts

of Shaldon, a village two miles on their way towards the
point of the shore they sought. Lizzy broke the silence
this time : ' I have to wait here to meet the carriers. I
don't know if they have come yet. As I told you, we go
to Lulwind Cove to-night, and it is two miles further than
Ringsworth.'

It turned out that the men had already come ; for
while she spoke two or three dozen heads broke the line
of the slope, and a company of them at once descended
from the bushes where they had been lying in wait. These
carriers were men whom Lizzy and other proprietors
regularly employed to bring the tubs from the boat to a
hiding-place inland. They were all young fellows of
Nether-Moynton, Shaldon, and the neighbourhood, quiet
and inoffensive persons, even though some held heavy sticks,
who simply engaged to carry the cargo for Lizzy and her
cousin Owlett, as they would have engaged in any other
labour for which they were fairly well paid.

At a word from her they closed in together. ' You
had better take it now,' she said to them ; and handed
to each a packet. It contained six shillings, their remuner-
ation for the night's undertaking, which was paid beforehand without reference to success or failure ; but, besides
this, they had the privilege of selling as agents when
the run was successfully made. As soon as it was done,
she said to them, ' The place is the old one, Dagger's
Grave, near Lulwind Cove ' ; the men till that moment
not having been told whither they were bound, for obvious
reasons. ' Mr. Owlett will meet you there,' added Lizzy.
' I shall follow behind, to see that we are not watched.'

The carriers went on, and Stockdale and Mrs. Newberry followed at a distance of a stone's throw. ' What
do these men do by day ? ' he said.

' Twelve or fourteen of them are labouring men. Some
are brickmakers, some carpenters, some shoemakers, some
thatchers. They are all known to me very well. Nine of
'em are of your own congregation.'

' I can't help that,' said Stockdale.

' O, I know you can't. I only told you. The others
are more church-inclined, because they supply the pa'son

with all the spirits he requires, and they don't wish to
show unfriendliness to a customer.'

'How do you choose 'em?' said Stockdale.

'We choose 'em for their closeness, and because they
are strong and surefooted, and able to carry a heavy
load a long way without being tired.'

Stockdale sighed as she enumerated each particular,
for it proved how far involved in the business a woman
must be who was so well acquainted with its conditions
and needs. And yet he felt more tenderly towards her
at this moment than he had felt all the foregoing day.
Perhaps it was that her experienced manner and bold
indifference stirred his admiration in spite of himself.

'Take my arm, Lizzy,' he murmured.

'I don't want it,' she said. 'Besides, we may never
be to each other again what we once have been.'

'That depends upon you,' said he, and they went on
again as before.

The hired carriers paced along over Shaldon Down with
as little hesitation as if it had been day, avoiding the cart-
way, and leaving the village of East Shaldon on the left, so
as to reach the crest of the hill at a lonely trackless place
not far from the ancient earthwork called Round Pound.
A quarter-hour more of brisk walking brought them within
sound of the sea, to the place called Dagger's Grave, not
many hundred yards from Lulwind Cove. Here they
paused, and Lizzy and Stockdale came up with them, when
they went on together to the verge of the cliff. One of the
men now produced an iron bar, which he drove firmly into
the soil a yard from the edge, and attached to it a rope
that he had uncoiled from his body. They all began to
descend, partly stepping, partly sliding down the incline,
as the rope slipped through their hands.

'You will not go to the bottom, Lizzy?' said Stockdale
anxiously.

'No. I stay here to watch,' she said. 'Mr. Owlett is
down there.'

The men remained quite silent when they reached the
shore; and the next thing audible to the two at the top
was the dip of heavy oars, and the dashing of waves against

a boat's bow. In a moment the keel gently touched the
shingle, and Stockdale heard the footsteps of the thirty-
six carriers running forwards over the pebbles towards the
point of landing.

There was a sousing in the water as of a brood of ducks
plunging in, showing that the men had not been particular
about keeping their legs, or even their waists, dry from the
brine : but it was impossible to see what they were doing,
and in a few minutes the shingle was trampled again.
The iron bar sustaining the rope, on which Stockdale's
hand rested, began to swerve a little, and the carriers
one by one appeared climbing up the sloping cliff, dripping
audibly as they came, and sustaining themselves by the
guide-rope. Each man on reaching the top was seen to be
carrying a pair of tubs, one on his back and one on his
chest, the two being slung together by cords passing round
the chine hoops, and resting on the carrier's shoulders.
Some of the stronger men carried three by putting an extra
one on the top behind, but the customary load was a pair,
these being quite weighty enough to give their bearer the
sensation of having chest and backbone in contact after a
walk of four or five miles.

' Where is Mr. Owlett ? ' said Lizzy to one of them.

' He will not come up this way,' said the carrier. ' He's
to bide on shore till we be safe off.' Then, without waiting for the rest, the foremost men plunged across the down,
and, when the last had ascended, Lizzy pulled up the rope,
wound it round her arm, wriggled the bar from the sod,
and turned to follow the carriers.

' You are very anxious about Owlett's safety,' said the
minister.

' Was there ever such a man ! ' said Lizzy. ' Why, isn't
he my cousin ? '

' Yes. Well, it is a bad night's work,' said Stockdale
heavily. ' But I'll carry the bar and rope for you.'

' Thank God, the tubs have got so far all right,' said she.

Stockdale shook his head, and, taking the bar, walked
by her side towards the downs ; and the moan of the sea
was heard no more.

' Is this what you meant the other day when you

spoke of having business with Owlett?' the young man asked.

'This is it,' she replied. 'I never see him on any other matter.'

'A partnership of that kind with a young man is very odd.'

'It was begun by my father and his, who were brother-laws.'

Her companion could not blind himself to the fact that where tastes and pursuits were so akin as Lizzy's and Owlett's, and where risks were shared, as with them, in every undertaking, there would be a peculiar appropriate-ness in her answering Owlett's standing question on matri-mony in the affirmative. This did not soothe Stockdale, its tendency being rather to stimulate in him an effort to make the pair as inappropriate as possible, and win her away from this nocturnal crew to correctness of conduct and a minister's parlour in some far-removed inland county.

They had been walking near enough to the file of carriers for Stockdale to perceive that, when they got into the road to the village, they split up into two companies of unequal size, each of which made off in a direction of its own. One company, the smaller of the two, went towards the church, and by the time that Lizzy and Stockdale reached their own house these men had scaled the church-yard wall, and were proceeding noiselessly over the grass within.

'I see that Mr. Owlett has arranged for one batch to be put in the church again,' observed Lizzy. 'Do you remem-ber my taking you there the first night you came?'

'Yes, of course,' said Stockdale. 'No wonder you had permission to broach the tubs—they were his, I suppose?'

'No, they were not—they were mine; I had permission from myself. The day after that they went several miles inland in a waggon-load of manure, and sold very well.'

At this moment the group of men who had made off to the left some time before began leaping one by one from the hedge opposite Lizzy's house, and the first man, who had no tubs upon his shoulders, came forward.

'Mrs. Newberry, isn't it?' he said hastily.

'Yes, Jim,' said she. 'What's the matter?'

'I find that we can't put any in Badger's Clump to-night, Lizzy,' said Owlett. 'The place is watched. We must sling the apple-tree in the orchet if there's time. We can't put any more under the church lumber than I have sent on there, and my mixen hev already more in en than is safe.'

'Very well,' she said. 'Be quick about it—that's all. What can I do?'

'Nothing at all, please. Ah, it is the minister!—you two that can't do anything had better get indoors and not be zeed.'

While Owlett thus conversed, in a tone so full of contraband anxiety and so free from lover's jealousy, the men who followed him had been descending one by one from the hedge; and it unfortunately happened that when the hindmost took his leap, the cord slipped which sustained his tubs; the result was that both the kegs fell into the road, one of them being stove in by the blow.

''Od drown it all!' said Owlett, rushing back.

'It is worth a good deal, I suppose?' said Stockdale.

'O no—about two guineas and half to us now,' said Lizzy excitedly. 'It isn't that—it is the smell! It is so blazing strong before it has been lowered by water, that it smells dreadfully when spilt in the road like that! I do hope Latimer won't pass by till it is gone off.'

Owlett and one or two others picked up the burst tub and began to scrape and trample over the spot, to disperse the liquor as much as possible; and then they all entered the gate of Owlett's orchard, which adjoined Lizzy's garden on the right. Stockdale did not care to follow them, for several on recognizing him had looked wonderingly at his presence, though they said nothing. Lizzy left his side and went to the bottom of the garden, looking over the hedge into the orchard, where the men could be dimly seen bustling about, and apparently hiding the tubs. All was done noiselessly, and without a light; and when it was over they dispersed in different directions, those who had taken their cargoes to the church having already gone off to their homes.

Lizzy returned to the garden-gate, over which Stockdale was still abstractedly leaning. ' It is all finished : I am going indoors now,' she said gently. ' I will leave the door ajar for you.'

' O no—you needn't,' said Stockdale ; ' I am coming too.'

But before either of them had moved, the faint clatter of horses' hoofs broke upon the ear, and it seemed to come from the point where the track across the down joined the hard road.

' They are just too late ! ' cried Lizzy exultingly.

' Who ? ' said Stockdale.

' Latimer, the riding-officer, and some assistant of his. We had better go indoors.'

They entered the house, and Lizzy bolted the door. ' Please don't get a light, Mr. Stockdale,' she said.

' Of course I will not,' said he.

' I thought you might be on the side of the king,' said Lizzy, with faintest sarcasm.

' I am,' said Stockdale. ' But, Lizzy Newberry, I love you, and you know it perfectly well, and you ought to know, if you do not, what I have suffered in my conscience on your account these last few days ! '

' I guess very well,' she said hurriedly. ' Yet I don't see why. Ah, you are better than I ! '

The trotting of the horses seemed to have again died away, and the pair of listeners touched each other's fingers in the cold ' Good-night ' of those whom something seriously divided. They were on the landing, but before they had taken three steps apart, the tramp of the horsemen suddenly revived, almost close to the house. Lizzy turned to the staircase window, opened the casement about an inch, and put her face close to the aperture. ' Yes, one of 'em is Latimer,' she whispered. ' He always rides a white horse. One would think it was the last colour for a man in that line.'

Stockdale looked, and saw the white shape of the animal as it passed by ; but before the riders had gone another ten yards Latimer reined in his horse, and said something to his companion which neither Stockdale nor Lizzy could hear. Its drift was, however, soon made evident, for the other man stopped also; and sharply turning the horses' heads they cautiously retraced their steps. When they were again opposite Mrs. Newberry's garden, Latimer dismounted, and the man on the dark horse did the same.

Lizzy and Stockdale, intently listening and observing the proceedings, naturally put their heads as close as possible to the slit formed by the slightly opened casement; and thus it occurred that at last their cheeks came positively into contact. They went on listening, as if they did not know of the singular incident which had happened to their faces, and the pressure of each to each rather increased than lessened with the lapse of time.

They could hear the Customs-men sniffing the air like hounds as they paced slowly along. When they reached the spot where the tub had burst, both stopped on the instant.

' Ay, ay, 'tis quite strong here,' said the second officer. ' Shall we knock at the door ? '

' Well, no,' said Latimer. ' Maybe this is only a trick to put us off the scent. They wouldn't kick up this stink anywhere near their hiding-place. I have known such things before.'

' Anyhow, the things, or some of 'em, must have been brought this way,' said the other.

' Yes,' said Latimer musingly. ' Unless 'tis all done to tole us the wrong way. I have a mind that we go home for to-night without saying a word, and come the first thing in the morning with more hands. I know they have storages about here, but we can do nothing by this owl's light. We will look round the parish and see if everybody is in bed, John; and if all is quiet, we will do as I say.'

They went on, and the two inside the window could hear them passing leisurely through the whole village, the street of which curved round at the bottom and entered the turnpike road at another junction. This way the officers followed, and the amble of their horses died quite away.

' What will you do ? ' said Stockdale, withdrawing from his position.

She knew that he alluded to the coming search by the officers to divert her attention from their own tender incident by the casement, which he wished to be passed over as a thing rather dreamt of than done. ' O, nothing,' she replied, with as much coolness as she could command under her disappointment at his manner. ' We often have such storms as this. You would not be frightened if you knew what fools they are. Fancy riding o' horse-back through the place ; of course they will hear and see nobody while they make that noise ; but they are always afraid to get off, in case some of our fellows should burst out upon 'em, and tie them up to the gate-post, as they have done before now. Good-night, Mr. Stockdale.'

She closed the window and went to her room, where a tear fell from her eyes ; and that not because of the alertness of the riding-officers.

THE GREAT SEARCH AT NETHER-MOYNTON

VI

STOCKDALE was so excited by the events of the evening, and the dilemma that he was placed in between conscience and love, that he did not sleep, or even doze, but remained as broadly awake as at noonday. As soon as the gray light began to touch ever so faintly the whiter objects in his bedroom he arose, dressed himself, and went downstairs into the road.

The village was already astir. Several of the carriers had heard the well-known canter of Latimer's horse while they were undressing in the dark that night, and had already communicated with each other and Owlett on the subject. The only doubt seemed to be about the safety of those tubs which had been left under the church gallery-stairs, and after a short discussion at the corner of the mill, it was agreed that these should be removed before it got lighter, and hidden in the middle of a double hedge bordering the adjoining field. However, before anything could be carried into effect, the footsteps of many men were heard coming down the lane from the highway.

' Damn it, here they be,' said Owlett, who, having already

drawn the hatch and started his mill for the day, stood
stolidly at the mill-door covered with flour, as if the interest
of his whole soul was bound up in the shaking walls around
him.

The two or three with whom he had been talking dispersed to their usual work, and when the Customs-officers,
and the formidable body of men they had hired, reached
the village cross, between the mill and Mrs. Newberry's
house, the village wore the natural aspect of a place beginning its morning labours.

'Now,' said Latimer to his associates, who numbered
thirteen men in all, 'what I know is that the things are
somewhere in this here place. We have got the day before
us, and 'tis hard if we can't light upon 'em and get 'em to
Budmouth Custom-house before night. First we will try
the fuel-houses, and then we'll work our way into the
chimmers, and then to the ricks and stables, and so creep
round. You have nothing but your noses to guide ye,
mind, so use 'em to-day if you never did in your lives
before.'

Then the search began. Owlett, during the early part,
watched from his mill-window, Lizzy from the door of
her house, with the greatest self-possession. A farmer
down below, who also had a share in the run, rode about
with one eye on his fields and the other on Latimer and his
myrmidons, prepared to put them off the scent if he should
be asked a question. Stockdale, who was no smuggler at
all, felt more anxiety than the worst of them, and went
about his studies with a heavy heart, coming frequently to
the door to ask Lizzy some question or other on the consequences to her of the tubs being found.

'The consequences,' she said quietly, 'are simply that
I shall lose 'em. As I have none in the house or garden,
they can't touch me personally.'

'But you have some in the orchard?'

'Mr. Owlett rents that of me, and he lends it to others.
So it will be hard to say who put any tubs there if they
should be found.'

There was never such a tremendous sniffing known as
that which took place in Nether-Moynton parish and its

vicinity this day. All was done methodically, and mostly on hands and knees. At different hours of the day they had different plans. From daybreak to breakfast-time the officers used their sense of smell in a direct and straight-forward manner only, pausing nowhere but at such places as the tubs might be supposed to be secreted in at that very moment, pending their removal on the following night. Among the places tested and examined were :—

Hollow trees	Cupboards	Culverts
Potato-graves	Clock-cases	Hedgerows
Fuel-houses	Chimney-flues	Faggot-ricks
Bedrooms	Rainwater-butts	Haystacks
Apple-lofts	Pigsties	Coppers and ovens.

After breakfast they recommenced with renewed vigour, taking a new line ; that is to say, directing their attention to clothes that might be supposed to have come in contact with the tubs in their removal from the shore, such garments being usually tainted with the spirit, owing to its oozing between the staves. They now sniffed at—

Smock-frocks	Smiths' and shoemakers' aprons
Old shirts and waistcoats	Knee-naps and hedging-gloves
Coats and hats	Tarpaulins
Breeches and leggings	Market-cloaks
Women's shawls and gowns	Scarecrows.

And as soon as the midday meal was over, they pushed their search into places where the spirits might have been thrown away in alarm :—

Horse-ponds	Mixens	Sinks in yards
Stable-drains	Wet ditches	Road-scrapings, and
Cinder-heaps	Cesspools	Back-door gutters.

But still these indefatigable Custom-house men discovered nothing more than the original tell-tale smell in the road opposite Lizzy's house, which even yet had not passed off.

' I'll tell ye what it is, men,' said Latimer, about three o'clock in the afternoon, ' we must begin over again. Find them tubs I will.'

The men, who had been hired for the day, looked at their hands and knees, muddy with creeping on all fours so frequently, and rubbed their noses, as if they had almost had enough of it; for the quantity of bad air which had passed into each one's nostril had rendered it nearly as insensible as a flue. However, after a moment's hesitation, they prepared to start anew, except three, whose power of smell had quite succumbed under the excessive wear and tear of the day.

By this time not a male villager was to be seen in the parish. Owlett was not at his mill, the farmers were not in their fields, the parson was not in his garden, the smith had left his forge, and the wheelwright's shop was silent.

'Where the divil are the folk gone?' said Latimer, waking up to the fact of their absence, and looking round. 'I'll have 'em up for this! Why don't they come and help us? There's not a man about the place but the Methodist parson, and he's an old woman. I demand assistance in the king's name!'

'We must find the jineral public afore we can demand that,' said his lieutenant.

'Well, well, we shall do better without 'em,' said Latimer, who changed his moods at a moment's notice. 'But there's great cause of suspicion in this silence and this keeping out of sight, and I'll bear it in mind. Now we will go across to Owlett's orchard and see what we can find there.'

Stockdale, who heard this discussion from the garden-gate, over which he had been leaning, was rather alarmed, and thought it a mistake of the villagers to keep so completely out of the way. He himself, like the Preventives, had been wondering for the last half-hour what could have become of them. Some labourers were of necessity engaged in distant fields, but the master-workmen should have been at home; though one and all, after just showing themselves at their shops, had apparently gone off for the day. He went in to Lizzy, who sat at a back window sewing, and said, 'Lizzy, where are the men?'

Lizzy laughed. 'Where they mostly are when they're run so hard as this.' She cast her eyes to heaven. 'Up there,' she said.

Stockdale looked up. 'What—on the top of the church tower?' he asked, seeing the direction of her glance.

' Yes.'

' Well, I expect they will soon have to come down,' said he gravely. ' I have been listening to the officers, and they are going to search the orchard over again, and then every nook in the church.'

Lizzy looked alarmed for the first time. ' Will you go and tell our folk ? ' she said. ' They ought to be let know.' Seeing his conscience struggling within him like a boiling pot, she added, ' No, never mind, I'll go myself.'

She went out, descended the garden, and climbed over the churchyard wall at the same time that the Preventive-men were ascending the road to the orchard. Stockdale could do no less than follow her. By the time that she reached the tower entrance he was at her side, and they entered together.

Nether-Moynton church-tower was, as in many villages, without a turret, and the only way to the top was by going up to the singers' gallery, and thence ascending by a ladder to a square trap-door in the floor of the bell-loft, above which a permanent ladder was fixed, passing through the bells to a hole in the roof. When Lizzy and Stockdale reached the gallery and looked up, nothing but the trap-door and the five holes for the bell-ropes appeared. The ladder was gone.

' There's no getting up,' said Stockdale.

' O yes, there is,' said she. ' There's an eye looking at us at this moment through a knot-hole in that trap-door.'

And as she spoke the trap opened, and the dark line of the ladder was seen descending against the whitewashed wall. When it touched the bottom Lizzy dragged it to its place, and said, ' If you'll go up, I'll follow.'

The young man ascended, and presently found himself among consecrated bells for the first time in his life, non-conformity having been in the Stockdale blood for some generations. He eyed them uneasily, and looked round for Lizzy. Owlett stood here, holding the top of the ladder.

' What, be you really one of us ? ' said the miller.

' It seems so,' said Stockdale sadly.

' He's not,' said Lizzy, who overheard. ' He's neither for nor against us. He'll do us no harm.'

She stepped up beside them, and then they went on to the next stage, which, when they had clambered over the dusty bell-carriages, was of easy ascent, leading towards the hole through which the pale sky appeared, and into the open air. Owlett remained behind for a moment, to pull up the lower ladder.

'Keep down your heads,' said a voice, as soon as they set foot on the flat.

Stockdale here beheld all the missing parishioners, lying on their stomachs on the tower roof, except a few who, elevated on their hands and knees, were peeping through the embrasures of the parapet. Stockdale did the same, and saw the village lying like a map below him, over which moved the figures of the Customs-men, each foreshortened to a crablike object, the crown of his hat forming a circular disc in the centre of him. Some of the men had turned their heads when the young preacher's figure arose among them.

'What, Mr. Stockdale?' said Matt Grey, in a tone of surprise.

'I'd as lief that it hadn't been,' said Jim Clarke. 'If the pa'son should see him a-trespassing here in his tower, 'twould be none the better for we, seeing how 'a do hate chapel-members. He'd never buy a tub of us again, and he's as good a customer as we have got this side o' Warm'll.'

'Where is the pa'son?' said Lizzy.

'In his house, to be sure, that he mid see nothing of what's going on—where all good folks ought to be, and this young man likewise.'

'Well, he has brought some news,' said Lizzy. 'They are going to search the orchard and church; can we do anything if they should find?'

'Yes,' said her cousin Owlett. 'That's what we've been talking o', and we have settled our line. Well, be dazed!'

The exclamation was caused by his perceiving that some of the searchers, having got into the orchard, and begun stooping and creeping hither and thither, were pausing in the middle, where a tree smaller than the rest was growing. They drew closer, and bent lower than ever upon the ground.

' O, my tubs ! ' said Lizzy faintly, as she peered through the parapet at them.

' They have got 'em, 'a b'lieve,' said Owlett.

The interest in the movements of the officers was so keen that not a single eye was looking in any other direction ; but at that moment a shout from the church beneath them attracted the attention of the smugglers, as it did also of the party in the orchard, who sprang to their feet and went towards the churchyard wall. At the same time those of the Government men who had entered the church unperceived by the smugglers cried aloud, ' Here be some of 'em at last.'

The smugglers remained in a blank silence, uncertain whether ' some of 'em ' meant tubs or men ; but again peeping cautiously over the edge of the tower they learnt that tubs were the things descried ; and soon these fated articles were brought one by one into the middle of the churchyard from their hiding-place under the gallery-stairs.

' They are going to put 'em on Hinton's vault till they find the rest ! ' said Lizzy hopelessly. The Customs-men had, in fact, begun to pile up the tubs on a large stone slab which was fixed there ; and when all were brought out from the tower, two or three of the men were left standing by them, the rest of the party again proceeding to the orchard.

The interest of the smugglers in the next manœuvres of their enemies became painfully intense. Only about thirty tubs had been secreted in the lumber of the tower, but seventy were hidden in the orchard, making up all that they had brought ashore as yet, the remainder of the cargo having been tied to a sinker and dropped overboard for another night's operations. The Preventives, having re-entered the orchard, acted as if they were positive that here lay hidden the rest of the tubs, which they were determined to find before nightfall. They spread themselves out round the field, and advancing on all fours as before, went anew round every apple-tree in the enclosure. The young tree in the middle again led them to pause, and at length the whole company gathered there in a way which signified that a second chain of reasoning had led to the same results as the first.

When they had examined the sod hereabouts for some minutes, one of the men rose, ran to a disused part of the church where tools were kept, and returned with the sexton's pickaxe and shovel, with which they set to work.

' Are they really buried there ? ' said the minister, for the grass was so green and uninjured that it was difficult to believe it had been disturbed. The smugglers were too interested to reply, and presently they saw, to their chagrin, the officers stand several on each side of the tree; and, stooping and applying their hands to the soil, they bodily lifted the tree and the turf around it. The apple-tree now showed itself to be growing in a shallow box, with handles for lifting at each of the four sides. Under the site of the tree a square hole was revealed, and an officer went and looked down.

'It is all up now,' said Owlett quietly. ' And now all of ye get down before they notice we are here; and be ready for our next move. I had better bide here till dark, or they may take me on suspicion, as 'tis on my ground. I'll be with ye as soon as daylight begins to pink in.'

' And I ? ' said Lizzy.

' You please look to the linch-pins and screws; then go indoors and know nothing at all. The chaps will do the rest.'

The ladder was replaced, and all but Owlett descended, the men passing off one by one at the back of the church, and vanishing on their respective errands. Lizzy walked boldly along the street, followed closely by the minister.

' You are going indoors, Mrs. Newberry ? ' he said.

She knew from the words ' Mrs. Newberry ' that the division between them had widened yet another degree.

' I am not going home,' she said. ' I have a little thing to do before I go in. Martha Sarah will get your tea.'

' O, I don't mean on that account,' said Stockdale. ' What *can* you have to do further in this unhallowed affair ? '

' Only a little,' she said.

' What is that ? I'll go with you.'

' No, I shall go by myself. Will you please go indoors ? I shall be there in less than an hour.'

'You are not going to run any danger, Lizzy?' said the young man, his tenderness reasserting itself.

'None whatever—worth mentioning,' answered she, and went down towards the Cross.

Stockdale entered the garden-gate, and stood behind it looking on. The Preventive-men were still busy in the orchard, and at last he was tempted to enter and watch their proceedings. When he came closer he found that the secret cellar, of whose existence he had been totally unaware, was formed by timbers placed across from side to side about a foot under the ground, and grassed over.

The officers looked up at Stockdale's fair and downy countenance, and evidently thinking him above suspicion, went on with their work again. As soon as all the tubs were taken out they began tearing up the turf, pulling out the timbers, and breaking in the sides, till the cellar was wholly dismantled and shapeless, the apple-tree lying with its roots high to the air. But the hole which had in its time held so much contraband merchandize was never completely filled up, either then or afterwards, a depression in the greensward marking the spot to this day.

THE WALK TO WARM'ELL CROSS AND AFTERWARDS

VII

As the goods had all to be carried to Budmouth that night, the next object of the Custom-house officers was to find horses and carts for the journey, and they went about the village for that purpose. Latimer strode hither and thither with a lump of chalk in his hand, marking broad-arrows so vigorously on every vehicle and set of harness that he came across, that it seemed as if he would chalk broad-arrows on the very hedges and roads. The owner of every conveyance so marked was bound to give it up for Government purposes. Stockdale, who had had enough of the scene, turned indoors thoughtful and depressed. Lizzy was already there, having come in at the back, though she had not yet taken off her bonnet. She looked tired, and her mood was not much brighter than his own. They had but little to say to each other; and the minister went away and attempted to read; but at this he could not succeed, and he shook the little bell for tea.

Lizzy herself brought in the tray, the girl having run off into the village during the afternoon, too full of excitement at the proceedings to remember her state of life. However, almost before the sad lovers had said anything to each other, Martha came in in a steaming state.

' O, there's such a stoor, Mrs. Newberry and Mr. Stockdale! The king's officers can't get the carts ready nohow at all! They pulled Thomas Artnell's, and William Rogers's, and Stephen Sprake's carts into the road, and off came the wheels, and down fell the carts; and they found there was no linch-pins in the arms; and then they tried Samuel Shane's waggon, and found that the screws were gone from he, and at last they looked at the dairyman's cart, and he's got none neither! They have gone now to the blacksmith's to get some made, but he's nowhere to be found! '

Stockdale looked at Lizzy, who blushed very slightly, and went out of the room, followed by Martha Sarah. But before they had got through the passage there was a rap at the front door, and Stockdale recognized Latimer's voice addressing Mrs. Newberry, who had turned back.

' For God's sake, Mrs. Newberry, have you seen Hardman the blacksmith up this way? If we could get hold of him, we'd e'en a'most drag him by the hair of his head to his anvil, where he ought to be.'

' He's an idle man, Mr. Latimer,' said Lizzy archly. ' What do you want him for? '

' Why, there isn't a horse in the place that has got more than three shoes on, and some have only two. The waggon-wheels be without strakes, and there's no linch-pins to the carts. What with that, and the bother about every set of harness being out of order, we shan't be off before night-fall—upon my soul we shan't. 'Tis a rough lot, Mrs. Newberry, that you've got about you here; but they'll play at this game once too often, mark my words they will! There's not a man in the parish that don't deserve to be whipped.'

It happened that Hardman was at that moment a little

further up the lane, smoking his pipe behind a holly-bush. When Latimer had done speaking he went on in this direction, and Hardman, hearing the riding-officer's steps, found curiosity too strong for prudence. He peeped out from the bush at the very moment that Latimer's glance was on it. There was nothing left for him to do but to come forward with unconcern.

'I've been looking for you for the last hour!' said Latimer with a glare in his eye.

'Sorry to hear that,' said Hardman. 'I've been out for a stroll, to look for more hid tubs, to deliver 'em up to Gover'ment.'

'O yes, Hardman, we know it,' said Latimer, with withering sarcasm. 'We know that you'll deliver 'em up to Gover'ment. We know that all the parish is helping us, and have been all day! Now you please walk along with me down to your shop, and kindly let me hire ye in the king's name.'

They went down the lane together, and presently there resounded from the smithy the ring of a hammer not very briskly swung. However, the carts and horses were got into some sort of travelling condition, but it was not until after the clock had struck six, when the muddy roads were glistening under the horizontal light of the fading day. The smuggled tubs were soon packed into the vehicles, and Latimer, with three of his assistants, drove slowly out of the village in the direction of the port of Budmouth, some considerable number of miles distant, the other men of the Preventive-guard being left to watch for the remainder of the cargo, which they knew to have been sunk somewhere between Ringsworth and Lulwind Cove, and to unearth Owlett, the only person clearly implicated by the discovery of the cave.

Women and children stood at the doors as the carts, each chalked with the Government pitchfork, passed in the increasing twilight; and as they stood they looked at the confiscated property with a melancholy expression that told only too plainly the relation which they bore to the trade.

'Well, Lizzy,' said Stockdale, when the crackle of the

wheels had nearly died away. ' This is a fit finish to your adventure. I am truly thankful that you have got off without suspicion, and the loss only of the liquor. Will you sit down and let me talk to you ? '

' By and by,' she said. ' But I must go out now.'

' Not to that horrid shore again ? ' he said blankly.

' No, not there. I am only going to see the end of this day's business.'

He did not answer to this, and she moved towards the door slowly, as if waiting for him to say something more.

' You don't offer to come with me,' she added at last. ' I suppose that's because you hate me after all this ! '

' Can you say it, Lizzy, when you know I only want to save you from such practices ? Come with you !—of course I will, if it is only to take care of you. But why will you go out again ? '

' Because I cannot rest indoors. Something is happening, and I must know what. Now, come ! ' And they went into the dusk together.

When they reached the turnpike-road she turned to the right, and he soon perceived that they were following the direction of the Preventive-men and their load. He had given her his arm, and every now and then she suddenly pulled it back, to signify that he was to halt a moment and listen. They had walked rather quickly along the first quarter of a mile, and on the second or third time of standing still she said, ' I hear them ahead—don't you ? '

' Yes,' he said ; ' I hear the wheels. But what of that ? '

' I only want to know if they get clear away from the neighbourhood.'

' Ah,' said he, a light breaking upon him. ' Something desperate is to be attempted !—and now I remember there was not a man about the village when we left.'

' Hark ! ' she murmured. The noise of the cart-wheels had stopped, and given place to another sort of sound.

' 'Tis a scuffle ! ' said Stockdale. ' There'll be murder ! Lizzy, let go my arm ; I am going on. On my conscience, I must not stay here and do nothing ! '

' There'll be no murder, and not even a broken head,'

she said. ' Our men are thirty to four of them : no harm
will be done at all.'

' Then there *is* an attack ! ' exclaimed Stockdale ; ' and
you knew it was to be. Why should you side with men
who break the laws like this ? '

' Why should you side with men who take from country
traders what they have honestly bought wi' their own
money in France ? ' said she firmly.

' They are not honestly bought,' said he.

' They are,' she contradicted. ' I and Mr. Owlett and
the others paid thirty shillings for every one of the tubs
before they were put on board at Cherbourg, and if a king
who is nothing to us sends his people to steal our property
we have a right to steal it back again.'

Stockdale did not stop to argue the matter but went
quickly in the direction of the noise, Lizzy keeping at his
side. ' Don't you interfere, will you, dear Richard ? ' she
said anxiously, as they drew near. ' Don't let us go any
closer : 'tis at Warm'ell Cross where they are seizing 'em.
You can do no good, and you may meet with a hard blow ! '

' Let us see first what is going on,' he said. But before
they had got much further the noise of the cart-wheels
began again ; and Stockdale soon found that they were
coming towards him. In another minute the three carts
came up, and Stockdale and Lizzy stood in the ditch to
let them pass.

Instead of being conducted by four men, as had happened when they went out of the village, the horses and
carts were now accompanied by a body of from twenty to
thirty, all of whom, as Stockdale perceived to his astonishment, had blackened faces. Among them walked six or
eight huge female figures, whom, from their wide strides,
Stockdale guessed to be men in disguise. As soon as the
party discerned Lizzy and her companion four or five fell
back, and when the carts had passed, came close to the
pair.

' There is no walking up this way for the present,' said
one of the gaunt women, who wore curls a foot long, dangling down the sides of her face, in the fashion of the time.
Stockdale recognized this lady's voice as Owlett's.

'Why not?' said Stockdale. 'This is the public highway.'

'Now look here, youngster,' said Owlett. 'O, 'tis the Methodist parson!—what, and Mrs. Newberry! Well, you'd better not go up that way, Lizzy. They've all run off, and folks have got their own again.'

The miller then hastened on and joined his comrades. Stockdale and Lizzy also turned back. 'I wish all this hadn't been forced upon us,' she said regretfully. 'But if those Coast-men had got off with the tubs, half the people in the parish would have been in want for the next month or two.'

Stockdale was not paying much attention to her words, and he said, 'I don't think I can go back like this. Those four poor Preventives may be murdered for all I know.'

'Murdered!' said Lizzy impatiently. 'We don't do murder here.'

'Well, I shall go as far as Warm'ell Cross to see,' said Stockdale decisively; and, without wishing her safe home or anything else, the minister turned back. Lizzy stood looking at him till his form was absorbed in the shades; and then, with sadness, she went in the direction of Nether-Moynton.

The road was lonely, and after nightfall at this time of the year there was often not a passer for hours. Stockdale pursued his way without hearing a sound beyond that of his own footsteps; and in due time he passed beneath the trees of the plantation which surrounded the Warm'ell Cross-road. Before he had reached the point of intersection he heard voices from the thicket.

'Hoi-hoi-hoi! Help, help!'

The voices were not at all feeble or despairing, but they were unmistakably anxious. Stockdale had no weapon, and before plunging into the pitchy darkness of the plantation he pulled a stake from the hedge, to use in case of need. When he got among the trees he shouted—'What's the matter—where are you?'

'Here,' answered the voices; and, pushing through the brambles in that direction, he came near the objects of his search.

' Why don't you come forward ? ' said Stockdale.

' We be tied to the trees ! '

' Who are you ? '

' Poor Will Latimer the Customs-officer ! ' said one plain-tively. ' Just come and cut these cords, there's a good man. We were afraid nobody would pass by to-night.'

Stockdale soon loosened them, upon which they stretched their limbs and stood at their ease.

' The rascals ! ' said Latimer, getting now into a rage, though he had seemed quite meek when Stockdale first came up. ' 'Tis the same set of fellows. I know they were Moynton chaps to a man.'

' But. we can't swear to 'em,' said another. ' Not one of 'em spoke.'

' What are you going to do ? ' said Stockdale.

' I'd fain go back to Moynton, and have at 'em again ! ' said Latimer.

' So would we ! ' said his comrades.

' Fight till we die ! ' said Latimer.

' We will, we will ! ' said his men.

' But,' said Latimer, more frigidly, as they came out of the plantation, ' we don't *know* that these chaps with black faces were Moynton men ? And proof is a hard thing.'

' So it is,' said the rest.

' And therefore we won't do nothing at all,' said Latimer, with complete dispassionateness. ' For my part, I'd sooner be them than we. The clitches of my arms are burning like fire from the cords those two strapping women tied round 'em. My opinion is, now I have had time to think o't, that you may serve your Gover'ment at too high a price. For these two nights and days I have not had an hour's rest ; and, please God, here's for home-along.'

The other officers agreed heartily to this course ; and, thanking Stockdale for his timely assistance, they parted from him at the Cross, taking themselves the western road, and Stockdale going back to Nether-Moynton.

During that walk the minister was lost in reverie of the most painful kind. As soon as he got into the house, and before entering his own rooms, he advanced to the door of the little back parlour in which Lizzy usually sat with her mother. He found her there alone. Stockdale went forward, and, like a man in a dream, looked down upon the table that stood between him and the young woman, who had her bonnet and cloak still on. As he did not speak, she looked up from her chair at him, with misgiving in her eye.

'Where are they gone?' he then said listlessly.

'Who?—I don't know. I have seen nothing of them since. I came straight in here.'

'If your men can manage to get off with those tubs, it will be a great profit to you, I suppose?'

'A share will be mine, a share my cousin Owlett's, a share to each of the two farmers, and a share divided amongst the men who helped us.'

'And you still think,' he went on slowly, 'that you will not give this business up?'

Lizzy rose, and put her hand upon his shoulder. 'Don't ask that,' she whispered. 'You don't know what you are asking. I must tell you, though I meant not to do it. What I make by that trade is all I have to keep my mother and myself with.'

He was astonished. 'I did not dream of such a thing,' he said. 'I would rather have scraped the roads, had I been you. What is money compared with a clear conscience?'

'My conscience is clear. I know my mother, but the king I have never seen. His dues are nothing to me. But it is a great deal to me that my mother and I should live.'

'Marry me, and promise to give it up. I will keep your mother.'

'It is good of you,' she said, moved a little. 'Let me think of it by myself. I would rather not answer now.'

She reserved her answer till the next day, and came into his room with a solemn face. 'I cannot do what you wished!' she said passionately. 'It is too much to ask. My whole life ha' been passed in this way.' Her words and manner showed that before entering she had been struggling with herself in private, and that the contention had been strong.

Stockdale turned pale, but he spoke quietly. 'Then,

Lizzy, we must part. I cannot go against my principles in this matter, and I cannot make my profession a mockery. You know how I love you, and what I would do for you ; but this one thing I cannot do.'

' But why should you belong to that profession ? ' she burst out. ' I have got this large house ; why can't you marry me, and live here with us, and not be a Methodist preacher any more ? I assure you, Richard, it is no harm, and I wish you could only see it as I do ! We only carry it on in winter : in summer it is never done at all. It stirs up one's dull life at this time o' the year, and gives excitement, which I have got so used to now that I should hardly know how to do 'ithout it. At nights, when the wind blows, instead of being dull and stupid, and not noticing whether it do blow or not, your mind is afield, even if you are not afield yourself ; and you are wondering how the chaps are getting on ; and you walk up and down the room, and look out o' window, and then you go out yourself, and know your way about as well by night as by day, and have hairbreadth escapes from old Latimer and his fellows, who are too stupid ever to really frighten us, and only make us a bit nimble.'

' He frightened you a little last night, anyhow : and I would advise you to drop it before it is worse.'

She shook her head. ' No, I must go on as I have begun. I was born to it. It is in my blood, and I can't be cured. O, Richard, you cannot think what a hard thing you have asked, and how sharp you try me when you put me between this and my love for 'ee ! '

Stockdale was leaning with his elbow on the mantel-piece, his hands over his eyes. ' We ought never to have met, Lizzy,' he said. ' It was an ill day for us ! I little thought there was anything so hopeless and impossible in our engagement as this. Well, it is too late now to regret consequences in this way. I have had the happiness of seeing you and knowing you at least.'

' You dissent from Church, and I dissent from State,' she said. ' And I don't see why we are not well matched.'

He smiled sadly, while Lizzy remained looking down, her eyes beginning to overflow.

That was an unhappy evening for both of them, and the days that followed were unhappy days. Both she and he went mechanically about their employments, and his depression was marked in the village by more than one of his denomination with whom he came in contact. But Lizzy, who passed her days indoors, was unsuspected of being the cause: for it was generally understood that a quiet engagement to marry existed between her and her cousin Owlett, and had existed for some time.

Thus uncertainly the week passed on; till one morning Stockdale said to her: 'I have had a letter, Lizzy. I must call you that till I am gone.'

'Gone?' said she blankly.

'Yes,' he said. 'I am going from this place. I felt it would be better for us both that I should not stay after what has happened. In fact, I couldn't stay here, and look on you from day to day, without becoming weak and faltering in my course. I have just heard of an arrangement by which the other minister can arrive here in about a week; and let me go elsewhere.'

That he had all this time continued so firmly fixed in his resolution came upon her as a grievous surprise. 'You never loved me!' she said bitterly.

'I might say the same,' he returned; 'but I will not. Grant me one favour. Come and hear my last sermon on the day before I go.'

Lizzy, who was a church-goer on Sunday mornings, frequently attended Stockdale's chapel in the evening with the rest of the double-minded; and she promised.

It became known that Stockdale was going to leave, and a good many people outside his own sect were sorry to hear it. The intervening days flew rapidly away, and on the evening of the Sunday which preceded the morning of his departure Lizzy sat in the chapel to hear him for the last time. The little building was full to overflowing, and he took up the subject which all had expected, that of the contraband trade so extensively practised among them. His hearers, in laying his words to their own hearts, did not perceive that they were most particularly directed against Lizzy, till the sermon waxed warm, and Stockdale nearly broke down with emotion. In truth his own earnestness, and her sad eyes looking up at him, were too much for the young man's equanimity. He hardly knew how he ended. He saw Lizzy, as through a mist, turn and go away with the rest of the congregation; and shortly afterwards followed her home.

She invited him to supper, and they sat down alone, her mother having, as was usual with her on Sunday nights, gone to bed early.

'We will part friends, won't we?' said Lizzy, with forced gaiety, and never alluding to the sermon: a reticence which rather disappointed him.

'We will,' he said, with a forced smile on his part; and they sat down.

It was the first meal that they had ever shared together in their lives, and probably the last that they would so share. When it was over, and the indifferent conversation could no longer be continued, he arose and took her hand. 'Lizzy,' he said, 'do you say we must part—do you?'

'You do,' she said solemnly. 'I can say no more.'

'Nor I,' said he. 'If that is your answer, good-bye!'

Stockdale bent over her and kissed her, and she involuntarily returned his kiss. 'I shall go early,' he said hurriedly. 'I shall not see you again.'

And he did leave early. He fancied, when stepping forth into the gray morning light, to mount the van which was to carry him away, that he saw a face between the parted curtains of Lizzy's window, but the light was faint, and the panes glistened with wet; so he could not be sure. Stockdale mounted the vehicle, and was gone; and on the following Sunday the new minister preached in the chapel of the Moynton Wesleyans.

One day, two years after the parting, Stockdale, now settled in a midland town, came into Nether-Moynton by carrier in the original way. Jogging along in the van that afternoon he had put questions to the driver, and the answers that he received interested the minister deeply. The result of them was that he went without the least hesitation to the door of his former lodging. It was about six o'clock

in the evening, and the same time of year as when he had
left ; now, too, the ground was damp and glistening, the
west was bright, and Lizzy's snowdrops were raising their
heads in the border under the wall.

Lizzy must have caught sight of him from the window,
for by the time that he reached the door she was there
holding it open: and then, as if she had not sufficiently
considered her act of coming out, she drew herself back,
saying with some constraint, ' Mr. Stockdale ! '

' You knew it was,' said Stockdale, taking her hand.
' I wrote to say I should call.'

' Yes, but you did not say when,' she answered.

' I did not.   I was not quite sure when my business
would lead me to these parts.'

' You only came because business brought you near ? '

' Well, that is the fact ; but I have often thought I
should like to come on purpose to see you. . . .   But
what's all this that has happened ?   I told you how it
would be, Lizzy, and you would not listen to me.'

' I would not,' she said sadly.   ' But I had been brought
up to that life ; and it was second nature to me.   However,
it is all over now.   The officers have blood-money for taking a man dead or alive, and the trade is go ng to nothing.
We were hunted down like rats.'

' Owlett is quite gone, I hear.'

' Yes.   He is in America.   We had a dreadful struggle
that last time, when they tried to take him.   It is a perfect
miracle that he lived through it ; and it is a wonder that
I was not killed.   I was shot in the hand.   It was not by
aim ;   the shot was really meant for my cousin ;   but I
was behind, looking on as usual, and the bullet came to
me.   It bled terribly, but I got home without fainting ;
and it healed after a time.   You know how he suffered ? '

' No,' said Stockdale.   ' I only heard that he just escaped
with his life.'

' He was shot in the back ;   but a rib turned the ball.
He was badly hurt.   We would not let him be took.   The
men carried him all night across the meads to Kingsbere,
and hid him in a barn, dressing his wound as well as they
could, till he was so far recovered as to be able to get about.

Then he was caught, and tried with the others at the assizes; but they all got off.[1] He had given up his mill for some time; and at last he went to Bristol, and took a passage to America, where he's settled.'

'What do you think of smuggling now?' said the minister gravely.

'I own that we were wrong,' said she. 'But I have suffered for it. I am very poor now, and my mother has been dead these twelve months. . . . But won't you come in, Mr. Stockdale?'

Stockdale went in; and it is to be supposed that they came to an understanding; for a fortnight later there was a sale of Lizzy's furniture, and after that a wedding at a chapel in a neighbouring town.

He took her away from her old haunts to the home that he had made for himself in his native county, where she studied her duties as a minister's wife with praiseworthy assiduity. It is said that in after years she wrote an excellent tract called *Render unto Cæsar; or, The Repentant Villagers*, in which her own experience was anonymously used as the introductory story. Stockdale got it printed, after making some corrections, and putting in a few powerful sentences of his own; and many hundreds of copies were distributed by the couple in the course of their married life.

April 1879.

NOTE.—The ending of this story with the marriage of Lizzy and the minister was almost *de rigueur* in an English magazine at the time of writing. But at this late date, thirty years after, it may not be amiss to give the ending that would have been preferred by the writer to the convention used above. Moreover it corresponds more closely with the true incidents of which the tale is a vague and flickering shadow. Lizzy did not, in fact, marry the minister, but— much to her credit in the author's opinion—stuck to Jim the smuggler, and emigrated with him after their marriage, an expatrial step rather forced upon him by his adventurous antecedents. They both died in Wisconsin between 1850 and 1860. (*May* 1912.)

---

[1] See the Preface to *Wessex Tales*.

LIFE'S LITTLE IRONIES

CONTAINING

AN IMAGINATIVE WOMAN—THE SON'S VETO—
FOR CONSCIENCE' SAKE—A TRAGEDY OF TWO
AMBITIONS—ON THE WESTERN CIRCUIT—TO
PLEASE HIS WIFE—THE FIDDLER OF THE
REELS—A FEW CRUSTED CHARACTERS

PREFATORY NOTE

TO

LIFE'S LITTLE IRONIES

OF the following collection the first story, ' An Imaginative Woman,' originally stood in *Wessex Tales*, but was brought into this volume as being more nearly its place, turning as it does upon a trick of Nature, so to speak, a physical possibility that may attach to a wife of vivid imaginings, as is well known to medical practitioners and other observers of such manifestations.

The two stories named ' A Tradition of Eighteen Hundred and Four ' and ' The Melancholy Hussar of the German Legion,' which were formerly printed in this series, were also transferred to *Wessex Tales*, where they more naturally belong.

The present narratives and sketches, though separately published at various antecedent dates, were first collected and issued in a volume in 1894.

T. .H.

May 1912.

AN IMAGINATIVE WOMAN

AN IMAGINATIVE WOMAN

WHEN William Marchmill had finished his inquiries for lodgings at the well-known watering-place of Solentsea in Upper Wessex, he returned to the hotel to find his wife. She, with the children, had rambled along the shore, and Marchmill followed in the direction indicated by the military-looking hall-porter.

'By Jove, how far you've gone! I am quite out of breath,' Marchmill said, rather impatiently, when he came up with his wife, who was reading as she walked, the three children being considerably further ahead with the nurse.

Mrs. Marchmill started out of the reverie into which the book had thrown her. 'Yes,' she said, 'you've been such a long time. I was tired of staying in that dreary hotel. But I am sorry if you have wanted me, Will.'

'Well, I have had trouble to suit myself. When you see the airy and comfortable rooms heard of, you find they are stuffy and uncomfortable. Will you come and see if what I've fixed on will do? There is not much room, I am afraid; but I can light on nothing better. The town is rather full.'

The pair left the children and nurse to continue their ramble, and went back together.

In age well-balanced, in personal appearance fairly matched, and in domestic requirements conformable, in temper this couple differed, though even here they did not often clash, he being equable, if not lymphatic, and she decidedly nervous and sanguine. It was to their tastes and fancies, those smallest, greatest particulars, that no common denominator could be applied. Marchmill considered his wife's likes and inclinations somewhat silly; she considered his sordid and material. The husband's business was that of a gunmaker in a thriving city north-

wards, and his soul was in that business always; the lady
was best characterized by that superannuated phrase of
elegance 'a votary of the muse.' An impressionable,
palpitating creature was Ella, shrinking humanely from
detailed knowledge of her husband's trade whenever she
reflected that everything he manufactured had for its
purpose the destruction of life. She could only recover
her equanimity by assuring herself that some, at least,
of his weapons were sooner or later used for the exter-
mination of horrid vermin and animals almost as cruel
to their inferiors in species as human beings were to
theirs.

She had never antecedently regarded this occupation of
his as any objection to having him for a husband. Indeed,
the necessity of getting life-leased at all cost, a cardinal
virtue which all good mothers teach, kept her from thinking of it at all till she had closed with William, had passed
the honeymoon, and reached the reflecting stage. Then,
like a person who has stumbled upon some object in the
dark, she wondered what she had got; mentally walked
round it, estimated it; whether it were rare or common;
contained gold, silver, or lead; were a clog or a pedestal,
everything to her or nothing.

She came to some vague conclusions, and since then had
kept her heart alive by pitying her proprietor's obtuseness
and want of refinement, pitying herself, and letting off
her delicate and ethereal emotions in imaginative occupa-
tions, day-dreams, and night-sighs, which perhaps would
not much have disturbed William if he had known of
them.

Her figure was small, elegant, and slight in build, trip-
ping, or rather bounding, in movement. She was dark-
eyed, and had that marvellously bright and liquid sparkle
in each pupil which characterizes persons of Ella's cast of
soul, and is too often a cause of heartache to the possessor's
male friends, ultimately sometimes to herself. Her husband was a tall, long-featured man, with a brown beard;
he had a pondering regard; and was, it must be added,
usually kind and tolerant to her. He spoke in squarely
shaped sentences, and was supremely satisfied with a

condition of sublunary things which made weapons a
necessity.

Husband and wife walked till they had reached the house
they were in search of, which stood in a terrace facing the
sea, and was fronted by a small garden of wind-proof and
salt-proof evergreens, stone steps leading up to the porch.
It had its number in the row, but, being rather larger than
the rest, was in addition sedulously distinguished as
Coburg House by its landlady, though everybody else
called it 'Thirteen, New Parade.' The spot was bright
and lively now; but in winter it became necessary to
place sandbags against the door, and to stuff up the
keyhole against the wind and rain, which had worn the
paint so thin that the priming and knotting showed
through.

The householder, who had been watching for the gentleman's return, met them in the passage, and showed the
rooms. She informed them that she was a professional
man's widow, left in needy circumstances by the rather
sudden death of her husband, and she spoke anxiously of the
conveniences of the establishment.

Mrs. Marchmill said that she liked the situation and
the house; but, it being small, there would not be accommodation enough, unless she could have all the rooms.

The landlady mused with an air of disappointment.
She wanted the visitors to be her tenants very badly,
she said, with obvious honesty. But unfortunately two
of the rooms were occupied permanently by a bachelor
gentleman. He did not pay season prices, it was true;
but as he kept on his apartments all the year round, and
was an extremely nice and interesting young man, who gave
no trouble, she did not like to turn him out for a month's
'let,' even at a high figure. 'Perhaps, however,' she added,
'he might offer to go for a time.'

They would not hear of this, and went back to the hotel,
intending to proceed to the agent's to inquire further.
Hardly had they sat down to tea when the landlady called.
Her gentleman, she said, had been so obliging as to offer
to give up his rooms for three or four weeks rather than
drive the new-comers away.

' It is very kind, but we won't inconvenience him in that way,' said the Marchmills.

' O, it won't inconvenience him, I assure you ! ' said the landlady eloquently. ' You see, he's a different sort of young man from most—dreamy, solitary, rather melancholy—and he cares more to be here when the south-westerly gales are beating against the door, and the sea washes over the Parade, and there's not a soul in the place, than he does now in the season. He'd just as soon be where, in fact, he's going temporarily, to a little cottage on the Island opposite, for a change.' She hoped therefore that they would come.

The Marchmill family accordingly took possession of the house next day, and it seemed to suit them very well. After luncheon Mr. Marchmill strolled out towards the pier, and Mrs. Marchmill, having despatched the children to their outdoor amusements on the sands, settled herself in more completely, examining this and that article, and testing the reflecting powers of the mirror in the wardrobe door.

In the small back sitting-room, which had been the young bachelor's, she found furniture of a more personal nature than in the rest. Shabby books, of correct rather than rare editions, were piled up in a queerly reserved manner in corners, as if the previous occupant had not conceived the possibility that any incoming person of the season's bringing could care to look inside them. The landlady hovered on the threshold to rectify anything that Mrs. Marchmill might not find to her satisfaction.

' I'll make this my own little room,' said the latter, ' because the books are here. By the way, the person who has left seems to have a good many. He won't mind my reading some of them, Mrs. Hooper, I hope ? '

' O dear no, ma'am. Yes, he has a good many. You see, he is in the literary line himself somewhat. He is a poet—yes, really a poet—and he has a little income of his own, which is enough to write verses on, but not enough for cutting a figure, even if he cared to.'

' A poet ! Oh, I did not know that.'

Mrs. Marchmill opened one of the books, and saw the

owner's name written on the title-page. 'Dear me!' she continued; 'I know his name very well—Robert Trewe —of course I do; and his writings! And it is *his* rooms we have taken, and *him* we have turned out of his home?'

Ella Marchmill, sitting down alone a few minutes later, thought with interested surprise of Robert Trewe. Her own latter history will best explain that interest. Herself the only daughter of a struggling man of letters, she had during the last year or two taken to writing poems, in an endeavour to find a congenial channel in which to let flow her painfully embayed emotions, whose former limpidity and sparkle seemed departing in the stagnation caused by the routine of a practical household and the gloom of bearing children to a commonplace father. These poems, subscribed with a masculine pseudonym, had appeared in various obscure magazines, and in two cases in rather prominent ones. In the second of the latter the page which bore her effusion at the bottom, in smallish print, bore at the top, in large print, a few verses on the same subject by this very man, Robert Trewe. Both of them had, in fact, been struck by a tragic incident reported in the daily papers, and had used it simultaneously as an inspiration, the editor remarking in a note upon the coincidence, and that the excellence of both poems prompted him to give them together.

After that event Ella, otherwise 'John Ivy,' had watched with much attention the appearance anywhere in print of verse bearing the signature of Robert Trewe, who, with a man's unsusceptibility on the question of sex, had never once thought of passing himself off as a woman. To be sure, Mrs. Marchmill had satisfied herself with a sort of reason for doing the contrary in her case; since nobody might believe in her inspiration if they found that the sentiments came from a pushing tradesman's wife, from the mother of three children by a matter-of-fact small-arms manufacturer.

Trewe's verse contrasted with that of the rank and file of recent minor poets in being impassioned rather than ingenious, luxuriant rather than finished. Neither *symboliste* nor *décadent*, he was a pessimist in so far as that character applies to a man who looks at the worst contingencies as well as the best in the human condition. Being little attracted by excellences of form and rhythm apart from content, he sometimes, when feeling outran his artistic speed, perpetrated sonnets in the loosely rhymed Elizabethan fashion, which every right-minded reviewer said he ought not to have done.

With sad and hopeless envy Ella Marchmill had often and often scanned the rival poet's work, so much stronger as it always was than her own feeble lines. She had imitated him, and her inability to touch his level would send her into fits of despondency. Months passed away thus, till she observed from the publishers' list that Trewe had collected his fugitive pieces into a volume, which was duly issued, and was much or little praised according to chance, and had a sale quite sufficient to pay for the printing.

This step onward had suggested to ' John Ivy ' the idea of collecting her pieces also, or at any rate of making up a book of her rhymes by adding many in manuscript to the few that had seen the light, for she had been able to get no great number into print. A ruinous charge was made for costs of publication; a few reviews noticed her poor little volume ; but nobody talked of it, nobody bought it, and it fell dead in a fortnight—if it had ever been alive.

The author's thoughts were diverted to another groove just then by the discovery that she was going to have a third child, and the collapse of her poetical venture had perhaps less effect upon her mind than it might have done if she had been domestically unoccupied. Her husband had paid the publisher's bill with the doctor's, and there it all had ended for the time. But, though less than a poet of her century, Ella was more than a mere multiplier of her kind, and latterly she had begun to feel the old afflatus once more. And now by an odd conjunction she found herself in the rooms of Robert Trewe.

She thoughtfully rose from her chair and searched the apartment with the interest of a fellow-tradesman. Yes, the volume of his own verse was among the rest. Though

quite familiar with its contents, she read it here as if it
spoke aloud to her, then called up Mrs. Hooper, the landlady, for some trivial service, and inquired again about the
young man.

'Well, I'm sure you'd be interested in him, ma'am, if
you could see him, only he's so shy that I don't suppose
you will.' Mrs. Hooper seemed nothing loth to minister
to her tenant's curiosity about her predecessor. 'Lived
here long? Yes, nearly two years. He keeps on his rooms
even when he's not here : the soft air of this place suits
his chest, and he likes to be able to come back at any
time. He is mostly writing or reading, and doesn't see
many people, though, for the matter of that, he is such a
good, kind young fellow that folks would only be too glad
to be friendly with him if they knew him. You don't meet
kind-hearted people every day.'

'Ah, he's kind-hearted . . . and good.'

'Yes; he'll oblige me in anything if I ask him. "Mr.
Trewe," I say to him sometimes, "you are rather out of
spirits." "Well, I am, Mrs. Hooper," he'll say, "though
I don't know how you should find it out." "Why not
take a little change?" I ask. Then in a day or two he'll
say that he will take a trip to Paris, or Norway, or somewhere; and I assure you he comes back all the better for it.'

'Ah, indeed! His is a sensitive nature, no doubt.'

'Yes. Still he's odd in some things. Once when he
had finished a poem of his composition late at night he
walked up and down the room rehearsing it ; and the floors
being so thin—jerry-built houses, you know, though I
say it myself—he kept me awake up above him till I
wished him further. . . . But we get on very well.'

This was but the beginning of a series of conversations
about the rising poet as the days went on. On one of
these occasions Mrs. Hooper drew Ella's attention to what
she had not noticed before : minute scribblings in pencil
on the wall-paper behind the curtains at the head of the
bed.

'O! let me look,' said Mrs. Marchmill, unable to conceal
a rush of tender curiosity as she bent her pretty face close
to the wall.

' These,' said Mrs. Hooper, with the manner of a woman
who knew things, ' are the very beginnings and first thoughts
of his verses. He has tried to rub most of them out, but
you can read them still. My belief is that he wakes up
in the night, you know, with some rhyme in his head,
and jots it down there on the wall lest he should forget it
by the morning. Some of these very lines you see here I
have seen afterwards in print in the magazines. Some
are newer ; indeed, I have not seen that one before. It
must have been done only a few days ago.'

' O yes ! . . .'

Ella Marchmill flushed without knowing why, and
suddenly wished her companion would go away, now that
the information was imparted. An indescribable consciousness of personal interest rather than literary made
her anxious to read the inscription alone ; and she accordingly waited till she could do so, with a sense that a great
store of emotion would be enjoyed in the act.

Perhaps because the sea was choppy outside the Island,
Ella's husband found it much pleasanter to go sailing and
steaming about without his wife, who was a bad sailor,
than with her. He did not disdain to go thus alone on
board the steamboats of the cheap-trippers, where there
was dancing by moonlight, and where the couples would
come suddenly down with a lurch into each other's arms ;
for, as he blandly told her, the company was too mixed
for him to take her amid such scenes. Thus, while this
thriving manufacturer got a great deal of change and sea-
air out of his sojourn here, the life, external at least, of
Ella was monotonous enough, and mainly consisted in
passing a certain number of hours each day in bathing and
walking up and down a stretch of shore. But the poetic
impulse having again waxed strong, she was possessed by
an inner flame which left her hardly conscious of what was
proceeding around her.

She had read till she knew by heart Trewe's last little
volume of verses, and spent a great deal of time in vainly
attempting to rival some of them, till, in her failure, she
burst into tears. The personal element in the magnetic
attraction exercised by this circumambient, unapproach-

able master of hers was so much stronger than the intellectual and abstract that she could not understand it. To be sure, she was surrounded noon and night by his customary environment, which literally whispered of him to her at every moment ; but he was a man she had never seen, and that all that moved her was the instinct to specialize a waiting emotion on the first fit thing that came to hand did not, of course, suggest itself to Ella.

In the natural way of passion under the too practical conditions which civilization has devised for its fruition, her husband's love for her had not survived, except in the form of fitful friendship, any more than, or even so much as, her own for him; and, being a woman of very living ardours, that required sustenance of some sort, they were beginning to feed on this chancing material, which was, indeed, of a quality far better than chance usually offers.

One day the children had been playing hide-and-seek in a closet, whence, in their excitement, they pulled out some clothing. Mrs. Hooper explained that it belonged to Mr. Trewe, and hung it up in the closet again. Possessed of her fantasy, Ella went later in the afternoon, when nobody was in that part of the house, opened the closet, unhitched one of the articles, a mackintosh, and put it on, with the waterproof cap belonging to it.

'The mantle of Elijah!' she said. 'Would it might inspire me to rival him, glorious genius that he is!'

Her eyes always grew wet when she thought like that, and she turned to look at herself in the glass. *His* heart had beat inside that coat, and *his* brain had worked under that hat at levels of thought she would never reach. The consciousness of her weakness beside him made her feel quite sick. Before she had got the things off her the door opened, and her husband entered the room.

'What the devil——'

She blushed, and removed them.

'I found them in the closet here,' she said, 'and put them on in a freak. What have I else to do? You are always away!'

'Always away? Well . . .'

That evening she had a further talk with the landlady,

who might herself have nourished a half-tender regard
for the poet, so ready was she to discourse ardently about
him.

'You are interested in Mr. Trewe, I know, ma'am,' she
said ; 'and he has just sent to say that he is going to call
to-morrow afternoon to look up some books of his that
he wants, if I'll be in, and he may select them from your
room ? '

'O yes ! '

'You could very well meet Mr. Trewe then, if you'd
like to be in the way ! '

She promised with secret delight, and went to bed
musing of him.

Next morning her husband observed : 'I've been thinking of what you said, Ell : that I have gone about a good
deal and left you without much to amuse you. Perhaps
it's true. To-day, as there's not much sea, I'll take you
with me on board the yacht.'

For the first time in her experience of such an offer
Ella was not glad. But she accepted it for the moment.
The time for setting out drew near, and she went to get
ready. She stood reflecting. The longing to see the poet
she was now distinctly in love with overpowered all other
considerations.

'I don't want to go,' she said to herself. 'I can't bear
to be away ! And I won't go.'

She told her husband that she had changed her mind
about wishing to sail. He was indifferent, and went his
way.

For the rest of the day the house was quiet, the children
having gone out upon the sands. The blinds waved in
the sunshine to the soft, steady stroke of the sea beyond
the wall ; and the notes of the Green Silesian band, a troop
of foreign gentlemen hired for the season, had drawn almost
all the residents and promenaders away from the vicinity
of Coburg House. A knock was audible at the door.

Mrs. Marchmill did not hear any servant go to answer
it, and she became impatient. The books were in the
room where she sat ; but nobody came up. She rang the
bell.

'There is some person waiting at the door,' she said.

'O no, ma'am! He's gone long ago. I answered it,' the servant replied, and Mrs. Hooper came in herself.

'So disappointing!' she said. 'Mr. Trewe not coming after all!'

'But I heard him knock, I fancy!'

'No; that was somebody inquiring for lodgings who came to the wrong house. I forgot to tell you that Mr. Trewe sent a note just before lunch to say I needn't get any tea for him, as he should not require the books, and wouldn't come to select them.'

Ella was miserable, and for a long time could not even re-read his mournful ballad on 'Severed Lives,' so aching was her erratic little heart, and so tearful her eyes. When the children came in with wet stockings, and ran up to her to tell her of their adventures, she could not feel that she cared about them half as much as usual.

. . . .

'Mrs. Hooper, have you a photograph of—the gentleman who lived here?' She was getting to be curiously shy in mentioning his name.

'Why, yes. It's in the ornamental frame on the mantel-piece in your own bedroom, ma'am.'

'No; the Royal Duke and Duchess are in that.'

'Yes, so they are; but he's behind them. He belongs rightly to that frame, which I bought on purpose; but as he went away he said : " Cover me up from those strangers that are coming, for God's sake. I don't want them staring at me, and I am sure they won't want me staring at them." So I slipped in the Duke and Duchess temporarily in front of him, as they had no frame, and Royalties are more suitable for letting furnished than a private young man. If you take 'em out you'll see him under. Lord, ma'am, he wouldn't mind if he knew it! He didn't think the next tenant would be such an attractive lady as you, or he wouldn't have thought of hiding himself, perhaps.'

'Is he handsome?' she asked timidly.

'I call him so. Some, perhaps, wouldn't.'

'Should I?' she asked, with eagerness.

' I think you would, though some would say he's more
striking than handsome ; a large-eyed, thoughtful fellow,
you know, with a very electric flash in his eye when he
looks round quickly, such as you'd expect a poet to be who
doesn't get his living by it.'

' How old is he ? '

' Several years older than yourself, ma'am ; about thirty-
one or two, I think.'

Ella was, as a matter of fact, a few months over thirty
herself ; but she did not look nearly so much. Though
so immature in nature, she was entering on that tract of
life in which emotional women begin to suspect that last
love may be stronger than first love ; and she would soon,
alas! enter on the still more melancholy tract when at
least the vainer ones of her sex shrink from receiving a
male visitor otherwise than with their backs to the window
or the blinds half down. She reflected on Mrs. Hooper's
remark, and said no more about age.

Just then a telegram was brought up. It came from
her husband, who had gone down the Channel as far as
Budmouth with his friends in the yacht, and would not be
able to get back till next day.

After her light dinner Ella idled about the shore with the
children till dusk, thinking of the yet uncovered photograph
in her room, with a serene sense of something ecstatic to
come. For, with the subtle luxuriousness of fancy in
which this young woman was an adept, on learning that
her husband was to be absent that night she had refrained
from incontinently rushing upstairs and opening the pic-
ture-frame, preferring to reserve the inspection till she
could be alone, and a more romantic tinge be imparted
to the occasion by silence, candles, solemn sea and stars
outside, than was afforded by the garish afternoon sunlight.

The children had been sent to bed, and Ella soon followed, though it was not yet ten o'clock. To gratify her
passionate curiosity she now made her preparations, first
getting rid of superfluous garments and putting on her
dressing-gown, then arranging a chair in front of the table
and reading several pages of Trewe's tenderest utter-

ances. Next she fetched the portrait-frame to the light, opened the back, took out the likeness, and set it up before her.

It was a striking countenance to look upon. The poet wore a luxuriant black moustache and imperial, and a slouched hat which shaded the forehead. The large dark eyes described by the landlady showed an unlimited capacity for misery ; they looked out from beneath well-shaped brows as if they were reading the universe in the microcosm of the confronter's face, and were not altogether overjoyed at what the spectacle portended.

Ella murmured in her lowest, richest, tenderest tone : ' And it's *you* who've so cruelly eclipsed me these many times ! '

As she gazed long at the portrait she fell into thought, till her eyes filled with tears, and she touched the cardboard with her lips. Then she laughed with a nervous lightness, and wiped her eyes.

She thought how wicked she was, a woman having a husband and three children, to let her mind stray to a stranger in this unconscionable manner. No, he was not a stranger ! She knew his thoughts and feelings as well as she knew her own ; they were, in fact, the self-same thoughts and feelings as hers, which her husband distinctly lacked ; perhaps luckily for himself, considering that he had to provide for family expenses.

' He's nearer my real self, he's more intimate with the real me than Will is, after all, even though I've never seen him,' she said.

She laid his book and picture on the table at the bedside, and when she was reclining on the pillow she re-read those of Robert Trewe's verses which she had marked from time to time as most touching and true. Putting these aside she set up the photograph on its edge upon the coverlet, and contemplated it as she lay. Then she scanned again by the light of the candle the half-obliterated pencillings on the wall-paper beside her head. There they were—phrases, couplets, *bouts-rimés*, beginnings and middles of lines, ideas in the rough, like Shelley's scraps, and the least of them so intense, so sweet, so palpitating, that it seemed as if his very breath, warm and loving, fanned her cheeks from those walls, walls that had surrounded his head times and times as they surrounded her own now. He must often have put up his hand so— with the pencil in it. Yes, the writing was sideways, as it would be if executed by one who extended his arm thus.

These inscribed shapes of the poet's world,

> 'Forms more real than living man,
> Nurslings of immortality,'

were, no doubt, the thoughts and spirit-strivings which had come to him in the dead of night, when he could let himself go and have no fear of the frost of criticism. No doubt they had often been written up hastily by the light of the moon, the rays of the lamp, in the blue-grey dawn, in full daylight perhaps never. And now her hair was dragging where his arm had lain when he secured the fugitive fancies; she was sleeping on a poet's lips, immersed in the very essence of him, permeated by his spirit as by an ether.

While she was dreaming the minutes away thus, a footstep came upon the stairs, and in a moment she heard her husband's heavy step on the landing immediately without.

'Ell, where are you?'

What possessed her she could not have described, but, with an instinctive objection to let her husband know what she had been doing, she slipped the photograph under the pillow just as he flung open the door with the air of a man who had dined not badly.

'O, I beg pardon,' said William Marchmill. 'Have you a headache? I am afraid I have disturbed you.'

'No, I've not got a headache,' said she. 'How is it you've come?'

'Well, we found we could get back in very good time after all, and I didn't want to make another day of it, because of going somewhere else to-morrow.'

'Shall I come down again?'

'O no. I'm as tired as a dog. I've had a good feed,

and I shall turn in straight off. I want to get out at six o'clock to-morrow if I can. . . . I shan't disturb you by my getting up; it will be long before you are awake.' And he came forward into the room.

While her eyes followed his movements, Ella softly pushed the photograph further out of sight.

'Sure you're not ill?' he asked, bending over her.

'No, only wicked!'

'Never mind that.' And he stooped and kissed her. 'I wanted to be with you to-night.'

Next morning Marchmill was called at six o'clock; and in waking and yawning she heard him muttering to himself: 'What the deuce is this that's been crackling under me so?' Imagining her asleep he searched round him and withdrew something. Through her half-opened eyes she perceived it to be Mr. Trewe.

'Well, I'm damned!' her husband exclaimed.

'What, dear?' said she.

'O, you are awake? Ha! ha!'

'What *do* you mean?'

'Some bloke's photograph—a friend of our landlady's, I suppose. I wonder how it came here; whisked off the mantelpiece by accident perhaps when they were making the bed.'

'I was looking at it yesterday, and it must have dropped in then.'

'O, he's a friend of yours? Bless his picturesque heart!'

Ella's loyalty to the object of her admiration could not endure to hear him ridiculed. 'He's a clever man!' she said, with a tremor in her gentle voice which she herself felt to be absurdly uncalled for. He is a rising poet—the gentleman who occupied two of these rooms before we came, though I've never seen him.'

'How do you know, if you've never seen him?'

'Mrs. Hooper told me when she showed me the photograph.'

'O, well, I must up and be off. I shall be home rather early. Sorry I can't take you to-day, dear. Mind the children don't go getting drowned.'

That day Mrs. Marchmill inquired if Mr. Trewe were likely to call at any other time.

' Yes,' said Mrs. Hooper. ' He's coming this day week to stay with a friend near here till you leave. He'll be sure to call.'

Marchmill did return quite early in the afternoon ; and, opening some letters which had arrived in his absence, declared suddenly that he and his family would have to leave a week earlier than they had expected to do—in short, in three days.

' Surely we can stay a week longer ? ' she pleaded. ' I like it here.'

' I don't. It is getting rather slow.'

' Then you might leave me and the children ! '

' How perverse you are, Ell ! What's the use ? And have to come to fetch you ! No : we'll all return together ; and we'll make out our time in North Wales or Brighton a little later on. Besides, you've three days longer yet.'

It seemed to be her doom not to meet the man for whose rival talent she had a despairing admiration, and to whose person she was now absolutely attached. Yet she determined to make a last effort : and having gathered from her landlady that Trewe was living in a lonely spot not far from the fashionable town on the Island opposite, she crossed over in the packet from the neighbouring pier the following afternoon.

What a useless journey it was ! Ella knew but vaguely where the house stood, and when she fancied she had found it, and ventured to inquire of a pedestrian if he lived there, the answer returned by the man was that he did not know. And if he did live there, how could she call upon him ? Some women might have the assurance to do it, but she had not. How crazy he would think her. She might have asked him to call upon her, perhaps ; but she had not the courage for that, either. She lingered mournfully about the picturesque seaside eminence till it was time to return to the town and enter the steamer for recrossing, reaching home for dinner without having been greatly missed.

At the last moment, unexpectedly enough, her husband said that he should have no objection to letting her and the children stay on till the end of the week, since she wished to do so, if she felt herself able to get home without him. She concealed the pleasure this extension of time gave her ; and Marchmill went off the next morning alone.

But the week passed, and Trewe did not call.

On Saturday morning the remaining members of the Marchmill family departed from the place which had been productive of so much fervour in her. The dreary, dreary train ; the sun shining in moted beams upon the hot cushions ; the dusty permanent way ; the mean rows of wire—these things were her accompaniment : while out of the window the deep blue sea-levels disappeared from her gaze, and with them her poet's home. Heavy-hearted, she tried to read, and wept instead.

Mr. Marchmill was in a thriving way of business, and he and his family lived in a large new house, which stood in rather extensive grounds a few miles outside the midland city wherein he carried on his trade. Ella's life was lonely here, as the suburban life is apt to be, particularly at certain seasons ; and she had ample time to indulge her taste for lyric and elegiac composition. She had hardly got back when she encountered a piece by Robert Trewe in the new number of her favourite magazine, which must have been written almost immediately before her visit to Solentsea, for it contained the very couplet she had seen pencilled on the wall-paper by the bed, and Mrs. Hooper had declared to be recent. Ella could resist no longer, but seizing a pen impulsively, wrote to him as a brother-poet, using the name of John Ivy, congratulating him in her letter on his triumphant executions in metre and rhythm of thoughts that moved his soul, as compared with her own browbeaten efforts in the same pathetic trade.

To this address there came a response in a few days, little as she had dared to hope for it—a civil and brief note, in which the young poet stated that, though he was not well acquainted with Mr. Ivy's verse, he recalled the name as being one he had seen attached to some very promising pieces ; that he was glad to gain Mr. Ivy's acquaintance by letter, and should certainly look with much interest for his productions in the future.

There must have been something juvenile or timid in her own epistle, as one ostensibly coming from a man, she declared to herself ; for Trewe quite adopted the tone of an elder and superior in this reply. But what did it matter ? He had replied ; he had written to her with his own hand from that very room she knew so well, for he was now back again in his quarters.

The correspondence thus begun was continued for two months or more, Ella Marchmill sending him from time to time some that she considered to be the best of her pieces, which he very kindly accepted, though he did not say he sedulously read them, nor did he send her any of his own in return. Ella would have been more hurt at this than she was if she had not known that Trewe laboured under the impression that she was one of his own sex.

Yet the situation was unsatisfactory. A flattering little voice told her that, were he only to see her, matters would be otherwise. No doubt she would have helped on this by making a frank confession of womanhood, to begin with, if something had not happened, to her delight, to render it unnecessary. A friend of her husband's, the editor of the most important newspaper in their city and county, who was dining with them one day, observed during their conversation about the poet that his (the editor's) brother the landscape-painter was a friend of Mr. Trewe's, and that the two men were at that very moment in Wales together.

Ella was slightly acquainted with the editor's brother. The next morning down she sat and wrote, inviting him to stay at her house for a short time on his way back, and requesting him to bring with him, if practicable, his companion Mr. Trewe, whose acquaintance she was anxious to make. The answer arrived after some few days. Her correspondent and his friend Trewe would have much satisfaction in accepting her invitation on their way southward, which would be on such and such a day in the following week.

Ella was blithe and buoyant. Her scheme had succeeded ; her beloved though as yet unseen one was coming. ' Behold, he standeth behind our wall ; he looked forth at the windows, showing himself through the lattice,' she thought ecstatically. ' And, lo, the winter is past, the rain is over and gone, the flowers appear on the earth, the time of the singing of birds is come, and the voice of the turtle is heard in our land.'

But it was necessary to consider the details of lodging and feeding him. This she did most solicitously, and awaited the pregnant day and hour.

It was about five in the afternoon when she heard a ring at the door and the editor's brother's voice in the hall. Poetess as she was, or as she thought herself, she had not been too sublime that day to dress with infinite trouble in a fashionable robe of rich material, having a faint resemblance to the *chiton* of the Greeks, a style just then in vogue among ladies of an artistic and romantic turn, which had been obtained by Ella of her Bond Street dressmaker when she was last in London. Her visitor entered the drawing-room. She looked towards his rear ; nobody else came through the door. Where, in the name of the God of Love, was Robert Trewe ?

' O, I'm sorry,' said the painter, after their introductory words had been spoken. ' Trewe is a curious fellow, you know, Mrs. Marchmill. He said he'd come ; then he said he couldn't. He's rather dusty. We've been doing a few miles with knapsacks, you know ; and he wanted to get on home.'

' He—he's not coming ? '

' He's not ; and he asked me to make his apologies.'

' When did you p-p-part from him ? ' she asked, her nether lip starting off quivering so much that it was like a *tremolo*-stop opened in her speech. She longed to run away from this dreadful bore and cry her eyes out.

' Just now, in the turnpike road yonder there.'

' What ! he has actually gone past my gates ? '

' Yes. When we got to them—handsome gates they are, too, the finest bit of modern wrought-iron work I have seen—when we came to them we stopped, talking there a little while, and then he wished me good-bye and went on. The truth is, he's a little bit depressed just now, and doesn't want to see anybody. He's a very good fel-

low, and a warm friend, but a little uncertain and gloomy
sometimes ; he thinks too much of things. His poetry is
rather too erotic and passionate, you know, for some
tastes ; and he has just come in for a terrible slating from
the —— *Review* that was published yesterday ; he saw a
copy of it at the station by accident. Perhaps you've
read it ? '

' No.'

' So much the better. O, it is not worth thinking of ;
just one of those articles written to order, to please the
narrow-minded set of subscribers upon whom the circula-
tion depends. But he's upset by it. He says it is the
misrepresentation that hurts him so ; that, though he
can stand a fair attack, he can't stand lies that he's power-
less to refute and stop from spreading. That's just Trewe's
weak point. He lives so much by himself that these things
affect him much more than they would if he were in the
bustle of fashionable or commercial life. So he wouldn't
come here, making the excuse that it all looked so new and
monied—if you'll pardon——'

' But—he must have known—there was sympathy here !
Has he never said anything about getting letters from this
address ? '

' Yes, yes, he has, from John Ivy—perhaps a relative
of yours, he thought, visiting here at the time ? '

' Did he—like Ivy, did he say ? '

' Well, I don't know that he took any great interest in
Ivy.'

' Or in his poems ? '

' Or in his poems—so far as I know, that is.'

Robert Trewe took no interest in her house, in her
poems, or in their writer. As soon as she could get away
she went into the nursery and tried to let off her emotion
by unnecessarily kissing the children, till she had a sudden
sense of disgust at being reminded how plain-looking they
were, like their father.

The obtuse and single-minded landscape-painter never
once perceived from her conversation that it was only
Trewe she wanted, and not himself. He made the best
of his visit, seeming to enjoy the society of Ella's husband,

who also took a great fancy to him, and showed him everywhere about the neighbourhood, neither of them noticing
Ella's mood.

The painter had been gone only a day or two when,
while sitting upstairs alone one morning, she glanced over
the London paper just arrived, and read the following
paragraph :—

'SUICIDE OF A POET

'Mr. Robert Trewe, who has been favourably known for some
years as one of our rising lyrists, committed suicide at his lodgings at
Solentsea on Saturday evening last by shooting himself in the right
temple with a revolver. Readers hardly need to be reminded that
Mr. Trewe has recently attracted the attention of a much wider
public than had hitherto known him, by his new volume of verse,
mostly of an impassioned kind, entitled "Lyrics to a Woman Unknown," which has been already favourably noticed in these pages
for the extraordinary gamut of feeling it traverses, and which has been
made the subject of a severe, if not ferocious, criticism in the ——
Review. It is supposed, though not certainly known, that the
article may have partially conduced to the sad act, as a copy of the
review in question was found on his writing-table ; and he has
been observed to be in a somewhat depressed state of mind since the
critique appeared.'

Then came the report of the inquest, at which the following letter was read, it having been addressed to a
friend at a distance :—

'DEAR ——,—Before these lines reach your hands I shall be
delivered from the inconveniences of seeing, hearing, and knowing
more of the things around me. I will not trouble you by giving my
reasons for the step I have taken, though I can assure you they were
sound and logical. Perhaps had I been blessed with a mother, or a
sister, or a female friend of another sort tenderly devoted to me, I
might have thought it worth while to continue my present existence.
I have long dreamt of such an unattainable creature, as you know;
and she, this undiscoverable, elusive one, inspired my last volume ;
the imaginary woman alone, for, in spite of what has been said in
some quarters, there is no real woman behind the title. She has
continued to the last unrevealed, unmet, unwon. I think it desirable to mention this in order that no blame may attach to any real
woman as having been the cause of my decease by cruel or cavalier
treatment of me. Tell my landlady that I am sorry to have caused
her this unpleasantness ; but my occupancy of the rooms will soon
be forgotten. There are ample funds in my name at the bank to
pay all expenses.

R. TREWE.'

Ella sat for a while as if stunned, then rushed into the
adjoining chamber and flung herself upon her face on the bed.

Her grief and distraction shook her to pieces ; and
she lay in this frenzy of sorrow for more than an hour.
Broken words came every now and then from her quivering
lips : ' O, if he had only known of me—known of me—
me ! . . . O, if I had only once met him—only once ; and
put my hand upon his hot forehead—kissed him—let him
know how I loved him—that I would have suffered shame
and scorn, would have lived and died, for him ! Perhaps
it would have saved his dear life ! . . . But no—it was
not allowed ! God is a jealous God ; and that happiness
was not for him and me ! '

All possibilities were over ; the meeting was stultified.
Yet it was almost visible to her in her fantasy even now,
though it could never be substantiated—

> ' The hour which might have been, yet might not be,
> Which man's and woman's heart conceived and bore,
> Yet whereof life was barren.'

. . . .

She wrote to the landlady at Solentsea in the third
person, in as subdued a style as she could command,
enclosing a postal order for a sovereign, and informing
Mrs. Hooper that Mrs. Marchmill had seen in the papers
the sad account of the poet's death, and having been, as
Mrs. Hooper was aware, much interested in Mr. Trewe during her stay at Coburg House, she would be obliged if Mrs.
Hooper could obtain a small portion of his hair before his
coffin was closed down, and send it her as a memorial
of him, as also the photograph that was in the frame.

By the return-post a letter arrived containing what had
been requested. Ella wept over the portrait and secured
it in her private drawer ; the lock of hair she tied with
white ribbon and put in her bosom, whence she drew it
and kissed it every now and then in some unobserved
nook.

' What's the matter ? ' said her husband, looking up
from his newspaper on one of these occaisons. ' Crying
over something ? A lock of hair ? Whose is it ? '

' He's dead ! ' she murmured.

' Who ? '

' I don't want to tell you, Will, just now, unless you insist ! ' she said, a sob hanging heavy in her voice.

' O, all right.'

' Do you mind my refusing ?   I will tell you some day.'

' It doesn't matter in the least, of course.'

He walked away whistling a few bars of no tune in particular ; and when he had got down to his factory in the city the subject came into Marchmill's head again.

He, too, was aware that a suicide had taken place recently at the house they had occupied at Solentsea. Having seen the volume of poems in his wife's hand of late, and heard fragments of the landlady's conversation about Trewe when they were her tenants, he all at once said to himself, ' Why of course it's he ! . . . How the devil did she get to know him ? What sly animals women are ! '

Then he placidly dismissed the matter, and went on with his daily affairs.   By this time Ella at home had come to a determination.   Mrs. Hooper, in sending the hair and photograph, had informed her of the day of the funeral ; and as the morning and noon wore on an overpowering wish to know where they were laying him took possession of the sympathetic woman.   Caring very little now what her husband or anyone else might think of her eccentricities, she wrote Marchmill a brief note, stating that she was called away for the afternoon and evening, but would return on the following morning.   This she left on his desk, and having given the same information to the servants, went out of the house on foot.

When Mr. Marchmill reached home early in the afternoon the servants looked anxious.   The nurse took him privately aside, and hinted that her mistress's sadness during the past few days had been such that she feared she had gone out to drown herself.   Marchmill reflected. Upon the whole he thought that she had not done that. Without saying whither he was bound he also started off, telling them not to sit up for him.   He drove to the railway-station, and took a ticket for Solentsea.

It was dark when he reached the place, though he had come by a fast train, and he knew that if his wife had preceded him thither it could only have been by a slower train, arriving not a great while before his own. The season at Solentsea was now past : the parade was gloomy, and the flys were few and cheap. He asked the way to the Cemetery, and soon reached it. The gate was locked, but the keeper let him in, declaring, however, that there was nobody within the precincts. Although it was not late, the autumnal darkness had now become intense ; and he found some difficulty in keeping to the serpentine path which led to the quarter where, as the man had told him, the one or two interments for the day had taken place. He stepped upon the grass, and, stumbling over some pegs, stooped now and then to discern if possible a figure against the sky. He could see none ; but lighting on a spot where the soil was trodden, beheld a crouching object beside a newly-made grave. She heard him, and sprang up.

' Ell, how silly this is ! ' he said indignantly. ' Running away from home—I never heard such a thing ! Of course I am not jealous of this unfortunate man ; but it is too ridiculous that you, a married woman with three children and a fourth coming, should go losing your head like this over a dead lover ! . . . Do you know you were locked in ? You might not have been able to get out all night.'

She did not answer.

' I hope it didn't go far between you and him, for your own sake.'

' Don't insult me, Will.'

' Mind, I won't have any more of this sort of thing ; do you hear ? '

' Very well,' she said.

He drew her arm within his own, and conducted her out of the Cemetery. It was impossible to get back that night ; and not wishing to be recognized in their present sorry condition he took her to a miserable little coffee-house close to the station, whence they departed early in the morning, travelling almost without speaking, under the sense that it was one of those dreary situations occurring in married life which words could not mend, and reaching their own door at noon.

The months passed, and neither of the twain ever ventured to start a conversation upon this episode. Ella seemed to be only too frequently in a sad and listless mood, which might almost have been called pining. The time was approaching when she would have to undergo the stress of childbirth for a fourth time, and that apparently did not tend to raise her spirits.

' I don't think I shall get over it this time ! ' she said one day.

' Pooh ! what childish foreboding ! Why shouldn't it be as well now as ever ? '

She shook her head. ' I feel almost sure I am going to die ; and I should be glad, if it were not for Nelly, and Frank, and Tiny.'

' And me ! '

' You'll soon find somebody to fill my place,' she murmured, with a sad smile. ' And you'll have a perfect right to ; I assure you of that.'

' Ell, you are not thinking still about that—poetical friend of yours ? '

She neither admitted nor denied the charge. ' I am not going to get over my illness this time,' she reiterated. ' Something tells me I shan't.'

This view of things was rather a bad beginning, as it usually is ; and, in fact, six weeks later, in the month of May, she was lying in her room, pulseless and bloodless, with hardly strength enough left to follow up one feeble breath with another, the infant for whose unnecessary life she was slowly parting with her own being fat and well. Just before her death she spoke to Marchmill softly :—

' Will, I want to confess to you the entire circumstances of that—about you know what—that time we visited Solentsea. I can't tell what possessed me—how I could forget you so, my husband ! But I had got into a morbid state : I thought you had been unkind ; that you had neglected me ; that you weren't up to my intellectual level, while he was, and far above it. I wanted a fuller appreciator, perhaps, rather than another lover——'

She could get no further then for very exhaustion ; and she went off in sudden collapse a few hours later, without having said anything more to her husband on the subject of her love for the poet. William Marchmill, in truth, like most husbands of several years' standing, was little disturbed by retrospective jealousies, and had not shown the least anxiety to press her for confessions concerning a man dead and gone beyond any power of inconveniencing him more.

But when she had been buried a couple of years it chanced one day that, in turning over some forgotten papers that he wished to destroy before his second wife entered the house, he lighted on a lock of hair in an envelope, with the photograph of the deceased poet, a date being written on the back in his late wife's hand. It was that of the time they spent at Solentsea.

Marchmill looked long and musingly at the hair and portrait, for something struck him. Fetching the little boy who had been the death of his mother, now a noisy toddler, he took him on his knee, held the lock of hair against the child's head, and set up the photograph on the table behind, so that he could closely compare the features each countenance presented. By a known but inexplicable trick of Nature there were undoubtedly strong traces of resemblance to the man Ella had never seen ; the dreamy and peculiar expression of the poet's face sat, as the transmitted idea, upon the child's, and the hair was of the same hue.

' I'm damned if I didn't think so ! ' murmured Marchmill. ' Then she *did* play me false with that fellow at the lodgings ! Let me see : the dates—the second week in August . . . the third week in May. . . . Yes . . . yes. . . . Get away, you poor little brat ! You are nothing to me ! '

1893.

THE SON'S VETO

THE SON'S VETO

I

To the eyes of a man viewing it from behind, the nut-brown hair was a wonder and a mystery. Under the black beaver hat surmounted by its tuft of black feathers, the long locks, braided and twisted and coiled like the rushes of a basket, composed a rare, if somewhat barbaric, example of ingenious art. One could understand such weavings and coilings being wrought to last intact for a year, or even a calendar month ; but that they should be all demolished regularly at bedtime, after a single day of permanence, seemed a reckless waste of successful fabrication.

And she had done it all herself, poor thing. She had no maid, and it was almost the only accomplishment she could boast of. Hence the unstinted pains.

She was a young invalid lady—not so very much of an invalid—sitting in a wheeled chair, which had been pulled up in the front part of a green enclosure, close to a bandstand where a concert was going on, during a warm June afternoon. It had place in one of the minor parks or private gardens that are to be found in the suburbs of London, and was the effort of a local association to raise money for some charity. There are worlds within worlds in the great city, and though nobody outside the immediate district had ever heard of the charity, or the band, or the garden, the enclosure was filled with an interested audience sufficiently informed on all these.

As the strains proceeded many of the listeners observed the chaired lady, whose back hair, by reason of her prominent position, so challenged inspection. Her face was not easily discernible, but the aforesaid cunning tress-weavings, the white ear and poll, and the curve of a cheek which was neither flaccid nor sallow, were signals that led to the expectation of good beauty in front. Such expectations are not infrequently disappointed as soon as the disclosure comes; and in the present case, when the lady, by a turn of the head, at length revealed herself, she was not so handsome as the people behind her had supposed, and even hoped—they did not know why.

For one thing (alas ! the commonness of this complaint), she was less young than they had fancied her to be. Yet attractive her face unquestionably was, and not at all sickly. The revelation of its details came each time she turned to talk to a boy of twelve or thirteen who stood beside her, and the shape of whose hat and jacket implied that he belonged to a well-known public school. The immediate bystanders could hear that he called her ' Mother.'

When the end of the recital was reached, and the audience withdrew, many chose to find their way out by passing at her elbow. Almost all turned their heads to take a full and near look at the interesting woman, who remained stationary in the chair till the way should be clear enough for her to be wheeled out without obstruction. As if she expected their glances, and did not mind gratifying their curiosity, she met the eyes of several of her observers by lifting her own, showing these to be soft, brown, and affectionate orbs, a little plaintive in their regard.

She was conducted out of the gardens, and passed along the pavement till she disappeared from view, the schoolboy walking beside her. To inquiries made by some persons who watched her away, the answer came that she was the second wife of the incumbent of a neighbouring parish, and that she was lame. She was generally believed to be a woman with a story—an innocent one, but a story of some sort or other.

In conversing with her on their way home the boy who walked at her elbow said that he hoped his father had not missed them.

' He have been so comfortable these last few hours that I am sure he cannot have missed us,' she replied.

' *Has*, dear mother—not *have* ! ' exclaimed the public-school boy, with an impatient fastidiousness that was almost harsh. ' Surely you know that by this time ! '

His mother hastily adopted the correction, and did not resent his making it, or retaliate, as she might well have done, by bidding him to wipe that crumby mouth of his, whose condition had been caused by surreptitious attempts to eat a piece of cake without taking it out of the pocket wherein it lay concealed. After this the pretty woman and the boy went onward in silence.

That question of grammar bore upon her history, and she fell into reverie, of a somewhat sad kind to all appearance. It might have been assumed that she was wondering if she had done wisely in shaping her life as she had shaped it, to bring out such a result as this.

In a remote nook in North Wessex, forty miles from London, near the thriving county-town of Aldbrickham, there stood a pretty village with its church and parsonage, which she knew well enough, but her son had never seen. It was her native village, Gaymead, and the first event bearing upon her present situation had occurred at that place when she was only a girl of nineteen.

How well she remembered it, that first act in her little tragi-comedy, the death of her reverend husband's first wife. It happened on a spring evening, and she who now and for many years had filled that first wife's place was then parlour-maid in the parson's house.

When everything had been done that could be done, and the death was announced, she had gone out in the dusk to visit her parents, who were living in the same village, to tell them the sad news. As she opened the white swing-gate and looked towards the trees which rose westward, shutting out the pale light of the evening sky, she discerned, without much surprise, the figure of a man standing in the hedge, though she roguishly exclaimed as a matter of form, ' O, Sam, how you frightened me ! '

He was a young gardener of her acquaintance. She told him the particulars of the late event, and they stood silent, these two young people, in that elevated, calmly philosophic mind which is engendered when a tragedy has happened close at hand, and has not happened to the philosophers themselves. But it had its bearing upon their relations.

' And will you stay on now at the Vicarage, just the
same ? ' asked he.

She had hardly thought of that. ' O yes—I suppose ! '
she said. ' Everything will be just as usual, I imagine ? '

He walked beside her towards her mother's. Presently
his arm stole round her waist. She gently removed it ;
but he placed it there again, and she yielded the point.
' You see, dear Sophy, you don't know that you'll stay
on ; you may want a home, and I shall be ready to offer
one some day, though I may not be ready just yet.'

' Why, Sam, how can you be so fast ! I've never even said
I liked 'ee ; and it is all your own doing, coming after
me ! '

' Still, it is nonsense to say I am not to have a try at
you like the rest.' He stooped to kiss her a farewell, for
they had reached her mother's door.

' No, Sam ; you shan't ! ' she cried, putting her hand
over his mouth. ' You ought to be more serious on such a
night as this.' And she bade him adieu without allowing
him to kiss her or to come indoors.

The vicar just left a widower was at this time a man
about forty years of age, of good family, and childless.
He had led a secluded existence in this college living,
partly because there were no resident landowners ; and
his loss now intensified his habit of withdrawal from outward observation. He was seen still less than heretofore,
kept himself still less in time with the rhythm and racket
of the movements called progress in the world without.
For many months after his wife's decease the economy of
his household remained as before ; the cook, the housemaid, the parlour-maid, and the man out-of-doors performed their duties or left them undone, just as Nature
prompted them—the vicar knew not which. It was then
represented to him that his servants seemed to have nothing to do in his small family of one. He was struck with
the truth of this representation, and decided to cut down
his establishment. But he was forestalled by Sophy, the
parlour-maid, who said one evening that she wished to
leave him.

' And why ? ' said the parson.

' Sam Hobson has asked me to marry him, sir.'

' Well—do you want to marry ? '

' Not much. But it would be a home for me. And we have heard that one of us will have to leave.'

A day or two after she said : ' I don't want to leave just yet, sir, if you don't wish it. Sam and I have quarrelled.'

He looked up at her. He had hardly ever observed her before, though he had been frequently conscious of her soft presence in the room. What a kitten-like, flexuous, tender creature she was ! She was the only one of the servants with whom he came into immediate and continuous relation. What should he do if Sophy were gone ?

Sophy did not go, but one of the others did, and things went on quietly again.

When Mr. Twycott, the vicar, was ill, Sophy brought up his meals to him, and she had no sooner left the room one day than he heard a noise on the stairs. She had slipped down with the tray, and so twisted her foot that she could not stand. The village surgeon was called in ; the vicar got better, but Sophy was incapacitated for a long time ; and she was informed that she must never again walk much or engage in any occupation which required her to stand long on her feet. As soon as she was comparatively well she spoke to him alone. Since she was forbidden to walk and bustle about, and, indeed, could not do so, it became her duty to leave. She could very well work at something sitting down, and she had an aunt a seamstress.

The parson had been very greatly moved by what she had suffered on his account, and he exclaimed, ' No, Sophy ; lame or not lame, I cannot let you go. You must never leave me again ! '

He came close to her, and, though she could never exactly tell how it happened, she became conscious of his lips upon her cheek. He then asked her to marry him. Sophy did not exactly love him, but she had a respect for him which almost amounted to veneration. Even if she had wished to get away from him she hardly dared refuse a personage

so reverend and august in her eyes, and she assented forthwith to be his wife.

Thus it happened that one fine morning, when the doors
of the church were naturally open for ventilation, and the
singing birds fluttered in and alighted on the tie-beams of
the roof, there was a marriage-service at the communion-
rails, which hardly a soul knew of. The parson and a
neighbouring curate had entered at one door, and Sophy
at another, followed by two necessary persons, whereupon
in a short time there emerged a newly-made husband and
wife.

Mr. Twycott knew perfectly well that he had committed
social suicide by this step, despite Sophy's spotless character, and he had taken his measures accordingly. An
exchange of livings had been arranged with an acquaintance
who was incumbent of a church in the south of London,
and as soon as possible the couple removed thither, aban-
doning their pretty country home, with trees and shrubs
and glebe, for a narrow, dusty house in a long, straight
street, and their fine peal of bells for the wretchedest one-
tongued clangour that ever tortured mortal ears. It was
all on her account. They were, however, away from every
one who had known her former position ; and also under
less observation from without than they would have had
to put up with in any country parish.

Sophy the woman was as charming a partner as a man
could possess, though Sophy the lady had her deficiencies.
She showed a natural aptitude for little domestic refine-
ments, so far as related to things and manners ; but in
what is called culture she was less intuitive. She had now
been married more than fourteen years, and her husband
had taken much trouble with her education ; but she still
held confused ideas on the use of ' was ' and ' were,' which
did not beget a respect for her among the few acquaintances she made. Her great grief in this relation was that
her only child, on whose education no expense had been
and would be spared, was now old enough to perceive these
deficiencies in his mother, and not only to see them but
to feel irritated at their existence.

Thus she lived on in the city, and wasted hours in braiding her beautiful hair, till her once apple cheeks waned to pink of the very faintest. Her foot had never regained its natural strength after the accident, and she was mostly obliged to avoid walking altogether. Her husband had grown to like London for its freedom and its domestic privacy; but he was twenty years his Sophy's senior, and had latterly been seized with a serious illness. On this day, however, he had seemed to be well enough to justify her accompanying her son Randolph to the concert.

II

The next time we get a glimpse of her is when she appears in the mournful attire of a widow.

Mr. Twycott had never rallied, and now lay in a well-packed cemetery to the south of the great city, where, if all the dead it contained had stood erect and alive, not one would have known him or recognized his name. The boy had dutifully followed him to the grave, and was now again at school.

Throughout these changes Sophy had been treated like the child she was in nature though not in years. She was left with no control over anything that had been her husband's beyond her modest personal income. In his anxiety lest her inexperience should be overreached he had safeguarded with trustees all he possibly could. The completion of the boy's course at the public school, to be followed in due time by Oxford and ordination, had been all previsioned and arranged, and she really had nothing to occupy her in the world but to eat and drink, and make a business of indolence, and go on weaving and coiling the nut-brown hair, merely keeping a home open for the son whenever he came to her during vacations.

Foreseeing his probable decease long years before her, her husband in his lifetime had purchased for her use a semi-detached villa in the same long, straight road whereon the church and parsonage faced, which was to be hers as long as she chose to live in it. Here she now resided, looking out upon the fragment of lawn in front, and through the railings at the ever-flowing traffic; or, bending forward over the window-sill on the first floor, stretching her eyes far up and down the vista of sooty trees, hazy air, and drab house-façades, along which echoed the noises common to a suburban main thoroughfare.

Somehow, her boy, with his aristocratic school-knowledge, his grammars, and his aversions, was losing those wide infantine sympathies, extending as far as to the sun and moon themselves, with which he, like other children, had been born, and which his mother, a child of nature herself, had loved in him ; he was reducing their compass to a population of a few thousand wealthy and titled people, the mere veneer of a thousand million or so of others who did not interest him at all. He drifted further and further away from her. Sophy's *milieu* being a suburb of minor tradesmen and under-clerks, and her almost only companions the two servants of her own house, it was not surprising that after her husband's death she soon lost the little artificial tastes she had acquired from him, and became—in her son's eyes—a mother whose mistakes and origin it was his painful lot as a gentleman to blush for. As yet he was far from being man enough—if he ever would be—to rate these sins of hers at their true infinitesimal value beside the yearning fondness that welled up and remained penned in her heart till it should be more fully accepted by him, or by some other person or thing. If he had lived at home with her he would have had all of it ; but he seemed to require so very little in present circumstances, and it remained stored.

Her life became insupportably dreary ; she could not take walks, and had no interest in going for drives, or, indeed, in travelling anywhere. Nearly two years passed without an event, and still she looked on that suburban road, thinking of the village in which she had been born, and whither she would have gone back—O how gladly !— even to work in the fields.

Taking no exercise she often could not sleep, and would rise in the night or early morning to look out upon the then vacant thoroughfare, where the lamps stood like sentinels waiting for some procession to go by. An approximation to such a procession was indeed made early every morning about one o'clock, when the country vehicles passed up with loads of vegetables for Covent Garden market. She often saw them creeping along at this silent and dusky hour—waggon after waggon, bearing green bastions of cabbages nodding to their fall, yet never falling, walls of baskets enclosing masses of beans and peas, pyramids of snow-white turnips, swaying howdahs of mixed produce—creeping along behind aged night-horses, who seemed ever patiently wondering between their hollow coughs why they had always to work at that still hour when all other sentient creatures were privileged to rest. Wrapped in a cloak it was soothing to watch and sympathize with them when depression and nervousness hindered sleep, and to see how the fresh green-stuff brightened to life as it came opposite the lamp, and how the sweating animals steamed and shone with their miles of travel.

They had an interest, almost a charm, for Sophy, these semi-rural people and vehicles moving in an urban atmosphere, leading a life quite distinct from that of the daytime toilers on the same road. One morning a man who accompanied a waggon-load of potatoes gazed rather hard at the house-fronts as he passed, and with a curious emotion she thought his form was familiar to her. She looked out for him again. His being an old-fashioned conveyance, with a yellow front, it was easily recognizable, and on the third night after she saw it a second time. The man alongside was, as she had fancied, Sam Hobson, formerly gardener at Gaymead, who would at one time have married her.

She had occasionally thought of him, and wondered if life in a cottage with him would not have been a happier lot than the life she had accepted. She had not thought of him passionately, but her now dismal situation lent an interest to his resurrection—a tender interest which it is impossible to exaggerate. She went back to bed, and began thinking. When did these market-gardeners, who travelled up to town so regularly at one or two in the morning, come back? She dimly recollected seeing their empty waggons, hardly noticeable amid the ordinary day-traffic, passing down at some hour before noon.

It was only April, but that morning, after breakfast, she had the window opened, and sat looking out, the feeble

sun shining full upon her. She affected to sew, but her
eyes never left the street. Between ten and eleven the
desired waggon, now unladen, reappeared on its return
journey. But Sam was not looking round him then, and
drove on in a reverie.

'Sam!' cried she.

Turning with a start, his face lighted up. He called to
him a little boy to hold the horse, alighted, and came and
stood under the window.

'I can't come down easily, Sam, or I would!' she said.
'Did you know I lived here?'

'Well, Mrs. Twycott, I knew you lived along here somewhere. I have often looked out for 'ee.'

He briefly explained his own presence on the scene. He
had long since given up his gardening in the village near
Aldbrickham, and was now manager at a market-gardener's
on the south side of London, it being part of his duty to
go up to Covent Garden with waggon-loads of produce
two or three times a week. In answer to her curious
inquiry, he admitted that he had come to this particular
district because he had seen in the Aldbrickham paper, a
year or two before, the announcement of the death in
South London of the aforetime vicar of Gaymead, which
had revived an interest in her dwelling-place that he could
not extinguish, leading him to hover about the locality till
his present post had been secured.

They spoke of their native village in dear old North
Wessex, the spots in which they had played together as
children. She tried to feel that she was a dignified personage now, that she must not be too confidential with
Sam. But she could not keep it up, and the tears hanging
in her eyes were indicated in her voice.

'You are not happy, Mrs. Twycott, I'm afraid?' he
said.

'O, of course not! I lost my husband only the year
before last.'

'Ah! I meant in another way. You'd like to be home
again?'

'This is my home—for life. The house belongs to me.
But I understand——' She let it out then. 'Yes, Sam.

I long for home—*our* home! I *should* like to be there, and never leave it, and die there.' But she remembered herself. ' That's only a momentary feeling. I have a son, you know, a dear boy. He's at school now.'

' Somewhere handy, I suppose? I see there's lots on 'em along this road.'

' O no! Not in one of these wretched holes! At a public school—one of the most distinguished in England.'

' Chok' it all! of course! I forget, ma'am, that you've been a lady for so many years.'

' No, I am not a lady,' she said sadly. ' I never shall be. But he's a gentleman, and that—makes it—O how difficult for me!'

III

The acquaintance thus oddly reopened proceeded apace. She often looked out to get a few words with him, by night or by day. Her sorrow was that she could not accompany her one old friend on foot a little way, and talk more freely than she could do while he paused before the house. One night, at the beginning of June, when she was again on the watch after an absence of some days from the window, he entered the gate and said softly, ' Now, wouldn't some air do you good? I've only half a load this morning. Why not ride up to Covent Garden with me? There's a nice seat on the cabbages, where I've spread a sack. You can be home again in a cab before anybody is up.'

She refused at first, and then, trembling with excitement, hastily finished her dressing, and wrapped herself up in cloak and veil, afterwards sidling downstairs by the aid of the handrail, in a way she could adopt on an emergency. When she had opened the door she found Sam on the step, and he lifted her bodily on his strong arm across the little forecourt into his vehicle. Not a soul was visible or audible in the infinite length of the straight, flat highway, with its ever-waiting lamps converging to points in each direction. The air was fresh as country air at this hour, and the stars shone, except to the north-eastward, where there was a whitish light—the dawn. Sam carefully placed her in the seat and drove on.

They talked as they had talked in old days, Sam pulling
himself up now and then, when he thought himself too
familiar. More than once she said with misgiving that
she wondered if she ought to have indulged in the freak.
' But I am so lonely in my house,' she added, ' and this
makes me so happy ! '

' You must come again, dear Mrs. Twycott. There is
no time o' day for taking the air like this.'

It grew lighter and lighter. The sparrows became busy
in the streets, and the city waxed denser around them.
When they approached the river it was day, and on the
bridge they beheld the full blaze of morning sunlight in the
direction of St. Paul's, the river glistening towards it, and
not a craft stirring.

Near Covent Garden he put her into a cab, and they
parted, looking into each other's faces like the very old
friends they were. She reached home without adventure,
limped to the door, and let herself in with her latch-key
unseen.

The air and Sam's presence had revived her : her cheeks
were quite pink—almost beautiful. She had something to
live for in addition to her son. A woman of pure instincts,
she knew there had been nothing really wrong in the journey, but supposed it conventionally to be very wrong
indeed.

Soon, however, she gave way to the temptation of going
with him again, and on this occasion their conversation
was distinctly tender, and Sam said he never should forget
her, notwithstanding that she had served him rather badly
at one time. After much hesitation he told her of a plan
it was in his power to carry out, and one he should like
to take in hand, since he did not care for London work :
it was to set up as a master greengrocer down at Aldbrickham, the county-town of their native place. He knew of an
opening—a shop kept by aged people who wished to retire.

' And why don't you do it, then, Sam ? ' she asked with
a slight heartsinking.

' Because I'm not sure if—you'd join me. I know you
wouldn't—couldn't ! Such a lady as ye've been so long,
you couldn't be a wife to a man like me.'

' I hardly suppose I could ! ' she assented, also frightened at the idea.

' If you could,' he said eagerly, ' you'd on'y have to sit in the back parlour and look through the glass partition when I was away sometimes—just to keep an eye on things. The lameness wouldn't hinder that. . . . I'd keep you as genteel as ever I could, dear Sophy—if I might think of it ! ' he pleaded.

' Sam, I'll be frank,' she said, putting her hand on his. ' If it were only myself I would do it, and gladly, though everything I possess would be lost to me by marrying again.'

' I don't mind that ! It's more independent.'

' That's good of you, dear, dear Sam. But there's something else. I have a son. . . . I almost fancy when I am miserable sometimes that he is not really mine, but one I hold in trust for my late husband. He seems to belong so little to me personally, so entirely to his dead father. He is so much educated and I so little that I do not feel dignified enough to be his mother. . . . Well, he would have to be told.'

' Yes. Unquestionably.' Sam saw her thought and her fear. ' Still, you can do as you like, Sophy—Mrs. Twycott,' he added. ' It is not you who are the child, but he.'

' Ah, you don't know ! Sam, if I could, I would marry you, some day. But you must wait a while, and let me think.'

It was enough for him, and he was blithe at their parting. Not so she. To tell Randolph seemed impossible. She could wait till he had gone up to Oxford, when what she did would affect his life but little. But would he ever tolerate the idea ? And if not, could she defy him ?

She had not told him a word when the yearly cricket-match came on at Lord's between the public schools, though Sam had already gone back to Aldbrickham. Mrs. Twycott felt stronger than usual : she went to the match with Randolph, and was able to leave her chair and walk about occasionally. The bright idea occurred to her that she could casually broach the subject while moving round

among the spectators, when the boy's spirits were high
with interest in the game, and he would weigh domestic
matters as feathers in the scale beside the day's victory.
They promenaded under the lurid July sun, this pair, so
wide apart, yet so near, and Sophy saw the large proportion of boys like her own, in their broad white collars and
dwarf hats, and all around the rows of great coaches under
which was jumbled the *débris* of luxurious luncheons :
bones, pie-crusts, champagne-bottles, glasses, plates, nap-
kins, and the family silver ; while on the coaches sat the
proud fathers and mothers ; but never a poor mother like
her. If Randolph had not appertained to these, had not
centred all his interests in them, had not cared exclusively
for the class they belonged to, how happy would things
have been ! A great huzza at some small performance
with the bat burst from the multitude of relatives, and
Randolph jumped wildly into the air to see what had
happened. Sophy fetched up the sentence that had
been already shaped ; but she could not get it out. The
occasion was, perhaps, an inopportune one. The contrast
between her story and the display of fashion to which
Randolph had grown to regard himself as akin would be
fatal. She awaited a better time.

It was on an evening when they were alone in their
plain suburban residence, where life was not blue but
brown, that she ultimately broke silence, qualifying her
announcement of a probable second marriage by assuring
him that it would not take place for a long time to come,
when he would be living quite independently of her.

The boy thought the idea a very reasonable one, and
asked if she had chosen anybody. She hesitated ; and he
seemed to have a misgiving. He hoped his stepfather
would be a gentleman, he said.

' Not what you call a gentleman,' she answered timidly.
' He'll be much as I was before I knew your father ' ; and
by degrees she acquainted him with the whole. The youth's
face remained fixed for a moment ; then he flushed, leant
on the table, and burst into passionate tears.

His mother went up to him, kissed all of his face that
she could get at, and patted his back as if he were still the

baby he once had been, crying herself the while. When he had somewhat recovered from his paroxysm he went hastily to his own room and fastened the door.

Parleyings were attempted through the keyhole, outside which she waited and listened. It was long before he would reply, and when he did it was to say sternly at her from within : ' I am ashamed of you ! It will ruin me ! A miserable boor ! a churl ! a clown ! It will degrade me in the eyes of all the gentlemen of England ! '

' Say no more—perhaps I am wrong ! I will struggle against it ! ' she cried miserably.

Before Randolph left her that summer a letter arrived from Sam to inform her that he had been unexpectedly fortunate in obtaining the shop. He was in possession ; it was the largest in the town, combining fruit with vegetables, and he thought it would form a home worthy even of her some day. Might he not run up to town to see her ?

She met him by stealth, and said he must still wait for her final answer. The autumn dragged on, and when Randolph was home at Christmas for the holidays she broached the matter again. But the young gentleman was inexorable.

It was dropped for months ; renewed again ; abandoned under his repugnance ; again attempted ; and thus the gentle creature reasoned and pleaded till four or five long years had passed. Then the faithful Sam revived his suit with some peremptoriness. Sophy's son, now an undergraduate, was down from Oxford one Easter, when she again opened the subject. As soon as he was ordained, she argued, he would have a home of his own, wherein she, with her bad grammar and her ignorance, would be an encumbrance to him. Better obliterate her as much as possible.

He showed a more manly anger now, but would not agree. She on her side was more persistent, and he had doubts whether she could be trusted in his absence. But by indignation and contempt for her taste he completely maintained his ascendency ; and finally taking her before a little cross and altar that he had erected in his bedroom

for his private devotions, there bade her kneel, and swear
that she would not wed Samuel Hobson without his con-
sent. ' I owe this to my father ! ' he said.

The poor woman swore, thinking he would soften as
soon as he was ordained and in full swing of clerical work.
But he did not. His education had by this time sufficiently ousted his humanity to keep him quite firm ; though
his mother might have led an idyllic life with her faithful
fruiterer and greengrocer, and nobody have been anything
the worse in the world.

Her lameness became more confirmed as time went on,
and she seldom or never left the house in the long southern
thoroughfare, where she seemed to be pining her heart
away. ' Why mayn't I say to Sam that I'll marry him ?
Why mayn't I ? ' she would murmur plaintively to herself
when nobody was near.

Some four years after this date a middle-aged man was
standing at the door of the largest fruiterer's shop in Aldbrickham. He was the proprietor, but to-day, instead of
his usual business attire, he wore a neat suit of black ;
and his window was partly shuttered. From the railway-
station a funeral procession was seen approaching : it
passed his door and went out of the town towards the
village of Gaymead. The man, whose eyes were wet, held
his hat in his hand as the vehicles moved by ; while from
the mourning-coach a young smooth-shaven priest in a
high waistcoat looked black as a cloud at the shopkeeper
standing there.

December 1891.

FOR CONSCIENCE' SAKE

FOR CONSCIENCE' SAKE

I

WHETHER the utilitarian or the intuitive theory of the moral sense be upheld it is beyond question that there are a few subtle-souled persons with whom the absolute gratuitousness of an act of reparation is an inducement to perform it ; while exhortation as to its necessity would breed excuses for leaving it undone. The case of Mr. Millborne and Mrs. Frankland particularly illustrated this, and perhaps something more.

There were few figures better known to the local crossing-sweeper than Mr. Millborne's in his daily comings and goings along a familiar and quiet London street, where he lived inside the door marked eleven, though not as householder. In age he was fifty at least, and his habits were as regular as those of a person can be who has no occupation but the study of how to keep himself employed. He turned almost always to the right on getting to the end of the street, then he went onward down Bond Street to his club, whence he returned by precisely the same course about six o'clock, on foot ; or, if he went to dine, later on in a cab. He was known to be a man of some means, though apparently not wealthy. Being a bachelor he seemed to prefer his present mode of living as a lodger in Mrs. Towney's best rooms, with the use of furniture which he had bought ten times over in rent during his tenancy, to having a house of his own.

None among his acquaintance tried to know him well, for his manner and moods did not excite curiosity or deep friendship. He was not a man who seemed to have anything on his mind, anything to conceal, anything to impart. From his casual remarks it was generally understood that he was country-born, a native of some place in Wessex ; that he had come to London as a young man in a banking-house, and had risen to a post of responsibility; when, by the death of his father, who had been fortunate in his investments, the son succeeded to an income which led him to retire from a business life somewhat early.

One evening, when he had been unwell for several days, Doctor Bindon came in, after dinner, from the adjoining medical quarter, and smoked with him over the fire. The patient's ailment was not such as to require much thought, and they talked together on indifferent subjects.

'I am a lonely man, Bindon—a lonely man,' Millborne took occasion to say, shaking his head gloomily. 'You don't know such loneliness as mine. . . . And the older I get the more I am dissatisfied with myself. And to-day I have been, through an accident, more than usually haunted by what, above all other events of my life, causes that dissatisfaction—the recollection of an unfulfilled promise made twenty years ago. In ordinary affairs I have always been considered a man of my word; and perhaps it is on that account that a particular vow I once made, and did not keep, comes back to me with a magnitude out of all proportion (I daresay) to its real gravity, especially at this time of day. You know the discomfort caused at night by the half-sleeping sense that a door or window has been left unfastened, or in the day by the remembrance of unanswered letters. So does that promise haunt me from time to time, and has done to-day particularly.'

There was a pause, and they smoked on. Millborne's eyes, though fixed on the fire, were really regarding attentively a town in the West of England.

'Yes,' he continued, 'I have never quite forgotten it, though during the busy years of my life it was shelved and buried under the pressure of my pursuits. And, as I say, to-day in particular, an incident in the law-report of a somewhat similar kind has brought it back again vividly. However, what it was I can tell you in a few words, though no doubt you, as a man of the world, will smile at the thinness of my skin when you hear it. . . . I came up to town at one-and-twenty, from Toneborough, in Outer Wessex, where I was born, and where, before I left, I had

won the heart of a young woman of my own age. I promised her marriage, took advantage of my promise, and—
am a bachelor.'

'The old story.'

The other nodded.

'I left the place, and thought at the time I had done a
very clever thing in getting so easily out of an entangle-
ment. But I have lived long enough for that promise to
return to bother me—to be honest, not altogether as a
pricking of the conscience, but as a dissatisfaction with
myself as a specimen of the heap of flesh called humanity.
If I were to ask you to lend me fifty pounds, which I would
repay you next midsummer, and I did not repay you, I
should consider myself a shabby sort of fellow, especially
if you wanted the money badly. Yet I promised that girl
just as distinctly ; and then coolly broke my word, as if
doing so were rather smart conduct than a mean action,
for which the poor victim herself, encumbered with a child,
and not I, had really to pay the penalty, in spite of certain
pecuniary aid that was given. . . . There, that's the
retrospective trouble that I am always unearthing ; and
you may hardly believe that though so many years have
elapsed, and it is all gone by and done with, and she must
be getting on for an old woman now, as I am for an old
man, it really often destroys my sense of self-respect
still.'

'O, I can understand it. All depends upon the tem-
perament. Thousands of men would have forgotten all
about it ; so would you, perhaps, if you had married and
had a family. Did she ever marry ? '

'I don't think so. O no—she never did. She left Toneborough, and later on appeared under another name at
Exonbury, in the next county, where she was not known.
It is very seldom that I go down into that part of the country, but in passing through Exonbury, on one occasion, I
learnt that she was quite a settled resident there, as a
teacher of music, or something of the kind. That much I
casually heard when I was there two or three years ago.
But I have never set eyes on her since our original acquaintance, and should not know her if I met her.'

'Did the child live?' asked the doctor.

'For several years, certainly,' replied his friend. 'I
cannot say if she is living now. It was a little girl. She
might be married by this time as far as years go.'

'And the mother—was she a decent, worthy young
woman?'

'O yes; a sensible, quiet girl, neither attractive nor
unattractive to the ordinary observer; simply commonplace. Her position at the time of our acquaintance was
not so good as mine. My father was a solicitor, as I think
I have told you. She was a young girl in a music-shop;
and it was represented to me that it would be beneath my
position to marry her. Hence the result.'

'Well, all I can say is that after twenty years it is probably too late to think of mending such a matter. It has
doubtless by this time mended itself. You had better dismiss it from your mind as an evil past your control. Of
course, if mother and daughter are alive, or either, you
might settle something upon them, if you were inclined,
and had it to spare.'

'Well, I haven't much to spare, and I have relations in
narrow circumstances—perhaps narrower than theirs. But
that is not the point. Were I ever so rich I feel I could
not rectify the past by money. I did not promise to enrich
her. On the contrary, I told her it would probably be
dire poverty for both of us. But I did promise to make
her my wife.'

'Then find her and do it,' said the doctor jocularly as
he rose to leave.

'Ah, Bindon! That, of course, is the obvious jest. But
I haven't the slightest desire for marriage; I am quite
content to live as I have lived. I am a bachelor by nature,
and instinct, and habit, and everything. Besides, though
I respect her still (for she was not an atom to blame), I
haven't any shadow of love for her. In my mind she
exists as one of those women you think well of, but find
uninteresting. It would be purely with the idea of putting wrong right that I should hunt her up, and propose
to do it off-hand.'

'You don't think of it seriously?' said his surprised friend.

' I sometimes think that I would, if it were practicable ; simply, as I say, to recover my sense of being a man of honour.'

' I wish you luck in the enterprise,' said Doctor Bindon. ' You'll soon be out of that chair, and then you can put your impulse to the test. But—after twenty years of silence—I should say, don't ! '

II

The doctor's advice remained counterpoised, in Millborne's mind, by the aforesaid mood of seriousness and sense of principle, approximating often to religious sentiment, which had been evolving itself in his breast for months, and even years.

The feeling, however, had no immediate effect upon Mr. Millborne's actions. He soon got over his trifling illness, and was vexed with himself for having, in a moment of impulse, confided such a case of conscience to anybody.

But the force which had prompted it, though latent, remained with him and ultimately grew stronger. The upshot was that about four months after the date of his illness and disclosure, Millborne found himself on a mild spring morning at Paddington Station, in a train that was starting for the west. His many intermittent thoughts on his broken promise from time to time, in those hours when loneliness brought him face to face with his own personality, had at last resulted in this course.

The decisive stimulus had been given when, a day or two earlier, on looking into a Post-Office Directory, he learnt that the woman he had not met for twenty years was still living on at Exonbury under the name she had assumed when, a year or two after her disappearance from her native town and his, she had returned from abroad as a young widow with a child, and taken up her residence at the former city. Her condition was apparently but little changed, and her daughter seemed to be with her, their names standing in the Directory as ' Mrs. Leonora Frankland and Miss Frankland, Teachers of Music and Dancing.'

Mr. Millborne reached Exonbury in the afternoon, and

his first business, before even taking his luggage into the town, was to find the house occupied by the teachers. Standing in a central and open place it was not difficult to discover, a well-burnished brass door-plate bearing their names prominently. He hesitated to enter without further knowledge, and ultimately took lodgings over a toy-shop opposite, securing a sitting-room which faced a similar drawing- or sitting-room at the Franklands', where the dancing lessons were given. Installed here he was enabled to make indirectly, and without suspicion, inquiries and observations on the character of the ladies over the way, which he did with much deliberateness.

He learnt that the widow, Mrs. Frankland, with her one daughter, Frances, was of cheerful and excellent repute, energetic and painstaking with her pupils, of whom she had a good many, and in whose tuition her daughter assisted her. She was quite a recognized townswoman, and though the dancing branch of her profession was perhaps a trifle worldly, she was really a serious-minded lady who, being obliged to live by what she knew how to teach, balanced matters by lending a hand at charitable bazaars, assisting at sacred concerts, and giving musical recitations in aid of funds for bewildering happy savages, and other such enthusiasms of this enlightened country. Her daughter was one of the foremost of the bevy of young women who decorated the churches at Easter and Christmas, was organist in one of those edifices, and had subscribed to the testimonial of a silver broth-basin that was presented to the Reverend Mr. Walker as a token of gratitude for his faithful and arduous intonations of six months as sub-precentor in the Cathedral. Altogether mother and daughter appeared to be a typical and innocent pair among the genteel citizens of Exonbury.

As a natural and simple way of advertising their profession they allowed the windows of the music-room to be a little open, so that you had the pleasure of hearing all along the street at any hour between sunrise and sunset fragmentary gems of classical music as interpreted by the young people of twelve or fourteen who took lessons there. But it was said that Mrs. Frankland made most of her income by letting out pianos on hire, and by selling them as agent for the makers.

The report pleased Millborne; it was highly creditable, and far better than he had hoped. He was curious to get a view of the two women who led such blameless lives.

He had not long to wait to get a glimpse of Leonora. It was when she was standing on her own doorstep, opening her parasol, on the morning after his arrival. She was thin, though not gaunt, with greying hair; and a good, well-wearing, thoughtful face had taken the place of the one which had temporarily attracted him in the days of his nonage. She wore black, and it became her in her character of widow. The daughter next appeared; she was a smoothed and rounded copy of her mother, with the same decision in her mien that Leonora had, and a bounding gait in which he traced a faint resemblance to his own at her age.

For the first time he absolutely made up his mind to call on them. But his antecedent step was to send Leonora a note the next morning, stating his proposal to visit her, and suggesting the evening as the time, because she seemed to be so greatly occupied in her professional capacity during the day. He purposely worded his note in such a form as not to require an answer from her which would be possibly awkward to write.

No answer came. Naturally he should not have been surprised at this; and yet he felt a little checked, even though she had only refrained from volunteering a reply that was not demanded.

At eight, the hour fixed by himself, he crossed over and was passively admitted by the servant. Mrs. Frankland, as she called herself, received him in the large music-and-dancing-room on the first-floor front, and not in any private little parlour as he had expected. This cast a distressingly business-like colour over their first meeting after so many years of severance. The woman he had wronged stood before him, well dressed, even to his metropolitan eyes, and her manner as she came up to him was dignified even to hardness. She certainly was not glad to see him. But what could he expect after a neglect of twenty years!

' How do you do, Mr. Millborne ? ' she said cheerfully, as to any chance caller. ' I am obliged to receive you here because my daughter has a friend downstairs.'

' Your daughter—and mine.'

' Ah—yes, yes,' she replied hastily, as if the addition had escaped her memory. ' But perhaps the less said about that the better, in fairness to me. You will consider me a widow, please.'

' Certainly, Leonora. . . .' He could not get on, her manner was so cold and indifferent. The expected scene of sad reproach, subdued to delicacy by the run of years, was absent altogether. He was obliged to come to the point without preamble.

' You are quite free, Leonora—I mean as to marriage ? There is nobody who has your promise, or——'

' O yes ; quite free, Mr. Millborne,' she said, somewhat surprised.

' Then I will tell you why I have come. Twenty years ago I promised to make you my wife ; and I am here to fulfil that promise. Heaven forgive my tardiness ! '

Her surprise was increased, but she was not agitated. She seemed to become gloomy, disapproving. ' I—fear I could not entertain such an idea at this time of life,' she said after a moment or two. ' It would complicate matters too greatly. I have a very fair income, and require no help of any sort. I have no wish to marry. . . . What could have induced you to come on such an errand now ? It seems quite extraordinary, if I may say so ! '

' It must—I daresay it does,' Millborne replied vaguely, ' and I must tell you that impulse—I mean in the sense of passion—has little to do with it. I wish to marry you, Leonora ; I much desire to marry you. But it is an affair of conscience, a case of fulfilment. I promised you, and it was dishonourable of me to go away. I want to remove that sense of dishonour before I die. No doubt we might get to love each other as warmly as we did in old times ? '

She dubiously shook her head. ' I appreciate your motives, Mr. Millborne ; but you must consider my position ; and you will see that, short of the personal wish to marry, which I don't feel, there is no reason why I should

change my state, even though by so doing I should ease
your conscience. My position in this town is a respected
one ; I have built it up by my own hard labours, and, in
short, I don't wish to alter it. My daughter, too, is just
on the verge of an engagement to be married, to a young
man who will make her an excellent husband. It will be
in every way a desirable match for her. He is downstairs
now.'

'Does she know—anything about me ? '

'O no, no ; God forbid ! Her father is dead and buried
to her. So that, you see, things are going on smoothly,
and I don't want to disturb their progress.'

He nodded. 'Very well,' he said, and rose to go. At
the door, however, he came back again.

'Still, Leonora,' he urged, 'I have come on purpose ;
and I don't see what disturbance would be caused. You
would simply marry an old friend. Won't you reconsider ?
It is no more than right that we should be united, remembering the girl.'

She shook her head, and patted with her foot nervously.

'Well, I won't detain you,' he added. 'I shall not be leaving Exonbury yet. You will allow me to see you again ? '

'Yes ; I don't mind,' she said reluctantly.

The obstacles he had encountered, though they did not
reanimate his dead passion for Leonora, did certainly make
it appear indispensable to his peace of mind to overcome
her coldness. He called frequently. The first meeting
with the daughter was a trying ordeal, though he did not
feel drawn towards her as he had expected to be ; she did
not excite his sympathies. Her mother confided to Frances
the errand of 'her old friend,' which was viewed by the
daughter with strong disfavour. His desire being thus
uncongenial to both, for a long time Millborne made not
the least impression upon Mrs. Frankland. His attentions
pestered her rather than pleased her. He was surprised
at her firmness, and it was only when he hinted at moral
reasons for their union that she was ever shaken. 'Strictly
speaking,' he would say, 'we ought, as honest persons, to
marry ; and that's the truth of it, Leonora.'

'I have looked at it in that light,' she said quickly.

' It struck me at the very first. But I don't see the force of the argument. I totally deny that after this interval of time I am bound to marry you for honour's sake. I would have married you, as you know well enough, at the proper time. But what is the use of remedies now ? '

They were standing at the window. A scantly-whiskered young man, in clerical attire, called at the door below. Leonora flushed with interest.

' Who is he ? ' said Mr. Millborne.

' My Frances's lover. I am so sorry—she is not at home ! Ah ! they have told him where she is, and he has gone to find her. . . . I hope that suit will prosper, at any rate ! '

' Why shouldn't it ? '

' Well, he cannot marry yet ; and Frances sees but little of him now he has left Exonbury. He was formerly doing duty here, but now he is curate of St. John's, Ivell, fifty miles up the line. There is a tacit agreement between them, but—there have been friends of his who object, because of our vocation. However, he sees the absurdity of such an objection as that, and is not influenced by it.'

' Your marriage with me would help the match, instead of hindering it, as you have said.'

' Do you think it would ? '

' It certainly would, by taking you out of this business altogether.'

By chance he had found the way to move her somewhat, and he followed it up. This view was imparted to Mrs. Frankland's daughter, and it led her to soften her opposition. Millborne, who had given up his lodging in Exonbury, journeyed to and fro regularly, till at last he overcame her negations, and she expressed a reluctant assent.

They were married at the nearest church ; and the goodwill—whatever that was—of the music-and-dancing connection was sold to a successor only too ready to jump into the place, the Millbornes having decided to live in London.

III

Millborne was a householder in his old district, though not in his old street, and Mrs. Millborne and their daughter had turned themselves into Londoners. Frances was well reconciled to the removal by her lover's satisfaction at the change. It suited him better to travel from Ivell a hundred miles to see her in London, where he frequently had other engagements, than fifty in the opposite direction where nothing but herself required his presence. So here they were, furnished up to the attics, in one of the small but popular streets of the West district, in a house whose front, till lately of the complexion of a chimney-sweep, had been scraped to show to the surprised wayfarer the bright yellow and red brick that had lain lurking beneath the soot of fifty years.

The social lift that the two women had derived from the alliance was considerable; but when the exhilaration which accompanies a first residence in London, the sensation of standing on a pivot of the world, had passed, their lives promised to be somewhat duller than when, at despised Exonbury, they had enjoyed a nodding acquaintance with three-fourths of the town. Mr. Millborne did not criticize his wife; he could not. Whatever defects of hardness and acidity his original treatment and the lapse of years might have developed in her, his sense of a realized idea, of a re-established self-satisfaction, was always thrown into the scale on her side, and outweighed all objections.

It was about a month after their settlement in town that the household decided to spend a week at a watering-place in the Isle of Wight, and while there the Reverend Percival Cope (the young curate aforesaid) came to see them, Frances in particular. No formal engagement of the young pair had been announced as yet, but it was clear that their mutual understanding could not end in anything but marriage without grievous disappointment to one of the parties at least. Not that Frances was sentimental. She was rather of the imperious sort, indeed; and, to say all, the young girl had not fulfilled her father's expectations of her. But he hoped and worked for her welfare as sincerely as any father could do.

Mr. Cope was introduced to the new head of the family, and stayed with them in the Island two or three days. On the last day of his visit they decided to venture on a

two hours' sail in one of the small yachts which lay there
for hire. The trip had not progressed far before all, except
the curate, found that sailing in a breeze did not quite
agree with them ; but as he seemed to enjoy the experience, the other three bore their condition as well as they
could without grimace or complaint, till the young man,
observing their discomfort, gave immediate directions to
tack about. On the way back to port they sat silent,
facing each other.

Nausea in such circumstances, like midnight watching,
fatigue, trouble, fright, has this marked effect upon the
countenance, that it often brings out strongly the diver-
gences of the individual from the norm of his race, accen-
tuating superficial peculiarities to radical distinctions.
Unexpected physiognomies will uncover themselves at
these times in well-known faces ; the aspect becomes
invested with the spectral presence of entombed and forgotten ancestors ; and family lineaments of special or
exclusive cast, which in ordinary moments are masked by a
stereotyped expression and mien, start up with crude insis-
tence to the view.

Frances, sitting beside her mother's husband, with Mr.
Cope opposite, was naturally enough much regarded by
the curate during the tedious sail home ; at first with
sympathetic smiles. Then, as the middle-aged father and
his child grew each gray-faced, as the pretty blush of Frances disintegrated into spotty stains, and the soft rotun-
dities of her features diverged from their familiar and
reposeful beauty into elemental lines, Cope was gradually
struck with the resemblance between a pair in their discomfort who in their ease presented nothing to the eye in
common. Mr. Millborne and Frances in their indisposition
were strangely, startlingly alike.

The inexplicable fact absorbed Cope's attention quite.
He forgot to smile at Frances, to hold her hand ; and when
they touched the shore he remained sitting for some
moments like a man in a trance.

As they went homeward, and recovered their complexions
and contours, the similarities one by one disappeared, and
Frances and Mr. Millborne were again masked by the

ommonplace differences of sex and age. It was as if, during the voyage, a mysterious veil had been lifted, temporarily revealing a strange pantomime of the past.

During the evening he said to her casually : ' Is your step-father a cousin of your mother, dear Frances ? '

' O no,' said she. ' There is no relationship. He was only an old friend of hers. Why did you suppose such a thing ? '

He did not explain, and the next morning started to resume his duties at Ivell.

Cope was an honest young fellow, and shrewd withal. At home in his quiet rooms in St. Peter's Street, Ivell, he pondered long and unpleasantly on the revelations of the cruise. The tale it told was distinct enough, and for the first time his position was an uncomfortable one. He had met the Franklands at Exonbury as parishioners, had been attracted by Frances, and had floated thus far into an engagement which was indefinite only because of his inability to marry just yet. The Franklands' past had apparently contained mysteries, and it did not coincide with his judgment to marry into a family whose mystery was of the sort suggested. So he sat and sighed, between his reluctance to lose Frances and his natural dislike of forming a connection with people whose antecedents would not bear the strictest investigation.

A passionate lover of the old-fashioned sort might possibly never have halted to weigh these doubts ; but though he was in the Church Cope's affections were fastidious— distinctly tempered with the alloys of the century's decadence. He delayed writing to Frances for some while, simply because he could not tune himself up to enthusiasm when worried by suspicions of such a kind.

Meanwhile the Millbornes had returned to London, and Frances was growing anxious. In talking to her mother of Cope she had innocently alluded to his curious inquiry if her mother and her step-father were connected by any tie of cousinship. Mrs. Millborne made her repeat the words. Frances did so, and watched with inquisitive eyes their effect upon her elder, which was a distinct one.

' What is there so startling in his inquiry then ? ' Frances

asked. 'Can it have anything to do with his not writing
to me?'

Her mother flinched, but did not inform her, and Frances
also was now drawn within the atmosphere of suspicion.
That night when standing by chance outside the chamber
of her parents she heard for the first time their voices
engaged in a sharp altercation.

The apple of discord had, indeed, been dropped into the
house of the Millbornes. The scene within the chamber-
door was Mrs. Millborne standing before her dressing-table,
looking across to her husband in the dressing-room adjoining, where he was sitting down, his eyes fixed on the floor.
'Why did you come and disturb my life a second time?'
she harshly asked. 'Why did you pester me with your
conscience, till I was driven to accept you to get rid of
your importunity? Frances and I were doing well: the
one desire of my life was that she should marry that good
young man. And now the match is broken off by your
cruel interference! Why did you show yourself in my
world again, and raise this scandal upon my hard-won
respectability—won by such weary years of labour as none
will ever know!' She bent her face upon the table and
wept passionately.

There was no reply from Mr. Millborne. Frances lay
awake nearly all that night, and when at breakfast-time
the next morning still no letter appeared from Mr. Cope,
she entreated her mother to go to Ivell and see if the young
man were ill.

Mrs. Millborne went, returning the same day. Frances,
anxious and haggard, met her at the station.

Was all well? Her mother could not say it was; though
he was not ill.

One thing she had found out, that it was a mistake to
hunt up a man when his inclinations were to hold aloof.
Returning with her mother in the cab Frances insisted
upon knowing what the mystery was which plainly had
alienated her lover. The precise words which had been
spoken at the interview with him that day at Ivell Mrs.
Millborne could not be induced to repeat; but thus far
she admitted, that the estrangement was fundamentally

owing to Mr. Millborne having sought her out and married her.

'And why did he seek you out—and why were you obliged to marry him?' asked the distressed girl. Then the evidences pieced themselves together in her acute mind, and, her colour gradually rising, she asked her mother if what they pointed to was indeed the fact. Her mother admitted that it was.

A flush of mortification succeeded to the flush of shame upon the young woman's face. How could a scrupulously correct clergyman and lover like Mr. Cope ask her to be his wife after this discovery of her irregular birth? She covered her eyes with her hands in a silent despair.

In the presence of Mr. Millborne they at first suppressed their anguish. But by and by their feelings got the better of them, and when he was asleep in his chair after dinner Mrs. Millborne's irritation broke out. The embittered Frances joined her in reproaching the man who had come as the spectre to their intended feast of Hymen, and turned its promise to ghastly failure.

'Why were you so weak, mother, as to admit such an enemy to your house—one so obviously your evil genius—much less accept him as a husband, after so long? If you had only told me all, I could have advised you better! But I suppose I have no right to reproach him, bitter as I feel, and even though he has blighted my life for ever!'

'Frances, I did hold out; I saw it was a mistake to have any more to say to a man who had been such an unmitigated curse to me! But he would not listen; he kept on about his conscience and mine, till I was bewildered, and said Yes! . . . Bringing us away from a quiet town where we were known and respected—what an ill-considered thing it was! O the content of those days! We had society there, people in our own position, who did not expect more of us than we expected of them. Here, where there is so much, there is nothing! He said London society was so bright and brilliant that it would be like a new world. It may be to those who are in it; but what is that to us two lonely women; we only see it flashing past! . . . O the fool, the fool that I was!'

Now Millborne was not so soundly asleep as to prevent
his hearing these animadversions that were almost execra-
tions, and many more of the same sort. As there was no
peace for him at home, he went again to his club, where,
since his reunion with Leonora, he had seldom if ever been
seen. But the shadow of the troubles in his household
interfered with his comfort here also ; he could not, as
formerly, settle down into his favourite chair with the
evening paper, reposeful in the celibate's sense that where
he was his world's centre had its fixture. His world was
now an ellipse, with a dual centrality, of which his own
was not the major.

The young curate of Ivell still held aloof, tantalizing
Frances by his elusiveness. Plainly he was waiting upon
events. Millborne bore the reproaches of his wife and
daughter almost in silence ; but by degrees he grew meditative, as if revolving a new idea. The bitter cry about
blighting their existence at length became so impassioned
that one day Millborne calmly proposed to return again
to the country ; not necessarily to Exonbury, but, if they
were willing, to a little old manor-house which he had found
was to be let, standing a mile from Mr. Cope's town of
Ivell.

They were surprised, and, despite their view of him as
the bringer of ill, were disposed to accede. ' Though I
suppose,' said Mrs. Millborne to him, ' it will end in Mr.
Cope's asking you flatly about the past, and your being
compelled to tell him ; which may dash all my hopes for
Frances. She gets more and more like you every day,
particularly when she is in a bad temper. People will see
you together, and notice it ; and I don't know what may
come of it ! '

' I don't think they will see us together,' he said ; but
he entered into no argument when she insisted otherwise.
The removal was eventually resolved on ; the town-house
was disposed of, and again came the invasion by furniture-
men and vans, till all the movables and servants were
whisked away. He sent his wife and daughter to an hotel
while this was going on, taking two or three journeys himself to Ivell to superintend the refixing, and the improve-

ment of the grounds. When all was done he returned to
them in town.

The house was ready for their reception, he told them,
and there only remained the journey. He accompanied
them and their personal luggage to the station only, having, he said, to remain in town a short time on business
with his lawyer. They went, dubious and discontented ;
for the much-loved Cope had made no sign.

' If we were going down to live here alone,' said Mrs.
Millborne to her daughter in the train ; ' and there was no
intrusive tell-tale presence ! . . . But let it be ! '

The house was a lovely little place in a grove of elms,
and they liked it much. The first person to call upon
them as new residents was Mr. Cope. He was delighted
to find that they had come so near, and (though he did not
say this) meant to live in such excellent style. He had
not, however, resumed the manner of a lover.

' Your father spoils all ! ' murmured Mrs. Millborne.

But three days later she received a letter from her husband, which caused her no small degree of astonishment.
It was written from Boulogne.

It began with a long explanation of settlements of his
property, in which he had been engaged since their departure. The chief feature in the business was that Mrs.
Millborne found herself the absolute mistress of a comfortable sum in personal estate, and Frances of a life-interest
in a larger sum, the principal to be afterwards divided
amongst her children if she had any. The remainder of
his letter ran as hereunder :—

' I have learnt that there are some derelictions of duty which
cannot be blotted out by tardy accomplishment. Our evil actions
do not remain isolated in the past, waiting only to be reversed : like
locomotive plants they spread and re-root, till to destroy the original
stem has no material effect in killing them. I made a mistake in
searching you out ; I admit it ; whatever the remedy may be in
such cases it is not marriage, and the best thing for you and me is
that you do not see me more. You had better not seek me, for you
will not be likely to find me : you are well provided for, and we may
do ourselves more harm than good by meeting again.
' F. M.'

Millborne, in short, disappeared from that day forward.

But a searching inquiry would have revealed that, soon after the Millbornes went to Ivell, an Englishman, who did not give the name of Millborne, took up his residence in Brussels ; a man who might have been recognized by Mrs. Millborne if she had met him. One afternoon in the ensuing summer, when this gentleman was looking over the English papers, he saw the announcement of Miss Frances Frankland's marriage. She had become the Reverend Mrs. Cope.

'Thank God ! ' said the gentleman.

But his momentary satisfaction was far from being happiness. As he formerly had been weighted with a bad conscience, so now was he burdened with the heavy thought which oppressed Antigone, that by honourable observance of a rite he had obtained for himself the reward of dishonourable laxity. Occasionally he had to be helped to his lodgings by his servant from the *Cercle* he frequented, through having imbibed a little too much liquor to be able to take care of himself. But he was harmless, and even when he had been drinking said little.

March 1891.

A TRAGEDY OF TWO AMBITIONS

A TRAGEDY OF TWO AMBITIONS

I

THE shouts of the village-boys came in at the window, accompanied by broken laughter from loungers at the inn-door ; but the brothers Halborough worked on.

They were sitting in a bedroom of the master-mill-wright's house, engaged in the untutored reading of Greek and Latin. It was no tale of Homeric blows and knocks, Argonautic voyaging, or Theban family woe that inflamed their imaginations and spurred them onward. They were plodding away at the Greek Testament, immersed in a chapter of the idiomatic and difficult Epistle to the Hebrews.

The Dog-day sun in its decline reached the low ceiling with slanting sides, and the shadows of the great goat's-willow swayed and interchanged upon the walls like a spectral army manœuvring. The open casement which admitted the remoter sounds now brought the voice of some one close at hand. It was their sister, a pretty girl of fourteen, who stood in the court below.

' I can see the tops of your heads ! What's the use of staying up there ? I like you not to go out with the street-boys ; but do come and play with me ! '

They treated her as an inadequate interlocutor, and put her off with some slight word. She went away disappointed. Presently there was a dull noise of heavy footsteps at the side of the house, and one of the brothers sat up. ' I fancy I hear him coming,' he murmured, his eyes on the window.

A man in the light drab clothes of an old-fashioned country tradesman approached from round the corner, reeling as he came. The elder son flushed with anger, rose from his books, and descended the stairs. The younger sat on, till, after the lapse of a few minutes, his brother re-entered the room.

' Did Rosa see him ? '

' No.'

' Nor anybody ? '

' No.'

' What have you done with him ? '

' He's in the straw-shed.   I got him in with some trouble, and he has fallen asleep.   I thought this would be the explanation of his absence !   No stones dressed for Miller Kench, the great wheel of the saw-mills waiting for new float-boards, even the poor folk not able to get their waggons wheeled.'

' What *is* the use of poring over this ! ' said the younger, shutting up Donnegan's *Lexicon* with a slap.   ' O if we had only been able to keep mother's nine hundred pounds, what we could have done ! '

' How well she had estimated the sum necessary !   Four hundred and fifty each, she thought.   And I have no doubt that we could have done it on that, with care.'

This loss of the nine hundred pounds was the sharp thorn of their crown.   It was a sum which their mother had amassed with great exertion and self-denial, by adding to a chance legacy such other small amounts as she could lay hands on from time to time ; and she had intended with the hoard to indulge the dear wish of her heart— that of sending her sons, Joshua and Cornelius, to one of the Universities, having been informed that from four hundred to four hundred and fifty each might carry them through their terms with such great economy as she knew she could trust them to practise.   But she had died a year or two before this time, worn out by too keen a strain towards these ends ; and the money, coming unreservedly into the hands of their father, had been nearly dissipated. With its exhaustion went all opportunity and hope of a university degree for the sons.

' It drives me mad when I think of it,' said Joshua, the elder.   ' And here we work and work in our own bungling way, and the utmost we can hope for is a term of years as national schoolmasters, and possible admission to a Theological college, and ordination as despised licentiates.'

The anger of the elder was reflected as simple sadness in the face of the other. ' We can preach the Gospel as well without a hood on our surplices as with one,' he said with feeble consolation.

' Preach the Gospel—true,' said Joshua with a slight pursing of mouth. ' But we can't rise ! '

' Let us make the best of it, and grind on.'

The other was silent, and they drearily bent over their books again.

The cause of all this gloom, the millwright Halborough, now snoring in the shed, had been a thriving master-machinist, notwithstanding his free and careless disposition, till a taste for a more than adequate quantity of strong liquor took hold of him ; since when his habits had inter-fered with his business sadly. Already millers went else-where for their gear, and only one set of hands was now kept going, though there were formerly two. Already he found a difficulty in meeting his men at the week's end, and though they had been reduced in number there was barely enough work to do for those who remained.

The sun dropped lower and vanished, the shouts of the village children ceased to resound, darkness cloaked the students' bedroom, and all the scene outwardly breathed peace. None knew of the fevered youthful ambitions that throbbed in two breasts within the quiet creeper-covered walls of the millwright's house.

In a few months the brothers left the village of their birth to enter themselves as students in a training college for schoolmasters ; first having placed their young sister Rosa under as efficient a tuition at a fashionable watering-place as the means at their disposal could command.

II

A man in semi-clerical dress was walking along the road which led from the railway-station into a provincial town. As he walked he read persistently, only looking up once now and then to see that he was keeping on the foot-track and to avoid other passengers. At those moments, who-ever had known the former students at the millwright's would have perceived that one of them, Joshua Halborough, was the peripatetic reader here.

What had been simple force in the youth's face was energized judgment in the man's. His character was gradually writing itself out in his countenance. That he was watching his own career with deeper and deeper interest, that he continually 'heard his days before him,' and cared to hear little else, might have been hazarded from what was seen there. His ambitions were, in truth, passionate, yet controlled; so that the germs of many more plans than ever blossomed to maturity had place in him; and forward visions were kept purposely in twilight, to avoid distraction.

Events so far had been encouraging. Shortly after assuming the mastership of his first school he had obtained an introduction to the Bishop of a diocese far from his native county, who had looked upon him as a promising young man and taken him in hand. He was now in the second year of his residence at the theological college of the cathedral-town, and would soon be presented for ordination.

He entered the town, turned into a back street, and then into a yard, keeping his book before him till he set foot under the arch of the latter place. Round the arch was written 'National School,' and the stonework of the jambs was worn away as nothing but boys and the waves of ocean will wear it. He was soon amid the sing-song accents of the scholars.

His brother Cornelius, who was the schoolmaster here, laid down the pointer with which he was directing attention to the Capes of Europe, and came forward.

'That's his brother Jos!' whispered one of the sixth-standard boys. 'He's going to be a pa'son. He's now at college.'

'Corney is going to be one, too, when he's saved enough money,' said another.

After greeting his brother, whom he had not seen for several months, the junior began to explain his system of teaching geography.

But Halborough the elder took no interest in the sub-

ject. 'How about your own studies?' he asked. 'Did
you get the books I sent?'

Cornelius had received them, and he related what he was
doing.

'Mind you work in the morning. What time do you get
up?'

The younger replied: 'Half-past five.'

'Half-past four is not a minute too soon this time of the
year. There is no time like the morning for construing.
I don't know why, but when I feel even too dreary to
read a novel I can translate—there is something mechanical
about it I suppose. Now, Cornelius, you are rather behind-
hand, and have some heavy reading before you if you mean
to get out of this next Christmas.'

'I am afraid I have.'

'We must soon sound the Bishop. I am sure you
will get a title without difficulty when he has heard all.
The sub-dean, the principal of my college, says that the
best plan will be for you to come there when his lordship
is present at an examination, and he'll get you a personal
interview with him. Mind you make a good impression
upon him. I found in my case that that was everything,
and doctrine almost nothing. You'll do for a deacon, Corney, if not for a priest.'

The younger remained thoughtful. 'Have you heard
from Rosa lately?' he asked; 'I had a letter this morning.'

'Yes. The little minx writes rather too often. She
is homesick—though Brussels must be an attractive place
enough. But she must make the most of her time over
there. I thought a year would be enough for her, after that
high-class school at Sandbourne, but I have decided to give
her two, and make a good job of it, expensive as the establishment is.'

Their two rather harsh faces had softened directly they
began to speak of their sister, whom they loved more
ambitiously than they loved themselves.

'But where is the money to come from, Joshua?'

'I have already got it.' He looked round, and finding
that some boys were near withdrew a few steps. 'I
have borrowed it at five per cent. from the farmer who

used to occupy the farm next our field. You remember him.'

' But about paying him ? '

' I shall pay him by degrees out of my stipend. No, Cornelius, it was no use to do the thing by halves. She promises to be a most attractive, not to say beautiful, girl. I have seen that for years ; and if her face is not her fortune, her face and her brains together will be, if I observe and contrive aright. That she should be, every inch of her, an accomplished and refined woman, was indispensable for the fulfilment of her destiny, and for moving onwards and upwards with us ; and she'll do it, you will see. I'd half starve myself rather than take her away from that school now.'

They looked round the school they were in. To Cornelius it was natural and familiar enough, but to Joshua, with his limited human sympathies, who had just dropped in from a superior sort of place, the sight jarred unpleasantly, as being that of something he had left behind. ' I shall be glad when you are out of this,' he said, ' and in your pulpit, and well through your first sermon.'

' You may as well say inducted into my fat living, while you are about it.'

' Ah, well—don't think lightly of the Church. There's a fine work for any man of energy in the Church, as you'll find,' he said fervidly. ' Torrents of infidelity to be stemmed, new views of old subjects to be expounded, truths in spirit to be substituted for truths in the letter. . . .' He lapsed into reverie with the vision of his career, persuading himself that it was ardour for Christianity which spurred him on, and not pride of place. He had shouldered a body of doctrine, and was prepared to defend it tooth and nail, solely for the honour and glory that warriors win.

' If the Church is elastic, and stretches to the shape of the time, she'll last, I suppose,' said Cornelius. ' If not——. Only think, I bought a copy of Paley's *Evidences*, best edition, broad margins, excellent preservation, at a bookstall the other day for—ninepence ; and I thought that at this rate Christianity must be in rather a bad way.'

'No, no!' said the other almost angrily. 'It only shows that such defences are no longer necessary. Men's eyes can see the truth without extraneous assistance. Besides, we are in for Christianity, and must stick to her whether or no. I am just now going right through Pusey's *Library of the Fathers*.'

'You'll be a bishop, Joshua, before you have done!'

'Ah!' said the other bitterly, shaking his head. 'Perhaps I might have been—I might have been! But where is my D.D. or LL.D.; and how be a bishop without that kind of appendage? Archbishop Tillotson was the son of a Sowerby clothier, but he was sent to Clare College. To hail Oxford or Cambridge as *alma mater* is not for me—for us! My God! when I think of what we should have been —what fair promise has been blighted by that cursed, worthless——'

'Hush, hush! . . . But I feel it, too, as much as you. I have seen it more forcibly lately. You would have obtained your degree long before this time—possibly fellowship—and I should have been on my way to mine.'

'Don't talk of it,' said the other. 'We must do the best we can.'

They looked out of the window sadly, through the dusty panes, so high up that only the sky was visible. By degrees the haunting trouble loomed again, and Cornelius broke the silence with a whisper : 'He has called on me!'

The living pulses died on Joshua's face, which grew arid as a clinker. 'When was that?' he asked quickly.

'Last week.'

'How did he get here—so many miles?'

'Came by railway. He came to ask for money.'

'Ah!'

'He says he will call on you.'

Joshua replied resignedly. The theme of their conversation spoilt his buoyancy for that afternoon. He returned in the evening, Cornelius accompanying him to the station ; but he did not read in the train which took him back to the Fountall Theological College, as he had done on the way out. That ineradicable trouble still remained as a squalid spot in the expanse of his life. He

sat with the other students in the cathedral choir next day ;
and the recollection of the trouble obscured the purple
splendour thrown by the panes upon the floor.

It was afternoon. All was as still in the Close as a
cathedral-green can be between the Sunday services, and
the incessant cawing of the rooks was the only sound.
Joshua Halborough had finished his ascetic lunch, and had
gone into the library, where he stood for a few moments
looking out of the large window facing the green. He
saw walking slowly across it a man in a fustian coat and a
battered white hat with a much-ruffled nap, having upon
his arm a tall gipsy-woman wearing long brass ear-rings.
The man was staring quizzically at the west front of the
cathedral, and Halborough recognized in him the form and
features of his father. Who the woman was he knew not.
Almost as soon as Joshua became conscious of these things,
the sub-dean, who was also the principal of the college, and
of whom the young man stood in more awe than of the
Bishop himself, emerged from the gate and entered a path
across the Close. The pair met the dignitary, and to
Joshua's horror his father turned and addressed the sub-
dean.

What passed between them he could not tell. But
as he stood in a cold sweat he saw his father place his
hand familiarly on the sub-dean's shoulder ; the shrinking
response of the latter, and his quick withdrawal, told his
feeling. The woman seemed to say nothing, but when the
sub-dean had passed by they came on towards the college
gate.

Halborough flew along the corridor and out at a side
door, so as to intercept them before they could reach the
front entrance, for which they were making. He caught
them behind a clump of laurel.

' By Jerry, here's the very chap ! Well, you're a fine
fellow, Jos, never to send your father as much as a twist
o' baccy on such an occasion, and to leave him to travel all
these miles to find 'ee out ! '

' First, who is this ? ' said Joshua Halborough with pale
dignity, waving his hand towards the buxom woman with
the great ear-rings.

'Dammy, the mis'ess! Your step-mother! Didn't
you know I'd married? She helped me home from market
one night, and we came to terms, and struck the bargain.
Didn't we, Selinar?'

'Oi, by the great Lord an' we did!' simpered the lady.

'Well, what sort of a place is this you are living in?'
asked the millwright. 'A kind of house-of-correction
apparently?'

Joshua listened abstractedly, his features set to resignation. Sick at heart he was going to ask them if they were
in want of any necessary, any meal, when his father cut
him short by saying, 'Why, we've called to ask ye to come
round and take pot-luck with us at the Cock-and-Bottle,
where we've put up for the day, on our way to see mis'ess's
friends at Binegar Fair, where they'll be lying under
canvas for a night or two. As for the victuals at the
Cock I can't testify to 'em at all; but for the drink, they've
the rarest drop of Old Tom that I've tasted for many a
year.'

'Thanks; but I am a teetotaller; and I have lunched,'
said Joshua, who could fully believe his father's testimony
to the gin, from the odour of his breath. 'You see we
have to observe regular habits here; and I couldn't be
seen at the Cock-and-Bottle just now.'

'O dammy, then don't come, your reverence. Perhaps
you won't mind standing treat for those who can be seen
there?'

'Not a penny,' said the younger firmly. 'You've had
enough already.'

'Thank you for nothing. By the bye, who was that
spindle-legged, shoe-buckled parson feller we met by
now? He seemed to think we should poison him!'

Joshua remarked coldly that it was the principal of his
college, guardedly inquiring, 'Did you tell him whom you
were come to see?'

His father did not reply. He and his strapping gipsy
wife—if she were his wife—stayed no longer, and disappeared in the direction of the High Street. Joshua
Halborough went back to the library. Determined as was
his nature, he wept hot tears upon the books, and was

immeasurably more wretched that afternoon than the
unwelcome millwright. In the evening he sat down and
wrote a letter to his brother, in which, after stating what
had happened, and expatiating upon this new disgrace in
the gipsy wife, he propounded a plan for raising money
sufficient to induce the couple to emigrate to Canada. ' It
is our only chance,' he said. ' The case as it stands is
maddening. For a successful painter, sculptor, musician,
author, who takes society by storm, it is no drawback,
it is sometimes even a romantic recommendation, to hail
from outcasts and profligates. But for a clergyman of the
Church of England ! Cornelius, it is fatal ! To succeed
in the Church, people must believe in you, first of all, as a
gentleman, secondly as a man of means, thirdly as a
scholar, fourthly as a preacher, fifthly, perhaps, as a Christian—but always first as a gentleman, with all their heart
and soul and strength. I would have faced the fact of
being a small machinist's son, and have taken my chance,
if he'd been in any sense respectable and decent. The
essence of Christianity is humility, and by the help of God
I would have brazened it out. But this terrible vagabond-
age and disreputable connection ! If he does not accept
my terms and leave the country, it will extinguish us and
kill me. For how can we live, and relinquish our high
aim, and bring down our dear sister Rosa to the level of a
gipsy's step-daughter ? '

III

There was excitement in the parish of Narrobourne
one day. The congregation had just come out from
morning service, and the whole conversation was of the
new curate, Mr. Halborough, who had officiated for the
first time, in the absence of the rector.
Never before had the feeling of the villagers approached
a level which could be called excitement on such a matter
as this. The droning which had been the rule in that
quiet old place for a century seemed ended at last. They
repeated the text to each other as a refrain : ' O Lord, be
Thou my helper ! ' Not within living memory till to-day
had the subject of the sermon formed the topic of conver-

sation from the church door to the churchyard gate, to the exclusion of personal remarks on those who had been present, and on the week's news in general.

The thrilling periods of the preacher hung about their minds all that day. The parish being steeped in indifferentism, it happened that when the youths and maidens, middle-aged and old people, who had attended church that morning, recurred as by a fascination to what Halborough had said, they did so more or less indirectly, and even with the subterfuge of a light laugh that was not real, so great was their shyness under the novelty of their sensations.

What was more curious than that these unconventional villagers should have been excited by a preacher of a new school after forty years of familiarity with the old hand who had had charge of their souls, was the effect of Halborough's address upon the occupants of the manor-house pew, including the owner of the estate. These thought they knew how to discount the mere sensational sermon, how to minimize flash oratory to its bare proportions ; but they had yielded like the rest of the assembly to the charm of the newcomer.

Mr. Fellmer, the landowner, was a young widower, whose mother, still in the prime of life, had returned to her old position in the family mansion since the death of her son's wife in the year after her marriage, at the birth of a fragile little girl. From the date of his loss to the present time, Fellmer had led an inactive existence in the seclusion of the parish ; a lack of motive seemed to leave him listless. He had gladly reinstated his mother in the gloomy house, and his main occupation now lay in stewarding his estate, which was not large. Mrs. Fellmer, who had sat beside him under Halborough this morning, was a cheerful, straightforward woman, who did her marketing and her almsgiving in person, was fond of old-fashioned flowers, and walked about the village on very wet days visiting the parishioners. These, the only two great ones of Narrobourne, were impressed by Joshua's eloquence as much as the cottagers.

Halborough had been briefly introduced to them on his

arrival some days before, and, their interest being kindled, they waited a few moments till he came out of the vestry, to walk down the churchyard-path with him. Mrs. Fellmer spoke warmly of the sermon, of the good fortune of the parish in his advent, and hoped he had found comfortable quarters.

Halborough, faintly flushing, said that he had obtained very fair lodgings in the roomy house of a farmer, whom he named.

She feared he would find it very lonely, especially in the evenings, and hoped they would see a good deal of him. When would he dine with them ? Could he not come that day—it must be so dull for him the first Sunday evening in country lodgings ?

Halborough replied that it would give him much pleasure, but that he feared he must decline. ' I am not altogether alone,' he said. ' My sister, who has just returned from Brussels, and who felt, as you do, that I should be rather dismal by myself, has accompanied me hither to stay a few days till she has put my rooms in order and set me going. She was too fatigued to come to church, and is waiting for me now at the farm.'

' O, but bring your sister—that will be still better ! I shall be delighted to know her. How I wish I had been aware ! Do tell her, please, that we had no idea of her presence.'

Halborough assured Mrs. Fellmer that he would certainly bear the message ; but as to her coming he was not so sure. The real truth was, however, that the matter would be decided by him, Rosa having an almost filial respect for his wishes. But he was uncertain as to the state of her wardrobe, and had determined that she should not enter the manor-house at a disadvantage that evening, when there would probably be plenty of opportunities in the future of her doing so becomingly.

He walked to the farm in long strides. This, then, was the outcome of his first morning's work as curate here. Things had gone fairly well with him. He had been ordained ; he was in a comfortable parish, where he would exercise almost sole supervision, the rector being infirm. He had made a deep impression at starting, and the absence of a hood seemed to have done him no harm. Moreover, by considerable persuasion and payment, his father and the dark woman had been shipped off to Canada, where they were not likely to interfere greatly with his interests.

Rosa came out to meet him. ' Ah ! you should have gone to church like a good girl,' he said.

' Yes—I wished I had afterwards. But I do so hate church as a rule that even your preaching was under-estimated in my mind. It was too bad of me ! '

The girl who spoke thus playfully was fair, tall, and sylph-like, in a muslin dress, and with just the coquettish *désinvolture* which an English girl brings home from abroad, and loses again after a few months of native life. Joshua was the reverse of playful ; the world was too important a concern for him to indulge in light moods. He told her in decided, practical phraseology of the invitation.

' Now, Rosa, we must go—that's settled—if you've a dress that can be made fit to wear all on the hop like this. You didn't, of course, think of bringing an evening dress to such an out-of-the-way place ? '

But Rosa had come from the wrong city to be caught napping in those matters. ' Yes, I did,' said she. ' One never knows what may turn up.'

' Well done ! Then off we go at seven.'

The evening drew on, and at dusk they started on foot, Rosa pulling up the edge of her skirt under her cloak out of the way of the dews, so that it formed a great wind-bag all round her, and carrying her satin shoes under her arm. Joshua would not let her wait till she got indoors before changing them, as she proposed, but insisted on her performing that operation under a tree, so that they might enter as if they had not walked. He was nervously formal about such trifles, while Rosa took the whole proceeding—walk, dressing, dinner, and all—as a pastime. To Joshua it was a serious step in life.

A more unexpected kind of person for a curate's sister was never presented at a dinner. The surprise of Mrs. Fellmer was unconcealed. She had looked forward to a

Dorcas, or Martha, or Rhoda at the outside, and a shade of misgiving crossed her face. It was possible that, had the young lady accompanied her brother to church, there would have been no dining at Narrobourne House that day.

Not so with the young widower, her son. He resembled a sleeper who had awaked in a summer noon expecting to find it only dawn. He could scarcely help stretching his arms and yawning in their faces, so strong was his sense of being suddenly aroused to an unforeseen thing. When they had sat down to table he at first talked to Rosa somewhat with the air of a ruler in the land ; but the woman lurking in the acquaintance soon brought him to his level, and the girl from Brussels saw him looking at her mouth, her hands, her contour, as if he could not quite comprehend how they got created : then he dropped into the more satisfactory stage which discerns no particulars.

He talked but little ; she said much. The homeliness of the Fellmers, to her view, though they were regarded with such awe down here, quite disembarrassed her. The squire had become so unpractised, had dropped so far into the shade during the last year or so of his life, that he had almost forgotten what the world contained till this evening reminded him. His mother, after her first moments of doubt, appeared to think that he must be left to his own guidance, and gave her attention to Joshua.

With all his foresight and doggedness of aim, the result of that dinner exceeded Halborough's expectations. In weaving his ambitions he had viewed his sister Rosa as a slight, bright thing to be helped into notice by his abilities ; but it now began to dawn upon him that the physical gifts of Nature to her might do more for them both than Nature's intellectual gifts to himself. While he was patiently boring the tunnel Rosa seemed about to fly over the mountain.

He wrote the next day to his brother, now occupying his own old rooms in the theological college, telling him exultingly of the unanticipated *début* of Rosa at the manor-house. The next post brought him a reply of congratulation, dashed with the counteracting intelligence that his father did not like Canada—that his gipsy wife had deserted him, which made him feel so dreary that he thought of returning home.

In his recent satisfaction at his own successes Joshua Halborough had well-nigh forgotten his chronic trouble —latterly screened by distance. But it now returned upon him ; he saw more in this brief announcement than his brother seemed to see. It was the cloud no bigger than a man's hand.

IV

The following December, a day or two before Christmas, Mrs. Fellmer and her son were walking up and down the broad gravel path which bordered the east front of the house. Till within the last half-hour the morning had been a drizzling one, and they had just emerged for a short turn before luncheon.

'You see, dear mother,' the son was saying, 'it is the peculiarity of my position which makes her appear to me in such a desirable light. When you consider how I have been crippled at starting, how my life has been maimed ; that I feel anything like publicity distasteful, that I have no political ambition, and that my chief aim and hope lie in the education of the little thing Annie has left me, you must see how desirable a wife like Miss Halborough would be, to prevent my becoming a mere vegetable.'

'If you adore her, I suppose you must have her ! ' replied his mother with dry indirectness. 'But you'll find that she will not be content to live on here as you do, giving her whole mind to a young child.'

'That's just where we differ. Her very disqualification, that of being a nobody, as you call it, is her recommendation in my eyes. Her lack of influential connections limits her ambition. From what I know of her, a life in this place is all that she would wish for. She would never care to go outside the park-gates if it were necessary to stay within.'

'Being in love with her, Albert, and meaning to marry her, you invent your practical reasons to make the case

respectable. Well, do as you will; I have no authority
over you, so why should you consult me? You mean
to propose on this very occasion, no doubt. Don't you,
now?'

'By no means. I am merely revolving the idea in my
mind. If on further acquaintance she turns out to be as
good as she has hitherto seemed—well, I shall see. Admit,
now, that you like her.'

'I readily admit it. She is very captivating at first
sight. But as a step-mother to your child! You seem
mighty anxious, Albert, to get rid of me!'

'Not at all. And I am not so reckless as you think.
I don't make up my mind in a hurry. But the thought
having occurred to me, I mention it to you at once, mother.
If you dislike it, say so.'

'I don't say anything. I will try to make the best
of it if you are determined. When does she come?'

'To-morrow.'

All this time there were great preparations in train
at the curate's, who was now a householder. Rosa, whose
two or three weeks' stay on two occasions earlier in the
year had so affected the squire, was coming again, and at
the same time her younger brother Cornelius, to make
up a family party. Rosa, who journeyed from the Midlands, could not arrive till late in the evening, but Cornelius was to get there in the afternoon, Joshua going out
to meet him in his walk across the fields from the railway.

Everything being ready in Joshua's modest abode he
started on his way, his heart buoyant and thankful, if
ever it was in his life. He was of such good report himself
that his brother's path into holy orders promised to be
unexpectedly easy; and he longed to compare experiences
with him, even though there was on hand a more exciting
matter still. From his youth he had held that, in old-
fashioned country places, the Church conferred social
prestige up to a certain point at a cheaper price than
any other profession or pursuit; and events seemed to be
proving him right.

He had walked about half-an-hour when he saw Cornelius
coming along the path; and in a few minutes the two

brothers met. The experiences of Cornelius had been less immediately interesting than those of Joshua, but his personal position was satisfactory, and there was nothing to account for the singularly subdued manner that he exhibited, which at first Joshua set down to the fatigue of over-study ; and he proceeded to the subject of Rosa's arrival in the evening, and the probable consequences of this her third visit. ' Before next Easter she'll be his wife, my boy,' said Joshua with grave exultation.

Cornelius shook his head. ' She comes too late ! ' he returned.

' What do you mean ? '

' Look here.' He produced the Fountall paper, and placed his finger on a paragraph, which Joshua read. It appeared under the report of Petty Sessions, and was a commonplace case of disorderly conduct, in which a man was sent to prison for seven days for breaking windows in that town.

' Well ? ' said Joshua.

' It happened during an evening that I was in the street ; and the offender is our father.'

' Not—how—I sent him more money on his promising to stay in Canada ? '

' He is home, safe enough.' Cornelius in the same gloomy tone gave the remainder of his information. He had witnessed the scene, unobserved of his father, and had heard him say that he was on his way to see his daughter, who was going to marry a rich gentleman. The only good fortune attending the untoward incident was that the millwright's name had been printed as Joshua Alborough.

' Beaten ! We are to be beaten on the eve of our ex- pected victory ! ' said the elder brother. ' How did he guess that Rosa was likely to marry ? Good Heaven ! Cornelius, you seem doomed to bring bad news always, do you not ? '

' I do,' said Cornelius. ' Poor Rosa ! '

It was almost in tears, so great was their heart-sickness and shame, that the brothers walked the remainder of the way to Joshua's dwelling. In the evening they set out to meet Rosa, bringing her to the village in a fly ; and when she had come into the house, and was sitting down with them, they almost forgot their secret anxiety in contemplating her, who knew nothing about it.

Next day the Fellmers came, and the two or three days after that were a lively time. That the squire was yielding to his impulses—making up his mind—there could be no doubt. On Sunday Cornelius read the service, and Joshua preached. Mrs. Fellmer was quite maternal towards Rosa, and it appeared that she had decided to welcome the inevitable with a good grace. The pretty girl was to spend yet another afternoon with the elder lady, super-intending some parish treat at the house in observance of Christmas, and afterwards to stay on to dinner, her brothers to fetch her in the evening. They were also invited to dine, but they could not accept owing to an engagement.

The engagement was of a sombre sort. They were going to meet their father, who would that day be re-leased from Fountall Gaol, and try to persuade him to keep away from Narrobourne. Every exertion was to be made to get him back to Canada, to his old home in the Midlands—anywhere, so that he would not impinge disastrously upon their courses, and blast their sister's prospects of the auspicious marriage which was just then hanging in the balance.

As soon as Rosa had been fetched away by her friends at the manor-house her brothers started on their expedi-tion, without waiting for dinner or tea. Cornelius, to whom the millwright always addressed his letters when he wrote any, drew from his pocket and re-read as he walked the curt note which had led to this journey being undertaken ; it was despatched by their father the night before, imme-diately upon his liberation, and stated that he was setting out for Narrobourne at the moment of writing ; that having no money he would be obliged to walk all the way ; that he calculated on passing through the intervening town of Ivell about six on the following day, where he should sup at the Castle Inn, and where he hoped they would meet him with a carriage-and-pair, or some other such conveyance, that he might not disgrace them by arriving like a tramp.

'That sounds as if he gave a thought to our position,' said Cornelius.

Joshua knew the satire that lurked in the paternal words, and said nothing. Silence prevailed during the greater part of their journey. The lamps were lighted in Ivell when they entered the streets, and Cornelius, who was quite unknown in this neighbourhood, and who, moreover, was not in clerical attire, decided that he should be the one to call at the Castle Inn. Here, in answer to his inquiry under the darkness of the archway, they told him that such a man as he had described left the house about a quarter of an hour earlier, after making a meal in the kitchen-settle. He was rather the worse for liquor.

'Then,' said Joshua, when Cornelius joined him outside with this intelligence, 'we must have met and passed him! And now that I think of it, we did meet some one who was unsteady in his gait, under the trees on the other side of Hendford Hill, where it was too dark to see him.'

They rapidly retraced their steps; but for a long stretch of the way home could discern nobody. When, however, they had gone about three-quarters of the distance, they became conscious of an irregular footfall in front of them, and could see a whitish figure in the gloom. They followed dubiously. The figure met another wayfarer—the single one that had been encountered upon this lonely road—and they distinctly heard him ask the way to Narrobourne. The stranger replied—what was quite true—that the nearest way was by turning in at the stile by the next bridge, and following the footpath which branched thence across the meadows.

When the brothers reached the stile they also entered the path, but did not overtake the subject of their worry till they had crossed two or three meads, and the lights from Narrobourne manor-house were visible before them through the trees. Their father was no longer walking; he was seated against the wet bank of an adjoining hedge. Observing their forms he shouted, 'I'm going to Narrobourne; who may you be?'

They went up to him, and revealed themselves, remind-

ing him of the plan which he had himself proposed in his
note, that they should meet him at Ivell.

'By Jerry, I'd forgot it!' he said. 'Well, what do
you want me to do?' His tone was distinctly quarrel-
some.

A long conversation followed, which became embittered at the first hint from them that he should not come
to the village. The millwright drew a quart bottle from
his pocket, and challenged them to drink if they meant
friendly and called themselves men. Neither of the two
had touched alcohol for years, but for once they thought
it best to accept, so as not to needlessly provoke him.

'What's in it?' said Joshua.

'A drop of weak gin-and-water. It won't hurt 'ee.
Drink from the bottle.' Joshua did so, and his father
pushed up the bottom of the vessel so as to make him
swallow a good deal in spite of himself. It went down into
his stomach like molten lead.

'Ha, ha, that's right!' said old Halborough. 'But
'twas raw spirit—ha, ha!'

'Why should you take me in so?' said Joshua, losing
his self-command, try as he would to keep calm.

'Because you took me in, my lad, in banishing me to
that cursed country under pretence that it was for my good.
You were a pair of hypocrites to say so. It was done to
get rid of me—no more nor less. But, by Jerry, I'm a
match for ye now! I'll spoil your souls for preaching.
My daughter is going to be married to the squire here.
I've heard the news—I saw it in a paper!'

'It is premature——'

'I know it is true; and I'm her father, and I shall
give her away, or there'll be a hell of a row, I can assure
'ee! Is that where the gennleman lives?'

Joshua Halborough writhed in impotent despair. Fellmer had not yet positively declared himself, his mother
was hardly won round; a scene with their father in the
parish would demolish as fair a palace of hopes as was
ever builded. The millwright rose. 'If that's where the
squire lives I'm going to call. Just arrived from Canady
with her fortune—ha, ha! I wish no harm to the gennleman,

and the gennleman will wish no harm to me. But I like
to take my place in the family, and stand upon my rights,
and lower people's pride ! '

' You've succeeded already ! Where's that woman
you took with you——'

' Woman ! She was my wife as lawful as the Constitution—a sight more lawful than your mother was till some
time after you were born ! '

Joshua had for many years before heard whispers that
his father had cajoled his mother in their early acquaintance, and had made somewhat tardy amends ; but never
from his father's lips till now. It was the last stroke, and
he could not bear it. He sank back against the hedge. ' It
is over ! ' he said. ' He ruins us all ! '

The millwright moved on, waving his stick triumphantly,
and the two brothers stood still. They could see his
drab figure stalking along the path, and over his head
the lights from the conservatory of Narrobourne House,
inside which Albert Fellmer might possibly be sitting with
Rosa at that moment, holding her hand, and asking her to
share his home with him.

The staggering whity-brown form, advancing to put a
blot on all this, had been diminishing in the shade ; and
now suddenly disappeared beside a weir. There was the
noise of a flounce in the water.

' He has fallen in ! ' said Cornelius, starting forward
to run for the place at which his father had vanished.

Joshua, awaking from the stupefied reverie into which
he had sunk, rushed to the other's side before he had
taken ten steps. ' Stop, stop, what are you thinking of ? '
he whispered hoarsely, grasping Cornelius's arm.

' Pulling him out ! '

' Yes, yes—so am I. But—wait a moment——'

' But, Joshua ! '

' Her life and happiness, you know—Cornelius—and
your reputation and mine—and our chance of rising
together, all three——'

He clutched his brother's arm to the bone ; and as
they stood breathless the splashing and floundering in
the weir continued ; over it they saw the hopeful lights

from the manor-house conservatory winking through
the trees as their bare branches waved to and fro. In
their pause there had been time to save him twice over.

The floundering and splashing grew weaker, and they
could hear gurgling words : ' Help—I'm drownded ! Rosie
—Rosie ! '

' We'll go—we *must* save him. O Joshua ! '

' Yes, yes ! we must ! '

Still they did not move, but waited, holding each
other, each thinking the same thought. Weights of lead
seemed to be affixed to their feet, which would no longer
obey their wills. The mead became silent. Over it they
fancied they could see figures moving in the conservatory.
The air up there seemed to emit gentle kisses.

Cornelius started forward at last, and Joshua almost
simultaneously. Two or three minutes brought them to
the brink of the stream. At first they could see nothing
in the water, though it was not so deep nor the night so
dark but that their father's light kerseymere coat would
have been visible if he had lain at the bottom. Joshua
looked this way and that.

' He has drifted into the culvert,' he said.

Below the foot-bridge of the weir the stream suddenly
narrowed to half its width, to pass under a barrel arch or
culvert constructed for waggons to cross into the middle
of the mead in haymaking time. It being at present the
season of high water the arch was full to the crown, against
which the ripples clucked every now and then. At this
point he had just caught sight of a pale object slipping
under. In a moment it was gone.

They went to the lower end, but nothing emerged. For
a long time they tried at both ends to effect some communication with the interior, but to no purpose.

' We ought to have come sooner ! ' said the conscience-
stricken Cornelius, when they were quite exhausted, and
dripping wet.

' I suppose we ought,' replied Joshua heavily. He
perceived his father's walking-stick on the bank ; hastily
picking it up he stuck it into the mud among the sedge.
Then they went on.

'Shall we—say anything about this accident?' whispered Cornelius as they approached the door of Joshua's house.

'What's the use? It can do no good. We must wait until he is found.'

They went indoors and changed their clothes; after which they started for the manor-house, reaching it about ten o'clock. Besides their sister there were only three guests; an adjoining landowner and his wife, and the infirm old rector.

Rosa, although she had parted from them so recently, grasped their hands in an ecstatic, brimming, joyful manner, as if she had not seen them for years. 'You look pale,' she said.

The brothers answered that they had had a long walk, and were somewhat tired. Everybody in the room seemed charged full with some sort of interesting knowledge: the squire's neighbour and neighbour's wife looked wisely around; and Fellmer himself played the part of host with a preoccupied bearing which approached fervour. They left at eleven, not accepting the carriage offered, the distance being so short and the roads dry. The squire came rather further into the dark with them than he need have done, and wished Rosa good-night in a mysterious manner, slightly apart from the rest.

When they were walking along Joshua said, with a desperate attempt at joviality, 'Rosa, what's going on?'

'O, I——' she began between a gasp and a bound. 'He——'

'Never mind—if it disturbs you.'

She was so excited that she could not speak connectedly at first, the practised air which she had brought home with her having disappeared. Calming herself she added, 'I am not disturbed, and nothing has happened. Only he said he wanted to ask me *something*, some day; and I said never mind that now. He hasn't asked yet, and is coming to speak to you about it. He would have done so to-night, only I asked him not to be in a hurry. But he will come to-morrow, I am sure!'

V

It was summer-time, six months later, and mowers and haymakers were at work in the meads. The manor-house, being opposite them, frequently formed a peg for conversation during these operations; and the doings of the squire, and the squire's young wife, the curate's sister —who was at present the admired of most of them, and the interest of all—met with their due amount of criticism.

Rosa was happy, if ever woman could be said to be so. She had not learnt the fate of her father, and sometimes wondered—perhaps with a sense of relief—why he did not write to her from his supposed home in Canada. Her brother Joshua had been presented to a living in a small town, shortly after her marriage, and Cornelius had thereupon succeeded to the vacant curacy of Narrobourne.

These two had awaited in deep suspense the discovery of their father's body; and yet the discovery had not been made. Every day they expected a man or a boy to run up from the meads with the intelligence; but he had never come. Days had accumulated to weeks and months; the wedding had come and gone: Joshua had tolled and read himself in at his new parish; and never a shout of amazement over the millwright's remains.

But now, in June, when they were mowing the meads, the hatches had to be drawn and the water let out of its channels for the convenience of the mowers. It was thus that the discovery was made. A man, stooping low with his scythe, caught a view of the culvert lengthwise, and saw something entangled in the recently bared weeds of its bed. A day or two after there was an inquest; but the body was unrecognizable. Fish and flood had been busy with the millwright; he had no watch or marked article which could be identified; and a verdict of the accidental drowning of a person unknown settled the matter.

As the body was found in Narrobourne parish, there it had to be buried. Cornelius wrote to Joshua, begging him to come and read the service, or to send some one; he himself could not do it. Rather than let in a stranger

Joshua came, and silently scanned the coroner's order handed him by the undertaker :—

' I, Henry Giles, Coroner for the Mid-Division of Outer Wessex, do hereby order the Burial of the Body now shown to the Inquest Jury as the Body of an Adult Male Person Unknown . . .,' etc.

Joshua Halborough got through the service in some way, and rejoined his brother Cornelius at his house. Neither accepted an invitation to lunch at their sister's ; they wished to discuss parish matters together. In the afternoon she came down, though they had already called on her, and had not expected to see her again. Her bright eyes, brown hair, flowery bonnet, lemon-coloured gloves, and flush beauty, were like an irradiation into the apartment, which they in their gloom could hardly bear.

' I forgot to tell you,' she said, ' of a curious thing which happened to me a month or two before my marriage— something which I have thought may have had a con- nection with the accident to the poor man you have buried to-day. It was on that evening I was at the manor-house waiting for you to fetch me ; I was in the winter-garden with Albert, and we were sitting silent together, when we fancied we heard a cry in the distant meadow. We opened the door, and while Albert ran to fetch his hat, leaving me standing there, the cry was repeated, and my excited senses made me think I heard my own name. When Albert came back all was silent, and we decided that it was only a drunken shout, and not a cry for help. We both forgot the incident, and it never has occurred to me till since the funeral to-day that it might have been this stranger's cry. The name of course was only fancy, or he might have had a wife or child with a name something like mine, poor man ! '

When she was gone the brothers were silent till Cornelius said, ' Now mark this, Joshua. Sooner or later she'll know.'

' How ? '

' From one of us. Do you think human hearts are iron- cased safes, that you suppose we can keep this secret for ever ? '

'Yes, I think they are, sometimes,' said Joshua.

'No. It will out. We shall tell.'

'What, and ruin her—kill her? Disgrace her children, and pull down the whole auspicious house of Fellmer about our ears? No! May I—drown where he was drowned before I do it! Never, never. Surely you can say the same, Cornelius!'

Cornelius seemed fortified, and no more was said. For a long time after that day he did not see Joshua, and before the next year was out a son and heir was born to the Fellmers. The villagers rang the three bells every evening for a week and more, and were made merry by Mr. Fellmer's ale; and when the christening came on Joshua paid Narrobourne another visit.

Among all the people who assembled on that day the brother clergymen were the least interested. Their minds were haunted by a spirit in kerseymere. In the evening they walked together in the fields.

'She's all right,' said Joshua. 'But here are you doing journey-work, Cornelius, and likely to continue at it till the end of the day, as far as I can see. I, too, with my petty living—what am I after all? . . . To tell the truth, the Church is a poor forlorn hope for people without influence, particularly when their enthusiasm begins to flag. A social regenerator has a better chance outside, where he is unhampered by dogma and tradition. As for me, I would rather have gone on mending mills, with my crust of bread and liberty.'

Almost automatically they had bent their steps along the margin of the river; they now paused. They were standing on the brink of the well-known weir. There were the hatches, there was the culvert; they could see the pebbly bed of the stream through the pellucid water. The notes of the church-bells were audible, still jangled by the enthusiastic villagers.

'Why, see—it was there I hid his walking-stick!' said Joshua, looking towards the sedge. The next moment, during a passing breeze, something flashed white on the spot to which the attention of Cornelius was drawn.

From the sedge rose a straight little silver-poplar, and

it was the leaves of this sapling which caused the flicker of whiteness.

'His walking-stick has grown!' Joshua added. 'It was a rough one—cut from the hedge, I remember.'

At every puff of wind the tree turned white, till they could not bear to look at it; and they walked away.

'I see him every night,' Cornelius murmured. . . . 'Ah, we read our *Hebrews* to little account, Jos! Ὑπέμεινε σταυρὸν, αἰσχύνης καταφρονήσας. To have *endured* the cross, *despising* the shame—there lay greatness! But now I often feel that I should like to put an end to trouble here in this selfsame spot.'

'I have thought of it myself,' said Joshua.

'Perhaps we shall, some day,' murmured his brother.

'Perhaps,' said Joshua moodily.

With that contingency to consider in the silence of their nights and days they bent their steps homewards.

December 1888.

ON THE WESTERN CIRCUIT

ON THE WESTERN CIRCUIT

I

THE man who played the disturbing part in the two quiet feminine lives hereunder depicted—no great man, in any sense, by the way—first had knowledge of them on an October evening, in the city of Melchester. He had been standing in the Close, vainly endeavouring to gain amid the darkness a glimpse of the most homogeneous pile of mediæval architecture in England, which towered and tapered from the damp and level sward in front of him. While he stood the presence of the Cathedral walls was revealed rather by the ear than by the eyes; he could not see them, but they reflected sharply a roar of sound which entered the Close by a street leading from the city square, and, falling upon the building, was flung back upon him.

He postponed till the morrow his attempt to examine the deserted edifice, and turned his attention to the noise. It was compounded of steam barrel-organs, the clanging of gongs, the ringing of hand-bells, the clack of rattles, and the undistinguishable shouts of men. A lurid light hung in the air in the direction of the tumult. Thitherward he went, passing under the arched gateway, along a straight street, and into the square.

He might have searched Europe over for a greater contrast between juxtaposed scenes. The spectacle was that of the eighth chasm of the Inferno as to colour and flame, and, as to mirth, a development of the Homeric heaven. A smoky glare, of the complexion of brass-filings, ascended from the fiery tongues of innumerable naphtha lamps affixed to booths, stalls, and other temporary erections which crowded the spacious market-square. In front of this irradiation scores of human figures, more or less in profile, were darting athwart

351

and across, up, down, and around, like gnats against a
sunset.

Their motions were so rhythmical that they seemed
to be moved by machinery. And it presently appeared
that they were moved by machinery indeed ; the figures
being those of the patrons of swings, see-saws, flying-
leaps, above all of the three steam roundabouts which
occupied the centre of the position. It was from the latter
that the din of steam-organs came.

Throbbing humanity in full light was, on second thoughts,
better than architecture in the dark. The young man,
lighting a short pipe, and putting his hat on one side and
one hand in his pocket, to throw himself into harmony
with his new environment, drew near to the largest and
most patronized of the steam circuses, as the roundabouts
were called by their owners. This was one of brilliant
finish, and it was now in full revolution. The musical
instrument around which and to whose tones the riders
revolved, directed its trumpet-mouths of brass upon the
young man, and the long plate-glass mirrors set at angles,
which revolved with the machine, flashed the gyrating
personages and hobby-horses kaleidoscopically into his eyes.

It could now be seen that he was unlike the majority
of the crowd. A gentlemanly young fellow, one of the
species found in large towns only, and London particularly,
built on delicate lines, well, though not fashionably dressed,
he appeared to belong to the professional class ; he had
nothing square or practical about his look, much that
was curvilinear and sensuous. Indeed, some would have
called him a man not altogether typical of the middle-class
male of a century wherein sordid ambition is the master-
passion that seems to be taking the time-honoured place of
love.

The revolving figures passed before his eyes with an
unexpected and quiet grace in a throng whose natural
movements did not suggest gracefulness or quietude as a
rule. By some contrivance there was imparted to each
of the hobby-horses a motion which was really the triumph
and perfection of roundabout inventiveness—a galloping
rise and fall, so timed that, of each pair of steeds, one

was on the spring while the other was on the pitch.   The
riders were quite fascinated by these equine undulations
in this most delightful holiday-game of our times.   There
were riders as young as six, and as old as sixty years, with
every age between.   At first it was difficult to catch a
personality, but by and by the observer's eyes centred
on the prettiest girl out of the several pretty ones revolving.

It was not that one with the light frock and light hat
whom he had been at first attracted by ; no, it was the
one with the black cape, gray skirt, light gloves and—no,
not even she, but the one behind her ; she with the crimson
skirt, dark jacket, brown hat and brown gloves.   Unmistakably that was the prettiest girl.

Having finally selected her, this idle spectator studied
her as well as he was able during each of her brief transits
across his visual field.   She was absolutely unconscious
of everything save the act of riding : her features were
rapt in an ecstatic dreaminess ; for the moment she did
not know her age or her history or her lineaments, much
less her troubles.   He himself was full of vague latter-day
glooms and popular melancholies, and it was a refreshing
sensation to behold this young thing then and there,
absolutely as happy as if she were in a Paradise.

Dreading the moment when the inexorable stoker,
grimily lurking behind the glittering rococo-work, should
decide that this set of riders had had their pennyworth,
and bring the whole concern of steam-engine, horses,
mirrors, trumpets, drums, cymbals, and such-like to pause
and silence, he waited for her every reappearance, glancing
indifferently over the intervening forms, including the two
plainer girls, the old woman and child, the two youngsters,
the newly-married couple, the old man with a clay pipe, the
sparkish youth with a ring, the young ladies in the chariot,
the pair of journeyman-carpenters, and others, till his
select country beauty followed on again in her place.
He had never seen a fairer product of nature, and at each
round she made a deeper mark in his sentiments.   The
stoppage then came, and the sighs of the riders were
audible.

He moved round to the place at which he reckoned she would alight; but she retained her seat. The empty saddles began to refill, and she plainly was deciding to have another turn. The young man drew up to the side of her steed, and pleasantly asked her if she had enjoyed her ride.

'O yes!' she said, with dancing eyes. 'It has been quite unlike anything I have ever felt in my life before!'

It was not difficult to fall into conversation with her. Unreserved—too unreserved—by nature, she was not experienced enough to be reserved by art, and after a little coaxing she answered his remarks readily. She had come to live in Melchester from a village on the Great Plain, and this was the first time that she had ever seen a steam-circus; she could not understand how such wonderful machines were made. She had come to the city on the invitation of Mrs. Harnham, who had taken her into her household to train her as a servant, if she showed any aptitude. Mrs. Harnham was a young lady who before she married had been Miss Edith White, living in the country near the speaker's cottage; she was now very kind to her through knowing her in childhood so well. She was even taking the trouble to educate her. Mrs. Harnham was the only friend she had in the world, and being without children had wished to have her near her in preference to anybody else, though she had only lately come; allowed her to do almost as she liked, and to have a holiday whenever she asked for it. The husband of this kind young lady was a rich wine-merchant of the town, but Mrs. Harnham did not care much about him. In the daytime you could see the house from where they were talking. She, the speaker, liked Melchester better than the lonely country, and she was going to have a new hat for next Sunday that was to cost fifteen and ninepence.

Then she inquired of her acquaintance where he lived, and he told her in London, that ancient and smoky city, where everybody lived who lived at all, and died because they could not live there. He came into Wessex two or three times a year for professional reasons; he had arrived from Wintoncester yesterday, and was going on into the

next county in a day or two. For one thing he did like
the country better than the town, and it was because it
contained such girls as herself.

Then the pleasure-machine started again, and, to the
light-hearted girl, the figure of the handsome young man,
the market-square with its lights and crowd, the houses
beyond, and the world at large, began moving round as
before, countermoving in the revolving mirrors on her right
hand, she being as it were the fixed point in an undulating,
dazzling, lurid universe, in which loomed forward most
prominently of all the form of her late interlocutor. Each
time that she approached the half of her orbit that lay
nearest him they gazed at each other with smiles, and
with that unmistakable expression which means so little
at the moment, yet so often leads up to passion, heartache, union, disunion, devotion, overpopulation, drudgery,
content, resignation, despair.

When the horses slowed anew he stepped to her side
and proposed another heat. ' Hang the expense for once;'
he said. ' I'll pay ! '

She laughed till the tears came.

' Why do you laugh, dear ? ' said he.

' Because—you are so genteel that you must have
plenty of money, and only say that for fun ! ' she returned.

' Ha-ha ! ' laughed the young man in unison, and gallantly producing his money she was enabled to whirl on
again.

As he stood smiling there in the motley crowd, with his
pipe in his hand, and clad in the rough pea-jacket and
wideawake that he had put on for his stroll, who would
have supposed him to be Charles Bradford Raye, Esquire,
stuff-gownsman, educated at Wintoncester, called to the
Bar at Lincoln's Inn, now going the Western Circuit,
merely detained in Melchester by a small arbitration
after his brethren had moved on to the next county-town ?

II

The square was overlooked from its remoter corner by
the house of which the young girl had spoken, a dignified
residence of considerable size, having several windows on

each floor. Inside one of these, on the first floor, the apartment being a large drawing-room, sat a lady, in appearance from twenty-eight to thirty years of age. The blinds were still undrawn, and the lady was absently surveying the weird scene without, her cheek resting on her hand. The room was unlit from within, but enough of the glare from the market-place entered it to reveal the lady's face. She was what is called an interesting creature rather than a handsome woman ; dark-eyed, thoughtful, and with sensitive lips.

A man sauntered into the room from behind and came forward.

'O, Edith, I didn't see you,' he said. 'Why are you sitting here in the dark ? '

'I am looking at the fair,' replied the lady in a languid voice.

'Oh ? Horrid nuisance every year ! I wish it could be put a stop to.'

'I like it.'

'H'm. There's no accounting for taste.'

For a moment he gazed from the window with her, for politeness' sake, and then went out again.

In a few minutes she rang.

'Hasn't Anna come in ? ' asked Mrs. Harnham.

'No, m'm.'

'She ought to be in by this time. I meant her to go for ten minutes only.'

'Shall I go and look for her, m'm ? ' said the housemaid alertly.

'No. It is not necessary : she is a good girl and will come soon.'

However, when the servant had gone Mrs. Harnham arose, went up to her room, cloaked and bonneted herself, and proceeded downstairs, where she found her husband.

'I want to see the fair,' she said ; 'and I am going to look for Anna. I have made myself responsible for her, and must see she comes to no harm. She ought to be indoors. Will you come with me ? '

'Oh, she's all right. I saw her on one of those whirligig things, talking to her young man as I came in. But I'll go if you wish, though I'd rather go a hundred miles the other way.'

'Then please do so. I shall come to no harm alone.'

She left the house and entered the crowd which thronged the market-place, where she soon discovered Anna, seated on the revolving horse. As soon as it stopped Mrs. Harnham advanced and said severely, 'Anna, how can you be such a wild girl ? You were only to be out for ten minutes.'

Anna looked blank, and the young man, who had dropped into the background, came to help her alight.

'Please don't blame her,' he said politely. 'It is my fault that she has stayed. She looked so graceful on the horse that I induced her to go round again. I assure you that she has been quite safe.'

'In that case I'll leave her in your hands,' said Mrs. Harnham, turning to retrace her steps.

But this for the moment it was not so easy to do. Something had attracted the crowd to a spot in their rear, and the wine-merchant's wife, caught by its sway, found herself pressed against Anna's acquaintance without power to move away. Their faces were within a few inches of each other, his breath fanned her cheek as well as Anna's. They could do no other than smile at the accident ; but neither spoke, and each waited passively. Mrs. Harnham then felt a man's hand clasping her fingers, and from the look of consciousness on the young fellow's face she knew the hand to be his : she also knew that from the position of the girl he had no other thought than that the imprisoned hand was Anna's. What prompted her to refrain from undeceiving him she could hardly tell. Not content with holding the hand, he playfully slipped two of his fingers inside her glove, against her palm. Thus matters continued till the pressure lessened ; but several minutes passed before the crowd thinned sufficiently to allow Mrs. Harnham to withdraw.

'How did they get to know each other, I wonder ? ' she mused as she retreated. ' Anna is really very forward —and he very wicked and nice.'

She was so gently stirred with the stranger's manner and

voice, with the tenderness of his idle touch, that instead of re-entering the house she turned back again and observed the pair from a screened nook. Really she argued (being little less impulsive than Anna herself) it was very excusable in Anna to encourage him, however she might have contrived to make his acquaintance ; he was so gentlemanly, so fascinating, had such beautiful eyes. The thought that he was several years her junior produced a reasonless sigh.

At length the couple turned from the roundabout towards the door of Mrs. Harnham's house, and the young man could be heard saying that he would accompany her home. Anna, then, had found a lover, apparently a very devoted one. Mrs. Harnham was quite interested in him. When they drew near the door of the wine-merchant's house, a comparatively deserted spot by this time, they stood invisible for a little while in the shadow of a wall, where they separated, Anna going on to the entrance, and her acquaintance returning across the square.

'Anna,' said Mrs. Harnham, coming up. 'I've been looking at you ! That young man kissed you at parting, I am almost sure.'

'Well,' stammered Anna ; 'he said, if I didn't mind— it would do me no harm, and—and—him a great deal of good ! '

'Ah, I thought so ! And he was a stranger till to-night ? '

'Yes, ma'am.'

'Yet I warrant you told him your name and everything about yourself ? '

'He asked me.'

'But he didn't tell you his ? '

'Yes, ma'am, he did ! ' cried Anna victoriously. 'It is Charles Bradford, of London.'

'Well, if he's respectable, of course I've nothing to say against your knowing him,' remarked her mistress, prepossessed, in spite of general principles, in the young man's favour. 'But I must reconsider all that, if he attempts to renew your acquaintance. A country-bred girl like you, who has never lived in Melchester till this month, who had hardly ever seen a black-coated man till you came here, to be so sharp as to capture a young Londoner like him ! '

' I didn't capture him. I didn't do anything,' said Anna, in confusion.

When she was indoors and alone Mrs. Harnham thought what a well-bred and chivalrous young man Anna's companion had seemed. There had been a magic in his wooing touch of her hand ; and she wondered how he had come to be attracted by the girl.

The next morning the emotional Edith Harnham went to the usual week-day service in Melchester cathedral. In crossing the Close through the fog she again perceived him who had interested her the previous evening, gazing up thoughtfully at the high-piled architecture of the nave : and as soon as she had taken her seat he entered and sat down in a stall opposite hers.

He did not particularly heed her ; but Mrs. Harnham was continually occupying her eyes with him, and wondered more than ever what had attracted him in her unfledged maid-servant. The mistress was almost as unaccustomed as the maiden herself to the end-of-the-age young man, or she might have wondered less. Raye, having looked about him a while, left abruptly, without regard to the service that was proceeding ; and Mrs. Harnham—lonely, impressionable creature that she was—took no further interest in praising the Lord. She wished she had married a London man who knew the subtleties of love-making as they were evidently known to him who had mistakenly caressed her hand.

III

The calendar at Melchester had been light, occupying the court only a few hours ; and the assizes at Casterbridge, the next county-town on the Western Circuit, having no business for Raye, he had not gone thither. At the next town after that they did not open till the following Monday, trials to begin on Tuesday morning. In the natural order of things Raye would have arrived at the latter place on Monday afternoon ; but it was not till the middle of Wednesday that his gown and gray wig, curled in tiers, in the best fashion of Assyrian bas-reliefs, were seen blowing and bobbing behind him as he hastily walked up the High Street from his lodgings. But though he entered the assize building there was nothing for him to do, and sitting at the blue baize table in the well of the court, he mended pens with a mind far away from the case in progress. Thoughts of unpremeditated conduct, of which a week earlier he would not have believed himself capable, threw him into a mood of dissatisfied depression.

He had contrived to see again the pretty rural maiden Anna, the day after the fair, had walked out of the city with her to the earthworks of Old Melchester, and feeling a violent fancy for her, had remained in Melchester all Sunday, Monday, and Tuesday; by persuasion obtaining walks and meetings with the girl six or seven times during the interval; had in brief won her, body and soul.

He supposed it must have been owing to the seclusion in which he had lived of late in town that he had given way so unrestrainedly to a passion for an artless creature whose inexperience had, from the first, led her to place herself unreservedly in his hands. Much he deplored trifling with her feelings for the sake of a passing desire; and he could only hope that she might not live to suffer on his account.

She had begged him to come to her again; entreated him; wept. He had promised that he would do so, and he meant to carry out that promise. He could not desert her now. Awkward as such unintentional connections were, the interspace of a hundred miles—which to a girl of her limited capabilities was like a thousand—would effectually hinder this summer fancy from greatly encumbering his life; while thought of her simple love might do him the negative good of keeping him from idle pleasures in town when he wished to work hard. His circuit journeys would take him to Melchester three or four times a year; and then he could always see her.

The pseudonym, or rather partial name, that he had given her as his before knowing how far the acquaintance was going to carry him, had been spoken on the spur of the moment, without any ulterior intention whatever. He had not afterwards disturbed Anna's error, but on leaving her he had felt bound to give her an address at a stationer's not far from his chambers, at which she might write to him under the initials ' C. B.'

In due time Raye returned to his London abode, having called at Melchester on his way and spent a few additional hours with his fascinating child of nature. In town he lived monotonously every day. Often he and his rooms were enclosed by a tawny fog from all the world besides, and when he lighted the gas to read or write by, his situation seemed so unnatural that he would look into the fire and think of that trusting girl at Melchester again and again. Often, oppressed by absurd fondness for her, he would enter the dim religious nave of the Law Courts by the north door, elbow other juniors habited like himself, and like him unretained ; edge himself into this or that crowded court where a sensational case was going on, just as if he were in it, though the police officers at the door knew as well as he knew himself that he had no more concern with the business in hand than the patient idlers at the gallery-door outside, who had waited to enter since eight in the morning because, like him, they belonged to the classes that live on expectation. But he would do these things to no purpose, and think how greatly the characters in such scenes contrasted with the pink and breezy Anna.

An unexpected feature in that peasant maiden's conduct was that she had not as yet written to him, though he had told her she might do so if she wished. Surely a young creature had never before been so reticent in such circumstances. At length he sent her a brief line, positively requesting her to write. There was no answer by the return post, but the day after a letter in a neat feminine hand, and bearing the Melchester post-mark, was handed to him by the stationer.

The fact alone of its arrival was sufficient to satisfy his imaginative sentiment. He was not anxious to open the epistle, and in truth did not begin to read it for nearly half-an-hour, anticipating readily its terms of passionate retrospect and tender adjuration. When at last he turned

his feet to the fireplace and unfolded the sheet, he was
surprised and pleased to find that neither extravagance nor
vulgarity was there. It was the most charming little
missive he had ever received from woman. To be sure the
language was simple and the ideas were slight ; but it was
so self-possessed ; so purely that of a young girl who felt
her womanhood to be enough for her dignity that he read
it through twice. Four sides were filled, and a few lines
written across, after the fashion of former days ; the paper,
too, was common, and not of the latest shade and surface.
But what of those things ? He had received letters from
women who were fairly called ladies, but never so sensible,
so human a letter as this. He could not single out any
one sentence and say it was at all remarkable or clever ;
the *ensemble* of the letter it was which won him ; and
beyond the one request that he would write or come to her
again soon there was nothing to show her sense of a claim
upon him.

To write again and develop a correspondence was the
last thing Raye would have preconceived as his conduct
in such a situation ; yet he did send a short, encouraging
line or two, signed with his pseudonym, in which he asked
for another letter, and cheeringly promised that he would
try to see her again on some near day, and would never
forget how much they had been to each other during their
short acquaintance.

IV

To return now to the moment at which Anna, at Melchester, had received Raye's letter.

It had been put into her own hand by the postman
on his morning rounds. She flushed down to her neck
on receipt of it, and turned it over and over. ' It is mine ? '
she said.

' Why, yes, can't you see it is ? ' said the postman,
smiling as he guessed the nature of the document and the
cause of the confusion.

' O yes, of course ! ' replied Anna, looking at the letter,
forcedly tittering, and blushing still more.

Her look of embarrassment did not leave her with the

postman's departure. She opened the envelope, kissed its contents, put away the letter in her pocket, and remained musing till her eyes filled with tears.

A few minutes later she carried up a cup of tea to Mrs. Harnham in her bed-chamber. Anna's mistress looked at her, and said : ' How dismal you seem this morning, Anna. What's the matter ? '

' I'm not dismal. I'm glad ; only I——' She stopped to stifle a sob.

' Well ? '

' I've got a letter—and what good is it to me, if I can't read a word in it ! '

' Why, I'll read it, child, if necessary.'

' But this is from somebody—I don't want anybody to read it but myself ! ' Anna murmured.

' I shall not tell anybody. Is it from that young man ? '

' I think so.' Anna slowly produced the letter, saying : ' Then will you read it to me, ma'am ? '

This was the secret of Anna's embarrassment and flutterings. She could neither read nor write. She had grown up under the care of an aunt by marriage, at one of the lonely hamlets on the Great Mid-Wessex Plain where, even in days of national education, there had been no school within a distance of two miles. Her aunt was an ignorant woman ; there had been nobody to investigate Anna's circumstances, nobody to care about her learning the rudiments ; though, as often in such cases, she had been well fed and clothed and not unkindly treated. Since she had come to live at Melchester with Mrs. Harnham, the latter, who took a kindly interest in the girl, had taught her to speak correctly, in which accomplishment Anna showed considerable readiness, as is not unusual with the illiterate ; and soon became quite fluent in the use of her mistress's phraseology. Mrs. Harnham also insisted upon her getting a spelling and copy book, and beginning to practise in these. Anna was slower in this branch of her education, and meanwhile here was the letter.

Edith Harnham's large dark eyes expressed some interest in the contents, though, in her character of mere inter-preter, she threw into her tone as much as she could of mechanical passiveness. She read the short epistle on to its concluding sentence, which idly requested Anna to send him a tender answer.

' Now—you'll do it for me, won't you, dear mistress ? ' said Anna eagerly. ' And you'll do it as well as ever you can, please ? Because I couldn't bear him to think I am not able to do it myself. I should sink into the earth with shame if he knew that ! '

From some words in the letter Mrs. Harnham was led to ask questions, and the answers she received confirmed her suspicions. Deep concern filled Edith's heart at perceiving how the girl had committed her happiness to the issue of this new-sprung attachment. She blamed herself for not interfering in a flirtation which had resulted so seriously for the poor little creature in her charge ; though at the time of seeing the pair together she had a feeling that it was hardly within her province to nip young affection in the bud. However, what was done could not be undone, and it behoved her now, as Anna's only protector, to help her as much as she could. To Anna's eager request that she, Mrs. Harnham, should compose and write the answer to this young London man's letter, she felt bound to accede, to keep alive his attachment to the girl if possible ; though in other circumstances she might have suggested the cook as an amanuensis.

A tender reply was thereupon concocted, and set down in Edith Harnham's hand. This letter it had been which Raye had received and delighted in. Written in the presence of Anna it certainly was, and on Anna's humble note-paper, and in a measure indited by the young girl ; but the life, the spirit, the individuality, were Edith Harnham's.

' Won't you at least put your name yourself ? ' she said. ' You can manage to write that by this time ? '

' No, no,' said Anna, shrinking back. ' I should do it so bad. He'd be ashamed of me, and never see me again ! '

The note, so prettily requesting another from him, had, as we have seen, power enough in its pages to bring one. He declared it to be such a pleasure to hear from her that

she must write every week. The same process of manufacture was accordingly repeated by Anna and her mistress,
and continued for several weeks in succession ; each letter
being penned and suggested by Edith, the girl standing by ;
the answer read and commented on by Edith, Anna standing by and listening again.

Late on a winter evening, after the dispatch of the sixth
letter, Mrs. Harnham was sitting alone by the remains
of her fire. Her husband had retired to bed, and she had
fallen into that fixity of musing which takes no count of
hour or temperature. The state of mind had been brought
about in Edith by a strange thing which she had done that
day. For the first time since Raye's visit Anna had gone
to stay over a night or two with her cottage friends on the
Plain, and in her absence had arrived, out of its time, a
letter from Raye. To this Edith had replied on her own
responsibility, from the depths of her own heart, without
waiting for her maid's collaboration. The luxury of writing
to him what would be known to no consciousness but
his was great, and she had indulged herself therein.

Why was it a luxury ?

Edith Harnham led a lonely life. Influenced by the
belief of the British parent that a bad marriage with its
aversions is better than free womanhood with its interests,
dignity, and leisure, she had consented to marry the elderly
wine-merchant as a *pis aller*, at the age of seven-and-twenty
—some three years before this date—to find afterwards
that she had made a mistake. That contract had left
her still a woman whose deeper nature had never been
stirred.

She was now clearly realizing that she had become
possessed to the bottom of her soul with the image of a man
to whom she was hardly so much as a name. From the
first he had attracted her by his looks and voice ; by his
tender touch ; and, with these as generators, the writing of
letter after letter and the reading of their soft answers
had insensibly developed on her side an emotion which
fanned his ; till there had resulted a magnetic reciprocity
between the correspondents, notwithstanding that one of
them wrote in a character not her own. That he had been

able to seduce another woman in two days was his crowning though unrecognized fascination for her as the she-animal.

They were her own impassioned and pent-up ideas —lowered to monosyllabic phraseology in order to keep up the disguise—that Edith put into letters signed with another name, much to the shallow Anna's delight, who, unassisted, could not for the world have conceived such pretty fancies for winning him, even had she been able to write them. Edith found that it was these, her own foisted-in sentiments, to which the young barrister mainly responded. The few sentences occasionally added from Anna's own lips made apparently no impression upon him.

The letter-writing in her absence Anna never discovered; but on her return the next morning she declared she wished to see her lover about something at once, and begged Mrs. Harnham to ask him to come.

There was a strange anxiety in her manner which did not escape Mrs. Harnham, and ultimately resolved itself into a flood of tears. Sinking down at Edith's knees, she made confession that the result of her relations with her lover it would soon become necessary to disclose.

Edith Harnham was generous enough to be very far from inclined to cast Anna adrift at this conjuncture. No true woman ever is so inclined from her own personal point of view, however prompt she may be in taking such steps to safeguard those dear to her. Although she had written to Raye so short a time previously, she instantly penned another Anna-note hinting clearly though delicately the state of affairs.

Raye replied by a hasty line to say how much he was concerned at her news: he felt that he must run down to see her almost immediately.

But a week later the girl came to her mistress's room with another note, which on being read informed her that after all he could not find time for the journey. Anna was broken with grief; but by Mrs. Harnham's counsel strictly refrained from hurling at him the reproaches and bitterness customary from young women so situated. One thing was imperative: to keep the young man's romantic interest in her alive. Rather therefore did Edith, in the name of her *protégée*, request him on no account to be distressed about the looming event, and not to inconvenience himself to hasten down. She desired above everything to be no weight upon him in his career, no clog upon his high activities. She had wished him to know what had befallen : he was to dismiss it again from his mind. Only he must write tenderly as ever, and when he should come again on the spring circuit it would be soon enough to discuss what had better be done.

It may well be supposed that Anna's own feelings had not been quite in accord with these generous expressions ; but the mistress's judgment had ruled, and Anna had acquiesced. 'All I want is that *niceness* you can so well put into your letters, my dear, dear mistress, and that I can't for the life o' me make up out of my own head ; though I mean the same thing and feel it exactly when you've written it down ! '

When the letter had been sent off, and Edith Harnham was left alone, she bowed herself on the back of her chair and wept.

'I wish his child was mine—I wish it was ! ' she murmured. 'Yet how can I say such a wicked thing ! '

V

The letter moved Raye considerably when it reached him. The intelligence itself had affected him less than her unexpected manner of treating him in relation to it. The absence of any word of reproach, the devotion to his interests, the self-sacrifice apparent in every line, all made up a nobility of character that he had never dreamt of finding in womankind.

'God forgive me ! ' he said tremulously. 'I have been a wicked wretch. I did not know she was such a treasure as this ! '

He reassured her instantly—declaring that he would not of course desert her, that he would provide a home for her somewhere. Meanwhile she was to stay where she was as long as her mistress would allow her.

But a misfortune supervened in this direction. Whether

an inkling of Anna's circumstances reached the knowledge
of Mrs. Harnham's husband or not cannot be said, but the
girl was compelled, in spite of Edith's entreaties, to leave
the house. By her own choice she decided to go back for
a while to the cottage on the Plain. This arrangement
led to a consultation as to how the correspondence should
be carried on ; and in the girl's inability to continue
personally what had been begun in her name, and in the
difficulty of their acting in concert as heretofore, she
requested Mrs. Harnham—the only well-to-do friend she
had in the world—to receive the letters and reply to them
off-hand, sending them on afterwards to herself on the
Plain, where she might at least get some neighbour to
read them to her, if a trustworthy one could be met with.
Anna and her box then departed for the Plain.

Thus it befell that Edith Harnham found herself in the
strange position of having to correspond, under no supervision by the real woman, with a man not her husband, in
terms which were virtually those of a wife, concerning a
corporeal condition that was not Edith's at all ; the man
being one for whom, mainly through the sympathies
involved in playing this part, she secretly cherished a
predilection, subtle and imaginative truly, but strong and
absorbing. She opened each letter, read it as if intended
for herself, and replied from the promptings of her own
heart and no other.

Throughout this correspondence, carried on in the girl's
absence, the high-strung Edith Harnham lived in the
ecstasy of fancy ; the vicarious intimacy engendered
such a flow of passionateness as was never exceeded. For
conscience' sake Edith at first sent on each of his letters
to Anna, and even rough copies of her replies ; but later
on these so-called copies were much abridged, and many
letters on both sides were not sent on at all.

Though sensuous, and, superficially at least, infested
with the self-indulgent vices of artificial society, there was
a substratum of honesty and fairness in Raye's character.
He had really a tender regard for the country girl, and it
grew more tender than ever when he found her apparently
capable of expressing the deepest sensibilities in the simplest

words. He meditated, he wavered, and finally resolved
to consult his sister, a maiden lady much older than himself, of lively sympathies and good intent. In making
this confidence he showed her some of the letters.

'She seems fairly educated,' Miss Raye observed. 'And
bright in ideas. She expresses herself with a taste that
must be innate.'

'Yes. She writes very prettily, doesn't she, thanks to
these elementary schools?'

'One is drawn out towards her, in spite of one's self,
poor thing.'

The upshot of the discussion was that though he had not
been directly advised to do it, Raye wrote, in his real
name, what he would never have decided to write on his
own responsibility; namely, that he could not live without her, and would come down in the spring and shelve
her looming difficulty by marrying her.

This bold acceptance of the situation was made known
to Anna by Mrs. Harnham driving out immediately to the
cottage on the Plain. Anna jumped for joy like a little
child. And poor, crude directions for answering appro-
priately were given to Edith Harnham, who on her return
to the city carried them out with warm intensifications.

'O!' she groaned, as she threw down the pen. 'Anna
—poor good little fool—hasn't intelligence enough to
appreciate him! How should she? While I—don't bear
his child!'

It was now February. The correspondence had continued altogether for four months, and the next letter from
Raye contained incidentally a statement of his position
and prospects. He said that in offering to wed her he
had, at first, contemplated the step of retiring from a profession which hitherto had brought him very slight emolu-
ment, and which, to speak plainly, he had thought might
be difficult of practice after his union with her. But the
unexpected mines of brightness and warmth that her
letters had disclosed to be lurking in her sweet nature had
led him to abandon that somewhat sad prospect. He
felt sure that, with her powers of development, after a
little private training in the social forms of London under

his supervision, and a little help from a governess if necessary, she would make as good a professional man's wife
as could be desired, even if he should rise to the woolsack.
Many a Lord Chancellor's wife had been less intuitively a
lady than she had shown herself to be in her lines to him.

'O—poor fellow, poor fellow!' mourned Edith Harnham.

Her distress now raged as high as her infatuation. It
was she who had wrought him to this pitch—to a marriage
which meant his ruin; yet she could not, in mercy to her
maid, do anything to hinder his plan. Anna was coming
to Melchester that week, but she could hardly show the
girl this last reply from the young man; it told too much
of the second individuality that had usurped the place of
the first.

Anna came, and her mistress took her into her own
room for privacy. Anna began by saying with some
anxiety that she was glad the wedding was so near.

'O, Anna!' replied Mrs. Harnham. 'I think we must
tell him all—that I have been doing your writing for you?
—lest he should not know it till after you become his wife,
and it might lead to dissension and recriminations——'

'O, mis'ess, dear mis'ess—please don't tell him now!'
cried Anna in distress. 'If you were to do it, perhaps he
would not marry me; and what should I do then? It
would be terrible what would come to me! And I am
getting on with my writing, too. I have brought with me
the copybook you were so good as to give me, and I practise every day, and though it is so, so hard, I shall do it
well at last, I believe, if I keep on trying.'

Edith looked at the copybook. The copies had been
set by herself, and such progress as the girl had made was
in the way of grotesque facsimile of her mistress's hand.
But even if Edith's flowing caligraphy were reproduced
the inspiration would be another thing.

'You do it so beautifully,' continued Anna, 'and say
all that I want to say so much better than I could say it,
that I do hope you won't leave me in the lurch just now!'

'Very well,' replied the other. 'But I—but I thought
I ought not to go on!'

'Why?'

Her strong desire to confide her sentiments led Edith to answer truly:

'Because of its effect upon me.'

'But it *can't* have any!'

'Why, child?'

'Because you are married already!' said Anna with lucid simplicity.

'Of course it can't,' said her mistress hastily; yet glad, despite her conscience, that two or three outpourings still remained to her. 'But you must concentrate your attention on writing your name as I write it here.'

VI

Soon Raye wrote about the wedding. Having decided to make the best of what he feared was a piece of romantic folly, he had acquired more zest for the grand experiment. He wished the ceremony to be in London, for greater privacy. Edith Harnham would have preferred it at Melchester; Anna was passive. His reasoning prevailed, and Mrs. Harnham threw herself with mournful zeal into the preparations for Anna's departure. In a last desperate feeling that she must at every hazard be in at the death of her dream, and see once again the man who by a species of telepathy had exercised such an influence on her, she offered to go up with Anna and be with her through the ceremony—'to see the end of her,' as her mistress put it with forced gaiety; an offer which the girl gratefully accepted; for she had no other friend capable of playing the part of companion and witness, in the presence of a gentlemanly bridegroom, in such a way as not to hasten an opinion that he had made an irremediable social blunder.

It was a muddy morning in March when Raye alighted from a four-wheel cab at the door of a registry-office in the S.W. district of London, and carefully handed down Anna and her companion Mrs. Harnham. Anna looked attractive in the somewhat fashionable clothes which Mrs. Harnham had helped her to buy, though not quite so attractive as, an innocent child, she had appeared in her country gown on the back of the wooden horse at Melchester Fair.

Mrs. Harnham had come up this morning by an early train, and a young man—a friend of Raye's—having met them at the door, all four entered the registry-office together. Till an hour before this time Raye had never known the wine-merchant's wife, except at that first casual encounter, and in the flutter of the performance before them he had little opportunity for more than a brief acquaintance. The contract of marriage at a registry is soon got through ; but somehow, during its progress, Raye discovered a strange and secret gravitation between himself and Anna's friend.

The formalities of the wedding—or rather ratification of a previous union—being concluded, the four went in one cab to Raye's lodgings, newly taken in a new suburb in preference to a house, the rent of which he could ill afford just then. Here Anna cut the little cake which Raye had bought at a pastrycook's on his way home from Lincoln's Inn the night before. But she did not do much besides. Raye's friend was obliged to depart almost immediately, and when he had left the only ones virtually present were Edith and Raye, who exchanged ideas with much animation. The conversation was indeed theirs only, Anna being as a domestic animal who humbly heard but understood not. Raye seemed startled in awakening to this fact, and began to feel dissatisfied with her inadequacy.

At last, more disappointed than he cared to own, he said, 'Mrs. Harnham, my darling is so flurried that she doesn't know what she is doing or saying. I see that after this event a little quietude will be necessary before she gives tongue to that tender philosophy which she used to treat me to in her letters.'

They had planned to start early that afternoon for Knollsea, to spend the few opening days of their married life there, and as the hour for departure was drawing near Raye asked his wife if she would go to the writing-desk in the next room and scribble a little note to his sister, who had been unable to attend through indisposition, informing her that the ceremony was over, thanking her for her little present, and hoping to know her well now that she was the writer's sister as well as Charles's.

'Say it in the pretty poetical way you know so well how to adopt,' he added, 'for I want you particularly to win her, and both of you to be dear friends.'

Anna looked uneasy, but departed to her task, Raye remaining to talk to their guest. Anna was a long while absent, and her husband suddenly rose and went to her.

He found her still bending over the writing-table, with tears brimming up in her eyes; and he looked down upon the sheet of note-paper with some interest, to discover with what tact she had expressed her good-will in the delicate circumstances. To his surprise she had progressed but a few lines, in the characters and spelling of a child of eight, and with the ideas of a goose.

'Anna,' he said, staring; 'what's this?'

'It only means—that I can't do it any better!' she answered, through her tears.

'Eh? Nonsense!'

'I can't!' she insisted, with miserable, sobbing hardihood. 'I—I—didn't write those letters, Charles! I only told *her* what to write! And not always that! But I am learning, O so fast, my dear, dear husband! And you'll forgive me, won't you, for not telling you before?' She slid to her knees, abjectly clasped his waist and laid her face against him.

He stood a few moments, raised her, abruptly turned, and shut the door upon her, rejoining Edith in the drawing-room. She saw that something untoward had been discovered, and their eyes remained fixed on each other.

'Do I guess rightly?' he asked, with wan quietude. '*You* were her scribe through all this?'

'It was necessary,' said Edith.

'Did she dictate every word you ever wrote to me?'

'Not every word.'

'In fact, very little?'

'Very little.'

'You wrote a great part of those pages every week from your own conceptions, though in her name!'

' Yes.'

' Perhaps you wrote many of the letters when you were alone, without communication with her ? '

' I did.'

He turned to the bookcase, and leant with his hand over his face ; and Edith, seeing his distress, became white as a sheet.

' You have deceived me—ruined me ! ' he murmured.

' O, don't say it ! ' she cried in her anguish, jumping up and putting her hand on his shoulder. ' I can't bear that ! '

' Delighting me deceptively ! Why did you do it—*why* did you ! '

' I began doing it in kindness to her ! How could I do otherwise than try to save such a simple girl from misery ? But I admit that I continued it for pleasure to myself.'

Raye looked up. ' Why did it give you pleasure ? ' he asked.

' I must not tell,' she said.

He continued to regard her, and saw that her lips suddenly began to quiver under his scrutiny, and her eyes to fill and droop. She started aside, and said that she must go to the station to catch the return train : could a cab be called immediately ?

But Raye went up to her, and took her unresisting hand. ' Well, to think of such a thing as this ! ' he said. ' Why, you and I are friends—lovers—devoted lovers—by correspondence ! '

' Yes ; I suppose.'

' More.'

' More ? '

' Plainly more. It is no use blinking that. Legally I have married her—God help us both !—in soul and spirit I have married you, and no other woman in the world ! '

' Hush ! '

' But I will not hush ! Why should you try to disguise the full truth, when you have already owned half of it ? Yes, it is between you and me that the bond is—not between me and her ! Now I'll say no more. But, O my cruel one, I think I have one claim upon you ! '

She did not say what, and he drew her towards him,

and bent over her. ' If it was all pure invention in those letters,' he said emphatically, ' give me your cheek only. If you meant what you said, let it be lips. It is for the first and last time, remember ! '

She put up her mouth, and he kissed her long. ' You forgive me ? ' she said, crying.

' Yes.'

' But you are ruined ! '

' What matter ! ' he said, shrugging his shoulders. ' It serves me right ! '

She withdrew, wiped her eyes, entered and bade good-bye to Anna, who had not expected her to go so soon, and was still wrestling with the letter. Raye followed Edith downstairs, and in three minutes she was in a hansom driving to the Waterloo station.

He went back to his wife. ' Never mind the letter, Anna, to-day,' he said gently. ' Put on your things. We, too, must be off shortly.'

The simple girl, upheld by the sense that she was indeed married, showed her delight at finding that he was as kind as ever after the disclosure. She did not know that before his eyes he beheld as it were a galley, in which he, the fastidious urban, was chained to work for the remainder of his life, with her, the unlettered peasant, chained to his side.

Edith travelled back to Melchester that day with a face that showed the very stupor of grief, her lips still tingling from the desperate pressure of his kiss. The end of her impassioned dream had come. When at dusk she reached the Melchester station her husband was there to meet her, but in his perfunctoriness and her preoccupation they did not see each other, and she went out of the station alone.

She walked mechanically homewards without calling a fly. Entering, she could not bear the silence of the house, and went up in the dark to where Anna had slept, where she remained thinking awhile. She then returned to the drawing-room, and not knowing what she did, crouched down upon the floor.

' I have ruined him ! ' she kept repeating. ' I have ruined him ; because I would not deal treacherously towards her ! '

In the course of half an hour a figure opened the door of the apartment.

'Ah—who's that?' she said, starting up, for it was dark.

'Your husband—who should it be?' said the worthy merchant.

'Ah—my husband!—I forgot I had a husband!' she whispered to herself.

'I missed you at the station,' he continued. 'Did you see Anna safely tied up? I hope so, for 'twas time.'

'Yes—Anna is married.'

Simultaneously with Edith's journey home Anna and her husband were sitting at the opposite windows of a second-class carriage which sped along to Knollsea. In his hand was a pocket-book full of creased sheets closely written over. Unfolding them one after another he read them in silence, and sighed.

'What are you doing, dear Charles?' she said timidly from the other window, and drew nearer to him as if he were a god.

'Reading over all those sweet letters to me signed "Anna,"' he replied with dreary resignation.

Autumn 1891.

TO PLEASE HIS WIFE

TO PLEASE HIS WIFE

I

THE interior of St. James's Church, in Havenpool Town, was slowly darkening under the close clouds of a winter afternoon. It was Sunday: service had just ended, the face of the parson in the pulpit was buried in his hands, and the congregation, with a cheerful sigh of release, were rising from their knees to depart.

For the moment the stillness was so complete that the surging of the sea could be heard outside the harbour-bar. Then it was broken by the footsteps of the clerk going towards the west door to open it in the usual manner for the exit of the assembly. Before, however, he had reached the doorway, the latch was lifted from without, and the dark figure of a man in a sailor's garb appeared against the light.

The clerk stepped aside, the sailor closed the door gently behind him, and advanced up the nave till he stood at the chancel-step. The parson looked up from the private little prayer which, after so many for the parish, he quite fairly took for himself, rose to his feet, and stared at the intruder.

'I beg your pardon, sir,' said the sailor, addressing the minister in a voice distinctly audible to all the congregation. 'I have come here to offer thanks for my narrow escape from shipwreck. I am given to understand that it is a proper thing to do, if you have no objection?'

The parson, after a moment's pause, said hesitatingly, 'I have no objection; certainly. It is usual to mention any such wish before service, so that the proper words may be used in the General Thanksgiving. But, if you wish, we can read from the form for use after a storm at sea.'

'Ay, sure; I ain't particular,' said the sailor.

The clerk thereupon directed the sailor to the page in the prayer-book where the collect of thanksgiving would be found, and the rector began reading it, the sailor kneeling where he stood, and repeating it after him word by word in a distinct voice. The people, who had remained agape and motionless at the proceeding, mechanically knelt down likewise ; but they continued to regard the isolated form of the sailor who, in the precise middle of the chancel-step, remained fixed on his knees, facing the east, his hat beside him, his hands joined, and he quite unconscious of his appearance in their regard.

When his thanksgiving had come to an end he rose ; the people rose also ; and all went out of church together. As soon as the sailor emerged, so that the remaining daylight fell upon his face, old inhabitants began to recognize him as no other than Shadrach Jolliffe, a young man who had not been seen at Havenpool for several years. A son of the town, his parents had died when he was quite young, on which account he had early gone to sea, in the Newfoundland trade.

He talked with this and that townsman as he walked, informing them that, since leaving his native place years before, he had become captain and owner of a small coasting-ketch, which had providentially been saved from the gale as well as himself. Presently he drew near to two girls who were going out of the churchyard in front of him ; they had been sitting in the nave at his entry, and had watched his doings with deep interest, afterwards discussing him as they moved out of church together. One was a slight and gentle creature; the other a tall, large-framed, deliberative girl. Captain Jolliffe regarded the loose curls of their hair, their backs and shoulders, down to their heels, for some time.

' Who may them two maids be ? ' he whispered to his neighbour.

' The little one is Emily Hanning ; the tall one Joanna Phippard.'

' Ah ! I recollect 'em now, to be sure.'

He advanced to their elbow, and genially stole a gaze at them.

' Emily, you don't know me ? ' said the sailor, turning his beaming brown eyes on her.

' I think I do, Mr. Jolliffe,' said Emily shyly.

The other girl looked straight at him with her dark eyes.

' The face of Miss Joanna I don't call to mind so well,' he continued. ' But I know her beginnings and kindred.'

They walked and talked together, Jolliffe narrating particulars of his late narrow escape, till they reached the corner of Sloop Lane, in which Emily Hanning dwelt, when, with a nod and smile, she left them.   Soon the sailor parted also from Joanna, and, having no especial errand or appointment, turned back towards Emily's house.   She lived with her father, who called himself an accountant, the daughter, however, keeping a little stationery-shop as a supplemental provision for the gaps of his somewhat uncertain business.   On entering Jolliffe found father and daughter about to begin tea.

' O, I didn't know it was tea-time,' he said.   ' Ay, I'll have a cup with much pleasure.'

He remained to tea and long afterwards, telling more tales of his seafaring life.   Several neighbours called to listen, and were asked to come in.   Somehow Emily Hanning lost her heart to the sailor that Sunday night, and in the course of a week or two there was a tender understanding between them.

One moonlight evening in the next month Shadrach was ascending out of the town by the long straight road eastward, to an elevated suburb where the more fashionable houses stood—if anything near this ancient port could be called fashionable—when he saw a figure before him whom, from her manner of glancing back, he took to be Emily. But, on coming up, he found she was Joanna Phippard. He gave a gallant greeting, and walked beside her.

' Go along,' she said, ' or Emily will be jealous ! '

He seemed not to like the suggestion, and remained.

What was said and what was done on that walk never could be clearly recollected by Shadrach ; but in some way or other Joanna contrived to wean him away from her gentler and younger rival. From that week onwards,

Jolliffe was seen more and more in the wake of Joanna
Phippard and less in the company of Emily, and it was
soon rumoured about the quay that old Jolliffe's son, who
had come home from sea, was going to be married to the
former young woman, to the great disappointment of the
latter.

Just after this report had gone about, Joanna dressed
herself for a walk one morning, and started for Emily's
house in the little cross-street. Intelligence of the deep
sorrow of her friend on account of the loss of Shadrach had
reached her ears also, and her conscience reproached her
for winning him away.

Joanna was not altogether satisfied with the sailor. She
liked his attentions, and she coveted the dignity of matri-
mony ; but she had never been deeply in love with Jolliffe.
For one thing, she was ambitious, and socially his position
was hardly so good as her own, and there was always the
chance of an attractive woman mating considerably above
her. It had long been in her mind that she would not
strongly object to give him back again to Emily if her
friend felt so very badly about him. To this end she had
written a letter of renunciation to Shadrach, which letter
she carried in her hand, intending to send it if personal
observation of Emily convinced her that her friend was
suffering.

Joanna entered Sloop Lane and stepped down into the
stationery-shop, which was below the pavement level.
Emily's father was never at home at this hour of the day,
and it seemed as though Emily were not at home either,
for the visitor could make nobody hear. Customers came
so seldom hither that a five minutes' absence of the proprietor counted for little. Joanna waited in the little
shop, where Emily had tastefully set out—as women can
—articles in themselves of slight value, so as to obscure
the meagreness of the stock-in-trade ; till she saw a figure
pausing without the window apparently absorbed in the
contemplation of the sixpenny books, packets of paper,
and prints hung on a string. It was Captain Shadrach
Jolliffe, peering in to ascertain if Emily were there alone.
Moved by an impulse of reluctance to meet him in a spot

which breathed of Emily, Joanna slipped through the door
that communicated with the parlour at the back. She
had frequently done so before, for in her friendship with
Emily she had the freedom of the house without ceremony.

Jolliffe entered the shop. Through the thin blind which
screened the glass partition she could see that he was disappointed at not finding Emily there. He was about to
go out again, when Emily's form darkened the doorway,
hastening home from some errand. At sight of Jolliffe
she started back as if she would have gone out again.

'Don't run away, Emily; don't!' said he. 'What
can make 'ee afraid?'

'I'm not afraid, Captain Jolliffe. Only—only I saw
you all of a sudden, and—it made me jump!' Her voice
showed that her heart had jumped even more than the
rest of her.

'I just called as I was passing,' he said.

'For some paper?' She hastened behind the counter.

'No, no, Emily; why do you get behind there? Why
not stay by me? You seem to hate me.'

'I don't hate you. How can I?'

'Then come out, so that we can talk like Christians.'

Emily obeyed with a fitful laugh, till she stood again
beside him in the open part of the shop.

'There's a dear,' he said.

'You mustn't say that, Captain Jolliffe; because the
words belong to somebody else.'

'Ah! I know what you mean. But, Emily, upon my
life I didn't know till this morning that you cared one bit
about me, or I should not have done as I have done. I
have the best of feelings for Joanna, but I know that from
the beginning she hasn't cared for me more than in a friendly
way; and I see now the one I ought to have asked to be
my wife. You know, Emily, when a man comes home
from sea after a long voyage he's as blind as a bat—he
can't see who's who in women. They are all alike to him,
beautiful creatures, and he takes the first that comes easy,
without thinking if she loves him, or if he might not soon
love another better than her. From the first I inclined
to you most, but you were so backward and shy that I

thought you didn't want me to bother 'ee, and so I went
to Joanna.'

' Don't say any more, Mr. Jolliffe, don't ! ' said she,
choking. ' You are going to marry Joanna next month,
and it is wrong to—to——'

' O, Emily, my darling ! ' he cried, and clasped her little
figure in his arms before she was aware.

Joanna, behind the curtain, turned pale, tried to withdraw her eyes, but could not.

' It is only you I love as a man ought to love the woman
he is going to marry ; and I know this from what Joanna
has said, that she will willingly let me off ! She wants to
marry higher, I know, and only said " Yes " to me out of
kindness. A fine, tall girl like her isn't the sort for a
plain sailor's wife ; you be the best suited for that.'

He kissed her and kissed her again, her flexible form
quivering in the agitation of his embrace.

' I wonder—are you sure—Joanna is going to break off
with you ? O, are you sure ? Because——'

' I know she would not wish to make us miserable. She
will release me.'

' O, I hope—I hope she will ! Don't stay any longer,
Captain Jolliffe ! '

He lingered, however, till a customer came for a penny
stick of sealing-wax, and then he withdrew.

Green envy had overspread Joanna at the scene. She
looked about for a way of escape. To get out without
Emily's knowledge of her visit was indispensable. She
crept from the parlour into the passage, and thence to the
back door of the house, where she let herself noiselessly
into the street.

The sight of that caress had reversed all her resolutions.
She could not let Shadrach go. Reaching home she burnt
the letter, and told her mother that if Captain Jolliffe
called she was too unwell to see him.

Shadrach, however, did not call. He sent her a note
expressing in simple language the state of his feelings ; and
asked to be allowed to take advantage of the hints she
had given him that her affection, too, was little more than
friendly, by cancelling the engagement.

Looking out upon the harbour and the island beyond he waited and waited in his lodgings for an answer that did not come. The suspense grew to be so intolerable that after dark he went up the High Street. He could not resist calling at Joanna's to learn his fate.

Her mother said her daughter was too unwell to see him, and to his questioning admitted that it was in consequence of a letter received from himself, which had distressed her deeply.

' You know what it was about, perhaps, Mrs. Phippard ? ' he said.

Mrs. Phippard owned that she did, adding that it put them in a very painful position. Thereupon Shadrach, fearing that he had been guilty of an enormity, explained that if his letter had pained Joanna it must be owing to a misunderstanding, since he had thought it would be a relief to her. If otherwise, he would hold himself bound by his word, and she was to think of the letter as never having been written.

Next morning he received an oral message from the young woman, asking him to fetch her home from a meeting that evening. This he did, and while walking from the Town Hall to her door, with her hand in his arm, she said :

' It is all the same as before between us, isn't it, Shadrach ? Your letter was sent in mistake ? '

' It is all the same as before,' he answered, ' if you say it must be.'

' I wish it to be,' she murmured, with hard lineaments, as she thought of Emily.

Shadrach was a religious and scrupulous man, who respected his word as his life. Shortly afterwards the wedding took place, Jolliffe having conveyed to Emily as gently as possible the error he had fallen into when estimating Joanna's mood as one of indifference.

II

A month after the marriage Joanna's mother died, and the couple were obliged to turn their attention to very practical matters. Now that she was left without a parent, Joanna could not bear the notion of her husband going to

sea again, but the question was, What could he do at
home ? They finally decided to take on a small grocer's
shop in High Street, the goodwill and stock of which were
waiting to be disposed of at that time. Shadrach knew
nothing of shopkeeping, and Joanna very little, but they
hoped to learn.

To the management of this grocery business they now
devoted all their energies, and continued to conduct it
for many succeeding years, without great success. Two
sons were born to them, whom their mother loved to idol-
atry, although she had never passionately loved her husband; and she lavished upon them all her forethought
and care. But the shop did not thrive, and the large
dreams she had entertained of her sons' education and
career became attenuated in the face of realities. Their
schooling was of the plainest, but, being by the sea, they
grew alert in all such nautical arts and enterprises as were
attractive to their age.

The great interest of the Jolliffes' married life, outside
their own immediate household, had lain in the marriage
of Emily. By one of those odd chances which lead those
that lurk in unexpected corners to be discovered, while
the obvious are passed by, the gentle girl had been seen
and loved by a thriving merchant of the town, a widower,
some years older than herself, though still in the prime of
life. At first Emily had declared that she never, never
could marry anyone ; but Mr. Lester had quietly per-
severed, and had at last won her reluctant assent. Two
children also were the fruits of this union, and, as they
grew and prospered, Emily declared that she had never
supposed that she could live to be so happy.

The worthy merchant's home, one of those large, substantial brick mansions frequently jammed up in old-
fashioned towns, faced directly on the High Street, nearly
opposite to the grocery shop of the Jolliffes, and it now
became the pain of Joanna to behold the woman whose
place she had usurped out of pure covetousness, looking
down from her position of comparative wealth upon the
humble shop-window with its dusty sugar-loaves, heaps
of raisins, and canisters of tea, over which it was her own

lot to preside. The business having so dwindled, Joanna
was obliged to serve in the shop herself, and it galled and
mortified her that Emily Lester, sitting in her large drawing-
room over the way, could witness her own dancings up and
down behind the counter at the beck and call of wretched
twopenny customers, whose patronage she was driven to
welcome gladly ; persons to whom she was compelled to
be civil in the street, while Emily was bounding along
with her children and her. governess, and conversing with
the genteelest people of the town and neighbourhood.
This was what she had gained by not letting Shadrach
Jolliffe, whom she had so faintly loved, carry his affection
elsewhere.

Shadrach was a good and honest man, and he had been
faithful to her in heart and in deed. Time had clipped
the wings of his love for Emily in his devotion to the mother
of his boys ; he had quite lived down that impulsive earlier
fancy, and Emily had become in his regard nothing more
than a friend. It was the same with Emily's feelings for
him. Possibly, had she found the least cause for jealousy,
Joanna would almost have been better satisfied. It was
in the absolute acquiescence of Emily and Shadrach in the
results she herself had contrived that her discontent found
nourishment.

Shadrach was not endowed with the narrow shrewdness
necessary for developing a retail business in the face of
many competitors. Did a customer inquire if the grocer
could really recommend the wondrous substitute for eggs
which a persevering bagman had forced into his stock, he
would answer that ' when you did not put eggs into a
pudding it was difficult to taste them there ' ; and when
he was asked if his ' real Mocha coffee ' was real Mocha,
he would say grimly, ' as understood in small shops.' The
way to wealth was not by this route.

One summer day, when the big brick house opposite.
was reflecting the oppressive sun's heat into the shop, and
nobody was present but husband and wife, Joanna looked
across at Emily's door, where a wealthy visitor's carriage
had drawn up. Traces of patronage had been visible in
Emily's manner of late.

'Shadrach, the truth is, you are not a business-man,' his wife sadly murmured. 'You were not brought up to shopkeeping, and it is impossible for a man to make a fortune at an occupation he has jumped into, as you did into this.'

Jolliffe agreed with her, in this as in everything else. 'Not that I care a rope's end about making a fortune,' he said cheerfully. 'I am happy enough, and we can rub on somehow.'

She looked again at the great house through the screen of bottled pickles.

'Rub on—yes,' she said bitterly. 'But see how well off Emmy Lester is, who used to be so poor! Her boys will go to College, no doubt; and think of yours—obliged to go to the Parish School!'

Shadrach's thoughts had flown to Emily.

'Nobody,' he said good-humouredly, 'ever did Emily a better turn than you did, Joanna, when you warned her off me and put an end to that little simpering nonsense between us, so as to leave it in her power to say "Aye" to Lester when he came along.'

This almost maddened her.

'Don't speak of bygones!' she implored, in stern sadness. 'But think, for the boys' and my sake, if not for your own, what are we to do to get richer?'

'Well,' he said, becoming serious, 'to tell the truth, I have always felt myself unfit for this business, though I've never liked to say so. I seem to want more room for sprawling; a more open space to strike out in than here among friends and neighbours. I could get rich as well as any man, if I tried my own way.'

'I wish you would! What is your way?'

'To go to sea again.'

She had been the very one to keep him at home, hating the semi-widowed existence of sailors' wives. But her ambition checked her instincts now, and she said:

'Do you think success really lies that way?'

'I am sure it lies in no other.'

'Do you want to go, Shadrach?'

'Not for the pleasure of it, I can tell 'ee. There's no

such pleasure at sea, Joanna, as I can find in my back
parlour here. To speak honest, I have no love for the
brine. I never had much. But if it comes to a question
of a fortune for you and the lads, it is another thing. That's
the only way to it for one born and bred a seafarer as I.'

' Would it take long to earn ? '

' Well, that depends ; perhaps not.'

The next morning Shadrach pulled from a chest of
drawers the nautical jacket he had worn during the first
months of his return, brushed out the moths, donned it,
and walked down to the quay. The port still did a fair
business in the Newfoundland trade, though not so much
as formerly.

It was not long after this that he invested all he possessed
in purchasing a part-ownership in a brig, of which he was
appointed captain. A few months were passed in coast-
trading, during which interval Shadrach wore off the land-
rust that had accumulated upon him in his grocery phase ;
and in the spring the brig sailed for Newfoundland.

Joanna lived on at home with her sons, who were now
growing up into strong lads, and occupying themselves in
various ways about the harbour and quay.

' Never mind, let them work a little,' their fond mother
said to herself. ' Our necessities compel it now, but when
Shadrach comes home they will be only seventeen and
eighteen, and they shall be removed from the port, and
their education thoroughly taken in hand by a tutor ; and
with the money they'll have they will perhaps be as near
to gentlemen as Emmy Lester's precious two, with their
algebra and their Latin ! '

The date for Shadrach's return drew near and arrived,
and he did not appear. Joanna was assured that there
was no cause for anxiety, sailing-ships being so uncertain
in their coming ; which assurance proved to be well
grounded, for late one wet evening, about a month after
the calculated time, the ship was announced as at hand,
and presently the slip-slop step of Shadrach as the sailor
sounded in the passage, and he entered. The boys had gone
out and had missed him, and Joanna was sitting alone.

As soon as the first emotion of reunion between the

couple had passed, Jolliffe explained the delay as owing
to a small speculative contract, which had produced good
results.

'I was determined not to disappoint 'ee,' he said; 'and
I think you'll own that I haven't!'

With this he pulled out an enormous canvas bag, full
and rotund as the money-bag of the giant whom Jack
slew, untied it, and shook the contents out into her lap
as she sat in her low chair by the fire. A mass of sovereigns
and guineas (there were guineas on the earth in those days)
fell into her lap with a sudden thud, weighing down her
gown to the floor.

'There!' said Shadrach complacently. 'I told 'ee,
dear, I'd do it; and have I done it or no?'

Somehow her face, after the first excitement of possession, did not retain its glory.

'It is a lot of gold, indeed,' she said. 'And—is this
all?'

'All? Why, dear Joanna, do you know you can count
to three hundred in that heap? It is a fortune!'

'Yes—yes. A fortune—judged by sea; but judged by
land——'

However, she banished considerations of the money for
the nonce. Soon the boys came in, and next Sunday
Shadrach returned thanks to God—this time by the more
ordinary channel of the italics in the General Thanksgiving.
But a few days after, when the question of investing the
money arose, he remarked that she did not seem so satisfied
as he had hoped.

'Well, you see, Shadrach,' she answered, '*we* count by
hundreds; *they* count by thousands' (nodding towards
the other side of the street). 'They have set up a carriage
and pair since you left.'

'O, have they?'

'My dear Shadrach, you don't know how the world
moves. However, we'll do the best we can with it. But
they are rich, and we are poor still!'

The greater part of a year was desultorily spent. She
moved sadly about the house and shop, and the boys were
still occupying themselves in and around the harbour.

' Joanna,' he said, one day, ' I see by your movements that it is not enough.'

' It is not enough,' said she. ' My boys will have to live by steering the ships that the Lesters own ; and I was once above her ! '

Jolliffe was not an argumentative man, and he only murmured that he thought he would make another voyage. He meditated for several days, and coming home from the quay one afternoon said suddenly :

' I could do it for 'ee, dear, in one more trip, for certain, if—if——'

' Do what, Shadrach ? '

' Enable 'ee to count by thousands instead of hundreds.'

' If what ? '

' If I might take the boys.'

She turned pale.

' Don't say that, Shadrach,' she answered hastily.

' Why ? '

' I don't like to hear it ! There's danger at sea. I want them to be something genteel, and no danger to them. I couldn't let them risk their lives at sea. O, I couldn't ever, ever ! '

' Very well, dear, it shan't be done.'

Next day, after a silence, she asked a question :

' If they were to go with you it would make a great deal of difference, I suppose, to the profit ? '

' 'Twould treble what I should get from the venture single-handed. Under my eye they would be as good as two more of myself.'

Later on she said : ' Tell me more about this.'

' Well, the boys are almost as clever as master-mariners in handling a craft, upon my life ! There isn't a more cranky place in the Northern Seas than about the sand-banks of this harbour, and they've practised here from their infancy. And they are so steady. I couldn't get their steadiness and their trustworthiness in half a dozen men twice their age.'

' And is it *very* dangerous at sea ; now, too, there are rumours of war ? ' she asked uneasily.

' O, well, there be risks. Still . . .'

The idea grew and magnified, and the mother's heart was crushed and stifled by it. Emmy was growing *too* patronizing ; it could not be borne. Shadrach's wife could not help nagging him about their comparative poverty. The young men, amiable as their father, when spoken to on the subject of a voyage of enterprise, were quite willing to embark ; and though they, like their father, had no great love for the sea, they became quite enthusiastic when the proposal was detailed.

Everything now hung upon their mother's assent. She withheld it long, but at last gave the word : the young men might accompany their father. Shadrach was unusually cheerful about it : Heaven had preserved him hitherto, and he had uttered his thanks. God would not forsake those who were faithful to him.

All that the Jolliffes possessed in the world was put into the enterprise. The grocery stock was pared down to the least that possibly could afford a bare sustenance to Joanna during the absence, which was to last through the usual ' New-f'nland spell.' How she would endure the weary time she hardly knew, for the boys had been with her formerly ; but she nerved herself for the trial.

The ship was laden with boots and shoes, ready-made clothing, fishing-tackle, butter, cheese, cordage, sailcloth, and many other commodities ; and was to bring back oil, furs, skins, fish, cranberries, and what else came to hand. But much speculative trading to other ports was to be undertaken between the voyages out and homeward, and thereby much money made.

III

The brig sailed on a Monday morning in spring ; but Joanna did not witness its departure. She could not bear the sight that she had been the means of bringing about. Knowing this, her husband told her overnight that they were to sail some time before noon next day ; hence when, awakening at five the next morning, she heard them bustling about downstairs, she did not hasten to descend, but lay trying to nerve herself for the parting, imagining they would leave about nine, as her husband had done on his previous voyage. When she did descend she beheld words chalked upon the sloping face of the bureau; but no husband or sons. In the hastily-scrawled lines Shadrach said they had gone off thus not to pain her by a leave-taking; and the sons had chalked under his words: ' Good-bye, mother !'

She rushed to the quay, and looked down the harbour towards the blue rim of the sea, but she could only see the masts and bulging sails of the *Joanna*; no human figures. ' 'Tis I have sent them !' she said wildly, and burst into tears. In the house the chalked ' Good-bye ' nearly broke her heart. But when she had re-entered the front room, and looked across at Emily's, a gleam of triumph lit her thin face at her anticipated release from the thraldom of subservience.

To do Emily Lester justice, her assumption of superiority was mainly a figment of Joanna's brain. That the circumstances of the merchant's wife were more luxurious than Joanna's, the former could not conceal; though whenever the two met, which was not very often now, Emily endeavoured to subdue the difference by every means in her power.

The first summer lapsed away; and Joanna meagrely maintained herself by the shop, which now consisted of little more than a window and a counter. Emily was, in truth, her only large customer; and Mrs. Lester's kindly readiness to buy anything and everything without questioning the quality had a sting of bitterness in it, for it was the uncritical attitude of a patron, and almost of a donor. The long dreary winter moved on; the face of the bureau had been turned to the wall to protect the chalked words of farewell, for Joanna could never bring herself to rub them out; and she often glanced at them with wet eyes. Emily's handsome boys came home for the Christmas holidays; the University was talked of for them; and still Joanna subsisted as it were with held breath, like a person submerged. Only one summer more, and the ' spell ' would end. Towards the close of the time Emily called on her quondam friend. She had heard that Joanna began to feel anxious; she had received no letter from

husband or sons for some months. Emily's silks rustled
arrogantly when, in response to Joanna's almost dumb
invitation, she squeezed through the opening of the counter
and into the parlour behind the shop.

'*You* are all success, and *I* am all the other way ! ' said
Joanna.

'But why do you think so ? ' said Emily. 'They are
to bring back a fortune, I hear.'

'Ah! will they come ? The doubt is more than a
woman can bear. All three in one ship—think of that !
And I have not heard of them for months ! '

'But the time is not up. You should not meet misfortune half-way.'

'Nothing will repay me for the grief of their absence ! '

'Then why did you let them go ? You were doing
fairly well.'

'I *made* them go ! ' she said, turning vehemently upon
Emily. 'And I'll tell you why ! I could not bear that
we should be only muddling on, and you so rich and thriving ! Now I have told you, and you may hate me if you
will ! '

'I shall never hate you, Joanna.'

And she proved the truth of her words afterwards. The
end of autumn came, and the brig should have been in
port ; but nothing like the *Joanna* appeared in the channel
between the sands. It was now really time to be uneasy.
Joanna Jolliffe sat by the fire, and every gust of wind
caused her a cold thrill. She had always feared and detested
the sea ; to her it was a treacherous, restless, slimy creature, glorying in the griefs of women. 'Still,' she said,
' they *must* come ! '

She recalled to her mind that Shadrach had said before
starting that if they returned safe and sound, with success
crowning their enterprise, he would go as he had gone
after his shipwreck, and kneel with his sons in the church,
and offer sincere thanks for their deliverance. She went
to church regularly morning and afternoon, and sat in
the most forward pew, nearest the chancel-step. Her eyes
were mostly fixed on that step, where Shadrach had knelt
in the bloom of his young manhood : she knew to an inch

the spot which his knees had pressed twenty winters before ;
his outline as he had knelt, his hat on the step beside him.
God was good. Surely her husband must kneel there
again : a son on each side as he had said ; George just here,
Jim just there. By long watching the spot as she wor-
shipped became as if she saw the three returned ones there
kneeling ; the two slim outlines of her boys, the more
bulky form between them ; their hands clasped, their
heads shaped against the eastern wall. The fancy grew
almost to an hallucination ; she could never turn her worn
eyes to the step without seeing them there.

Nevertheless they did not come. Heaven was merciful,
but it was not yet pleased to relieve her soul. This was
her purgation for the sin of making them the slaves of her
ambition. But it became more than purgation soon, and
her mood approached despair. Months had passed since
the brig had been due, but it had not returned.

Joanna was always hearing or seeing evidences of their
arrival. When on the hill behind the port, whence a view
of the open Channel could be obtained, she felt sure that a
little speck on the horizon, breaking the eternally level
waste of waters southward, was the truck of the *Joanna's*
mainmast. Or when indoors, a shout or excitement of
any kind at the corner of the Town Cellar, where the High
Street joined the Quay, caused her to spring to her feet
and cry : ' 'Tis they ! '

But it was not. The visionary forms knelt every Sunday afternoon on the chancel-step, but not the real. Her
shop had, as it were, eaten itself hollow. In the apathy
which had resulted from her loneliness and grief she had
ceased to take in the smallest supplies, and thus had sent
away her last customer.

In this strait Emily Lester tried by every means in her
power to aid the afflicted woman ; but she met with constant repulses.

' I don't like you ! I can't bear to see you ! ' Joanna
would whisper hoarsely when Emily came to her and made
advances.

' But I want to help and soothe you, Joanna,' Emily
would say.

'You are a lady, with a rich husband and fine sons!
What can you want with a bereaved crone like me!'

'Joanna, I want this: I want you to come and live in
my house, and not stay alone in this dismal place any
longer.'

'And suppose they come and don't find me at home?
You wish to separate me and mine! No, I'll stay here.
I don't like you, and I can't thank you, whatever kindness
you do me!'

However, as time went on Joanna could not afford to
pay the rent of the shop and house without an income.
She was assured that all hope of the return of Shadrach
and his sons was vain, and she reluctantly consented to
accept the asylum of the Lesters' house. Here she was
allotted a room of her own on the second floor, and went
and came as she chose, without contact with the family.
Her hair greyed and whitened, deep lines channelled her
forehead, and her form grew gaunt and stooping. But
she still expected the lost ones, and when she met Emily
on the staircase she would say morosely: 'I know why
you've got me here! They'll come, and be disappointed
at not finding me at home, and perhaps go away again;
and then you'll be revenged for my taking Shadrach away
from 'ee!'

Emily Lester bore these reproaches from the grief-
stricken soul. She was sure—all the people of Havenpool
were sure—that Shadrach and his sons had gone to the
bottom. For years the vessel had been given up as lost.
Nevertheless, when awakened at night by any noise, Joanna
would rise from bed and glance at the shop opposite by
the light from the flickering lamp, to make sure it was not
they.

It was a damp and dark December night, six years after
the departure of the brig *Joanna*. The wind was from
the sea, and brought up a fishy mist which mopped the
face like moist flannel. Joanna had prayed her usual
prayer for the absent ones with more fervour and confidence
than she had felt for months, and had fallen asleep about
eleven. It must have been between one and two when
she suddenly started up. She had certainly heard steps

in the street, and the voices of Shadrach and her sons
calling at the door of the grocery shop. She sprang out
of bed, and, hardly knowing what clothing she dragged
on herself, hastened down Emily's large and carpeted
staircase, put the candle on the hall-table, unfastened the
bolts and chain, and stepped into the street. The mist,
blowing up the street from the Quay, hindered her seeing
the shop, although it was so near ; but she had crossed to
it in a moment. How was it ? Nobody stood there.
The wretched woman walked wildly up and down with
her bare feet—there was not a soul. She returned and
knocked with all her might at the door which had once
been her own—they might have been admitted for the
night, unwilling to disturb her till the morning. It was
not till several minutes had elapsed that the young man
who now kept the shop looked out of an upper window,
and saw the skeleton of something human standing below
half-dressed.

' Has anybody come ? ' asked the form.

' O, Mrs. Jolliffe, I didn't know it was you,' said the
young man kindly, for he was aware how her baseless
expectations moved her. ' No ; nobody has come.'

June 1891.

THE FIDDLER OF THE REELS

THE FIDDLER OF THE REELS

'Talking of Exhibitions, World's Fairs, and what not,' said the old gentleman, 'I would not go round the corner to see a dozen of them nowadays. The only exhibition that ever made, or ever will make, any impression upon my imagination was the first of the series, the parent of them all, and now a thing of old times—the Great Exhibition of 1851, in Hyde Park, London. None of the younger generation can realize the sense of novelty it produced in us who were then in our prime. A noun substantive went so far as to become an adjective in honour of the occasion. It was "exhibition" hat, "exhibition" razor-strop, "exhibition" watch; nay, even "exhibition" weather, "exhibition" spirits, sweethearts, babies, wives—for the time.

'For South Wessex, the year formed in many ways an extraordinary chronological frontier or transit-line, at which there occurred what one might call a precipice in Time. As in a geological "fault," we had presented to us a sudden bringing of ancient and modern into absolute contact, such as probably in no other single year since the Conquest was ever witnessed in this part of the country.'

These observations led us onward to talk of the different personages, gentle and simple, who lived and moved within our narrow and peaceful horizon at that time; and of three people in particular, whose queer little history was oddly touched at points by the Exhibition, more concerned with it than that of anybody else who dwelt in those outlying shades of the world, Stickleford, Mellstock, and Egdon. First in prominence among these three came Wat Ollamoor —if that were his real name—whom the seniors in our party had known well.

He was a woman's man, they said,—supremely so—

401

externally little else. To men he was not attractive; perhaps a little repulsive at times. Musician, dandy, and company-man in practice; veterinary surgeon in theory, he lodged awhile in Mellstock village, coming from nobody knew where; though some said his first appearance in this neighbourhood had been as fiddle-player in a show at Greenhill Fair.

Many a worthy villager envied him his power over unsophisticated maidenhood—a power which seemed sometimes to have a touch of the weird and wizardly in it. Personally he was not ill-favoured, though rather un-English, his complexion being a rich olive, his rank hair dark and rather clammy—made still clammier by secret ointments, which, when he came fresh to a party, caused him to smell like ' boys'-love' (southernwood) steeped in lamp-oil. On occasion he wore curls—a double row—running almost horizontally around his head. But as these were sometimes noticeably absent, it was concluded that they were not altogether of Nature's making. By girls whose love for him had turned to hatred he had been nicknamed 'Mop,' from this abundance of hair, which was long enough to rest upon his shoulders; as time passed the name more and more prevailed.

His fiddling possibly had the most to do with the fascination he exercised, for, to speak fairly, it could claim for itself a most peculiar and personal quality, like that in a moving preacher. There were tones in it which bred the immediate conviction that indolence and averseness to systematic application were all that lay between ' Mop ' and the career of a second Paganini.

While playing he invariably closed his eyes; using no notes, and, as it were, allowing the violin to wander on at will into the most plaintive passages ever heard by rustic man. There was a certain lingual character in the supplicatory expressions he produced, which would wellnigh have drawn an ache from the heart of a gate-post. He could make any child in the parish, who was at all sensitive to music, burst into tears in a few minutes by simply fiddling one of the old dance-tunes he almost entirely affected—country jigs, reels, and ' Favourite Quick Steps ' of the last century—some mutilated remains of which even now reappear as nameless phantoms in new quadrilles and gallops, where they are recognized only by the curious, or by such old-fashioned and far-between people as have been thrown with men like Wat Ollamoor in their early life.

His date was a little later than that of the old Mellstock quire-band which comprised the Dewys, Mail, and the rest —in fact, he did not rise above the horizon thereabout till those well-known musicians were disbanded as ecclesiastical functionaries. In their honest love of thoroughness they despised the new man's style. Theophilus Dewy (Reuben the tranter's younger brother) used to say there was no 'plumness' in it—no bowing, no solidity—it was all fantastical. And probably this was true. Anyhow, Mop had, very obviously, never bowed a note of church-music from his birth; he never once sat in the gallery of Mellstock Church where the others had tuned their venerable psalmody so many hundreds of times; had never, in all likelihood, entered a church at all. All were devil's tunes in his repertory. 'He could no more play the Wold Hundredth to his true time than he could play the brazen serpent,' the tranter would say. (The brazen serpent was supposed in Mellstock to be a musical instrument particularly hard to blow.)

Occasionally Mop could produce the aforesaid moving effect upon the souls of grown-up persons, especially young women of fragile and responsive organization. Such an one was Car'line Aspent. Though she was already engaged to be married before she met him, Car'line, of them all, was the most influenced by Mop Ollamoor's heart-stealing melodies, to her discomfort, nay, positive pain and ultimate injury. She was a pretty, invocating, weak-mouthed girl, whose chief defect as a companion with her sex was a tendency to peevishness now and then. At this time she was not a resident in Mellstock parish where Mop lodged, but lived some miles off at Stickleford, further down the river.

How and where she first made acquaintance with him and his fiddling is not truly known, but the story was that

it either began or was developed on one spring evening,
when, in passing through Lower Mellstock, she chanced
to pause on the bridge near his house to rest herself, and
languidly leaned over the parapet. Mop was standing on
his door-step, as was his custom, spinning the insidious
thread of semi- and demi-semiquavers from the E string
of his fiddle for the benefit of passers-by, and laughing as
the tears rolled down the cheeks of the little children
hanging around him. Car'line pretended to be engrossed
with the rippling of the stream under the arches, but in
reality she was listening, as he knew. Presently the aching
of the heart seized her simultaneously with a wild desire
to glide airily in the mazes of an infinite dance. To shake
off the fascination she resolved to go on, although it would
be necessary to ·pass him as he played. On stealthily
glancing ahead at the performer, she found to her relief
that his eyes were closed in abandonment to instrumenta-
tion, and she strode on boldly. But when closer her step
grew timid, her tread convulsed itself more and more
accordantly with the time of the melody, till she very
nearly danced along. Gaining another glance at him when
immediately opposite, she saw that *one* of his eyes was
open, quizzing her as he smiled at her emotional state.
Her gait could not divest itself of its compelled capers till
she had gone a long way past the house; and Car'line was
unable to shake off the strange infatuation for hours.

After that day, whenever there was to be in the neighbourhood a dance to which she could get an invitation,
and where Mop Ollamoor was to be the musician, Car'line
contrived to be present, though it sometimes involved a
walk of several miles; for he did not play so often in
Stickleford as elsewhere.

The next evidences of his influence over her were singular
enough, and it would require a neurologist to fully explain
them. She would be sitting quietly, any evening after
dark, in the house of her father, the parish clerk, which
stood in the middle of Stickleford village street, this being
the highroad between Lower Mellstock and Moreford, five
miles eastward. Here, without a moment's warning, and
in the midst of a general conversation between her father,

sister, and the young man before alluded to, who devotedly
wooed her in ignorance of her infatuation, she would start
from her seat in the chimney-corner as if she had received a
galvanic shock, and spring convulsively towards the ceiling ; then she would burst into tears, and it was not till
some half-hour had passed that she grew calm as usual.
Her father, knowing her hysterical tendencies, was always
excessively anxious about this trait in his youngest girl,
and feared the attack to be a species of epileptic fit.   Not
so her sister Julia.   Julia had found out what was the
cause.   At the moment before the jumping, only an excep-
tionally sensitive ear situated in the chimney-nook could
have caught from down the flue the beat of a man's footstep along the highway without.   But it was in that footfall, for which she had been waiting, that the origin of
Car'line's involuntary springing lay.   The pedestrian was
Mop Ollamoor, as the girl well knew ; but his business
that way was not to visit her ; he sought another woman
whom he spoke of as his Intended, and who lived at Moreford, two miles further on.   On one, and only one, occasion did it happen that Car'line could not control her utterance ; it was when her sister alone chanced to be present.
' O—O—O— ! ' she cried.   ' He's going to *her*, and not
coming to *me* ! '

   To do the fiddler justice, he had not at first thought
greatly of, or spoken much to, this girl of impressionable
mould.   But he had soon found out her secret, and could
not resist a little by-play with her too easily hurt heart,
as an interlude between his more serious lovemakings at
Moreford., The two became well acquainted, though only
by stealth, hardly a soul in Stickleford except her sister,
and her lover Ned Hipcroft, being aware of the attachment.
Her father disapproved of her coldness to Ned ; her sister,
too, hoped she might get over this nervous passion for a
man of whom so little was known.   The ultimate result
was that Car'line's manly and simple wooer Edward found
his suit becoming practically hopeless.   He was a respectable mechanic, in a far sounder position than Mop the
nominal horse-doctor ; but when, before leaving her, Ned
put his flat and final question, would she marry him, then

and there, now or never, it was with little expectation of obtaining more than the negative she gave him. Though her father supported him and her sister supported him, he could not play the fiddle so as to draw your soul out of your body like a spider's thread, as Mop did, till you felt as limp as withywind, and yearned for something to cling to. Indeed, Hipcroft had not the slightest ear for music; could not sing two notes in tune, much less play them.

The No he had expected and got from her, in spite of a preliminary encouragement, gave Ned a new start in life. It had been uttered in such a tone of sad entreaty that he resolved to persecute her no more; she should not even be distressed by a sight of his form in the distant perspective of the street and lane. He left the place, and his natural course was to London.

The railway to South Wessex was in process of construction, but it was not as yet opened for traffic; and Hipcroft reached the capital by a six days' trudge on foot, as many a better man had done before him. He was one of the last of the artisan class who used that now extinct method of travel to the great centres of labour, so customary then from time immemorial.

In London he lived and worked regularly at his trade. More fortunate than many, his disinterested willingness recommended him from the first. During the ensuing four years he was never out of employment. He neither advanced nor receded in the modern sense; he improved as a workman, but he did not shift one jot in social position. About his love for Car'line he maintained a rigid silence. No doubt he often thought of her; but being always occupied, and having no relations at Stickleford, he held no communication with that part of the country, and showed no desire to return. In his quiet lodging in Lambeth he moved about after working-hours with the facility of a woman, doing his own cooking, attending to his stocking-heels, and shaping himself by degrees to a lifelong bachelorhood. For this conduct one is bound to advance the canonical reason that time could not efface from his heart the image of little Car'line Aspent—and it may be in part true; but there was also the inference that his was a nature not greatly dependent upon the ministrations of the other sex for its comforts.

The fourth year of his residence as a mechanic in London was the year of the Hyde-Park Exhibition already mentioned, and at the construction of this huge glass-house, then unexampled in the world's history, he worked daily. It was an era of great hope and activity among the nations and industries. Though Hipcroft was, in his small way, a central man in the movement, he plodded on with his usual outward placidity. Yet for him, too, the year was destined to have its surprises, for when the bustle of getting the building ready for the opening day was past, the ceremonies had been witnessed, and people were flocking thither from all parts of the globe, he received a letter from Car'line. Till that day the silence of four years between himself and Stickleford had never been broken.

She informed her old lover, in an uncertain penmanship which suggested a trembling hand, of the trouble she had been put to in ascertaining his address, and then broached the subject which had prompted her to write. Four years ago, she said with the greatest delicacy of which she was capable, she had been so foolish as to refuse him. Her wilful wrong-headedness had since been a grief to her many times, and of late particularly. As for Mr. Ollamoor, he had been absent almost as long as Ned—she did not know where. She would gladly marry Ned now if he were to ask her again, and be a tender little wife to him till her life's end.

A tide of warm feeling must have surged through Ned Hipcroft's frame on receipt of this news, if we may judge by the issue. Unquestionably he loved her still, even if not to the exclusion of every other happiness. This from his Car'line, she who had been dead to him these many years, alive to him again as of old, was in itself a pleasant, gratifying thing. Ned had grown so resigned to, or satisfied with, his lonely lot, that he probably would not have shown much jubilation at anything. Still, a certain ardour of preoccupation, after his first surprise, revealed how deeply her confession of faith in him had stirred him. Measured and methodical in his ways, he did not answer the letter that day, nor the next, nor the next. He was having ' a good think.' When he did answer it, there was a great deal of sound reasoning mixed in with the unmistakable tenderness of his reply; but the tenderness itself was sufficient to reveal that he was pleased with her straightforward frankness; that the anchorage she had once obtained in his heart was renewable, if it had not been continuously firm.

He told her—and as he wrote his lips twitched humor-ously over the few gentle words of raillery he indited among the rest of his sentences—that it was all very well for her to come round at this time of day. Why wouldn't she have him when he wanted her? She had no doubt learned that he was not married, but suppose his affections had since been fixed on another? She ought to beg his pardon. Still, he was not the man to forget her. But considering how he had been used, and what he had suffered, she could not quite expect him to go down to Stickleford and fetch her. But if she would come to him, and say she was sorry, as was only fair; why, yes, he would marry her, knowing what a good little woman she was at the core. He added that the request for her to come to him was a less one to make than it would have been when he first left Stickle-ford, or even a few months ago; for the new railway into South Wessex was now open, and there had just begun to be run wonderfully contrived special trains, called excur-sion-trains, on account of the Great Exhibition; so that she could come up easily alone.

She said in her reply how good it was of him to treat her so generously, after her hot-and-cold treatment of him; that though she felt frightened at the magnitude of the journey, and was never as yet in a railway-train, having only seen one pass at a distance, she embraced his offer with all her heart; and would, indeed, own to him how sorry she was, and beg his pardon, and try to be a good wife always, and make up for lost time.

The remaining details of when and where were soon settled, Car'line informing him, for her ready identification in the crowd, that she would be wearing ' my new sprigged-laylock cotton gown,' and Ned gaily responding that, having married her the morning after her arrival, he would make a day of it by taking her to the Exhibition. One early summer afternoon, accordingly, he came from his place of work, and hastened towards Waterloo Station to meet her. It was as wet and chilly as an English June day can occasionally be, but as he waited on the platform in the drizzle he glowed inwardly, and seemed to have something to live for again.

The 'excursion-train'—an absolutely new departure in the history of travel—was still a novelty on the Wessex line, and probably everywhere. Crowds of people had flocked to all the stations on the way up to witness the unwonted sight of so long a train's passage, even where they did not take advantage of the opportunity it offered. The seats for the humbler class of travellers in these early experiments in steam-locomotion, were open trucks, without any protection whatever from the wind and rain; and damp weather having set in with the afternoon, the unfortunate occupants of these vehicles were, on the train drawing up at the London terminus, found to be in a pitiable condition from their long journey; blue-faced, stiff-necked, sneezing, rain-beaten, chilled to the marrow, many of the men being hatless; in fact, they resembled people who had been out all night in an open boat on a rough sea, rather than inland excursionists for pleasure. The women had in some degree protected themselves by turning up the skirts of their gowns over their heads, but as by this arrangement they were additionally exposed about the hips, they were all more or less in a sorry plight.

In the bustle and crush of alighting forms of both sexes which followed the entry of the huge concatenation into the station, Ned Hipcroft soon discerned the slim little figure his eye was in search of, in the sprigged lilac, as described. She came up to him with a frightened smile—still pretty, though so damp, weather-beaten, and shivering from long exposure to the wind.

'O Ned!' she sputtered, 'I—I——' He clasped her in his arms and kissed her, whereupon she burst into a flood of tears.

'You are wet, my poor dear! I hope you'll not get

cold,' he said. And surveying her and her multifarious surrounding packages, he noticed that by the hand she led a toddling child—a little girl of three or so—whose hood was as clammy and tender face as blue as those of the other travellers.

'Who is this—somebody you know?' asked Ned curiously.

'Yes, Ned. She's mine.'

'Yours?'

'Yes—my own.'

'Your own child?'

'Yes!'

'But who's the father?'

'The young man I had after you courted me.'

'Well—as God's in——'

'Ned, I didn't name it in my letter, because, you see, it would have been so hard to explain! I thought that when we met I could tell you how she happened to be born, so much better than in writing! I hope you'll excuse it this once, dear Ned, and not scold me, now I've come so many, many miles!'

'This means Mr. Mop Ollamoor, I reckon!' said Hipcroft, gazing palely at them from the distance of the yard or two to which he had withdrawn with a start.

Car'line gasped. 'But he's been gone away for years!' she supplicated. 'And I never had a young man before! And I was so onlucky to be catched the first time he took advantage o' me, though some of the girls down there go on like anything!'

Ned remained in silence, pondering.

'You'll forgive me, dear Ned?' she added, beginning to sob outright. 'I haven't taken 'ee in after all, because—because you can pack us back again, if you want to; though 'tis hundreds o' miles, and so wet, and night a-coming on, and I with no money!'

'What the devil can I do!' Hipcroft groaned.

A more pitiable picture than the pair of helpless creatures presented was never seen on a rainy day, as they stood on the great, gaunt, puddled platform, a whiff of drizzle blowing under the roof upon them now and then;

the pretty attire in which they had started from Stickleford in the early morning bemuddled and sodden, weariness
on their faces, and fear of him in their eyes ; for the child
began to look as if she thought she too had done some
wrong, remaining in an appalled silence till the tears rolled
down her chubby cheeks.

' What's the matter, my little maid ? ' said Ned mechanically.

' I do want to go home ! ' she let out, in tones that told
of a bursting heart. ' And my totties be cold, an' I shan't
have no bread an' butter no more ! '

' I don't know what to say to it all ! ' declared Ned, his
own eye moist as he turned and walked a few steps with
his head down ; then regarded them again point-blank.
From the child escaped troubled breaths and silently well-
ing tears.

' Want some bread and butter, do 'ee ? ' he said, with
factitious hardness.

' Ye—e—s ! '

' Well, I dare say I can get 'ee a bit ! Naturally, you
must want some. And you, too, for that matter, Car'line.'

' I do feel a little hungered. But I can keep it off,' she
murmured.

' Folk shouldn't do that,' he said gruffly. . . . ' There,
come along ! ' He caught up the child, as he added, ' You
must bide here to-night, anyhow, I s'pose ! What can
you do otherwise ? I'll get 'ee some tea and victuals ;
and as for this job, I'm sure I don't know what to say !
This is the way out.'

They pursued their way, without speaking, to Ned's
lodgings, which were not far off. There he dried them
and made them comfortable, and prepared tea ; they
thankfully sat down. The ready-made household of
which he suddenly found himself the head imparted a
cosy aspect to his room, and a paternal one to himself.
Presently he turned to the child and kissed her now
blooming cheeks ; and, looking wistfully at Car'line, kissed
her also.

' I don't see how I can send you back all them miles,'
he growled, ' now you've come all the way o' purpose to

join me. But you must trust me, Car'line, and show you've real faith in me. Well, do you feel better now, my little woman ? '

The child nodded beamingly, her mouth being otherwise occupied.

' I did trust you, Ned, in coming ; and I shall always ! '

Thus, without any definite agreement to forgive her, he tacitly acquiesced in the fate that Heaven had sent him ; and on the day of their marriage (which was not quite so soon as he had expected it could be, on account of the time necessary for banns) he took her to the Exhibition when they came back from church, as he had promised. While standing near a large mirror in one of the courts devoted to furniture, Car'line started, for in the glass appeared the reflection of a form exactly resembling Mop Ollamoor's— so exactly, that it seemed impossible to believe anybody but that artist in person to be the original. On passing round the objects which hemmed in Ned, her, and the child from a direct view, no Mop was to be seen. Whether he were really in London or not at that time was never known ; and Car'line always stoutly denied that her readiness to go and meet Ned in town arose from any rumour that Mop had also gone thither ; which denial there was no reasonable ground for doubting.

And then the year glided away, and the Exhibition folded itself up and became a thing of the past. The park trees that had been enclosed for six months were again exposed to the winds and storms, and the sod grew green anew. Ned found that Car'line resolved herself into a very good wife and companion, though she had made herself what is called cheap to him ; but in that she was like another domestic article, a cheap tea-pot, which often brews better tea than a dear one. One autumn Hipcroft found himself with but little work to do, and a prospect of less for the winter. Both being country born and bred, they fancied they would like to live again in their natural atmosphere. It was accordingly decided between them that they should leave the pent-up London lodging, and that Ned should seek out employment near his native place, his wife and her daughter staying with Car'line's

father during the search for occupation and an abode of
their own.

Tinglings of pride pervaded Car'line's spasmodic little
frame as she journeyed down with Ned to the place she
had left two or three years before, in silence and under a
cloud.   To return to where she had once been despised, a
smiling London wife with a distinct London accent, was a
triumph which the world did not witness every day.

The train did not stop at the petty roadside station that
lay nearest to Stickleford, and the trio went on to Casterbridge. Ned thought it a good opportunity to make a
few preliminary inquiries for employment at workshops in
the borough where he had been known ; and feeling cold
from her journey, and it being dry underfoot and only
dusk as yet, with a moon on the point of rising, Car'line
and her little girl walked on towards Stickleford, leaving
Ned to follow at a quicker pace, and pick her up at a certain
half-way house, widely known as an inn.

The woman and child pursued the well-remembered way
comfortably enough, though they were both becoming
wearied. In the course of three miles they had passed
Heedless-William's Pond, the familiar landmark by Bloom's
End, and were drawing near the Quiet Woman, a lone
roadside hostel on the lower verge of the Egdon Heath,
since and for many years abolished. In stepping up
towards it Car'line heard more voices within than had
formerly been customary at such an hour, and she learned
that an auction of fat stock had been held near the spot
that afternoon. The child would be the better for a rest
as well as herself, she thought, and she entered.

The guests and customers overflowed into the passage,
and Car'line had no sooner crossed the threshold than a
man whom she remembered by sight came forward with a
glass and mug in his hands towards a friend leaning against
the wall ; but, seeing her, very gallantly offered her a
drink of the liquor, which was gin-and-beer hot, pouring
her out a tumblerful and saying, in a moment or two :
' Surely, 'tis little Car'line Aspent that was—down at
Stickleford ? '

She assented, and, though she did not exactly want this

beverage, she drank it since it was offered, and her entertainer begged her to come in further and sit down. Once
within the room she found that all the persons present
were seated close against the walls, and there being a chair
vacant she did the same. An explanation of their position
occurred the next moment. In the opposite corner stood
Mop, rosining his bow and looking just the same as ever.
The company had cleared the middle of the room for
dancing, and they were about to dance again. As she
wore a veil to keep off the wind she did not think he had
recognized her, or could possibly guess the identity of the
child ; and to her satisfied surprise she found that she could
confront him quite calmly—mistress of herself in the dignity her London life had given her. Before she had quite
emptied her glass the dance was called, the dancers formed
in two lines, the music sounded, and the figure began.

Then matters changed for Car line. A tremor quickened
itself to life in her, and her hand so shook that she could
hardly set down her glass. It was not the dance nor the
dancers, but the notes of that old violin which thrilled the
London wife, these having still all the witchery that she
had so well known of yore, and under which she had used
to lose her power of independent will. How it all came
back ! There was the fiddling figure against the wall ;
the large, oily, mop-like head of him, and beneath the
mop the face with closed eyes.

After the first moments of paralyzed reverie the familiar
tune in the familiar rendering made her laugh and shed
tears simultaneously. Then a man at the bottom of the
dance, whose partner had dropped away, stretched out
his hand and beckoned to her to take the place. She did
not want to dance ; she entreated by signs to be left where
she was, but she was entreating of the tune and its player
rather than of the dancing man. The saltatory tendency
which the fiddler and his cunning instrument had ever
been able to start in her was seizing Car'line just as it had
done in earlier years, possibly assisted by the gin-and-beer
hot. Tired as she was she grasped her little girl by the
hand, and plunging in at the bottom of the figure, whirled
about with the rest. She found that her companions were

mostly people of the neighbouring hamlets and farms—
Bloom's End, Mellstock, Lewgate, and elsewhere ; and by
degrees she was recognized as she convulsively danced on,
wishing that Mop would cease and let her heart rest from
the aching he caused, and her feet also.

After long and many minutes the dance ended, when
she was urged to fortify herself with more gin-and-beer ;
which she did, feeling very weak and overpowered with
hysteric emotion. She refrained from unveiling, to keep
Mop in ignorance of her presence, if possible. Several of
the guests having left, Car'line hastily wiped her lips and
also turned to go ; but, according to the account of some
who remained, at that very moment a five-handed reel was
proposed, in which two or three begged her to join.

She declined on the plea of being tired and having to
walk to Stickleford, when Mop began aggressively tweed-
ling ' My Fancy-Lad,' in D major, as the air to which the
reel was to be footed. He must have recognized her,
though she did not know it, for it was the strain of all
seductive strains which she was least able to resist—the
one he had played when she was leaning over the bridge
at the date of their first acquaintance. Car'line stepped
despairingly into the middle of the room with the other
four.

Reels were resorted to hereabouts at this time by the
more robust spirits, for the reduction of superfluous energy
which the ordinary figure-dances were not powerful enough
to exhaust. As everybody knows, or does not know, the
five reelers stood in the form of a cross, the reel being performed by each line of three alternately, the persons who
successively came to the middle place dancing in both
directions. Car'line soon found herself in this place, the
axis of the whole performance, and could not get out of
it, the tune turning into the first part without giving her
opportunity. And now she began to suspect that Mop
did know her, and was doing this on purpose, though
whenever she stole a glance at him his closed eyes betok-
ened obliviousness to everything outside his own brain.
She continued to wend her way through the figure of 8
that was formed by her course, the fiddler introducing

into his notes the wild and agonizing sweetness of a living voice in one too highly wrought ; its pathos running high and running low in endless variation, projecting through her nerves excruciating spasms, a sort of blissful torture. The room swam ; the tune was endless ; and in about a quarter of an hour the only other woman in the figure dropped out exhausted, and sank panting on a bench.

The reel instantly resolved itself into a four-handed one. Car'line would have given anything to leave off ; but she had, or fancied she had, no power, while Mop played such tunes ; and thus another ten minutes slipped by, a haze of dust now clouding the candles, the floor being of stone, sanded. Then another dancer fell out—one of the men— and went into the passage in a frantic search for liquor. To turn the figure into a three-handed reel was the work of a second, Mop modulating at the same time into ' The Fairy Dance,' as better suited to the contracted movement, and no less one of those foods of love which, as manufactured by his bow, had always intoxicated her.

In a reel for three there was no rest whatever, and four or five minutes were enough to make her remaining two partners, now thoroughly blown, stamp their last bar, and, like their predecessors, limp off into the next room to get something to drink. Car'line, half-stifled inside her veil, was left dancing alone, the apartment now being empty of everybody save herself, Mop, and their little girl.

She flung up the veil, and cast her eyes upon him, as if imploring him to withdraw himself and his acoustic magnetism from the atmosphere. Mop opened one of his own orbs, as though for the first time, fixed it peeringly upon her, and smiling dreamily, threw into his strains the reserve of expression which he could not afford to waste on a big and noisy dance. Crowds of little chromatic subtleties, capable of drawing tears from a statue, proceeded straightway from the ancient fiddle, as if it were dying of the emotion which had been pent up within it ever since its banishment from some Italian or German city where it first took shape and sound. There was that in the look of Mop's one dark eye which said : ' You cannot leave off, dear, whether you would or no ! ' and it bred in her a paroxysm of desperation that defied him to tire her down.

She thus continued to dance alone, defiantly as she thought, but in truth slavishly and abjectly, subject to every wave of the melody, and probed by the gimlet-like gaze of her fascinator's open eye ; keeping up at the same time a feeble smile in his face, as a feint to signify it was still her own pleasure which led her on. A terrified embarrassment as to what she could say to him if she were to leave off, had its unrecognized share in keeping her going. The child, who was beginning to be distressed by the strange situation, came up and whimpered : ' Stop, mother, stop, and let's go home ! ' as she seized Car'line's hand.

Suddenly Car'line sank staggering to the floor, and rolling over on her face, prone she remained. Mop's fiddle thereupon emitted an elfin shriek of finality ; stepping quickly down from the nine-gallon beer-cask which had formed his rostrum, he went to the little girl, who disconsolately bent over her mother.

The guests who had gone into the back room for liquor and change of air, hearing something unusual, trooped back hitherward, where they endeavoured to revive poor, weak Car'line by blowing her with the bellows and opening the window. Ned, her husband, who had been detained in Casterbridge, as aforesaid, came along the road at this juncture, and hearing excited voices through the open casement, and, to his great surprise, the mention of his wife's name, he entered amid the rest upon the scene. Car'line was now in convulsions, weeping violently, and for a long time nothing could be done with her. While he was sending for a cart to take her onward to Stickleford Hipcroft anxiously inquired how it had all happened ; and then the assembly explained that a fiddler formerly known in the locality had lately visited his old haunts, and had taken upon himself without invitation to play that evening at the inn and raise a dance.

Ned demanded the fiddler's name, and they said Ollamoor.

' Ah ! ' exclaimed Ned, looking round him. ' Where is he, and where—where's my little girl ? '

Ollamoor had disappeared, and so had the child. Hip-croft was in ordinary a quiet and tractable fellow, but a determination which was to be feared settled in his face now. ' Blast him ! ' he cried. ' I'll beat his skull in for'n, if I swing for it to-morrow ! '

He had rushed to the poker which lay on the hearth, and hastened down the passage, the people following. Outside the house, on the other side of the highway, a mass of dark heath-land rose sullenly upward to its not easily accessible interior, a ravined plateau, whereon jutted into the sky, at the distance of a couple of miles, the fir-woods of Mistover backed by the Yalbury coppices—a place of Dantesque gloom at this hour, which would have afforded secure hiding for a battery of artillery, much less a man and a child.

Some other men plunged thitherward with him, and more went along the road. They were gone about twenty minutes altogether, returning without result to the inn. Ned sat down in the settle, and clasped his forehead with his hands.

' Well—what a fool the man is, and hev been all these years, if he thinks the child his, as a' do seem to ! ' they whispered. ' And everybody else knowing otherwise ! '

' No, I don't think 'tis mine ! ' cried Ned hoarsely, as he looked up from his hands. ' But she *is* mine, all the same ! Ha'n't I nussed her ? Ha'n't I fed her and teached her ? Ha'n't I played wi' her ? O, little Carry—gone with that rogue—gone ! '

' You ha'n't lost your mis'ess, anyhow,' they said to console him. ' She's throwed up the sperrits, and she is feeling better, and she's more to 'ee than a child that isn't yours.'

' She isn't ! She's not so particular much to me, especi-ally now she's lost the little maid ! But Carry's the whole world to me ! '

' Well, ver' like you'll find her to-morrow.'

' Ah—but shall I ? Yet he *can't* hurt her—surely he can't ! Well—how's Car'line now ? I am ready. Is the cart here ? '

She was lifted into the vehicle, and they sadly lumbered

on toward Stickleford. Next day she was calmer ; but
the fits were still upon her ; and her will seemed shattered.
For the child she appeared to show singularly little anxiety,
though Ned was nearly distracted by his passionate paternal love for a child not his own.   It was nevertheless quite
expected that the impish Mop would restore the lost one
after a freak of a day or two ; but time went on, and
neither he nor she could be heard of, and Hipcroft murmured
that perhaps he was exercising upon her some unholy
musical charm, as he had done upon Car'line herself.
Weeks passed, and still they could obtain no clue either
to the fiddler's whereabouts or to the girl's ; and how he
could have induced her to go with him remained a mystery.

Then Ned, who had obtained only temporary employment in the neighbourhood, took a sudden hatred towards
his native district, and a rumour reaching his ears through
the police that a somewhat similar man and child had
been seen at a fair near London, he playing a violin, she
dancing on stilts, a new interest in the capital took possession of Hipcroft with an intensity which would scarcely
allow him time to pack before returning thither. He did
not, however, find the lost one, though he made it the
entire business of his over-hours to stand about in by-streets
in the hope of discovering her, and would start up in the
night, saying, ' That rascal's torturing her to maintain
him ! '   To which his wife would answer peevishly, ' Don't
'ee raft yourself so, Ned !   You prevent my getting a bit
o' rest !   He won't hurt her ! ' and fall asleep again.

That Carry and her father had emigrated to America
was the general opinion ; Mop, no doubt, finding the girl a
highly desirable companion when he had trained her to
keep him by her earnings as a dancer. There, for that
matter, they may be performing in some capacity now,
though he must be an old scamp verging on three-score-
and-ten, and she a woman of four-and-forty.

May 1893.

A FEW CRUSTED CHARACTERS

A FEW CRUSTED CHARACTERS

INTRODUCTION

IT is a Saturday afternoon of blue and yellow autumn-time, and the scene is the High Street of a well-known market-town. A large carrier's van stands in the quadrangular fore-court of the White Hart Inn, upon the sides of its spacious tilt being painted, in weather-beaten letters : ' Burthen, Carrier to Longpuddle.' These vans, so numerous hereabout, are a respectable, if somewhat lumbering, class of conveyance, much resorted to by decent travellers not overstocked with money, the better among them roughly corresponding to the old French *diligences*.

The present one is timed to leave the town at four in the afternoon precisely, and it is now half-past three by the clock in the turret at the top of the street. In a few seconds errand-boys from the shops begin to arrive with packages, which they fling into the vehicle, and turn away whistling, and care for the packages no more. At twenty minutes to four an elderly woman places her basket upon the shafts, slowly mounts, takes up a seat inside, and folds her hands and her lips. She has secured her corner for the journey, though there is as yet no sign of a horse being put in, nor of a carrier. At the three-quarters, two other women arrive, in whom the first recognizes the post-mistress of Upper Longpuddle and the registrar's wife, they recognizing her as the aged groceress of the same village. At five minutes to the hour there approach Mr. Profitt, the schoolmaster, in a soft felt hat, and Christopher Twink,

</>

the master-thatcher; and as the hour strikes there rapidly
drop in the parish clerk and his wife, the seedsman and
his aged father, the registrar; also Mr. Day, the world-
ignored local landscape-painter, an elderly man who resides
in his native place, and has never sold a picture outside
it, though his pretensions to art have been nobly supported
by his fellow-villagers, whose confidence in his genius has
been as remarkable as the outer neglect of it, leading them
to buy his paintings so extensively (at the price of a few
shillings each, it is true) that every dwelling in the parish
exhibits three or four of those admired productions on its
walls.

Burthen, the carrier, is by this time seen bustling round
the vehicle; the horses are put in, the proprietor arranges
the reins and springs up into his seat as if he were used
to it—which he is.

' Is everybody here ? ' he asks preparatorily over his
shoulder to the passengers within.

As those who were not there did not reply in the negative the muster was assumed to be complete, and after a
few hitches and hindrances the van with its human freight
was got under way. It jogged on at an easy pace till it
reached the bridge which formed the last outpost of the
town. The carrier pulled up suddenly.

' Bless my soul ! ' he said, ' I've forgot the curate ! '

All who could do so gazed from the little back-window
of the van, but the curate was not in sight.

' Now I wonder where that there man is ? ' continued
the carrier.

' Poor man, he ought to have a living at his time of
life.'

' And he ought to be punctual,' said the carrier. ' " Four
o'clock sharp is my time for starting," I said to 'en. And
he said, " I'll be there." Now he's not here; and as a
serious old church-minister he ought to be as good as his
word. Perhaps Mr. Flaxton knows, being in the same
line of life ? ' He turned to the parish clerk.

' I was talking an immense deal with him, that's true,
half an hour ago,' replied that ecclesiastic, as one of whom
it was no erroneous supposition that he should be on inti-

mate terms with another of the cloth. 'But he didn't say
he would be late.'

The discussion was cut off by the appearance round the
corner of the van of rays from the curate's spectacles, followed hastily by his face and a few white whiskers, and
the swinging tails of his long gaunt coat. Nobody reproached him, seeing how he was reproaching himself; and
he entered breathlessly and took his seat.

'Now be we all here?' said the carrier again. They
started a second time, and moved on till they were about
three hundred yards out of the town, and had nearly reached
the second bridge, behind which, as every native remem-
bers, the road takes a turn, and travellers by this highway
disappear finally from the view of gazing burghers.

'Well, as I'm alive!' cried the postmistress from the
interior of the conveyance, peering through the little
square back-window along the road townward.

'What?' said the carrier.

'A man hailing us!'

Another sudden stoppage. 'Somebody else?' the carrier asked.

'Ay, sure!' All waited silently, while those who could
gaze out did so.

'Now, who can that be?' Burthen continued. 'I just
put it to ye, neighbours, can any man keep time with such
hindrances? Bain't we full a'ready? Who in the world
can the man be?'

'He's a sort of gentleman,' said the schoolmaster, his
position commanding the road more comfortably than that
of his comrades.

The stranger, who had been holding up his umbrella
to attract their notice, was walking forward leisurely
enough, now that he found, by their stopping, that it had
been secured. His clothes were decidedly not of a local
cut, though it was difficult to point out any particular
mark of difference. In his left hand he carried a small
leather travelling-bag. As soon as he had overtaken the
van he glanced at the inscription on its side, as if to assure
himself that he had hailed the right conveyance, and asked
if they had room.

The carrier replied that though they were pretty well laden he supposed they could carry one more, whereupon the stranger mounted, and took the seat cleared for him within. And then the horses made another move, this time for good, and swung along with their burden of fourteen souls all told.

'You bain't one of these parts, sir ? ' said the carrier. 'I could tell that as far as I could see 'ee.'

'Yes, I am one of these parts,' said the stranger.

'Oh ? H'm.'

The silence which followed seemed to imply a doubt of the truth of the new-comer's assertion. ' I was speaking of Upper Longpuddle, more particular,' continued the carrier hardily, ' and I think I know most faces of that valley.'

'I was born at Longpuddle, and nursed at Longpuddle, and my father and grandfather before me,' said the passenger quietly.

'Why, to be sure,' said the aged groceress in the background, ' it isn't John Lackland's son—never—it can't be —he who went to foreign parts five-and-thirty years ago with his wife and family ?   Yet—what do I hear ?—that's his father's voice ! '

'That's the man,' replied the stranger.   ' John Lackland was my father, and I am John Lackland's son.   Five-and-thirty years ago, when I was a boy of eleven, my parents emigrated across the seas, taking me and my sister with them.   Kytes's boy Tony was the one who drove us and our belongings to Casterbridge on the morning we left ; and his was the last Longpuddle face I saw.   We sailed the same week across the ocean, and there we've been ever since, and there I've left those I went with—all three.'

'Alive or dead ? '

'Dead,' he replied in a low voice. ' And I have come back to the old place, having nourished a thought—not a definite intention, but just a thought—that I should like to return here in a year or two, to spend the remainder of my days.'

'Married man, Mr. Lackland ? '

'No.'

'And have the world used 'ee well, sir—or rather John, knowing 'ee as a child ? In these rich new countries that we hear of so much, you've got rich with the rest ? '

'I am not very rich,' Mr. Lackland said. 'Even in new countries, you know, there are failures. The race is not always to the swift, nor the battle to the strong ; and even if it sometimes is, you may be neither swift nor strong. However, that's enough about me. Now, having answered your inquiries, you must answer mine ; for being in London, I have come down here entirely to discover what Longpuddle is looking like, and who are living there. That was why I preferred a seat in your van to hiring a carriage for driving across.'

'Well, as for Longpuddle, we rub on there much as usual. Old figures have dropped out o' their frames, so to speak it, and new ones have been put in their places. You mentioned Tony Kytes as having been the one to drive your family and your goods to Casterbridge in his father's waggon when you left. Tony is, I believe, living still, but not at Longpuddle. He went away and settled at Lewgate, near Mellstock, after his marriage. Ah, Tony was a sort o' man ! '

'His character had hardly come out when I knew him.'

'No. But 'twas well enough, as far as that goes—except as to women. I shall never forget his courting—never ! '

The returned villager waited silently, and the carrier went on :—

TONY KYTES, THE ARCH-DECEIVER

'I shall never forget Tony's face. 'Twas a little, round, firm, tight face, with a seam here and there left by the smallpox, but not enough to hurt his looks in a woman's eye, though he'd had it badish when he was a boy. So very serious looking and unsmiling 'a was, that young man, that it really seemed as if he couldn't laugh at all without great pain to his conscience. He looked very hard at a small speck in your eye when talking to 'ee. And there was no more sign of a whisker or beard on Tony Kytes's face than on the palm of my hand. He used to

sing " The Tailor's Breeches " with a religious manner, as
if it were a hymn :—

    ' " O the petticoats went off, and the breeches they went on ! "

and all the rest of the scandalous stuff.   He was quite
the women's favourite, and in return for their likings he
loved 'em in shoals.

    ' But in course of time Tony got fixed down to one in
particular, Milly Richards, a nice, light, small, tender little
thing ; and it was soon said that they were engaged to
be married.   One Saturday he had been to market to do
business for his father, and was driving home the waggon
in the afternoon.   When he reached the foot of the very
hill we shall be going over in ten minutes who should he
see waiting for him at the top but Unity Sallet, a handsome girl, one of the young women he'd been very tender
towards before he'd got engaged to Milly.

    ' As soon as Tony came up to her she said, " My dear
Tony, will you give me a lift home ? "

    ' " That I will, darling," said Tony.   " You don't sup-
pose I could refuse 'ee ? "

    ' She smiled a smile, and up she hopped, and on drove
Tony.

    ' " Tony," she says, in a sort of tender chide, " why
did ye desert me for that other one ?   In what is she better
than I ?   I should have made 'ee a finer wife, and a more
loving one, too.   'Tisn't girls that are so easily won at
first that are the best.   Think how long we've known
each other—ever since we were children almost—now
haven't we, Tony ? "

    ' " Yes, that we have," says Tony, a-struck with the
truth o't.

    ' " And you've never seen anything in me to complain
of, have ye, Tony ?   Now tell the truth to me ! "

    ' " I never have, upon my life," says Tony.

    ' " And—can you say I'm not pretty, Tony ?   Now look
at me ! "

    ' He let his eyes light upon her for a long while.   " I
really can't," says he.   " In fact, I never knowed you was
so pretty before ! "

' " Prettier than she ? "

'What Tony would have said to that nobody knows, for before he could speak, what should he see ahead, over the hedge past the turning, but a feather he knew well— the feather in Milly's hat—she to whom he had been thinking of putting the question as to giving out the banns that very week.

' " Unity," says he, as mild as he could, " here's Milly coming. Now I shall catch it mightily if she sees 'ee riding here with me ; and if you get down she'll be turning the corner in a moment, and, seeing 'ee in the road, she'll know we've been coming on together. Now, dearest Unity, will ye, to avoid all unpleasantness, which I know ye can't bear any more than I, will ye lie down in the back part of the waggon, and let me cover you over with the tarpaulin till Milly has passed ? It will all be done in a minute. Do !—and I'll think over what we've said, and perhaps I shall put a loving question to you after all, instead of to Milly. 'Tisn't true that it is all settled between her and me."

'Well, Unity Sallet agreed, and lay down at the back end of the waggon, and Tony covered her over, so that the waggon seemed to be empty but for the loose tarpaulin ; and then he drove on to meet Milly.

' " My dear Tony ! " cries Milly, looking up with a little pout at him as he came near. " How long you've been coming home ! Just as if I didn't live at Upper Longpuddle at all ! And I've come to meet you as you asked me to do, and to ride back with you, and talk over our future home—since you asked me, and I promised. But I shouldn't have come else, Mr. Tony ! "

' " Ay, my dear, I did ask 'ee—to be sure I did, now I think of it—but I had quite forgot it. To ride back with me, did you say, dear Milly ? "

' " Well, of course ! What can I do else ? Surely you don't want me to walk, now I've come all this way ? "

' " O no, no ! I was thinking you might be going on to town to meet your mother. I saw her there—and she looked as if she might be expecting 'ee."

' " O no ; she's just home. She came across the fields,
and so got back before you."

' " Ah ! I didn't know that," says Tony. And there
was no help for it but to take her up beside him.

' They talked on very pleasantly, and looked at the
trees, and beasts, and birds, and insects, and at the plough-
men at work in the fields, till presently who should they
see looking out of the upper window of a house that stood
beside the road they were following, but Hannah Jolliver,
another young beauty of the place at that time, and the
very first woman that Tony had fallen in love with—before
Milly and before Unity, in fact—the one that he had almost
arranged to marry instead of Milly. She was a much
more dashing girl than Milly Richards, though he'd not
thought much of her of late. The house Hannah was
looking from was her aunt's.

' " My dear Milly—my coming wife, as I may call 'ee,"
says Tony in his modest way, and not so loud that Unity
could overhear, " I see a young woman a-looking out of
window, who I think may accost me. The fact is, Milly,
she had a notion that I was wishing to marry her, and
since she's discovered I've promised another, and a prettier
than she, I'm rather afeard of her temper if she sees us
together. Now, Milly, would you do me a favour—my
coming wife, as I may say ? "

' " Certainly, dearest Tony," says she.

' " Then would ye creep under the empty sacks just here
in the front of the waggon, and hide there out of sight till
we've passed the house ? She hasn't seen us yet. You
see, we ought to live in peace and goodwill since 'tis almost
Christmas, and 'twill prevent angry passions rising, which
we always should do."

' " I don't mind, to oblige you, Tony," Milly said ; and
though she didn't care much about doing it, she crept
under, and crouched down just behind the seat, Unity
being snug at the other end. So they drove on till they
got near the road-side cottage. Hannah had soon seen
him coming, and waited at the window, looking down upon
him. She tossed her head a little disdainful and smiled
off-hand.

' " Well, aren't you going to be civil enough to ask me to ride home with you ! " she says, seeing that he was for driving past with a nod and a smile.

' " Ah, to be sure ! What was I thinking of ? " said Tony, in a flutter. " But you seem as if you was staying at your aunt's ? "   ·

' " No, I am not," she said. " Don't you see I have my bonnet and jacket on ? I have only called to see her on my way home. How can you be so stupid, Tony ? "

' " In that case—ah—of course you must come along wi' me," says Tony, feeling a dim sort of sweat rising up inside his clothes. And he reined in the horse, and waited till she'd come downstairs, and then helped her up beside him, her feet outside. He drove on again, his face as long as a face that was a round one by nature well could be.

' Hannah looked round sideways into his eyes. " This is nice, isn't it, Tony ? " she says. " I like riding with you."

' Tony looked back into her eyes. " And I with you," he said after a while. In short, having considered her, he warmed up, and the more he looked at her the more he liked her, till he couldn't for the life of him think why he had ever said a word about marriage to Milly or Unity while Hannah Jolliver was in question. So they sat a little closer and closer, their feet upon the foot-board and their shoulders touching, and Tony thought over and over again how handsome Hannah was. He spoke tenderer and tenderer, and called her " dear Hannah " in a whisper at last.

' " You've settled it with Milly by this time, I suppose ? " said she.

' " N—no, not exactly."

' " What ? How low you talk, Tony."

' " Yes—I've a kind of hoarseness. I said, not exactly."

' " I suppose you mean to ? "

' " Well, as to that—— " His eyes rested on her face, and hers on his. He wondered how he could have been such a fool as not to follow up Hannah. " My sweet Hannah ! " he bursts out, taking her hand, not being really able to help it, and forgetting Milly and Unity, and

all the world besides. " Settled it ? I don't think I
have ! "

'" Hark ! " says Hannah.

'" What ? " says Tony, letting go her hand.

'" Surely I heard a sort of little screaming squeak under
those sacks ? Why, you've been carrying corn, and there's
mice in this waggon, I declare ! " She began to haul up
the tails of her gown.

'" O no, 'tis the axle," said Tony in an assuring way.
" It do go like that sometimes in dry weather."

'" Perhaps it was. . . . Well, now, to be quite honest,
dear Tony, do you like her better than me ? Because—
because, although I've held off so independent, I'll own at
last that I do like 'ee, Tony, to tell the truth ; and I wouldn't
say no if you asked me—you know what."

' Tony was so won over by this pretty offering mood of a
girl who had been quite the reverse (Hannah had a backward way with her at times, if you can mind) that he just
glanced behind, and then whispered very soft, " I haven't
quite promised her, and I think I can get out of it, and
ask you that question you speak of."

'" Throw over Milly ?—all to marry me ! How delightful ! " broke out Hannah, quite loud, clapping her hands.

' At this there was a real squeak—an angry, spiteful
squeak, and afterward a long moan, as if something had
broke its heart, and a movement of the empty sacks.

'" Something's there ! " said Hannah, starting up.

'" It's nothing. really," says Tony in a soothing voice,
and praying inwardly for a way out of this. " I wouldn't
tell 'ee at first, because I wouldn't frighten 'ee. But,
Hannah, I've really a couple of ferrets in a bag under
there, for rabbiting, and they quarrel sometimes. I don't
wish it knowed, as 'twould be called poaching. Oh, they
can't get out, bless 'ee—you are quite safe ! And—and—
what a fine day it is, isn't it, Hannah, for this time of year ?
Be you going to market next Saturday ? How is your
aunt now ? " And so on, says Tony, to keep her from
talking any more about love in Milly's hearing.

' But he found his work cut out for him, and wondering
again how he should get out of this ticklish business, he

looked about for a chance. Nearing home he saw his
father in a field not far off, holding up his hand as if he
wished to speak to Tony.

' " Would you mind taking the reins a moment, Hannah,"
he said, much relieved, " while I go and find out what
father wants ? "

' She consented, and away he hastened into the field.
only too glad to get breathing time. He found that his
father was looking at him with rather a stern eye.

' " Come, come, Tony," says old Mr. Kytes, as soon as
his son was alongside him, " this won't do, you know."

' " What ? " says Tony.

' " Why, if you mean to marry Milly Richards, do it,
and there's an end o't. But don't go driving about the
country with Jolliver's daughter and making a scandal. I
won't have such things done."

' " I only asked her—that is, she asked me, to ride home."

' " She ?   Why, now, if it had been Milly, 'twould have
been quite proper ; but you and Hannah Jolliver going
about by yourselves——"

' " Milly's there, too, father."

' " Milly ?   Where ? "

' " Under the corn-sacks !   Yes, the truth is, father, I've
got rather into a nunnywatch, I'm afeard ! Unity Sallet
is there, too—yes, at the other end, under the tarpaulin.
All three are in that waggon, and what to do with 'em I
know no more than the dead !   The best plan is, as I'm
thinking, to speak out loud and plain to one of 'em before
the rest, and that will settle it ; not but what 'twill cause
'em to kick up a bit of a miff, for certain. Now which
would you marry, father, if you was in my place ? "

' " Whichever of 'em did *not* ask to ride with thee."

' " That was Milly, I'm bound to say, as she only mounted
by my invitation. But Milly——"

' " Then stick to Milly, she's the best. . . . But look
at that ! "

' His father pointed toward the waggon. " She can't
hold that horse in. You shouldn't have left the reins in
her hands. Run on and take the horse's head, or there'll
be some accident to them maids ! "

'Tony's horse, in fact, in spite of Hannah's tugging at the reins, had started on his way at a brisk walking pace, being very anxious to get back to the stable, for he had had a long day out. Without another word Tony rushed away from his father to overtake the horse.

'Now of all things that could have happened to wean him from Milly there was nothing so powerful as his father's recommending her. No; it could not be Milly, after all. Hannah must be the one, since he could not marry all three as he longed to do. This he thought while running after the waggon. But queer things were happening inside it.

'It was, of course, Milly who had screamed under the sack-bags, being obliged to let off her bitter rage and shame in that way at what Tony was saying, and never daring to show, for very pride and dread o' being laughed at, that she was in hiding. She became more and more restless, and in twisting herself about, what did she see but another woman's foot and white stocking close to her head. It quite frightened her, not knowing that Unity Sallet was in the waggon likewise. But after the fright was over she determined to get to the bottom of all this, and she crept and crept along the bed of the waggon, under the tarpaulin, like a snake, when lo and behold she came face to face with Unity.

'"Well, if this isn't disgraceful!" says Milly in a raging whisper to Unity.

'"'Tis," says Unity, "to see you hiding in a young man's waggon like this, and no great character belonging to either of ye!"

'"Mind what you are saying!" replied Milly, getting louder. "I am engaged to be married to him, and haven't I a right to be here? What right have you, I should like to know? What has he been promising you? A pretty lot of nonsense, I expect! But what Tony says to other women is all mere wind, and no concern to me!"

'"Don't you be too sure!" says Unity. "He's going to have Hannah, and not you, nor me either; I could hear that."

'Now at these strange voices sounding from under the

cloth Hannah was thunderstruck a'most into a swound; and it was just at this time that the horse moved on. Hannah tugged away wildly, not knowing what she was doing; and as the quarrel rose louder and louder Hannah got so horrified that she let go the reins altogether. The horse went on at his own pace, and coming to the corner where we turn round to drop down the hill to Lower Long-puddle he turned too quick, the off wheels went up the bank, the waggon rose sideways till it was quite on edge upon the near axles, and out rolled the three maidens into the road in a heap. The horse looked round and stood still.

'When Tony came up, frightened and breathless, he was relieved enough to see that neither of his darlings was hurt, beyond a few scratches from the brambles of the hedge. But he was rather alarmed when he heard how they were going on at one another.

'"Don't ye quarrel, my dears—don't ye!" says he, taking off his hat out of respect to 'em. And then he would have kissed them all round, as fair and square as a man could, but they were in too much of a taking to let him, and screeched and sobbed till they was quite spent.

'"Now I'll speak out honest, because I ought to," says Tony, as soon as he could get heard. "And this is the truth," says he. "I've asked Hannah to be mine, and she is willing, and we are going to put up the banns next——"

'Tony had not noticed that Hannah's father was coming up behind, nor had he noticed that Hannah's face was beginning to bleed from the scratch of a bramble. Hannah had seen her father, and had run to him, crying worse than ever.

'"My daughter is *not* willing, sir!" says Mr. Jolliver hot and strong. "Be you willing, Hannah? I ask ye to have spirit enough to refuse him, if yer virtue is left to 'ee and you run no risk?"

'"She's as sound as a bell for me, that I'll swear!" says Tony, flaring up. "And so's the others, come to that, though you may think it an onusual thing in me!"

'"I have spirit, and I do refuse him!" says Hannah, partly because her father was there, and partly, too, in a

tantrum because of the discovery, and the scar that might
be left on her face. " Little did I think when I was so
soft with him just now that I was talking to such a false
deceiver ! "

' " What, you won't have me, Hannah ? " says Tony,
his jaw hanging down like a dead man's.

' " Never—I would sooner marry no—nobody at all ! "
she gasped out, though with her heart in her throat, for
she would not have refused Tony if he had asked her quietly,
and her father had not been there, and her face had not
been scratched by the bramble. And having said that,
away she walked upon her father's arm, thinking and hoping he would ask her again.

' Tony didn't know what to say next. Milly was sobbing her heart out ; but as his father had strongly recommended her he couldn't feel inclined that way. So he
turned to Unity.

' " Well, will you, Unity dear, be mine ? " he says.

' " Take her leavings ? Not I ! " says Unity. " I'd
scorn it ! " And away walks Unity Sallet likewise, though
she looked back when she'd gone some way, to see if he
was following her.

' So there at last were left Milly and Tony by themselves, she crying in watery streams, and Tony looking
like a tree struck by lightning.

' " Well, Milly," he says at last, going up to her, " it do
seem as if fate had ordained that it should be you and I,
or nobody. And what must be must be, I suppose. Hey,
Milly ? "

' " If you like, Tony. You didn't really mean what
you said to them ? "

' " Not a word of it ! " declares Tony, bringing down his
fist upon his palm.

' And then he kissed her, and put the waggon to rights,
and they mounted together ; and their banns were put up
the very next Sunday. I was not able to go to their wedding, but it was a rare party they had, by all account.
Everybody in Longpuddle was there almost ; you among
the rest, I think, Mr. Flaxton ? ' The speaker turned to
the parish clerk.

' I was,' said Mr. Flaxton. ' And that party was the cause of a very curious change in some other people's affairs; I mean in Steve Hardcome's and his cousin James's.'

' Ah ! the Hardcomes,' said the stranger.   ' How familiar that name is to me ! What of them ? '

The clerk cleared his throat and began :—

THE HISTORY OF THE HARDCOMES

' Yes, Tony's was the very best wedding-randy that ever I was at; and I've been at a good many, as you may suppose '—turning to the newly-arrived one—' having, as a church-officer, the privilege to attend all christening, wedding, and funeral parties—such being our Wessex custom.

' 'Twas on a frosty night in Christmas week, and among the folk invited were the said Hardcomes o' Climmerston —Steve and James—first cousins, both of them small farmers, just entering into business on their own account. With them came, as a matter of course, their intended wives, two young women of the neighbourhood, both very pretty and sprightly maidens, and numbers of friends from Abbot's-Cernel, and Weatherbury, and Mellstock, and I don't know where—a regular houseful.

' The kitchen was cleared of furniture for dancing, and the old folk played at " Put " and " All-fours " in the parlour, though at last they gave that up to join in the dance. The top of the figure was by the large front window of the room, and there were so many couples that the lower part of the figure reached through the door at the back, and into the darkness of the out-house; in fact, you couldn't see the end of the row at all, and 'twas never known exactly how long that dance was, the lowest couples being lost among the faggots and brushwood in the out-house.

' When we had danced a few hours, and the crowns of we taller men were swelling into lumps with bumping the beams of the ceiling, the first fiddler laid down his fiddle-bow, and said he should play no more, for he wished to dance. And in another hour the second fiddler laid down his, and said he wanted to dance, too; so there was only

the third fiddler left, and he was a' old, veteran man, very
weak in the wrist. However, he managed to keep up a
faltering tweedle-dee ; but there being no chair in the
room, and his knees being as weak as his wrists, he was
obliged to sit upon as much of the little corner-table as
projected beyond the corner-cupboard fixed over it, which
was not a very wide seat for a man advanced in years.

' Among those who danced most continually were the
two engaged couples, as was natural to their situation.
Each pair was very well matched, and very unlike the
other. James Hardcome's intended was called Emily
Darth, and both she and James were gentle, nice-minded,
in-door people, fond of a quiet life. Steve and his chosen,
named Olive Pawle, were different ; they were of a more
bustling nature, fond of racketing about and seeing what
was going on in the world. The two couples had arranged
to get married on the same day, and that not long thence ;
Tony's wedding being a sort of stimulant, as is often the
case ; I've noticed it professionally many times.

' They danced with such a will as only young people in
that stage of courtship can dance ; and it happened that
as the evening wore on James had for his partner Stephen's
plighted one, Olive, at the same time that Stephen was
dancing with James's Emily. It was noticed that in spite
o' the exchange the young men seemed to enjoy the dance
no less than before. By and by they were treading another
tune in the same changed order as we had noticed earlier,
and though at first each one had held the other's mistress
strictly at half-arm's length, lest there should be shown
any objection to too close quarters by the lady's proper
man, as time passed there was a little more closeness
between 'em ; and presently a little more closeness still.

' The later it got the more did each of the two cousins
dance with the wrong young girl, and the tighter did he
hold her to his side as he whirled her round ; and, what
was very remarkable, neither seemed to mind what the
other was doing. The party began to draw towards its
end, and I saw no more that night, being one of the first
to leave, on account of my morning's business. But I
learnt the rest of it from those that knew.

' After finishing a particularly warming dance with the changed partners, as I've mentioned, the two young men looked at one another, and in a moment or two went out into the porch together.

' " James," says Steve, " what were you thinking of when you were dancing with my Olive ? "

' " Well," said James, " perhaps what you were thinking of when you were dancing with my Emily."

' " I was thinking," said Steve, with some hesitation, " that I wouldn't mind changing for good and all ! "

' " It was what I was feeling likewise," said James.

' " I willingly agree to it, if you think we could manage it."

' " So do I. But what would the girls say ? "

' " 'Tis my belief," said Steve, " that they wouldn't particularly object. Your Emily clung as close to me as if she already belonged to me, dear girl."

' " And your Olive to me," says James. " I could feel her heart beating like a clock."

' Well, they agreed to put it to the girls when they were all four walking home together. And they did so. When they parted that night the exchange was decided on—all having been done under the hot excitement of that evening's dancing. Thus it happened that on the following Sunday morning, when the people were sitting in church with mouths wide open to hear the names published as they had expected, there was no small amazement to hear them coupled the wrong way, as it seemed. The congregation whispered, and thought the parson had made a mistake ; till they discovered that his reading of the names was verily the true way. As they had decided, so they were married, each one to the other's original property.

' Well, the two couples lived on for a year or two ordinarily enough, till the time came when these young people began to grow a little less warm to their respective spouses, as is the rule of married life ; and the two cousins wondered more and more in their hearts what had made 'em so mad at the last moment to marry crosswise as they did, when they might have married straight, as was planned by Nature, and as they had fallen in love. 'Twas Tony's

party that had done it, plain enough, and they half wished
they had never gone there.   James, being a quiet, fireside,
perusing man, felt at times a wide gap between himself
and Olive, his wife, who loved riding and driving and outdoor jaunts to a degree;   while Steve, who was always
knocking about hither and thither, had a very domestic
wife, who worked samplers, and made hearthrugs, scarcely
ever wished to cross the threshold, and only drove out
with him to please him.

'However, they said very little about this mismating to
any of their acquaintances, though sometimes Steve would
look at James's wife, and sigh, and James would look at
Steve's wife and do the same.   Indeed, at last the two
men were frank enough towards each other not to mind
mentioning it quietly to themselves, in a long-faced, sorry-
smiling, whimsical sort of way, and would shake their
heads together over their foolishness in upsetting a well-
considered choice on the strength of an hour's fancy in the
whirl and wildness of a dance.   Still, they were sensible
and honest young fellows enough, and did their best to
make shift with their lot as they had arranged it, and not
to repine at what could not now be altered or mended.

'So things remained till one fine summer day they went
for their yearly little outing together, as they had made it
their custom to do for a long while past.   This year they
chose Budmouth-Regis as the place to spend their holiday
in; and off they went in their best clothes at nine o'clock
in the morning.

'When they had reached Budmouth-Regis they walked
two and two along the shore—their new boots going
squeakity-squash upon the clammy velvet sands.   I can
seem to see 'em now!   Then they looked at the ships in
the harbour; and then went up to the Look-out; and then
had dinner at an inn, and then again walked two and two,
squeakity-squash, upon the velvet sands.   As evening
drew on they sat on one of the public seats upon the Esplanade, and listened to the band; and then they said, "What
shall we do next?"

'"Of all things," said Olive (Mrs. James Hardcome,
that is), "I should like to row in the bay!   We could

listen to the music from the water as well as from here, and have the fun of rowing besides."

' " The very thing ; so should I," says Stephen, his tastes being always like hers.'

Here the clerk turned to the curate.

' But you, sir, know the rest of the strange particulars of that strange evening of their lives better than anybody else, having had much of it from their own lips, which I had not ; and perhaps you'll oblige the gentleman ? '

' Certainly, if it is wished,' said the curate. And he took up the clerk's tale :—

' Stephen's wife hated the sea, except from land, and couldn't bear the thought of going into a boat. James, too, disliked the water, and said that for his part he would much sooner stay on and listen to the band in the seat they occupied, though he did not wish to stand in his wife's way if she desired a row. The end of the discussion was that James and his cousin's wife Emily agreed to remain where they were sitting and enjoy the music, while they watched the other two hire a boat just beneath, and take their water-excursion of half an hour or so, till they should choose to come back and join the sitters on the Esplanade ; when they would all start homeward together.

' Nothing could have pleased the other two restless ones better than this arrangement ; and Emily and James watched them go down to the boatman below and choose one of the little yellow skiffs, and walk carefully out upon the little plank that was laid on trestles to enable them to get alongside the craft. They saw Stephen hand Olive in, and take his seat facing her ; when they were settled they waved their hands to the couple watching them, and then Stephen took the pair of sculls and pulled off to the tune beat by the band, she steering through the other boats skimming about, for the sea was as smooth as glass that evening, and pleasure-seekers were rowing everywhere.

' " How pretty they look moving on, don't they ? " said Emily to James (as I've been assured). " They both enjoy it equally. In everything their likings are the same."

' " That's true," said James.

' " They would have made a handsome pair if they had married," said she.

' " Yes," said he.   " 'Tis a pity we should have parted 'em."

' " Don't talk of that, James," said she.   " For better or for worse we decided to do as we did, and there's an end of it."

' They sat on after that without speaking, side by side, and the band played as before ; the people strolled up and down ; and Stephen and Olive shrank smaller and smaller as they shot straight out to sea.   The two on shore used to relate how they saw Stephen stop rowing a moment, and take off his coat to get at his work better ; but James's wife sat quite still in the stern, holding the tiller-ropes by which she steered the boat.   When they had got very small indeed she turned her head to shore.

' " She is waving her handkerchief to us," said Stephen's wife, who thereupon pulled out her own, and waved it as a return signal.

' The boat's course had been a little awry while Mrs. James neglected her steering to wave her handkerchief to her husband and Mrs. Stephen ; but now the light skiff went straight onward again, and they could soon see nothing more of the two figures it contained than Olive's light mantle and Stephen's white shirt-sleeves behind.

' The two on the shore talked on.   " 'Twas very curious —our changing partners at Tony Kytes's wedding," Emily declared.   " Tony was of a fickle nature by all account, and it really seemed as if his character had infected us that night.   Which of you two was it that first proposed not to marry as we were engaged ? "   •

' " H'm—I can't remember at this moment," says James.   " We talked it over, you know ; and no sooner said than done."

' " 'Twas the dancing," said she.   " People get quite crazy sometimes in a dance."

' " They do," he owned.

' " James—do you think they care for one another still ? " asks Mrs. Stephen.

' James Hardcome mused and admitted that perhaps a little tender feeling might flicker up in their hearts for a moment now and then. " Still, nothing of any account," he said.

' " I sometimes think that Olive is in Steve's mind a good deal," murmurs Mrs. Stephen ; " particularly when she pleases his fancy by riding past our window at a gallop on one of the draught-horses. . . .   I never could do anything of that sort ; I could never get over my fear of a horse."

' " And I am no horseman, though I pretend to be on her account," murmured James Hardcome. " But isn't it almost time for them to turn and sweep round to the shore, as the other boating folk have done ?   I wonder what Olive means by steering away straight to the horizon like that ?   She has hardly swerved from a direct line seaward since they started."

' " No doubt they are talking, and don't think of where they are going," suggests Stephen's wife.

' " Perhaps so," said James. " I didn't know Steve could row like that."

' " O yes," says she.   " He often comes here on business, and generally has a pull round the bay."

' " I can hardly see the boat or them," says James again ; " and it is getting dark."

' The heedless pair afloat now formed a mere speck in the films of the coming night, which thickened apace, till it completely swallowed up their distant shapes. They had disappeared while still following the same straight course away from the world of land-livers, as if they were intending to drop over the sea-edge into space, and never return to earth again.

' The two on the shore continued to sit on, punctually abiding by their agreement to remain on the same spot till the others returned. The Esplanade lamps were lit one by one, the bandsmen folded up their stands and departed, the yachts in the bay hung out their riding lights, and the little boats came back to shore one after another, their hirers walking on to the sands by the plank they had climbed to go afloat ; but among these Stephen and Olive did not appear.

'" What a time they are ! " said Emily. " I am getting
quite chilly. I did not expect to have to sit so long in the
evening air."

' Thereupon James Hardcome said that he did not
require his overcoat, and insisted on lending it to her.

' He wrapped it round Emily's shoulders.

'" Thank you, James," she said. " How cold Olive
must be in that thin jacket ! "

' He said he was thinking so, too. " Well, they are sure
to be quite close at hand by this time, though we can't see
'em. The boats are not all in yet. Some of the rowers
are fond of paddling along the shore to finish out their
hour of hiring."

'" Shall we walk by the edge of the water," said she,
" to see if we can discover them ? "

' He assented, reminding her that they must not lose
sight of the seat, lest the belated pair should return and
miss them, and be vexed that they had not kept the
appointment.

' They walked a sentry-beat up and down the sands
immediately opposite the seat ; and still the others did not
come. James Hardcome at last went to the boatman,
thinking that after all his wife and cousin might have come
in under shadow of the dusk without being perceived,
and might have forgotten the appointment at the bench.

'" All in ? " asked James.

'" All but one boat," said the lessor. " I can't think
where that couple is keeping to. They might run foul of
something or other in the dark."

' Again Stephen's wife and Olive's husband waited,
with more and more anxiety. But no little yellow boat
returned. Was it possible they could have landed further
down the Esplanade ?

'" It may have been done to escape paying," said the
boat-owner. " But they didn't look like people who would
do that."

' James Hardcome knew that he could found no hope
on such a reason as that. But now, remembering what
had been casually discussed between Steve and himself
about their wives from time to time, he admitted for the

first time the possibility that their old tenderness had been
revived by their face-to-face position more strongly than
either had anticipated at starting—the excursion having
been so obviously undertaken for the pleasure of the performance only—and that they had landed at some steps
he knew of further down towards the pier, to be longer alone
together.

' Still he disliked to harbour the thought, and would not
mention its existence to his companion. He merely said
to her, " Let us walk further on."

' They did so, and lingered between the boat-stage and
the pier till Stephen Hardcome's wife was uneasy, and was
obliged to accept James's offered arm. Thus the night
advanced. Emily was presently so worn out by fatigue
that James felt it necessary to conduct her home ; there
was, too, a remote chance that the truants had landed
in the harbour on the other side of the town, or elsewhere,
and hastened home in some unexpected way, in the belief
that their consorts would not have waited so long.

' However, he left a direction in the town that a look-out
should be kept, though this was arranged privately, the
bare possibility of an elopement being enough to make
him reticent ; and, full of misgivings, the two remaining
ones hastened to catch the last train out of Budmouth-
Regis ; and when they got to Casterbridge drove back to
Upper Longpuddle.'

' Along this very road as we do now,' remarked the parish
clerk.

' To be sure—along this very road,' said the curate.
' However, Stephen and Olive were not at their homes ;
neither had entered the village since leaving it in the
morning. Emily and James Hardcome went to their
respective dwellings to snatch a hasty night's rest, and at
daylight the next morning they drove again to Casterbridge and entered the Budmouth train, the line being just
opened.

' Nothing had been heard of the couple there during this
brief absence. In the course of a few hours some young
men testified to having seen such a man and woman rowing
in a frail hired craft, the head of the boat kept straight

to sea; they had sat looking in each other's faces as if
they were in a dream, with no consciousness of what they
were doing, or whither they were steering. It was not
till late that day that more tidings reached James's ears.
The boat had been found drifting bottom upward a long
way from land. In the evening the sea rose somewhat,
and a cry spread through the town that two bodies were
cast ashore in Lulwind Bay, several miles to the eastward.
They were brought to Budmouth, and inspection revealed
them to be the missing pair. It was said that they had
been found tightly locked in each other's arms, his lips
upon hers, their features still wrapt in the same calm
and dream-like repose which had been observed in their
demeanour as they had glided along.

'Neither James nor Emily questioned the original
motives of the unfortunate man and woman in putting
to sea. They were both above suspicion as to intention.
Whatever their mutual feelings might have led them on
to, underhand behaviour at starting was foreign to the
nature of either. Conjecture pictured that they might
have fallen into tender reverie while gazing each into a pair
of eyes that had formerly flashed for him and her alone,
and, unwilling to avow what their mutual sentiments
were, they had done no more than continue thus, oblivious
of time and space, till darkness suddenly overtook them
far from land. But nothing was truly known. It had
been their destiny to die thus. The two halves, intended
by Nature to make the perfect whole, had failed in that
result during their lives, though " in their death they were
not divided." Their bodies were brought home, and buried
on one day. I remember that, on looking round the
churchyard while reading the service, I observed nearly
all the parish at their funeral.'

'It was so, sir,' said the clerk.

'The remaining two,' continued the curate (whose voice
had grown husky while relating the lovers' sad fate),
'were a more thoughtful and far-seeing, though less
romantic, couple than the first. They were now mutually
bereft of a companion, and found themselves by this
accident in a position to fulfil their destiny according to

Nature's plan and their own original and calmly-formed intention. James Hardcome took Emily to wife in the course of a year and a half; and the marriage proved in every respect a happy one. I solemnized the service, Hardcome having told me, when he came to give notice of the proposed wedding, the story of his first wife's loss almost word for word as I have told it to you.'

'And are they living in Longpuddle still?' asked the new-comer.

'O no, sir,' interposed the clerk. 'James has been dead these dozen years, and his mis'ess about six or seven. They had no children. William Privett used to be their odd man till he died.'

'Ah—William Privett! He dead, too?—dear me!' said the other. 'All passed away!'

'Yes, sir. William was much older than I. He'd ha' been over eighty if he had lived till now.'

'There was something very strange about William's death—very strange indeed!' sighed a melancholy man in the back of the van. It was the seedsman's father, who had hitherto kept silence.

'And what might that have been?' asked Mr. Lackland.

THE SUPERSTITIOUS MAN'S STORY

'William, as you may know, was a curious, silent man; you could feel when he came near 'ee; and if he was in the house òr anywhere behind your back without your seeing him, there seemed to be something clammy in the air, as if a cellar door was opened close by your elbow. Well, one Sunday, at a time that William was in very good health to all appearance, the bell that was ringing for church went very heavy all of a sudden; the sexton, who told me o't, said he'd not known the bell go so heavy in his hand for years—and he feared it meant a death in the parish. That was on the Sunday, as I say. During the week after, it chanced that William's wife was staying up late one night to finish her ironing, she doing the washing for Mr. and Mrs. Hardcome. Her husband had finished his supper and gone to bed as usual some hour or two before. While she ironed she heard him coming downstairs ; he stopped to put on his boots at the stair-foot, where he always left them, and then came on into the living-room where she was ironing, passing through it towards the door, this being the only way from the staircase to the outside of the house. No word was said on either side, William not being a man given to much speaking, and his wife being occupied with her work. He went out and closed the door behind him. As her husband had now and then gone out in this way at night before when unwell, or unable to sleep for want of a pipe, she took no particular notice, and continued at her ironing. This she finished shortly after, and as he had not come in she waited a while for him, putting away the irons and things, and preparing the table for his breakfast in the morning. Still he did not return, and supposing him not far off, and wanting to get to bed herself, tired as she was, she left the door unbarred and went to the stairs, after writing on the back of the door with chalk : *Mind and do the door* (because he was a forgetful man).

' To her great surprise, and I might say alarm, on reaching the foot of the stairs his boots were standing there as they always stood when he had gone to rest ; going up to their chamber she found him in bed sleeping as sound as a rock. How he could have got back again without her seeing or hearing him was beyond her comprehension. It could only have been by passing behind her very quietly while she was bumping with the iron. But this notion did not satisfy her : it was surely impossible that she should not have seen him come in through a room so small. She could not unravel the mystery, and felt very queer and uncomfortable about it. However, she would not disturb him to question him then, and went to bed herself.

' He rose and left for his work very early the next morning, before she was awake, and she waited his return to breakfast with much anxiety for an explanation, for thinking over the matter by daylight made it seem only the more startling. When he came in to the meal he said, before she could put her question, " What's the meaning of them words chalked on the door ? "

' She told him, and asked him about his going out the

night before. William declared that he had never left the
bedroom after entering it, having in fact undressed, lain
down, and fallen asleep directly, never once waking till
the clock struck five, and he rose up to go to his labour.

' Betty Privett was as certain in her own mind that
he did go out as she was of her own existence, and was
little less certain that he did not return. She felt too
disturbed to argue with him, and let the subject drop as
though she must have been mistaken. When she was
walking down Longpuddle street later in the day she met
Jim Weedle's daughter Nancy, and said, " Well, Nancy,
you do look sleepy to-day ! "

' " Yes, Mrs. Privett," says Nancy. " Now don't tell
anybody, but I don't mind letting you know what the
reason o't is. Last night, being Old Midsummer Eve,
some of us went to church porch, and didn't get home till
near one."

' " Did ye ? " says Mrs. Privett. " Old Midsummer
yesterday, was it ? Faith I didn't think whe'r 'twas Midsummer or Michaelmas ; I'd too much work to do."

' " Yes. And we were frightened enough, I can tell 'ee,
by what we saw."

' " What did ye see ? "

' (You may not remember, sir, having gone off to foreign
parts so young, that on Midsummer Night it is believed
hereabout that the faint shapes of all the folk in the parish
who are going to be at death's door within the year can
be seen entering the church. Those who get over their
illness come out again after a while ; those that are doomed
to die do not return.)

' " What did you see ? " asked William's wife.

' " Well," says Nancy, backwardly—" we needn't tell
what we saw, or who we saw."

' " You saw my husband," says Betty Privett, in a quiet
way.

' " Well, since you put it so," says Nancy, hanging
fire, " we—thought we did see him ; but it was darkish,
and we was frightened, and of course it might not have been
he."

' " Nancy, you needn't mind letting it out, though 'tis

kept back in kindness. And he didn't come out of church again : I know it as well as you."

'Nancy did not answer yes or no to that, and no more was said. But three days after, William Privett was mowing with John Chiles in Mr. Hardcome's meadow, and in the heat of the day they sat down to eat their bit o' nunch under a tree, and empty their flagon. Afterwards both of 'em fell asleep as they sat. John Chiles was the first to wake, and as he looked towards his fellow-mower he saw one of those great white miller's-souls as we call 'em—that is to say, a miller-moth—come from William's open mouth while he slept, and fly straight away. John thought it odd enough, as William had worked in a mill for several years when he was a boy. He then looked at the sun, and found by the place o't that they had slept a long while, and as William did not wake, John called to him and said it was high time to begin work again. He took no notice, and then John went up and shook him, and found he was dead.

'Now on that very day old Philip Hookhorn was down at Longpuddle Spring dipping up a pitcher of water ; and as he turned away, who should he see coming down to the spring on the other side but William, looking very pale and odd. This surprised Philip Hookhorn very much, for years before that time William's little son—his only child —had been drowned in that spring while at play there, and this had so preyed upon William's mind that he'd never been seen near the spring afterwards, and had been known to go half a mile out of his way to avoid the place. On inquiry, it was found that William in body could not have stood by the spring, being in the mead two miles off ; and it also came out that the time at which he was seen at the spring was the very time when he died.'

'A rather melancholy story,' observed the emigrant, after a minute's silence.

'Yes, yes. Well, we must take ups and downs together,' said the seedsman's father.

'You don't know, Mr. Lackland, I suppose, what a rum start that was between Andrey Satchel and Jane

Vallens and the pa'son and clerk o' Scrimpton ? ' said
the master-thatcher, a man with a spark of subdued liveliness in his eye, who had hitherto kept his attention
mainly upon small objects a long way ahead, as he sat in
front of the van with his feet outside. ' Theirs was a
queerer experience of a pa'son and clerk than some folks
get, and may cheer 'ee up a little after this dampness that's
been flung over yer soul.'

The returned one replied that he knew nothing of the
history, and should be happy to hear it, quite recollecting
the personality of the man Satchel.

' Ah, no; this Andrey Satchel is the son of the Satchel
that you knew ; this one has not been married more than
two or three years, and 'twas at the time o' the wedding
that the accident happened that I could tell 'ee of, or
anybody else here, for that matter.'

' No, no ; you must tell it, neighbour, if anybody,' said
several ; a request in which Mr. Lackland joined, adding
that the Satchel family was one he had known well before
leaving home.

' I'll just mention, as you be a stranger,' whispered
the carrier to Lackland, ' that Christopher's stories will
bear pruning.'

The emigrant nodded.

' Well, I can soon tell it,' said the master-thatcher,
schooling himself to a tone of actuality. ' Though as it'
has more to do with the pa'son and clerk than with Andrey
himself, it ought to be told by a better churchman than I.

ANDREY SATCHEL AND THE PARSON AND CLERK

' It all arose, you must know, from Andrey being fond
of a drop of drink at that time—though he's a sober enough
man now by all account, so much the better for him.
Jane, his bride, you see, was somewhat older than Andrey ;
how much older I don't pretend to say ; she was not one
of our parish, and the register alone may be able to tell
that. But, at any rate, her being a little ahead of her
young man in mortal years, coupled with other bodily
circumstances owing to that young man——'

(' Ah, poor thing ! ' sighed the women.)

'—made her very anxious to get the thing done before he changed his mind; and 'twas with a joyful countenance (they say) that she, with Andrey and his brother and sister-in-law, marched off to church one November morning as soon as 'twas day a'most, to be made one with Andrey for the rest of her life. He had left our place long before it was light, and the folks that were up all waved their lanterns at him, and flung up their hats as he went.

'The church of her parish was a mile and more from where she lived, and, as it was a wonderful fine day for the time of year, the plan was that as soon as they were married they would make out a holiday by driving straight off to Port Bredy, to see the ships and the sea and the sojers, instead of coming back to a meal at the house of the distant relation she lived wi', and moping about there all the afternoon.

'Well, some folks noticed that Andrey walked with rather wambling steps to church that morning; the truth o't was that his nearest neighbour's child had been christened the day before, and Andrey, having stood godfather, had stayed all night keeping up the christening, for he had said to himself, " Not if I live to be a thousand shall I again be made a godfather one day, and a husband the next, and perhaps a father the next, and therefore I'll make the most of the blessing." So that when he started from home in the morning he had not been in bed at all. The result was, as I say, that when he and his bride-to-be walked up the church to get married, the pa'son (who was a very strict man inside the church, whatever he was outside) looked hard at Andrey, and said, very sharp:

'"How's this, my man? You are in liquor. And so early, too. I'm ashamed of you!"

'"Well, that's true, sir," says Andrey. "But I can walk straight enough for practical purposes. I can walk a chalk line," he says (meaning no offence), " as well as some other folk: and "— (getting hotter)—" I reckon that if you, Pa'son Billy Toogood, had kept up a christening all night so thoroughly as I have done, you wouldn't be able to stand at all; d—— me if you would!"

' This answer made Pa'son Billy—as they used to call
him—rather spitish, not to say hot, for he was a warm-
tempered man if provoked, and he said, very decidedly:
" Well, I cannot marry you in this state ; and I will not !
Go home and get sober ! " And he slapped the book
together like a rat-trap.

' Then the bride burst out crying as if her heart would
break, for very fear that she would lose Andrey after all
her hard work to get him, and begged and implored the
pa'son to go on with the ceremony. But no.

' " I won't be a party to your solemnizing matrimony
with a tipsy man," says Mr. Toogood. " It is not right
and decent. I am sorry for you, my young woman, seeing
the condition you are in, but you'd better go home again.
I wonder how you could think of bringing him here drunk
like this ! "

' " But if—if he don't come drunk he won't come at all,
sir ! " she says, through her sobs.

' " I can't help that," says the pa'son ; and plead as she
might, it did not move him. Then she tried him another
way.

' " Well, then, if you'll go home, sir, and leave us here,
and come back to the church in an hour or two, I'll undertake to say that he shall be as sober as a judge," she cries.
" We'll bide here, with your permission ; for if he once
goes out of this here church unmarried, all Van Amburgh's
horses won't drag him back again ! "

' " Very well," says the parson. " I'll give you two
hours, and then I'll return."

' " And please, sir, lock the door, so that we can't escape ! "
says she.

' " Yes," says the parson.

' " And let nobody know that we are here."

' The pa'son then took off his clane white surplice,
and went away ; and the others consulted upon the best
means for keeping the matter a secret, which it was not
a very hard thing to do, the place being so lonely, and the
hour so early. The witnesses, Andrey's brother and
brother's wife, neither one o' which cared about Andrey's
marrying Jane, and had come rather against their will,

said they couldn't wait two hours in that hole of a place, wishing to get home to Longpuddle before dinner-time. They were altogether so crusty that the clerk said there was no difficulty in their doing as they wished. They could go home as if their brother's wedding had actually taken place and the married couple had gone onward for their day's pleasure jaunt to Port Bredy as intended. He, the clerk, and any casual passer-by would act as witnesses when the pa'son came back.

'This was agreed to, and away Andrey's relations went, nothing loath, and the clerk shut the church door and prepared to lock in the couple. The bride went up and whispered to him, with her eyes a-streaming still.

'"My dear good clerk," she says, "if we bide here in the church, folk may see us through the windows, and find out what has happened; and 'twould cause such a talk and scandal that I never should get over it: and perhaps, too, dear Andrey might try to get out and leave me! Will ye lock us up in the tower, my dear good clerk?" she says. "I'll tole him in there if you will."

'The clerk had no objection to do this to oblige the poor young woman, and they toled Andrey into the tower, and the clerk locked 'em both up straightway, and then went home, to return at the end of the two hours.

'Pa'son Toogood had not been long in his house after leaving the church when he saw a gentleman in pink and top-boots ride past his windows, and with a sudden flash of heat he called to mind that the hounds met that day just on the edge of his parish. The pa'son was one who dearly loved sport, and much he longed to be there.

'In short, except o' Sundays and at tide-times in the week, Pa'son Billy was the life o' the hunt. 'Tis true that he was poor, and that he rode all of a heap, and that his black mare was rat-tailed and old, and his tops older, and all over of one colour, whitey-brown, and full o' cracks. But he'd been in at the death of three thousand foxes. And—being a bachelor man—every time he went to bed in summer he used to open the bed at bottom and crawl up head foremost, to mind en of the coming winter and the good sport he'd have, and the foxes going to earth.

And whenever there was a christening at the Squire's, and he had dinner there afterwards, as he always did, he never failed to christen the chiel over again in a bottle of port wine.

'Now the clerk was the pa'son's groom and gardener and general manager, and had just got back to his work in the garden when he, too, saw the hunting man pass, and presently saw lots more of 'em, noblemen and gentry, and then he saw the hounds, the huntsman, Jim Treadhedge, the whipper-in, and I don't know who besides. The clerk loved going to cover as frantical as the pa'son, so much so that whenever he saw or heard the pack he could no more rule his feelings than if they were the winds of heaven. He might be bedding, or he might be sowing— all was forgot. So he throws down his spade and rushes in to the pa'son, who was by this time as frantical to go as he.

' " That there mare of yours, sir, do want exercise bad, very bad, this morning ! " the clerk says, all of a tremble. " Don't ye think I'd better trot her round the downs for an hour, sir ? "

' " To be sure, she does want exercise badly. I'll trot her round myself," says the pa'son.

' " Oh—you'll trot her yerself ? Well, there's the cob, sir. Really that cob is getting oncontrollable through biding in a stable so long ! If you wouldn't mind my putting on the saddle——"

' " Very well. Take him out, certainly," says the pa'son, never caring what the clerk did so long as he himself could get off immediately. So, scrambling into his riding-boots and breeches as quick as he could, he rode off towards the meet, intending to be back in an hour. No sooner was he gone than the clerk mounted the cob, and was off after him. When the pa'son got to the meet he found a lot of friends, and was as jolly as he could be : the hounds found a'most as soon as they threw off, and there was great excitement. So, forgetting that he had meant to go back at once, away rides the pa'son with the rest o' the hunt, all across the fallow ground that lies between Lippet Wood and Green's Copse ; and as he galloped he looked behind for a moment, and there was the clerk close to his heels.

' " Ha, ha, clerk—you here ? " he says.

' " Yes, sir, here be I," says t'other.

' " Fine exercise for the horses ! "

' " Ay, sir—hee, hee ! " says the clerk.

' So they went on and on, into Green's Copse, then across to Higher Jirton ; then on across this very turnpike-road to Waterston Ridge, then away towards Yalbury Wood : up hill and down dale, like the very wind, the clerk close to the pa'son, and the pa'son not far from the hounds. Never was there a finer run knowed with that pack than they had that day ; and neither pa'son nor clerk thought one word about the unmarried couple locked up in the church tower waiting to get j'ined.

' " These hosses of yours, sir, will be much improved by this ! " says the clerk as he rode along, just a neck behind the pa'son. " 'Twas a happy thought of your reverent mind to bring 'em out to-day. Why, it may be frosty and slippery in a day or two, and then the poor things mid not be able to leave the stable for weeks."

' " They may not, they may not, it is true. A merciful man is merciful to his beast," says the pa'son.

' " Hee, hee ! " says the clerk, glancing sly into the pa'son's eye.

' " Ha, ha ! " says the pa'son, a-glancing back into the clerk's. " Halloo ! " he shouts, as he sees the fox break cover at that moment.

' " Halloo ! " cries the clerk. " There he goes ! Why, dammy, there's two foxes——"

' " Hush, clerk, hush ! Don't let me hear that word again ! Remember our calling."

' " True, sir, true. But really, good sport do carry away a man so, that he's apt to forget his high persuasion ! " And the next minute the corner of the clerk's eye shot again into the corner of the pa'son's, and the pa'son's back again to the clerk's. " Hee, hee ! " said the clerk.

' " Ha, ha ! " said Pa'son Toogood.

' " Ah, sir," says the clerk again, " this is better than crying Amen to your Ever-and-ever on a winter's morning ! "

' " Yes, indeed, clerk ! To everything there's a season,"

says Pa'son Toogood, quite pat, for he was a learned Christian man when he liked, and had chapter and ve'se at his tongue's end, as a pa'son should.

' At last, late in the day, the hunting came to an end by the fox running into a' old woman's cottage, under her table, and up the clock-case. The pa'son and clerk were among the first in at the death, their faces a-staring in at the old woman's winder, and the clock striking as he'd never been heard to strik' before. Then came the question of finding their way home.

' Neither the pa'son nor the clerk knowed how they were going to do this, for their beasts were wellnigh tired down to the ground. But they started back-along as well as they could, though they were so done up that they could only drag along at a' amble, and not much of that at a time.

' " We shall never, never get there ! " groaned Mr. Toogood, quite bowed down.

' " Never ! " groans the clerk. " 'Tis a judgment upon us for our iniquities ! "

' " I fear it is," murmurs the pa'son.

' Well, 'twas quite dark afore they entered the pa'sonage gate, having crept into the parish as quiet as if they'd stole a hammer, little wishing their congregation to know what they'd been up to all day long. And as they were so dog-tired, and so anxious about the horses, never once did they think of the unmarried couple. As soon as ever the horses had been stabled and fed, and the pa'son and clerk had had a bit and a sup theirselves, they went to bed.

' Next morning when Pa'son Toogood was at breakfast, thinking of the glorious sport he'd had the day before, the clerk came in a hurry to the door and asked to see him.

' " It has just come into my mind, sir, that we've forgot all about the couple that we was to have married yesterday ! "

' The half-chawed victuals dropped from the pa'son's mouth as if he'd been shot. " Bless my soul," says he, " so we have ! How very awkward ! "

' " It is, sir ; very. Perhaps we've ruined the 'ooman ! "

' " Ah—to be sure—I remember ! She ought to have
been married before."

' " If anything has happened to her up in that there
tower, and no doctor or nuss——" '

(' Ah—poor thing ! ' sighed the women.)

' "—'twill be a quarter-sessions matter for us, not to
speak of the disgrace to the Church ! "

' " Good God, clerk, don't drive me wild ! " says the
pa'son. " Why the hell didn't I marry 'em, drunk or
sober ! " (Pa'sons used to cuss in them days like plain
honest men.) " Have you been to the church to see
what happened to them, or inquired in the village ? "

' " Not I, sir ! It only came into my head a moment
ago, and I always like to be second to you in church matters. You could have knocked me down with a sparrow's
feather when I thought o't, sir ; I assure 'ee you could ! "

' Well, the pa'son jumped up from his breakfast, and
together they went off to the church.

' " It is not at all likely that they are there now," says
Mr. Toogood, as they went ; " and indeed I hope they
are not. They be pretty sure to have escaped and gone
home."

' However, they opened the church-hatch, entered the
churchyard, and looking up at the tower there they seed
a little small white face at the belfry-winder, and a little
small hand waving. 'Twas the bride.

' " God my life, clerk," says Mr. Toogood. " I don't
know how to face 'em ! " And he sank down upon a
tombstone. " How I wish I hadn't been so cussed particular ! "

' " Yes—'twas a pity we didn't finish it when we'd begun," the clerk said. " Still, since the feelings of your
holy priestcraft wouldn't let ye, the couple must put up
with it."

' " True, clerk, true ! Does she look as if anything
premature had took place ? "

' " I can't see her no lower down than her arm-pits,
sir."

' " Well—how do her face look ? "

' " It do look mighty white ! "

' " Well, we must know the worst ! Dear me, how the small of my back do ache from that ride yesterday ! . . . But to more godly business ! "

' They went on into the church, and unlocked the tower stairs, and immediately poor Jane and Andrey busted out like starved mice from a cupboard, Andrey limp and sober enough now, and his bride pale and cold, but otherwise as usual.

' " What," says the pa'son with a great breath of relief, " you haven't been here ever since ? "

' " Yes, we have, sir ! " says the bride, sinking down upon a seat in her weakness. " Not a morsel, wet or dry, have we had since ! It was impossible to get out without help, and here we've stayed ! "

' " But why didn't you shout, good souls ? " said the pa'son.

' " She wouldn't let me," says Andrey.

' " Because we were so ashamed at what had led to it," sobs Jane. " We felt that if it were noised abroad it would cling to us all our lives ! Once or twice Andrey had a good mind to toll the bell, but then he said : ' No ; I'll starve first. I won't bring disgrace on my name and yours, my dear.' And so we waited and waited, and walked round and round ; but never did you come till now ! "

' " To my regret ! " says the pa'son. " Now, then, we will soon get it over."

' " I—I should like some victuals," said Andrey ; " 'twould gie me courage to do it, if it is only a crust o' bread and a' onion ; for I am that leery that I can feel my stomach rubbing against my backbone."

' " I think we had better get it done," said the bride, a bit anxious in manner ; " since we are all here convenient, too ! "

' Andrey gave way about the victuals, and the clerk called in a second witness who wouldn't be likely to gossip about it, and soon the knot was tied, and the bride looked smiling and calm forthwith, and Andrey limper than ever.

' " Now," said Pa'son Toogood, " you two must come

to my house, and have a good lining put to your insides
before you go a step further."

'They were very glad of the offer, and went out of the
churchyard by one path while the pa'son and clerk went
out by the other, and so did not attract notice, it being
still early. They entered the rectory as if they'd just
come back from their trip to Port Bredy; and then they
knocked in the victuals and drink till they could hold no
more.

'It was a long while before the story of what they had
gone through was known, but it was talked of in time, and
they themselves laugh over it now; though what Jane
got for her pains was no great bargain after all. 'Tis true
she saved her name.'

'Was that the same Andrey who went to the squire's
house as one of the Christmas fiddlers?' asked the seedsman.

'No, no,' replied Mr. Profitt, the schoolmaster. 'It
was his father did that. Ay, it was all owing to his being
such a man for eating and drinking.' Finding that he
had the ear of the audience, the schoolmaster continued
without delay:—

OLD ANDREY'S EXPERIENCE AS A MUSICIAN

'I was one of the quire-boys at that time, and we and the
players were to appear at the manor-house as usual that
Christmas week, to play and sing in the hall to the Squire's
people and visitors (among 'em being the archdeacon, Lord
and Lady Baxby, and I don't know who); afterwards going, as we always did, to have a good supper in the servants'
hall. Andrew knew this was the custom, and meeting
us when we were starting to go, he said to us: "Lord, how I
should like to join in that meal of beef, and turkey, and
plum-pudding, and ale, that you happy ones be going to
just now! One more or less will make no difference to the
Squire. I am too old to pass as a singing boy, and too
bearded to pass as a singing girl; can ye lend me a fiddle,
neighbours, that I may come with ye as a bandsman?"

'Well, we didn't like to be hard upon him, and lent

him an old one, though Andrew knew no more of music than the Giant o' Cernel; and armed with the instrument he walked up to the Squire's house with the others of us at the time appointed, and went in boldly, his fiddle under his arm. He made himself as natural as he could in opening the music-books and moving the candles to the best points for throwing light upon the notes; and all went well till we had played and sung " While shepherds watch," and " Star, arise," and " Hark the glad sound." Then the Squire's mother, a tall gruff old lady, who was much interested in church-music, said quite unexpectedly to Andrew : " My man, I see you don't play your instrument with the rest. How is that ? "

' Every one of the quire was ready to sink into the earth with concern at the fix Andrew was in. We could see that he had fallen into a cold sweat, and how he would get out of it we did not know.

' " I've had a misfortune, mem," he says, bowing as meek as a child. " Coming along the road I fell down and broke my bow."

' " O, I am sorry to hear that," says she. " Can't it be mended ? "

' " O no, mem," says Andrew. " 'Twas broke all to splinters."

' " I'll see what I can do for you," says she.

' And then it seemed all over, and we played " Rejoice, ye drowsy mortals all," in D and two sharps. But no sooner had we got through it than she says to Andrew :

' " I've sent up into the attic, where we have some old musical instruments, and found a bow for you." And she hands the bow to poor wretched Andrew, who didn't even know which end to take hold of. " Now we shall have the full accompaniment," says she.

' Andrew's face looked as if it were made of rotten apple as he stood in the circle of players in front of his book ; for if there was one person in the parish that everybody was afraid of, 'twas this hook-nosed old lady. However, by keeping a little behind the next man he managed to make pretence of beginning, sawing away with his bow without ·letting it touch the strings, so that it looked as if he were driving into the tune with heart and soul. 'Tis a question if he wouldn't have got through all right if one of the Squire's visitors (no other than the archdeacon) hadn't noticed that he held the fiddle upside down, the nut under his chin, and the tail-piece in his hand; and they began to crowd round him, thinking 'twas some new way of performing.

'This revealed everything; the Squire's mother had Andrew turned out of the house as a vile impostor, and there was great interruption to the harmony of the proceedings, the Squire declaring he should have notice to leave his cottage that day fortnight. However, when we got to the servants' hall there sat Andrew, who had been let in at the back door by the orders of the Squire's wife, after being turned out at the front by the orders of the Squire, and nothing more was heard about his leaving his cottage. But Andrew never performed in public as a musician after that night; and now he's dead and gone, poor man, as we all shall be!'

'I had quite forgotten the old choir, with their fiddles and bass-viols,' said the home-comer, musingly. 'Are they still going on the same as of old?'

'Bless the man!' said Christopher Twink, the master-thatcher; 'why, they've been done away with these twenty year. A young teetotaller plays the organ in church now, and plays it very well; though 'tis not quite such good music as in old times, because the organ is one of them that go with a winch, and the young teetotaller says he can't always throw the proper feeling into the tune without wellnigh working his arms off.'

'Why did they make the change, then?'

'Well, partly because of fashion, partly because the old musicians got into a sort of scrape. A terrible scrape 'twas, too—wasn't it, John? I shall never forget it—never! They lost their character as officers of the church as complete as if they'd never had any character at all.'

'That was very bad for them.'

'Yes.' The master-thatcher attentively regarded past times as if they lay about a mile off, and went on:—

ABSENT-MINDEDNESS IN A PARISH CHOIR

' It happened on Sunday after Christmas—the last Sunday ever they played in Longpuddle church gallery, as it turned out, though they didn't know it then. As you may know, sir, the players formed a very good band— almost as good as the Mellstock parish players that were led by the Dewys ; and that's saying a great deal. There was Nicholas Puddingcome, the leader, with the first fiddle ; there was Timothy Thomas, the bass-viol man ; John Biles, the tenor fiddler ; Dan'l Hornhead, with the serpent ; Robert Dowdle, with the clarionet ; and Mr. Nicks, with the oboe—all sound and powerful musicians, and strong-winded men—they that blowed. For that reason they were very much in demand Christmas week for little reels and dancing parties : for they could turn a jig or a horn-pipe out of hand as well as ever they could turn out a psalm, and perhaps better, not to speak irreverent. In short, one half-hour they could be playing a Christmas carol in the Squire's hall to the ladies and gentlemen, and drinking tay and coffee with 'em as modest as saints ; and the next, at The Tinker's Arms, blazing away like wild horses with the " Dashing White Sergeant " to nine couple of dancers and more, and swallowing rum-and-cider hot as flame.

' Well, this Christmas they'd been out to one rattling randy after another every night, and had got next to no sleep at all. Then came the Sunday after Christmas, their fatal day. 'Twas so mortal cold that year that they could hardly sit in the gallery ; for though the congregation down in the body of the church had a stove to keep off the frost, the players in the gallery had nothing at all. So Nicholas said at morning service, when 'twas freezing an inch an hour, " Please the Lord I won't stand this numbing weather no longer : this afternoon we'll have something in our insides to make us warm, if it cost a king's ransom.''

' So he brought a gallon of hot brandy and beer, ready mixed, to church with him in the afternoon, and by keeping the jar well wrapped up in Timothy Thomas's bass-viol bag it kept drinkably warm till they wanted it, which was just a thimbleful in the Absolution, and another after the Creed, and the remainder at the beginning o' the sermon. When they'd had the last pull they felt quite comfortable and warm, and as the sermon went on—most unfortunately for 'em it was a long one that afternoon—they fell asleep, every man jack of 'em ; and there they slept on as sound as rocks.

' 'Twas a very dark afternoon, and by the end of the sermon all you could see of the inside of the church were the pa'son's two candles alongside of him in the pulpit, and his spaking face behind 'em. The sermon being ended at last, the pa'son gie'd out the Evening Hymn. But no quire set about sounding up the tune, and the people began to turn their heads to learn the reason why, and then Levi Limpet, a boy who sat in the gallery, nudged Timothy and Nicholas, and said, " Begin ! begin ! "

' " Hey ? what ? " says Nicholas, starting up ; and the church being so dark and his head so muddled he thought he was at the party they had played at all the night before, and away he went, bow and fiddle, at " The Devil among the Tailors," the favourite jig of our neighbourhood at that time. The rest of the band, being in the same state of mind and nothing doubting, followed their leader with all their strength, according to custom. They poured out that there tune till the lower bass notes of " The Devil among the Tailors " made the cobwebs in the roof shiver like ghosts ; then Nicholas, seeing nobody moved, shouted out as he scraped (in his usual commanding way at dances when the folk didn't know the figures), " Top couples cross hands ! And when I make the fiddle squeak at the end, every man kiss his pardner under the mistletoe ! "

' The boy Levi was so frightened that he bolted down the gallery stairs and out homeward like lightning. The pa'son's hair fairly stood on end when he heard the evil tune raging through the church, and thinking the quire had gone crazy he held up his hand and said : " Stop, stop, stop ! Stop, stop ! What's this ? " But they didn't hear'n for the noise of their own playing, and the more he called the louder they played.

'Then the folks came out of their pews, wondering down to the ground, and saying: "What do they mean by such wickedness! We shall be consumed like Sodom and Gomorrah!"

'And the Squire, too, came out of his pew lined wi' green baize, where lots of lords and ladies visiting at the house were worshipping along with him, and went and stood in front of the gallery, and shook his fist in the musicians' faces, saying, "What! In this reverent edifice! What!"

'And at last they heard'n through their playing, and stopped.

' "Never such an insulting, disgraceful thing—never!" says the Squire, who couldn't rule his passion.

' "Never!" says the pa'son, who had come down and stood beside him.

' "Not if the Angels of Heaven," says the Squire (he was a wickedish man, the Squire was, though now for once he happened to be on the Lord's side)—"not if the Angels of Heaven come down," he says, "shall one of you villainous players ever sound a note in this church again; for the insult to me, and my family, and my visitors, and the pa'son, and God Almighty, that you've a-perpetrated this afternoon!"

'Then the unfortunate church band came to their senses, and remembered where they were; and 'twas a sight to see Nicholas Puddingcome and Timothy Thomas and John Biles creep down the gallery stairs with their fiddles under their arms, and poor Dan'l Hornhead with his serpent, and Robert Dowdle with his clarionet, all looking as little as ninepins; and out they went. The pa'son might have forgi'ed 'em when he learned the truth o't, but the Squire would not. That very week he sent for a barrel-organ that would play two-and-twenty new psalm-tunes, so exact and particular that, however sinful inclined you was, you could play nothing but psalm-tunes whatsomever. He had a really respectable man to turn the winch, as I said, and the old players played no more.'

'And, of course, my old acquaintance, the annuitant, Mrs. Winter, who always seemed to have something on

her mind, is dead and gone ? ' said the home-comer, after a
lóng silence.

Nobody in the van seemed to recollect the name.

' O yes, she must be dead long since : she was seventy
when I as a child knew her,' he added.

' I can recollect Mrs. Winter very well, if nobody else
can,' said the aged groceress.   ' Yes, she's been dead these
five-and-twenty year at least.   You knew what it was upon
her mind, sir, that gave her that hollow-eyed look, I
suppose ? '

' It had something to do with a son of hers, I think
I once was told.   But I was too young to know particulars.'

The groceress sighed as she conjured up a vision of days
long past.   ' Yes,' she murmured, ' it had all to do with a
son.'   Finding that the van was still in a listening mood,
she spoke on :—

THE WINTERS AND THE PALMLEYS

' To go back to the beginning—if one must—there were
two women in the parish when I was a child, who were
to a certain extent rivals in good looks.   Never mind
particulars, but in consequence of this they were at daggers-
drawn, and they did not love each other any better when
one of them tempted the other's lover away from her
and married him.   He was a young man of the name of
Winter, and in due time they had a son.

' The other woman did not marry for many years :
but when she was about thirty a quiet man named Palmley
asked her to be his wife, and she‚ accepted him.   You
don't mind when the Palmleys were Longpuddle folk, but
I do well.   She had a son also, who was, of course, nine
or ten years younger than the son of the first.   The child
proved to be of rather weak intellect, though his mother
loved him as the apple of her eye.

' This woman's husband died when the child was eight
years old, and left his widow and boy in poverty.   Her
former rival, also a widow now, but fairly well provided
for, offered for pity's sake to take the child as errand-
boy, small as he was, her own son, Jack, being hard upon
seventeen.   Her poor neighbour could do no better than

let the child go there.   And to the richer woman's house little Palmley straightway went.

'Well, in some way or other—how, it was never exactly known—the thriving woman, Mrs. Winter, sent the little boy with a message to the next village one December day, much against his will.   It was getting dark, and the child prayed to be allowed not to go, because he would be afraid coming home.   But the mistress insisted, more out of thoughtlessness than cruelty, and the child went.   On his way back he had to pass through Yalbury Wood, and something came out from behind a tree and frightened him into fits.   The child was quite ruined by it ; he became quite a drivelling idiot, and soon afterward died.

'Then the other woman had nothing left to live for, and vowed vengeance against that rival who had first won away her lover, and now had been the cause of her bereavement. This last affliction was certainly not intended by her thriving acquaintance, though it must be owned that when it was done she seemed but little concerned.   Whatever vengeance poor Mrs. Palmley felt, she had no opportunity of carrying it out, and time might have softened her feelings into forgetfulness of her supposed wrongs as she dragged on her lonely life.   So matters stood when, a year after the death of the child, Mrs. Palmley's niece, who had been born and bred in the city of Exonbury, came to live with her.

'This young woman—Miss Harriet Palmley—was a proud and handsome girl, very well brought up, and more stylish and genteel than the people of our village, as was natural, considering where she came from.   She regarded herself as much above Mrs. Winter and her son in position as Mrs. Winter and her son considered themselves above poor Mrs. Palmley.   But love is an unceremonious thing, and what in the world should happen but that young Jack Winter must fall woefully and wildly in love with Harriet Palmley almost as soon as he saw her.

'She, being better educated than he, and caring nothing for the village notion of his mother's superiority to her aunt, did not give him much encouragement.   But Long-puddle being no very large world, the two could not help seeing a good deal of each other while she was staying there, and, disdainful young woman as she was, she did seem to take a little pleasure in his attentions and advances.

'One day when they were picking apples together, he asked her to marry him. She had not expected anything so practical as that at so early a time, and was led by her surprise into a half-promise ; at any rate, she did not absolutely refuse him, and accepted some little presents that he made her.

'But he saw that her view of him was rather as a simple village lad than as a young man to look up to, and he felt that he must do something bold to secure her. So he said one day, "I am going away, to try to get into a better position than I can get here." In two or three weeks he wished her good-bye, and went away to Monksbury, to superintend a farm, with a view to start as a farmer himself ; and from there he wrote regularly to her, as if their marriage were an understood thing.

'Now Harriet liked the young man's presents and the admiration of his eyes ; but on paper he was less attractive to her. Her mother had been a schoolmistress, and Harriet had besides a natural aptitude for pen-and-ink work, in days when to be a ready writer was not such a common thing as it is now, and when actual handwriting was valued as an accomplishment in itself. Jack Winter's performances in the shape of love-letters quite jarred her city nerves and her finer taste, and when she answered one of them, in the lovely running hand that she took such pride in, she very strictly and loftily bade him to practise with a pen and spelling-book if he wished to please her. Whether he listened to her request or not nobody knows, but his letters did not improve. He ventured to tell her in his clumsy way that if her heart were more warm towards him she would not be so nice about his handwriting and spelling ; which indeed was true enough.

'Well, in Jack's absence the weak flame that had been set alight in Harriet's heart soon sank low, and at last went out altogether. He wrote and wrote, and begged and prayed her to give a reason for her coldness ; and then she told him plainly that she was town born, and he was not sufficiently well educated to please her.

' Jack Winter's want of pen-and-ink training did not make him less thin-skinned than others ; in fact, he was terribly tender and touchy about anything. This reason that she gave for finally throwing him over grieved him, shamed him, and mortified him more than can be told in these times, the pride of that day in being able to write with beautiful flourishes, and the sorrow at not being able to do so, raging so high.   Jack replied to her with an angry note, and then she hit back with smart little stings, telling him how many words he had misspelt in his last letter, and declaring again that this alone was sufficient justification for any woman to put an end to an understanding with him. Her husband must be a better scholar.

' He bore her rejection of him in silence, but his suffering was sharp—all the sharper in being untold. She communicated with Jack no more ; and as his reason for going out into the world had been only to provide a home worthy of her, he had no further object in planning such a home now that she was lost to him. He therefore gave up the farming occupation by which he had hoped to make himself a master-farmer, and left the spot to return to his mother.

' As soon as he got back to Longpuddle he found that Harriet had already looked wi' favour upon another lover. He was a young road-contractor, and Jack could not but admit that his rival was both in manners and scholarship much ahead of him. Indeed, a more sensible match for the beauty who had been dropped into the village by fate could hardly have been found than this man, who could offer her so much better a chance than Jack could have done, with his uncertain future and narrow abilities for grappling with the world. The fact was so clear to him that he could hardly blame her.

' One day by accident Jack saw on a scrap of paper the handwriting of Harriet's new beloved. It was flowing like a stream, well spelt, the work of a man accustomed to the ink-bottle and the dictionary, of a man already called in the parish a good scholar. And then it struck all of a sudden into Jack's mind what a contrast the letters of this young man must make to his own miserable old letters,

and how ridiculous they must make his lines appear. He
groaned and wished he had never written to her, and
wondered if she had ever kept his poor performances.
Possibly she had kept them, for women are in the habit
of doing that, he thought, and whilst they were in her
hands there was always a chance of his honest, stupid love-
assurances to her being joked over by Harriet with her
present lover, or by anybody who should accidentally
uncover them.

' The nervous, moody young man could not bear the
thought of it, and at length decided to ask her to return
them, as was proper when engagements were broken off.
He was some hours in framing, copying, and recopying
the short note in which he made his request, and having
finished it he sent it to her house. His messenger came
back with the answer, by word of mouth, that Miss Palmley
bade him say she should not part with what was hers,
and wondered at his boldness in troubling her.

' Jack was much affronted at this, and determined to go
for his letters himself. He chose a time when he knew she
was at home, and knocked and went in without much
ceremony ; for though Harriet was so high and mighty,
Jack had small respect for her aunt, Mrs. Palmley, whose
little child had been his boot-cleaner in earlier days. Harriet was in the room, this being the first time they had met
since she had jilted him. He asked for his letters with a
stern and bitter look at her.

' At first she said he might have them for all that she
cared, and took them out of the bureau where she kept
them. Then she glanced over the outside one of the
packet, and suddenly altering her mind, she told him
shortly that his request was a silly one, and slipped the
letters into her aunt's work-box, which stood open on the
table, locking it and saying with a bantering laugh that
of course she thought it best to keep 'em, since they might
be useful to produce as evidence that she had good cause
for declining to marry him.

' He blazed up hot. " Give me those letters ! " he said.
" They are mine ! "

' " No, they are not," she replied ; " they are mine."

' " Whos'ever they are I want them back," says he.
" I don't want to be made sport of for my penmanship :
you've another young man now ! He has your confidence,
and you pour all your tales into his ear. You'll be showing
them to him ! "

' " Perhaps," said my lady Harriet, with calm coolness,
like the heartless woman that she was.

' Her manner so maddened him that he made a step
towards the work-box, but she snatched it up, locked it
in the bureau, and turned upon him triumphant. For a
moment he seemed to be going to wrench the key of the
bureau out of her hand ; but he stopped himself, and
swung round upon his heel and went away.

' When he was out-of-doors alone, and it got night,
he walked about restless, and stinging with the sense of
being beaten at all points by her. He could not help
fancying her telling her new lover or her acquaintances
of this scene with himself, and laughing with them over
those poor blotted, crooked lines of his that he had been
so anxious to obtain. As the evening passed on he worked
himself into a dogged resolution to have them back at any
price, come what might.

' At the dead of night he came out of his mother's house
by the back door, and creeping through the garden hedge
went along the field adjoining till he reached the back of
her aunt's dwelling. The moon struck bright and flat
upon the walls, 'twas said, and every shiny leaf of the creepers
was like a little looking-glass in the rays. From long
acquaintance Jack knew the arrangement and position of
everything in Mrs. Palmley's house as well as in his own
mother's. The back window close to him was a casement with little leaded squares, as it is to this day, and
was, as now, one of two lighting the sitting-room. The
other, being in front, was closed up with shutters, but
this back one had not even a blind, and the moonlight
as it streamed in showed every article of the furniture to
him outside. To the right of the room is the fireplace,
as you may remember ; to the left was the bureau at that
time ; inside the bureau was Harriet's work-box, as he
supposed (though it was really her aunt's), and inside the

work-box were his letters. Well, he took out his pocket-knife, and without noise lifted the leading of one of the panes, so that he could take out the glass, and putting his hand through the hole he unfastened the casement, and climbed in through the opening. All the household— that is to say, Mrs. Palmley, Harriet, and the little maid-servant—were asleep. Jack went straight to the bureau, so he said, hoping it might have been unfastened again —it not being kept locked in ordinary—but Harriet had never unfastened it since she secured her letters there the day before. Jack told afterward how he thought of her asleep upstairs, caring nothing for him, and of the way she had made sport of him and of his letters ; and having advanced so far, he was not to be hindered now. By forcing the large blade of his knife under the flap of the bureau, he burst the weak lock ; within was the rosewood work-box just as she had placed it in her hurry to keep it from him. There being no time to spare for getting the letters out of it then, he took it under his arm, shut the bureau, and made the best of his way out of the house, latching the casement behind him, and refixing the pane of glass in its place.

' Winter found his way back to his mother's as he had come, and being dog-tired, crept upstairs to bed, hiding the box till he could destroy its contents. The next morning early he set about doing this, and carried it to the linhay at the back of his mother's dwelling. Here by the hearth he opened the box, and began burning one by one the letters that had cost him so much labour to write and shame to think of, meaning to return the box to Harriet, after repairing the slight damage he had caused it by opening it without a key, with a note—the last she would ever receive from him—telling her triumphantly that in refusing to return what he had asked for she had calculated too surely upon his submission to her whims.

' But on removing the last letter from the box he received a shock ; for underneath it, at the very bottom, lay money—several golden guineas—" Doubtless Harriet's pocket-money," he said to himself ; though it was not, but Mrs. Palmley's. Before he had got over his qualms at this discovery he heard footsteps coming through the house-passage to where he was. In haste he pushed the box and what was in it under some brushwood which lay in the linhay; but Jack had been already seen. Two constables entered the out-house, and seized him as he knelt before the fireplace, securing the work-box and all it contained at the same moment. They had come to apprehend him on a charge of breaking into the dwelling-house of Mrs. Palmley on the night preceding : and almost before the lad knew what had happened to him they were leading him along the lane that connects that end of the village with this turn-pike-road, and along they marched him between 'em all the way to Casterbridge jail.

'Jack's act amounted to night burglary—though he had never thought of it—and burglary was felony, and a capital offence in those days. His figure had been seen by some one against the bright wall as he came away from Mrs. Palmley's back window, and the box and money were found in his possession, while the evidence of the broken bureau-lock and tinkered window-pane was more than enough for circumstantial detail. Whether his protestation that he went only for his letters, which he believed to be wrongfully kept from him, would have availed him anything if supported by other evidence I do not know ; but the one person who could have borne it out was Harriet, and she acted entirely under the sway of her aunt. That aunt was deadly towards Jack Winter. Mrs. Palmley's time had come. Here was her revenge upon the woman who had first won away her lover, and next ruined and deprived her of her heart's treasure—her little son. When the assize week drew on, and Jack had to stand his trial, Harriet did not appear in the case at all, which was allowed to take its course, Mrs. Palmley testifying to the general facts of the burglary. Whether Harriet would have come forward if Jack had appealed to her is not known ; possibly she would have done it for pity's sake ; but Jack was too proud to ask a single favour of a girl who had jilted him ; and he let her alone. The trial was a short one, and the death sentence was passed.

'The day o' young Jack's execution was a cold dusty

Saturday in March. He was so boyish and slim that they were obliged in mercy to hang him in the heaviest fetters kept in the jail, lest his heft should not break his neck, and they weighed so upon him that he could hardly drag himself up to the drop. At that time the gover'ment was not strict about burying the body of an executed person within the precincts of the prison, and at the earnest prayer of his poor mother his body was allowed to be brought home. All the parish waited at their cottage doors in the evening for its arrival : I remember how, as a very little girl, I stood by my mother's side. About eight o'clock, as we hearkened on our door-stones in the cold bright starlight, we could hear the faint crackle of a waggon from the direction of the turnpike-road. The noise was lost as the waggon dropped into a hollow, then it was plain again as it lumbered down the next long incline, and presently it entered Longpuddle. The coffin was laid in the belfry for the night, and the next day, Sunday, be-tween the services, we buried him. A funeral sermon was preached the same afternoon, the text chosen being, " He was the only son of his mother, and she was a widow." . . . Yes, they were cruel times !

' As for Harriet, she and her lover were married in due time ; but by all account her life was no jocund one. She and her good-man found that they could not live comfortably at Longpuddle, by reason of her connection with Jack's misfortunes, and they settled in a distant town, and were no more heard of by us ; Mrs. Palmley, too, found it advisable to join 'em shortly after. The dark-eyed, gaunt old Mrs. Winter, remembered by the emigrant gentleman here, was, as you will have foreseen, the Mrs. Winter of this story ; and I can well call to mind how lonely she was, how afraid the children were of her, and how she kept herself as a stranger among us, though she lived so long.'

' Longpuddle has had her sad experiences as well as her sunny ones,' said Mr. Lackland.

' Yes, yes. But I am thankful to say not many like that, though good and bad have lived among us.'

' There was Georgy Crookhill—he was one of the shady sort, as I have reason to know,' observed the registrar, with the manner of a man who would like to have his say also.

' I used to hear what he was as a boy at school.'

' Well, as he began so he went on. It never got so far as a hanging matter with him, to be sure ; but he had some narrow escapes of penal servitude ; and once it was a case of the biter bit.'

INCIDENT IN THE LIFE OF MR. GEORGE CROOKHILL

' One day,' the registrar continued, ' Georgy was ambling out of Melchester on a miserable screw, the fair being just over, when he saw in front of him a fine-looking young farmer riding out of the town in the same direction. He was mounted on a good strong handsome animal, worth fifty guineas if worth a crown. When they were going up Bissett Hill, Georgy made it his business to overtake the young farmer. They passed the time o' day to one another ; Georgy spoke of the state of the roads, and jogged alongside the well-mounted stranger in very friendly conversation. The farmer had not been inclined to say much to Georgy at first, but by degrees he grew quite affable, too—as friendly as Georgy was towards him. He told Crookhill that he had been doing business at Melchester fair, and was going on as far as Shottsford-Forum that night, so as to reach Caster-bridge market the next day. When they came to Wood-yates Inn they stopped to bait their horses, and agreed to drink together ; with this they got more friendly than ever, and on they went again. Before they had nearly reached Shottsford it came on to rain, and as they were now passing through the village of Trantridge, and it was quite dark, Georgy persuaded the young farmer to go no further that night ; the rain would most likely give them a chill. For his part he had heard that the little inn here was comfortable, and he meant to stay. At last the young farmer agreed to put up there also ; and they dismounted, and entered, and had a good supper together, and talked over their affairs like men who had known and proved each other a long time. When it was the hour for retiring they went upstairs to a double-bedded room which Georgy Crookhill had asked the landlord to let them share, so sociable were they.

'Before they fell asleep they talked across the room about one thing and another, running from this to that till the conversation turned upon disguises, and changing clothes for particular ends. The farmer told Georgy that he had often heard tales of people doing it; but Crookhill professed to be very ignorant of all such tricks; and soon the young farmer sank into slumber.

'Early in the morning, while the tall young farmer was still asleep (I tell the story as 'twas told me), honest Georgy crept out of his bed by stealth, and dressed himself in the farmer's clothes, in the .pockets of the said clothes being the farmer's money. Now though Georgy particularly wanted the farmer's nice clothes and nice horse, owing to a little transaction at the fair which made it desirable that he should not be too easily recognized, his desires had their bounds: he did not wish to take his young friend's money, at any rate more of it than was necessary for paying his bill. This he abstracted, and leaving the farmer's purse containing the rest on the bedroom table, went downstairs. The inn folks had not particularly noticed the faces of their customers, and the one or two who were up at this hour had no thought but that Georgy was the farmer; so when he had paid the bill very liberally, and said he must be off, no objection was made to his getting the farmer's horse saddled for himself; and he rode away upon it as if it were his own.

'About half an hour after, the young farmer awoke, and looking across the room saw that his friend Georgy had gone away in clothes which didn't belong to him, and had kindly left for himself the seedy ones worn by Georgy. At this he sat up in a deep thought for some time, instead of hastening to give an alarm. "The money, the money is gone," he said to himself, "and that's bad. But so are the clothes."

'He then looked upon the table and saw that the money, or most of it, had been left behind.

'"Ha, ha, ha!" he cried, and began to dance about the room. "Ha, ha, ha!" he said again, and made beautiful smiles to himself in the shaving-glass and in the brass candlestick; and then swung about his arms for all the world as if he were going through the sword exercise.

'When he had dressed himself in Georgy's clothes and gone downstairs, he did not seem to mind at all that they took him for the other; and even when he saw that he had been left a bad horse for a good one, he was not inclined to cry out. They told him his friend had paid the bill, at which he seemed much pleased, and without waiting for breakfast he mounted Georgy's horse and rode away likewise, choosing the nearest by-lane in preference to the highroad, without knowing that Georgy had chosen that by-lane also.

'He had not trotted more than two miles in the personal character of Georgy Crookhill when, suddenly rounding a bend that the lane made thereabout, he came upon a man struggling in the hands of two village constables. It was his friend Georgy, the borrower of his clothes and horse. But so far was the young farmer from showing any alacrity in rushing forward to claim his property that he would have turned the poor beast he rode into the wood adjoining, if he had not been already perceived.

'"Help, help, help!" cried the constables. "Assistance in the name of the Crown!"

'The young farmer could do nothing but ride forward. "What's the matter?" he inquired, as coolly as he could.

'"A deserter—a deserter!" said they. "One who's to be tried by court-martial and shot without parley. He deserted from the Dragoons at Cheltenham some days ago, and was tracked; but the search-party can't find him anywhere, and we told 'em if we met him we'd hand him on to 'em forthwith. The day after he left the barracks the rascal met a respectable farmer and made him drunk at an inn, and told him what a fine soldier he would make, and coaxed him to change clothes, to see how well a military uniform would become him. This the simple farmer did; when our deserter said that for a joke he would leave the room and go to the landlady, to see if she would know him in that dress. He never came back, and Farmer Jollice found himself in soldier's clothes, the money in his pockets gone, and, when he got to the stable, his horse gone, too."

' " A scoundrel ! " says the young man in Georgy's clothes. " And is this the wretched caitiff ? " (pointing to Georgy).

' " No, no ! " cries Georgy, as innocent as a babe of this matter of the soldier's desertion. " He's the man ! He was wearing Farmer Jollice's suit o' clothes, and he slept in the same room wi' me, and brought up the subject of changing clothes, which put it into my head to dress myself in his suit before he was awake. He's got on mine ! "

' " D'ye hear the villain ? " groans the tall young man to the constables. " Trying to get out of his crime by charging the first innocent man with it that he sees ! No, master soldier—that won't do ! "

' " No, no ! That won't do ! " the constables chimed in. " To have the impudence to say such as that, when we caught him in the act almost ! But, thank God, we've got the handcuffs on him at last."

' " We have, thank God," said the tall young man. " Well, I must move on. Good luck to ye with your prisoner ! " And off he went, as fast as his poor jade would carry him.

' The constables then, with Georgy handcuffed between 'em, and leading the horse, marched off in the other direction, towards the village where they had been accosted by the escort of soldiers sent to bring the deserter back, Georgy groaning : " I shall be shot, I shall be shot ! " They had not gone more than a mile before they met them.

' " Hoi, there ! " says the head constable.

' " Hoi, yerself ! " says the corporal in charge.

' " We've got your man," says the constable.

' " Where ? " says the corporal.

' " Here, between us," said the constable. " Only you don't recognize him out o' uniform."

' The corporal looked at Georgy hard enough ; then shook his head and said he was not the absconder.

' " But the absconder changed clothes with Farmer Jollice, and took his horse ; and this man has 'em, d'ye see ! "

' " 'Tis not our man," said the soldiers. " He's a tall young fellow with a mole on his right cheek, and a military bearing, which this man decidedly has not."

' " I told the two officers of justice that 'twas the other ! " pleaded Georgy. " But they wouldn't believe me."

' And so it became clear that the missing dragoon was the tall young farmer, and not Georgy Crookhill— a fact which Farmer Jollice himself corroborated when he arrived on the scene. As Georgy had only robbed the robber, his sentence was comparatively light. The deserter from the Dragoons was never traced : his double shift of clothing having been of the greatest advantage to him in getting off ; though he left Georgy's horse behind him a few miles ahead, having found the poor creature more hindrance than aid.'

The man from abroad seemed to be less interested in the questionable characters of Longpuddle and their strange adventures than in the ordinary inhabitants and the ordinary events, though his local fellow-travellers preferred the former as subjects of discussion. He now for the first time asked concerning young persons of the opposite sex—or rather those who had been young when he left his native land. His informants, adhering to their own opinion that the remarkable was better worth telling than the ordinary, would not allow him to dwell upon the simple chronicles of those who had merely come and gone. They asked him if he remembered Netty Sargent.

' Netty Sargent—I do, just remember her. She was a young woman living with her uncle when I left, if my childish recollection may be trusted.'

' That was the maid. She was a oneyer, if you like, sir. Not any harm in her, you know, but up to everything. You ought to hear how she got the copyhold of her house extended. Oughtn't he, Mr. Day ? '

' He ought,' replied the world-ignored old painter.

' Tell him, Mr. Day. Nobody can do it better than

you, and you know the legal part better than some of
us.'

Day apologized, and began :—

NETTY SARGENT'S COPYHOLD

'She continued to live with her uncle, in the lonely
house by the copse, just as at the time you knew her ;
a tall spry young woman. Ah, how well one can remember
her black hair and dancing eyes at that time, and her
sly way of screwing up her mouth when she meant to
tease ye ! Well, she was hardly out of short frocks before
the chaps were after her, and by long and by late she was
courted by a young man whom perhaps you did not know
—Jasper Cliff was his name—and, though she might
have had many a better fellow, he so greatly took her fancy
that 'twas Jasper or nobody for her. He was a selfish
customer, always thinking less of what he was going to do
than of what he was going to gain by his doings. Jasper's
eyes might have been fixed upon Netty, but his mind was
upon her uncle's house ; though he was fond of her in his
way—I admit that.

'This house, built by her great-great-grandfather, with
its garden and little field, was copyhold—granted upon
lives in the old way, and had been so granted for generations. Her uncle's was the last life upon the property ;
so that at his death, if there was no admittance of new
lives, it would all fall into the hands of the lord of the
manor. But 'twas easy to admit—a slight " fine," as
'twas called, of a few pounds, was enough to entitle him
to a new deed o' grant by the custom of the manor ; and
the lord could not hinder it.

'Now there could be no better provision for his niece
and only relative than a sure house over her head, and
Netty's uncle should have seen to the renewal in time,
owing to the peculiar custom of forfeiture by the dropping
of the last life before the new fine was paid ; for the Squire
was very anxious to get hold of the house and land ; and
every Sunday when the old man came into the church
and passed the Squire's pew, the Squire would say, " A
little weaker in his knees, a little crookeder in his back

—and the re-admittance not applied for : ha ! ha ! I shall be able to make a complete clearing of that corner of the manor some day ! "

' 'Twas extraordinary, now we look back upon it, that old Sargent should have been so dilatory ; yet some people are like it ; and he put off calling at the Squire's agent's office with the fine week after week, saying to himself, " I shall have more time next market-day than I have now." One unfortunate hindrance was that he didn't very well like Jasper Cliff, and as Jasper kept urging Netty, and Netty on that account kept urging her uncle, the old man was inclined to postpone the reliveing as long as he could, to spite the selfish young lover. At last old Mr. Sargent fell ill, and then Jasper could bear it no longer : he produced the fine-money himself, and handed it to Netty, and spoke to her plainly.

' " You and your uncle ought to know better. You should press him more. There's the money. If you let the house and ground slip between ye, I won't marry ; hang me if I will ! For folks won't deserve a husband that can do such things."

' The worried girl took the money and went home, and told her uncle that it was no house no husband for her. Old Mr. Sargent pooh-poohed the money, for the amount was not worth consideration, but he did now bestir himself, for he saw she was bent upon marrying Jasper, and he did not wish to make her unhappy, since she was so determined. It was much to the Squire's annoyance that he found Sargent had moved in the matter at last ; but he could not gainsay it, and the documents were prepared (for on this manor the copyholders had writings with their holdings, though on some manors they had none). Old Sargent being now too feeble to go to the agent's house, the deed was to be brought to his house signed, and handed over as a receipt for the money ; the counterpart to be signed by Sargent, and sent back to the Squire.

' The agent had promised to call on old Sargent for this purpose at five o'clock, and Netty put the money into her desk to have it close at hand. While doing this she heard a slight cry from her uncle, and turning round, saw that he had fallen forward in his chair. She went and lifted him, but he was unconscious ; and unconscious he remained. Neither medicine nor stimulants would bring him to himself. She had been told that he might possibly go off in that way, and it seemed as if the end had come. Before she had started for the doctor his face and extremities grew quite cold and white, and she saw that help would be useless. He was stone-dead.

'Netty's situation rose upon her distracted mind in all its seriousness. The house, garden, and field were lost—by a few hours—and with them a home for herself and her lover. She would not think so meanly of Jasper as to suppose that he would adhere to the resolution declared in a moment of impatience ; but she trembled, nevertheless. Why could not her uncle have lived a couple of hours longer, since he had lived so long ? It was now past three o'clock ; at five the agent was to call, and, if all had gone well, by ten minutes past five the house and holding would have been securely hers for her own and Jasper's lives, these being two of the three proposed to be added by paying the fine. How that wretched old Squire would rejoice at getting the little tenancy into his hands ! He did not really require it, but constitution-ally hated these tiny copyholds and leaseholds and free-holds, which made islands of independence in the fair, smooth ocean of his estates.

'Then an idea struck into the head of Netty how to accomplish her object in spite of her uncle's negligence. It was a dull December afternoon : and the first step in her scheme—so the story goes, and I see no reason to doubt it——'

''Tis true as the light,' affirmed Christopher Twink. 'I was just passing by.'

'The first step in her scheme was to fasten the outer door, to make sure of not being interrupted. Then she set to work by placing her uncle's small, heavy oak table before the fire ; then she went to her uncle's corpse, sitting in the chair as he had died—a stuffed arm-chair, on casters, and rather high in the seat, so it was told me —and wheeled the chair, uncle and all, to the table, placing

him with his back towards the window, in the attitude of
bending over the said oak table, which I knew as a boy
as well as I know any piece of furniture in my own house.
On the table she laid the large family Bible open before
him, and placed his forefinger on the page ; and then she
opened his eyelids a bit, and put on him his spectacles, so
that from behind he appeared for all the world as if he were
reading the Scriptures.   Then she unfastened the door and
sat down, and when it grew dark she lit a candle, and put
it on the table beside her uncle's book.

  ' Folk may well guess how the time passed with her till
the agent came, and how, when his knock sounded upon
the door, she nearly started out of her skin—at least
that's as it was told me. Netty promptly went to the
door.

  ' " I am sorry, sir," she says, under her breath ; " my
uncle is not so well to-night, and I'm afraid he can't see
you."

  ' " H'm !—that's a pretty tale," says the steward.   " So
I've come all this way about this trumpery little job for
nothing ! "

  ' " O no, sir—I hope not," says Netty.   " I suppose
the business of granting the new deed can be done just the
same ? "

  ' " Done ? Certainly not. He must pay the renewal
money, and sign the parchment in my presence."

  ' She looked dubious. " Uncle is so dreadful nervous
about law business," says she, " that, as you know, he's
put it off and put it off for years ; and now to-day really
I've feared it would verily drive him out of his mind.   His
poor three teeth quite chattered when I said to him that
you would be here soon with the parchment writing.
He always was afraid of agents, and folks that come for
rent, and such-like."

  ' " Poor old fellow—I'm sorry for him.   Well, the thing
can't be done unless I see him and witness his signature."

  ' " Suppose, sir, that you see him sign, and he don't
see you looking at him ?   I'd soothe his nerves by saying
you weren't strict about the form of witnessing, and didn't
wish to come in.   So that it was done in your bare presence

it would be sufficient, would it not ? As he's such an old, shrinking, shivering man, it would be a great considerateness on your part if that would do."

' " In my bare presence would do, of course—that's all I come for. But how can I be a witness without his seeing me ? "

' " Why, in this way, sir ; if you'll oblige me by just stepping here." She conducted him a few yards to the left, till they were opposite the parlour window. The blind had been left up purposely, and the candlelight shone out upon the garden bushes. Within the agent could see, at the other end of the room, the back and side of the old man's head, and his shoulders and arm, sitting with the book and candle before him, and his spectacles on his nose, as she had placed him.

' " He's reading his Bible, as you see, sir," she says, quite in her meekest way.

' " Yes. I thought he was a careless sort of man in matters of religion ? "

' " He always was fond of his Bible," Netty assured him. " Though I think he's nodding over it just at this moment. However, that's natural in an old man, and unwell. Now you could stand here and see him sign, couldn't you, sir, as he's such an invalid ? "

' " Very well," said the agent, lighting a cigar. " You have ready by you the merely nominal sum you'll have to pay for the admittance, of course ? "

' " Yes," said Netty. " I'll bring it out." She fetched the cash, wrapped in paper, and handed it to him, and when he had counted it the steward took from his breast pocket the precious parchments and gave one to her to be signed.

' " Uncle's hand is a little paralyzed," she said. " And what with his being half asleep, too, really I don't know what sort of a signature he'll be able to make."

' " Doesn't matter, so that he signs."

' " Might I hold his hand ? "

' " Ay, hold his hand, my young woman—that will be near enough."

' Netty re-entered the house, and the agent continued

smoking outside the window. Now came the ticklish part of Netty's performance. The steward saw her put the inkhorn—" horn," says I in my old-fashioned way—the inkstand, before her uncle, and touch his elbow as if to arouse him, and speak to him, and spread out the deed ; when she had pointed to show him where to sign she dipped the pen and put it into his hand. To hold his hand she artfully stepped behind him, so that the agent could only see a little bit of his head, and the hand she held ; but he saw the old man's hand trace his name on the document. As soon as 'twas done she came out to the steward with the parchment in her hand, and the steward signed as witness by the light from the parlour window. Then he gave her the deed signed by the Squire, and left ; and next morning Netty told the neighbours that her uncle was dead in his bed.'

' She must have undressed him and put him there.'

' She must. O, that girl had a nerve, I can tell ye ! Well, to cut a long story short, that's how she got back the house and field that were, strictly speaking, gone from her ; and by getting them, got her a husband.

' Every virtue has its reward, they say. Netty had hers for her ingenious contrivance to gain Jasper. Two years after they were married he took to beating her—not hard, you know ; just a smack or two, enough to set her in a temper, and let out to the neighbours what she had done to win him, and how she repented of her pains. When the old Squire was dead, and his son came into the property, this confession of hers began to be whispered about. But Netty was a pretty young woman, and the Squire's son was a pretty young man at that time, and wider-minded than his father, having no objection to little holdings ; and he never took any proceedings against her.'

There was now a lull in the discourse, and soon the van descended the hill leading into the long straggling village. When the houses were reached the passengers dropped off one by one, each at his or her own door. Arrived at the inn, the returned emigrant secured a bed, and having eaten a light meal, sallied forth upon the scene he had known so well in his early days. Though flooded with the light of the rising moon, none of the objects wore the attractiveness in this their real presentation that had ever accompanied their images in the field of his imagination when he was more than two thousand miles removed from them. The peculiar charm attaching to an old village in an old country, as seen by the eyes of an absolute foreigner, was lowered in his case by magnified expectations from infantine memories. He walked on, looking at this chimney and that old wall, till he came to the churchyard, which he entered.

The head-stones, whitened by the moon, were easily decipherable ; and now for the first time Lackland began to feel himself amid the village community that he had left behind him five-and-thirty years before. Here, beside the Sallets, the Darths, the Pawles, the Privetts, the Sargents, and others of whom he had just heard, were names he remembered even better than those : the Jickses, and the Crosses, and the Knights, and the Olds. Doubtless representatives 'of these families, or some of them, were yet among the living ; but to him they would all be as strangers. Far from finding his heart ready-supplied with roots and tendrils here, he perceived that in returning to this spot it would be incumbent upon him to re-establish himself from the beginning, precisely as though he had never known the place, nor it him. Time had not condescended to wait his pleasure, nor local life his greeting.

The figure of Mr. Lackland was seen at the inn, and in the village street, and in the fields and lanes about Upper Longpuddle, for a few days after his arrival, and then, ghost-like, it silently disappeared. He had told some of the villagers that his immediate purpose in coming had been fulfilled by a sight of the place, and by conversation with its inhabitants ; but that his ulterior purpose—of coming to spend his latter days among them —would probably never be carried out. It is now a dozen or fifteen years since his visit was paid, and his face has not again been seen.

March 1891